*home is
where
you are*

Home Is Where You Are

Second paperback edition: July 2022

Cover art by Elle Maxwell

Cover copyright © 2020 by Elle Maxwell

ISBN: 978-1-7355646-6-1

www.melissagracewrites.com

home is
where
you are

MELISSA GRACE

For Granny.
A piece of you will always reside in the heart of every strong woman I write about.
But more importantly, in the heart of the woman who writes about them.
Love you special.

"Find out who you are and do it on purpose."

—*Dolly Parton*

ONE

Liv

"THAT'S IT," my best friend Ella Claiborne said. She slammed her coffee mug on the wrought iron patio table so hard it shook. "I'm getting you out of this house."

It was the first Sunday of October and an unusually cool one at that. Autumn in Nashville was often just an extension of summer, but a cold front had left the mid-state overcast with highs in the upper fifties.

"I *am* out of the house," I protested. I pulled the sleeves of my sweater over my hands to ward off the afternoon chill. "I'm on the patio."

"Olivia Faith Sinclair," Ella scolded me, and I winced. It was the first time anyone had said my full name, complete with my maiden name, since my divorce had been finalized six months ago. Her tone softened as she read my expression. "You know what I meant."

"I've been out of the house plenty." The wind blew the *Nashville Scene* magazine on the table open, and I avoided Ella's stern gaze by picking it up and fumbling through it. "It's not like I've not been working. You would know." I was the owner and head baker of Livvie Cakes Bakery and Cupcakery, one of the most popular bakeries in the greater Nashville area. Ella worked alongside me handling the business and marketing side of things. We were nestled in the heart of the 12 South neighborhood, which was just down the street from my little white bungalow. The bungalow I had to purchase when my husband decided he didn't want to be married anymore—at least not to me.

"You work twelve-hour days, and then you come home to an empty house where you eat Pop-Tarts for dinner in your sweatpants and watch *Grey's Anatomy*." She tucked a piece of her blonde hair behind her ear. "I'd hardly call that getting out."

"My house is not empty. Mama's here." Mama was the ornery tuxedo cat I'd adopted from the humane association a couple of months ago. "She doesn't even hiss at me when I feed her now. We're making great progress."

"Well, Mama won't be the only hostile kitty around here if you keep going the way you're going." She flashed her eyes down to my lady parts and grinned that mischievous grin of hers. It was the same one that got me in heaps of trouble when we were younger, back when I was fun. That version of me felt long gone.

"Bold of you to assume my kitty hasn't been hostile for years now." I snorted and flipped a page of the magazine only to see a picture of my ex-husband staring back at me. I swallowed hard, taking in the face I knew like the back of my hand. Now that face was standing beside a gorgeous, busty, and fiery redhead that could have easily been a real-life Jessica Rabbit in her sparkly red dress.

Benton Wyatt was handsome in a Patrick Dempsey sort of way. He was tall and sinewy with wavy salt and pepper hair.

His handsome face never seemed to age even though he was a few years older than me. He also happened to be one of the most sought after record executives in country music. His label, 6th & 15th Records, housed some of country music's hottest artists.

It was a world that felt both familiar and completely foreign to me. When I met Ben, I wasn't even old enough to drink. I was just a girl with a dream and a guitar. Not long after we got married, I walked off the stage for the last time. My dreams no longer fit with the ones he had.

Ben knew talent when he saw it, and that's how I knew talent wasn't something I possessed. Because he never saw it in me. Sure, I could sing on karaoke night or around a bonfire with friends and people would always be impressed, but I didn't have *it*. That magical, indescribable quality that turned ordinary people into superstars.

I chewed my bottom lip, skimming over the caption that informed me Jessica Rabbit was actually Shelby Kirkland, a 20-something up and coming country artist who recently signed with 6th & 15th.

Ella snatched the magazine from my grasp and scanned it with her pale blue eyes. "That son of a bitch."

"She's quite lovely," I said bitterly. "Perhaps she has a fully functioning uterus." I picked up my coffee cup and cradled it in my hands. Ella looked at me, her brows furrowed with concern.

Starting a family had been a point of contention for me and Ben. We both wanted one, but my body had been hellbent on not cooperating.

"I'm not letting you do this to yourself anymore." Ella closed the magazine and slapped it on the table. "He's moving on, and it's time you did too." She leaned forward, placing her hands on my knees. "The blaming and the self-loathing? It stops right fucking now."

"I'm not self-loathing." I pouted and caught a glimpse of my reflection in the glass of the patio door.

That was a fucking lie, and I knew it.

"That's horse shit, Liv." One of the things I loved and hated most about Ella was her knack for always calling me on my shit. "You gave up your dreams. You gave up your entire life for that man, Olivia, and I'm not letting you waste another second on that hoity-toity fuck face. I'm getting you out of this house, and that is final."

I grumbled as I stared at the gnat that found its way inside my mug, drowning in the mighty sea of my oat milk latte.

"Why don't we go to Santa's Pub tonight and do some karaoke? I haven't heard you sing in forever."

"I don't think so." I shook my head. That was the last thing I wanted to do. I still hadn't been able to bring myself to pull out my road-worn Taylor guitar. When I moved, I shoved the hard case in the back of my closet behind my winter coat so that it could no longer look at me with the disappointment I felt. "Besides, what would you do with Grace?"

"First of all, she's seventeen." Ella extracted the coffee mug from my hands and placed it on the table, forcing me to focus on her. "The kid is going off to college next year. It's not like she needs a babysitter."

"Not karaoke. Not this time." I pleaded as a knowing smile spread across her face. "What." It was a statement, not a question.

"I know how I'm getting you out of the house," she informed me all too cheerfully. "You know those concert tickets and backstage passes I splurged on for Grace's birthday? Well, the show is tomorrow, and now her friend Lexi can't go because she's got mono."

"I could have told Lexi that kissing boys was a bad idea."

"My dear, Lexi's loss is your gain," Ella continued, completely ignoring me. "You're going with us."

"Won't that cramp Grace's style? Being out on the town with two old ladies?"

"We are not old," Ella rolled her eyes.

"Doesn't she have another friend she can invite? What about Becca?"

"She and Becca are on the outs right now. Anyway, when was the last time the three of us went on an adventure like this together?"

"When we took her to that *Walking Dead* convention last summer and nearly got trampled by hundreds of women trying to get a look at Norman Reedus."

"And wasn't that fun?"

Fun was certainly not how I remembered it, but I knew that arguing was pointless. Ella had already made up her mind. "What band was it again?"

"Midnight in Dallas," she squealed. "I practically had to sell my soul to get these tickets."

I stared at her blankly. "Sounds like the name of a Lifetime movie."

She picked up the magazine and swatted me over the head with it. "Even *you* know who Midnight in Dallas is. They only swept the freaking Grammys this year. Remember that song we heard at the shop last week that you couldn't stop listening to? 'Fortress'? That's their newest one."

"The one with the sexy voice?" I asked, my interest admittedly a little piqued. I remembered the sound of that soulful voice. I couldn't get it out of my head last week as I worked on our new Pumpkin Praline cupcake recipe. At the time, I didn't know if the song was by a band or solo artist. All I knew was the voice behind it was like a velvet robe for the soul.

"That's the one!" Her excitement overflowed like an uncorked bottle of champagne, and I knew there was no turning back. "We'll get dressed up, go to dinner at Adele's, and then head to the Ryman. It'll be great."

"You do realize I haven't dressed up basically this entire decade, right?"

"You're not getting out of this," Ella said, eyeing me. "You always look amazing. You don't give yourself enough credit, Liv. You can wear jeans and a T-shirt and still look like a fucking rockstar."

"That's good news seeing how that's almost all I own."

"So you'll go?" Ella reached for my hands and gave them an excited squeeze.

I sighed, but I knew I couldn't say no. Ella needed this night out as much as I did. "Yes. Yes, I'll go."

I CUED UP A MIDNIGHT IN DALLAS RADIO STATION ON MY phone while I worked the next morning. I found myself swaying to the sounds of that soulful, sexy as hell voice while I swirled a pastry bag over dozens of cupcakes. Their sound fit right in with the usual suspects on my playlists these days: The Lumineers, Lord Huron, The Civil Wars, Hozier, and even Ed Sheeran. Don't get me wrong. My heart would always bleed country, but lately, my soul had been venturing over into indie rock and even a little pop.

Mondays were generally our slowest day of the week. Ella

was off since Grace's school had an Inservice Day, so it felt extra quiet. We had some large orders come in that morning, so I worked right through lunch, completely lost in the music. It wasn't until Katie Kelley, our other pastry chef, spoke up that I even realized what time it was.

"Hey, Liv." Katie's sweet, soft-spoken voice broke through the Midnight in Dallas trance I was in. "Didn't you say you needed to dip out a little early? It's a quarter to four already." Her honey-colored ponytail flipped as she turned to point at the clock.

"Shit." I sighed. Days like today I was glad to be only a short walk from home. "I have a couple dozen left to go."

"Girl, get out of here." Katie waved me off, taking the pastry bag from my hands. "I've got this, *and* I'm opening up tomorrow. Don't you worry about a thing. You and Ella have fun tonight."

When Katie joined our team four years ago, Ella and I had been able to breathe a lot easier. She was only a few years younger than us, and she came with very little baking experience, but now she was a dear friend, brilliant pastry chef, and our most trusted employee. Katie was the friend who showed up with delicious home-cooked meals for me after Ben asked for a divorce. She was a little on the shy side, but dependable to a fault. Last spring when Ella and I both managed to come down with the flu, Katie showed up on our doorsteps with care packages of homemade chicken soup, Gatorade, tea, and trashy magazines. She did this all while keeping things running smoothly at the bakery *and* making thirteen wedding cakes for one of our busiest weekends of the season.

"You're a lifesaver." I kissed her on the cheek before whipping off my apron and exchanging it for my tiny leopard-print cross body purse on the hook by the back door.

"You better come back with some good stories tomorrow," Katie called after me.

"Right," I mumbled. I turned the knob on the back door, giving it a shove with my hip, and I was off. I jogged down the sidewalk along the road behind the bakery. Everything surrounding the businesses of 12th Avenue South was purely residential with cozy, renovated bungalows, and a few new townhouses. Parking was hard to come by due to the eclectic mix of eateries and boutiques that lined 12th Avenue, so cars were always stacked like dominos along the tree-lined street.

The leaves that had already fallen crunched beneath my feet as I practically sprinted the entire two and a half blocks home. I quickly let myself in the front door, narrowly avoiding Mama's tail as I skittered past her.

"Sorry, Mama." She hissed as I threw my bag on the small table inside the foyer and ran down the hall to my bedroom. My phone chirped with a text notification from my back pocket, and I knew exactly who it was before I even looked at it.

Ella: We're picking you up in the Lyft at 5:15. You better look hot!

I rolled my eyes as I ticked off my quick reply.

Liv: If by hot you mean in the middle of a hot flash, I'm already there.

She shot back an eye-roll emoji, and I pulled up a pop radio station on my phone before tossing it on the bed. I half-stripped, half-danced my way to the bathroom to the sound of "Drop It Low" by Ester Dean.

I took the fastest shower of my life, but took the time to blow out my long, dark hair, which was already far more than I usually did. Humming along to the radio, I piled mascara on as though my life depended on it. I finished by slicking on a lipstick that I probably bought back when Taylor Swift was still singing country songs. I threw on some ripped black jeans, a Queen shirt, and a jacket since the unusually cool weather showed no signs of leaving anytime soon.

I headed over to the dresser and spritzed myself with my favorite fragrance, catching a glimpse of myself in the mirror as I returned the perfume to its home beside an old photograph of me and Ella.

Not half bad for a thirty-something divorcee with a hostile kitty.

My phone pinged from the bed, and I giggled to myself. I grabbed it and ran back down the hallway as Mama scrambled across the floor with an annoyed meow.

"I'll see you later, Mama," I said to her, snatching my purse from the foyer and starting toward the door. I was still shoving my feet inside my boots when the door rattled shut behind me. I bounded down the sidewalk toward Ella and Grace in the backseat of an SUV with the Lyft sign illuminated on the dash.

"So the meet and greet is *before* the show?" Ella asked Grace, furrowing her brow. "Are you sure?"

"Yes, mom," Grace assured her for the third time since we'd arrived at the Ryman Auditorium. After a quick dinner at Adele's, one of our favorite places for dinner and Sunday brunch, we hopped in another Lyft for the short drive over to the venue.

The Ryman Auditorium was a show stopper, no matter who was on the schedule. With its stained-glass windows and perfect acoustics, it was known as the Mother Church for a reason. Every show there felt like coming home in a way that can only be described as spiritual.

Even being from Nashville, I'd only been to the Ryman a handful of times. The most recent being the last time I'd accompanied Ben to an event about five years ago. One of his artists, a young blonde who'd been hailed as the next Carrie Underwood, was playing for the first time. I sat in the front row watching as Ben beamed up at her proudly, wondering if he would ever look at me that way. I shook my head in an effort to remove the memory from my mind.

After we checked in with our tickets and passes, we were instructed to follow a tall, dark-haired usher to the backstage area. We felt the audience erupt as we wound our way behind our guide through roadies and concert-goers in the underbelly of the auditorium. The sound of a bass drum began to thud, and the opening notes of a song began to play.

Grace squealed, her loose blonde waves shimmying over her shoulders as she grabbed Ella's arm and looped her other arm through mine. "That must be Sam Corbyn."

"Who is that again?" I leaned into her ear so as not to display my ignorance too loudly.

"The opening act." She sighed, her eyes going all star crossed. "He sings that 'Blue Skies' song. *And* he's British. He's so hot!"

"Well, God save the Queen." I laughed, my spirit buoyed by her excitement.

I looked at the framed photographs and old posters that adorned the walls from concerts past and imagined the many talents that walked these halls. Once upon a time, I longed to be one of them. Playing the Mother Church was one of those honors that every singer/songwriter hoped for. I pushed the thought from my mind as our guide came to a stop behind a short line of fans who chattered nervously amongst them-selves. An expressionless and muscular bodyguard in all black with a sleeve of tattoos stood watch outside the door.

"This is our stop." The usher gestured at the closed door that we were all now waiting outside of. "They're letting each group in one at a time to chat with the guys and take some photos. When you're done, if you'll go back up the way you came, the ushers at the main floor entrance will show you to your seats."

"Thank you," Ella said as he waved, disappearing down the hall and into the crowd. "I wonder if these guys are as good-looking in person as they are on Instagram. I was checking them out earlier and they are H-A-W-T." She spelled out the last word, causing me and Grace to burst into laughter. I wasn't sure, but I could have sworn the bodyguard's lip twitched.

"What does that even mean?" I snorted between laughs.

"What?" Ella asked. "It's what the young people say."

"*Mom.*" Grace shook her head. "We do *not* say that." We watched with interest as the door opened and two squealing girls stumbled out. They took off down the hall as a group of four teenagers slipped inside the room.

"I'm just saying." Ella raked her fingers through her golden hair, adjusting her off the shoulder sweater so that it showed off her bronzed skin. "You've got two single ladies here on the prowl."

"I sure hope you mean you and Grace." I raised my brow pointedly in her direction.

"Um, no. I mean you and me," she fired back. "Grace isn't allowed to date till she's thirty. I'm pretty sure these guys are too old for her anyway."

"Derek just turned twenty-eight." Grace sighed dreamily.

"He's not *that* old." She'd informed us over dinner that the bass player and youngest band member, Derek, was her favorite. She also spent a solid fifteen minutes showing us his Instagram page that was filled with artsy and romantic photos he'd taken.

I laughed. "Oh to be twenty-eight and *not that old* again."

The bodyguard's lips twitched into a smile.

"You're not old, Aunt Liv," Grace assured me. "I mean you're old, but you don't, like, act old. Besides, you're a total smokeshow."

"A what?" Ella and I asked in unison.

"It means hot." Grace rolled her eyes and giggled. "You know? H-A-W-T." The bodyguard either snorted or laughed. I wasn't sure which, but I was glad someone else found this amusing.

"Well, that's the truth." Ella pouted. "But what about me? Am I a smokeshow?"

"You look good too, mom."

"A total smokeshow," I agreed. The door opened again spilling out the four excited teens, and the group in front of us entered the room.

"We're next." Ella smiled nervously, whipping out a compact and a tube of lipstick from her clutch. She expertly applied the bold, red color and checked her reflection before passing the compact over to Grace's waiting hand.

"You both look beautiful," I assured them as Grace slicked a nude lip gloss over her lips before offering the compact to me. I shook my head, and she handed it back to her mom. "I'm good. I'm afraid this is as good as it gets."

"You sure?" Ella asked, waving the compact at me. "Remember, remember, the hostile kitty's splendor! I'm sure that's how the saying goes."

"Mom!" Grace dissolved into laughter.

This time, the guard *definitely* let out a chuckle.

Grace was used to a certain amount of this kind of talk. Grace and Ella had essentially grown up together, and though Ella was certainly an amazing mom, she was also a friend to Grace. She wasn't afraid to talk like a grown-up around her, and she encouraged her daughter to talk to her about anything and everything. Though she knew Grace was a virgin, she wanted her to feel safe enough to talk to her about sex when that time came.

"What?" Ella shrugged. "You'll understand one day, sweetie. It's kind of an 'if you don't use it, you lose it' sort of thing."

I turned to face Ella, my back to the door. "First of all, I'm pretty sure the saying you were looking for is 'remember, remember, the 5th of November' from *V For Vendetta.*" Ella's eyes widened, and her gaze seemed to travel above my head. "And I'm pretty sure it had nothing to do with my *hostile kitty.*" I made a sweeping motion down my core, hearing the bodyguard snort from behind me.

"Hey, ladies." A warm, velvety voice came from behind me, and I felt a vicious heat begin to rise to my cheeks. I knew that voice all too well. I'd only been listening to it all day. I turned to see the face that matched the voice, and my breath caught in my throat. He had to be at least six foot two, and I could see the subtle outline of his well-defined abs through his tight white T-shirt. The cotton fabric stretched against the smooth curve of his biceps and gave way to a set of muscular forearms that could have been chiseled out of stone. Finally, my eyes settled on a face that was framed perfectly by a jawline that could cut a girl's heart wide open. His eyes were the color of a storm rolling in. Tiny flecks of grey sparkled like lighting in clouds of deep blue. His light brown hair was short on the sides and longer on top. It looked messy yet still somehow perfect as he ran his hands through it. Even *his hands* were perfect for crying out loud. His mouth curled into an inviting, boyish smile.

"Oh my God!" Grace squeaked. "You're Jaxon Slade."

"Guilty as charged." Jaxon raised his brow, not taking his eyes off me.

"I'm Grace." She introduced herself animatedly before gesturing toward her mom. "This is my mom, Ella."

"Her very cool, super hot mom," Ella added, reaching her hand out to shake his. He took her hand and flashed his wide grin in her direction.

"And this is my Aunt Liv," Grace said finally, squeezing my shoulder.

"She's *very* cool." Ella's voice was at least a full octave higher as she chattered nervously. "Soooo much cooler than me *and* a total smokeshow."

He extended his hand toward me. I felt Ella shove me in the back, cueing me to respond or do anything besides stand there with my mouth open like a trout on a hook.

"I'm Olivia Sinclair," I managed to croak as I took his hand. I felt the calluses of his fingertips slide against my palm, setting off an electric current that coursed through my body. I was suddenly reminded that my kitty wasn't hostile at all. In fact, it was ready to send out the welcome wagon. "Or Liv. You can call me Liv."

"Olivia… *Liv.*" He said both my name and nickname slowly, my hand still locked in his warm grasp. "Why don't you guys come and meet the band?"

He stepped closer to me, allowing Grace admission to the dressing room.

"This was the last group," the bodyguard said as Ella entered the room behind Grace. She spun around and gave me a thumbs-up, an overjoyed expression plastered across her face. "I'm gonna go grab a drink, so lock the door. I'll knock when it's time to go." The bodyguard smirked and disappeared down the hallway.

Jaxon's smile reached the corners of his eyes. When he laughed, I felt it through my entire body. "I see we saved the best for last."

TWO

Jax

_____

LIV MET my gaze with a shy smile before quickly averting her eyes to the floor, her shoes—anywhere that wasn't me. I became acutely aware of my own heartbeat as it thudded faster and faster in my ears.

Wow. This girl was beautiful. The way her fair skin flushed with embarrassment was adorable. Her shiny chestnut hair cascaded over her shoulders, almost reaching her hips. She wore a T-shirt with Queen emblazoned across the front, which told me she also had great taste in music. The fabric of her shirt outlined the perfect curve of her body, tapering at her waist. My eyes settled for a split second on the alleged 'hostile kitty' she mentioned. My cheeks flushed, and I stifled a laugh.

I wondered why it was so hostile.

My eyes shifted to her left hand to check for a ring, and I was shocked to find it totally bare. I was even more shocked by how relieved I was.

"Should we go in?" The sound of Liv's voice interrupted

my thoughts. She chewed her bottom lip, and my heart thundered in response. "I wouldn't want you to get mobbed. I mean, I could try to fend off a crowd, but I don't know if I'm quite as intimidating as your tattooed friend with the muscles as big as my head."

"Oh, yeah, come on in." I cleared my throat, stepping to the side for her to walk past me into the dressing room. As she did, the sweet scent of orange blossoms beckoned me to follow behind her. I pulled the door closed and locked it as instructed.

The other two girls, Grace and her mom Ella, were already chatting animatedly with the rest of the guys.

"Guys," I said. "This is Liv."

"Hello, Liv," our manager greeted her, stepping forward to take her hand. "Cash Montgomery. I'm the guy that keeps these fellas in line." His phone rang, and he quietly excused himself to take the call in the corner of the room.

Our bass player extended his hand to shake Liv's outstretched one. "Nice to meet you. I'm Derek."

"I dig the Queen shirt, Liv." I watched as Luca Sterling took her hand in his and kissed it. My jaw clenched involuntarily. I knew that compliment meant our lead guitarist had already been checking Liv out, and that annoyed the shit out of me. He was the brooding, individualistic type. He knew the effect he had on the ladies, but Liv seemed unfazed.

"And this is Dallas." I gently guided her toward our drummer. He was the spirited one of the group, and even though Luca was the oldest, Dallas was our leader. No decisions got made without his approval.

"Wait," Liv said as she shook his hand. "Dallas as in Midnight in Dallas? Is that where the name came from?"

"Yep," he answered, his mouth stretching into a broad grin. "Derek here is my cousin, and his last name is Knights with a K. When the two of us started out as a duo in college, we were Dallas Knights, which was honestly fucking weird because nobody knew how to spell it. Also, because Derek is a terrible singer. When Jaxon and Luca joined us, we knew we had to rebrand if we were ever going to go anywhere as a band."

"Midnight became the witching hour for us." I jumped in, longing to see her eyes back on mine. What color were her eyes? Green? Hazel? I wanted to look closer, but I didn't want her to think I was a total weirdo. "We used to rehearse in Dallas' old garage well past midnight, and that's when our best ideas came to us."

"Hence Midnight in Dallas," Luca explained with a laugh. "Because Midnights in Dallas' Garage didn't have the same ring to it."

Derek leaned against the counter. "The artists formerly known as Dallas Knights."

"And that's how Midnight in Dallas was born." Dallas chuckled.

"So what brings you guys out tonight?" I asked Liv, but Grace answered.

"These tickets were my birthday present."

"They went on sale a week before her birthday in March, and I nearly took down Ticketmaster to get them." Ella looked over at her daughter proudly. "You guys are her favorite band. I was prepared to do whatever I had to in order to make that happen, including, but not limited to, becoming a stowaway on your tour bus. Aren't y'all glad it didn't come to that?"

"Listen, Ella," Luca flirted. "Don't threaten me with a good time."

"Hey, no threats here," Ella said with a shrug. "Only promises."

"Ooooh," Dallas hooted. "Sounds like Miss Ella came to play."

"Please remember when you find her hiding somewhere on your bus looking all fatal attraction that you encouraged this." Liv raised her brow at Dallas. "I will have no sympathy for any of you."

"I promise to send postcards from the road." Ella stuck her tongue out at Liv. "Take care of Grace for me." Grace playfully punched her mom in the arm.

"So, it sounds like you may be fairly new to our music?" I asked Liv, nudging her with my arm. I wanted to reclaim her attention and have any excuse to keep her talking to me.

"I am." She smiled sheepishly. Her smile made my knees weak for reasons I didn't understand. I only knew I wanted to see it again. "I love music, but I've been a little out of the loop lately. I heard 'Fortress' for the first time last week, and I loved it. It's been in my head ever since, and I listened to your stuff all day today. You guys are really good."

"Fortress" had been an instant hit with its slow, steady beat that built up to a stunning guitar solo, courtesy of Luca. The entire song felt like you were climbing up a mountain. By the time you reached the bridge, you were standing on top of the world, soaking in a panoramic view. It started off sad, but by the end, you couldn't help but feel a sense of hope.

"We had to get this one out of the house," Ella spoke up, pointing at Liv. "She hasn't been out in *ages*."

"*Mom.*" Grace elbowed her mother, and Liv's eyes fell. There was a sadness that crept onto her face that said there was much more to this story, and it was a story I wanted to know all about.

"So, it's a girls night?" I asked, wanting to put Liv back at ease. "Where are you ladies sitting?"

Liv pulled her ticket from her back pocket, inspecting it. "Main floor, row S."

"I think we can do one better than that." I raised my brow in question to the rest of the guys. They nodded their agreement to whatever plan I was cooking up on the fly.

"No way," Grace gasped, her eyes lit up with excitement. It was then I knew exactly what I had to do. I hoped on all that was holy that she wouldn't think I was a total creeper.

"Way," I said with as much smoothness as I could muster. "I think we could make room for you guys to watch the show from the side of the stage, but I'm going to need one small favor in return."

"Yes! Anything!" Grace shrieked. "Whatever it is, yes." Liv and Ella eyed me suspiciously. Not nearly as suspiciously as the rest of the band. What the fuck was I even doing?

"I'm gonna need your Aunt Liv's phone number." I smiled down at Liv and chewed my lip nervously, as a soft flush of pink crept onto Liv's face. Dallas looked at me with wide eyes, clearly not expecting me to go in this direction. Hell, even I wasn't entirely sure what I was doing. Cash glanced up from his phone call and shot me a questioning look.

"Excuse me?" Liv asked. "You want my number because why?"

"Here it is." Before Liv could protest any further, Grace had already pulled up the number on her phone and had it in my hands.

"Grace," Liv hissed.

I whipped my phone out of my back pocket, snapping a photo of the screen with Olivia Sinclair's number on it.

"I love you, Aunt Livvie." Grace beamed as I handed her phone back to her.

"It's settled then," I announced, still completely unsure how I'd managed to pull off this little stunt. "Lovely doing business with you, Miss Grace."

"Thank you." She chirped happily as Liv stood with a bemused look in her eyes. "It was my pleasure."

"Hold up a second." Liv crossed her arms, narrowing her eyes at me. "Don't I get a say in this?"

"Um, yes." My voice faltered as I raked my hand through my hair, trying my best to look charming. I'd never done anything like this before, and I couldn't explain what made me do it now. I was afraid I'd crossed a line, but there was something about her that made me feel like I couldn't let her walk out of this dressing room and never see her again.

"If you want to keep my number, you've got to dedicate a song to Grace on stage tonight." She tilted her chin up at me with playful defiance.

My mouth twitched into a grin. "I think we can make that happen."

Grace shrieked. "Really? Please let it be 'Fortress.' It's my favorite."

There was a knock on the door, followed by a low voice. "It's showtime, fellas."

Derek opened the door, and the room was suddenly alight with activity.

"Wait," Luca said. "We've gotta take a photo first."

"Right." Ella shook her head, completely flustered. She had clearly been so engrossed with watching what was going down with me and Liv that she'd forgotten this was a meet and greet. Honestly, so had I. "Which one of you guys has the longest arms? I'll never be able to get us all in the picture."

"That would be me." I took the phone from her as everyone piled in close and faced me. Grace wrapped herself around Derek, and Luca enveloped Ella in a giant hug. Before Dallas could even try to move in on Liv, I tucked her under my arm and felt her tentatively settle her arm around me.

"I see how it is." Dallas feigned offense. "Nobody's got love for Dallas."

"Without Dallas, there *is* no Midnight in Dallas, so you better get your ass over here," Liv joked, holding her free arm out to him.

"That's more like it." Dallas laughed, sliding in next to her. I was appreciative of her kindness toward Dallas, and admittedly, a little jealous.

"Here we go." I tightened my arm around the curve of Liv's waist. "One... two... three."

Cash ended his call, laughing at us all smushed together. "You guys look great," he said, slipping his phone back inside his pocket.

I glanced at the photo before handing the phone back to Ella, and my chest tightened seeing Liv nestled under my arm. "Wait!" I dug my phone out of the pocket of my jeans. "I want to take one with mine too." Dallas exchanged a curious look with me as everyone piled back in their places. This time, Dallas and Luca sandwiched Ella. "We, uh, like to take a photo from each meet and greet. You know, for Instagram."

Luca couldn't hide his snort as the lie escaped my lips, but the girls didn't seem to notice.

"Doin' it for the Gram." Grace resumed her position next to Derek.

"We can take as many of these as you want, sweetheart." Ella joked, throwing her arms around the guys. "This is the most action I've had in at least a decade."

"I'll take it for you," Cash offered, eyeing me as he reached for the phone. He was clearly clued into my batshit crazy behavior.

"Thanks, man," I said casually. With that, I pulled Liv into my chest and folded my arms around her. She smelled delicious, like citrus and champagne, and all I wanted was to get drunk on her. I felt her relax in my arms as Cash counted us down and took the photos.

"Alright, everybody." Cash handed my phone back to me and clasped his hands together. "It's showtime." Assistants entered the room in a flurry of movement along with Brady, who began herding us all toward the door.

"It was nice meeting you guys," Ella exclaimed, giving Luca and Dallas another hug.

"The pleasure was entirely ours," Dallas insisted, shaking his hair down from its ponytail and fist-bumping Grace. "You ladies are welcome to stowaway on our bus anytime."

"Don't encourage her, Dallas," Liv warned with a laugh. "I don't have that kind of bail money."

"Y'all are the best," Grace drawled, as Derek enveloped her in another hug.

Liv turned to me, chewing her bottom lip. I wanted to know what those lips tasted like. They looked soft and inviting as they curled into a sweet smile. "Seriously, thank you. And... you know you don't have to... I don't expect you to..." She stumbled over her words, and it was the cutest thing I'd ever seen. I already wanted to call her even though she was standing right in front of me. "It was really great meeting you, Jaxon."

"You can call me Jax."

"Jax." She stuck her hand out to shake mine. "Thanks again."

I took her slender hand and held onto it a little longer than I probably should have. "Cash, will you take these lovely ladies to watch the show from the stage please?"

With that, Cash whisked them away. Before they turned the corner toward the stage, I saw her look back at me, and I could swear, she smiled.

THREE

Liv

"YOU LADIES ARE GETTING the VIP treatment tonight." Cash wound us through the backstage area where people bounced back and forth like pinballs moving equipment behind the scenes. The opening act was still playing, and the closer we got to the front of the side stage area, the more the sounds of the crowd swelled around us.

"Thank you for this," I said, catching up to him. "Does this happen often? Fans getting chosen to watch the show backstage?" Though I was sure this had to be a regular occurrence, there was a certain innocence in the way Jax looked at me that made me question it.

"Honestly? No," he admitted, running a hand through his whiskey-colored hair. "The only people that have ever been invited to watch the show from the stage are family members and maybe a few close friends. You guys must have made quite the impression."

Ella's eyes widened, and she elbowed me swiftly in the side. I felt Grace tug on my jacket.

"Antoni!" Cash caught the attention of a gorgeous man

wearing a headset and carrying a clipboard, who at the sound of his name, fell into stride beside us. He wore a sharp black suit with purple sparkles on the lapel and exuded the confidence of a man that could be running this joint. His dark hair was gelled to perfection, and his five o'clock shadow was meticulously groomed. "This is Liv, Ella, and her daughter Grace. They're going to be hanging out stage right tonight. Would you mind getting them something to drink? A couple of glasses of champagne and let's see if we can get a virgin cocktail for Miss Grace. I want you to load them up with some merch too."

"On it, boss," Antoni said before practically vanishing into thin air.

"You really don't have to do that." Ella tried to stop Antoni, but he disappeared before she could even finish her sentence.

"Nonsense. We want to," Cash insisted, bringing us all to a stop. "Here we are. Best seat in the house."

Grace squealed with delight, her eyes sparkling. When I turned toward the stage and my eyes adjusted to the lights, I saw exactly why. We had a perfect view of Sam Corbyn's mop of red hair. He and his band were in the middle of an upbeat performance with a heavy bass drum. I shifted my gaze to look out into the crowd and felt my heart catch in my throat. The fans were on their feet, clapping along and singing the lyrics back as Sam pointed his microphone toward them. Their energy was palpable and so damn happy. I detected something that felt a lot like regret bubbling deep inside me.

I felt Jax's perfect hand on my shoulder before I heard him. "What do you think?" He leaned in so I could hear him over the crowd. His velvet voice was so close I could feel the warmth of his breath on my ear. I turned to face him, and butterflies swirled around in my stomach as I gazed up into his soulful, stormy eyes. His expression was so sweet and excited as he awaited my response that my heart was ready to swan dive right onto his black Chuck Taylors.

"This is really amazing." I glanced back at Grace who was dancing as Ella chatted with Cash. "Thank you so much. You seriously made Grace's night."

"And what about you?" He flashed me that dazzling grin, making my heart flutter.

"Seeing her happy makes me happy." I loved Grace as if she were my own, and seeing her so overjoyed and animated made me happy.

"Well, that won't do."

"Wait. What?"

"I want to make *your* night too, Olivia Sinclair."

"Oh, I didn't mean—"

"Nope. I'm gonna make your night too. Those are the rules." His eyes sparkled, and he shrugged nonchalantly.

"And whose rules are these exactly?" I laughed. Whether I was laughing at how adorable he was, or at how absolutely fucking absurd this was, I wasn't sure.

"Mine." He smiled at me in a way that made me understand why women used to throw their panties at rockstars. Did people still do that? If not, they should. "I've got to go play this show real quick, but after that, I'm gonna make your night. I promise."

Before I could protest, he jogged over to where the rest of the band was huddled. His eyes found mine again before I made my way back to where Grace, Ella, and Cash stood.

Ella gaped at me as Grace grabbed my hand and squealed in my ear.

"I'm going to go check in with the guys," Cash told us. "And I'll check on that champagne."

"Thanks, Cash." Ella chirped, yanking me closer as he stepped away. "WHAT IS GOING ON?"

"I think Jaxon Slade has a crush on Aunt Liv," Grace sang, bumping me with her hip.

"Yeah, in my dreams maybe." I snorted. "First of all, I have to be older than him. *Have to be.* Second of all, *have you seen him?* I'm pretty sure he's the great, great, great, great-grandchild of Adonis."

"He's gorgeous *and* famous." Grace rested the back of her hand on her forehead and pretended to faint.

"He's gorgeous, but *so are you.*" Ella poked me in the shoulder for emphasis. "You don't give yourself enough credit."

"Y'all, this guy is famous. He's probably dating some supermodel that carries a small dog in her purse. He's cute, but I'm sure he just enjoys flirting." I shook my head. "This is not a thing. Don't make this a thing."

"Oh, it's a *thing,*" Ella fired back. "You heard what Cash said. They don't invite just anyone to do this."

"He did it for Grace," I insisted. "For her birthday."

"But he wanted *your* phone number," Grace reminded me. She had me there. I couldn't explain why Jaxon Slade had insisted on having my phone number, but I knew it didn't matter. There was no way I'd ever hear from him, and that was perfectly fine because this was not a thing that happened in real life.

"You guys are crazy." I let out an exasperated sigh. "This isn't a thing. It's not."

Ella narrowed her eyes at me. "What did he say to you over there?"

"He asked what I thought about the view."

"Uh-huh." Ella would not be deterred. This was no longer a conversation. It was an interrogation. "And?"

"I said it was amazing. I thanked him and said he'd made Grace's night."

"*And?* What else?" Grace raised an eyebrow at me. Damn. The girl was exactly like her mother.

"*And* he asked if he'd made my night too."

"And?" Ella grabbed ahold of my arms. "What did you say?"

"I said that seeing Grace happy made me happy. He said that simply wouldn't do, and he was going to make my night too because those are the rules." I curved my fingers into air quotes.

"Oh my God!" Grace bounced with excitement. "A rockstar is in love with you!"

"*That's* a little premature, don't you think?" I shook my head. "And insane. He's a hot rockstar and I'm… me."

"So what?" Ella brushed me off. "Famous people fall in love with normal people all the time. Look at George Clooney."

"The fact that you are now comparing me with Amal Clooney should be a clue as to how far we've strayed from reality."

"Nope." Ella shook her head incredulously. "Stop that. You think you don't deserve some hot, incredibly sweet, successful person that thinks you're amazing, but you do. Liv, you do deserve that."

"Then it's a good thing I've got the two hottest dates in this place right here." I linked my arms through theirs. "Let's just enjoy the show and this amazing view."

Grace sighed dreamily. "You could be dating a rockstar."

"You're going out with him." Ella squinted at me.

"He hasn't even asked me to go anywhere." I threw my hands up. "You guys have lost it. I'm not—"

"Champagne for the lovely ladies." Cash approached with two sparkling flutes in his hands, saving me from any further conversation about Jaxon Slade. Antoni was on his heels with a tall, sparkly glass in one hand and a black shopping bag packed to the brim, with what I assumed was the merch Cash had mentioned, in the other.

"I got a Shirley Ginger for you, honey." Antoni shimmied his shoulders. "Nothing like a good mocktail."

"Thank you so much," I said gratefully. We took the drinks and the bag from their hands, thanking them profusely. "Y'all have done too much. We really appreciate it."

"Truly, it's our pleasure." Cash smiled brightly. "You guys mind some company? We're usually working throughout the show, but the band is on a little break after tonight, so things aren't as crazy as usual."

"Of course," I said, perhaps a little too eagerly. I knew that as long Cash was there with us, there would be no further mention of Jax.

"You guys are in for a treat." He moved to stand by Ella. "These guys put on such a great show. Jax's voice is even better live."

Well, shit. You had one job, Cash.

"Jax is *quite* impressive." Ella smirked in my direction, letting me know that though I may have avoided the topic for now, this conversation was far from over.

CASH WAS RIGHT. MIDNIGHT IN DALLAS PUT ON A HELL OF A
show. I don't think the audience sat down the entire ninety
minutes they played. As promised, Jax's voice was other-
worldly. Every word he sang felt like salve on a wound. By
the time they stepped on stage for their final encore, Cash,
Ella, Grace, and I had felt every end of the emotional spectrum. We'd even managed to pull Antoni in to dance with us
for a couple of songs.

I watched the way the crowd responded to Jax, how he
seemed to hold them in the palm of his hand. My hands
twitched with memory, and I suddenly felt a familiar ache to
feel my fingertips on the neck of my old guitar.

I watched as Cash twirled Ella, her head thrown back with
laughter, and the sheer bliss plastered on Grace's face as she
sang along to every word, and I felt grateful. Ella had been
right the day before. I had been wallowing in my misery for
the last six months. Really, if I'd been honest with myself, I'd
been drowning in it a lot longer than that. It felt good to come
back to the land of the living with the two people I loved most
in the world.

But just as the carriage turned back into a pumpkin in
Cinderella, I felt the sadness beginning to grip at my heart. It
threatened to morph me back into the sad sack I'd been the
day before.

Antoni bumped my hip with his. "Why the long face,
gorgeous?"

"Hmm?" I looked up into his chocolatey eyes that seemed
to see right through me. "Oh, nothing. Sorry. I guess I spaced
out there for a second." He studied me as though he were
trying to decide whether he believed me or not. Even if he
didn't, he decided not to press the issue any further.

He clutched his headset to his ear, listening intently. "Duty calls." He groaned before disappearing through the backstage area.

Midnight in Dallas closed their set with "Fortress." As promised, Jax dedicated it to Grace who dissolved into a puddle of happiness. From the response of the crowd, the song appeared to be a fan favorite. Upon closer inspection, the lyrics told the story of a girl who'd built a fortress to protect her from pain. In doing so, she discovered she'd locked out the whole world, and the hurt she'd tried so hard to run from had become her only friend.

At one point, Jax stopped singing, and the audience filled in every word in perfect harmony. Because Nashville, of course. The show ended in a much deserved decibel-crushing explosion of applause and screams.

"That was fucking amazing," Ella said breathlessly as the band ran off the stage opposite to where we were stationed.

"I told you." Cash nudged her arm and beamed with excitement. "Man, that was fun. Thanks for letting me hang out with you guys."

"Are you kidding me?" I asked. "Thanks for letting *us* hang out with *you*."

"I am ruined for all other concerts in the future." Grace laughed. "Ruined."

"I'm so glad you guys enjoyed it." Cash's eyes settled on Ella.

I pulled my phone out of my back pocket. I made a mental note to mention how many times Cash's eyes found their way to Ella during the course of the evening when she inevitably tried to bring up this Jax business again.

"We should probably get going." I was admittedly a little sad that our evening had come to an end.

Ella pouted. "It's going to be a bitch trying to get a Lyft outta here."

"Why don't I have Antoni give you guys a ride?" Cash asked. "I'd offer myself, but I've got to wrap up a few things here."

"That's so sweet of you," Ella said, "but we don't want you guys going through all that trouble for us."

"It's so nice of you to offer, though," I added. "You guys really rolled out the red carpet for us."

"Really, it's no trouble." Cash dismissed the notion with a wave of his hand. "Besides, it would make me feel better to know you ladies made it home safe." He placed a gentle hand on Ella's arm and began to move us through the bustle of the backstage area. He began tapping out a text on his phone, presumably to Antoni, as he guided us through the clusters of people. "I insist. He's parked out by the bus and our security detail, so you won't even have to get out in that mess of people."

"Cash, you're so damn sweet." Ella smiled gratefully. "Such a gentleman."

Grace and I echoed our thanks as he navigated us down the now empty corridor with the framed photos and posters that led beyond the dressing room. My phone buzzed in my back pocket, and I narrowly avoided dropping it as I extracted it from my jeans. A number I didn't recognize flashed across the screen, and I immediately felt heat threaten to rise into my cheeks. Ella looked back at me, her face laced with an 'I told you so' smugness as Grace squeezed my arm. It was far too late for a telemarketer. Surely it wasn't...

No. Absolutely not. There was no way in hell.

"Hello?" I answered cautiously.

"Where do you think you're going?" Jax's warm voice came through the phone.

"Hi, Jax." I laughed nervously as Ella and Grace exchanged a knowing glance. "We're heading home. Cash has Antoni giving us a ride." At the sound of his name, Cash cocked his head curiously.

"Correction," he said. "Giving Ella and Grace a ride home. You've got a prior commitment."

"Excuse me?"

"I told you earlier. I'm still gonna make your night. It must be done. Sorry. I don't make the rules."

"You need to get your story straight because ninety minutes ago you *did* make the rules."

"Turn around." His voice was soft, but I could hear his smile through the phone. The hairs on the back of my neck raised with anticipation. I stopped mid-step and turned around, my mouth curving into an involuntary smile. He was standing in the middle of the hallway outside the dressing room while the bodyguard stood watch a little further down. "Hi." He grinned as he started toward me.

"Hi." I dropped the phone to my side as he approached.

"Did you guys enjoy the show?"

"Y'all were amazing," Grace gushed. "This was seriously the best night of my life."

"I'm glad." He chuckled before addressing Ella and Grace. "Listen, ladies, I made a promise to Liv earlier that I'd like to keep. Do you mind if I take her off your hands for the rest of the night? That is, if she'll agree to come with me." He looked over at me hopefully, and my mind began to spin out of control. He really wasn't going to let this go.

"On one condition." Ella poked her finger into his chest. "You have to make sure she gets home safe. I don't care how famous or how cute you are, mister. You let anything happen to my best friend and the only song you'll be singing is the death march. Understood?"

"Understood." He saluted her. "I vow to protect her with my life."

Ella narrowed her eyes, analyzing him for a moment. "You have my blessing, but it's up to Liv."

He looked at me expectantly, his palms pressed together in a praying gesture in front of his chest. "What do you say?" I didn't know what in the world Jaxon Slade wanted with me. A man like him belonged next to the Jessica Rabbits of the world, not a woman like me.

"You should go, Aunt Liv." Grace prodded me.

"Thanks, Grace." He put an arm around her. "Please?" I couldn't help but laugh as he made Grace an accessory to his plan. They made sad puppy dog eyes in my direction. I glanced over at Ella who subtly motioned toward Jax with her eyes. I knew if I declined this invitation, I would never hear the end of it. I had to admit, I was curious too.

"Fine," I agreed. "I'll go with you."

His eyes lit up, and he hugged Grace. "You did it, Grace! I owe you one."

"VIP at every show in Nashville from here on out." She held her pinky finger out to him without missing a beat.

"Deal." He held out his pinky and linked it with hers. "But you guys have to bring Liv."

"Deal." She moved to give me a hug. "Love you, Aunt Liv."

"I love you too." I kissed her on the top of her head. "You little shit."

Ella reached out to embrace me too, giving Jax one last inspection with her eyes. "Is your phone charged?"

"Yes, mom." I snickered.

"Call me if you need me." Ella kissed my cheek. "I love you, babe. I'll text you soon to check on you, and if this fool pulls any funny business—"

"I'm not gon—" Jax started to defend himself, but Ella cut him off.

"*And if this fool pulls any funny business,* I'm fully prepared to take his life." She pointed two fingers at her eyes and then back at him to indicate that she was watching him. "I said what I said." Cash chuckled from where he stood beside her, clearly as amused by this entire situation as I was.

Jax held his hands up in surrender. "I promise."

With one last wave, Cash led Grace and Ella through the exit to the outside, and I was left standing face to face with Jax. He raised his brow, looking at me like a kid at Christmas.

He stared at me thoughtfully for a moment, looking me over in a way that made me wonder what he was thinking. I was beginning to wonder if I'd made a horrible mistake when he offered his arm to me. "Are you ready?"

Taking his arm, I felt every nerve in my body stand to attention. "Ready."

"I'VE GOT TO GRAB MY STUFF AND LET THE GUYS KNOW I'M out of here." He interrupted my thoughts as we reentered the dressing room we'd been in together only a couple of hours before. How was I standing here with Jaxon Slade about to embark on God knows what kind of adventure? Was this even real?

"Liv!" I was brought back to reality as Dallas stood, wrapping his tattooed arms around me in a hug. Jax stepped over to the long counter against the wall and rummaged through one of the gym bags strewn out on the counter, finally landing on a wallet and a set of keys. I watched with probably far too much interest as he shrugged his muscular shoulders into a distressed denim jacket. "You're still here. What did you guys think of the show?"

"You guys were amazing," I said. "Grace was over the moon."

"She's a cool kid." Dallas grinned, glancing sideways at Jax who had returned to my side and placed his hand on the small of my back. "You sure you want to go off with this fool tonight?"

"Nope. Not when you put it like that." I smiled nervously.

"I'm messing with you." He laughed. "Jax is my best friend. You're in good hands."

"Liv's here!" A ripped and shirtless Luca cheered as he entered the room. His alabaster skin and dark hair made his blue eyes appear as though they could pierce your soul. "Sorry, I'm all sweaty." He leaned in to hug me, not seeming the least bit sorry.

"You seem to have lost your shirt," I joked, unsure where to put my hands. "I believe I saw some out there on the merch table. You want me to go grab you one?"

"I like you, Liv," he said with a low chuckle. "You're a local, right? Where should I go tonight? Should I hit up Broadway?"

"Not if you don't want to get accosted by a bunch of drunk tourists singing 'Sweet Caroline' on a pedal tavern," I said flatly.

"Are there lots of pretty girls on these pedal taverns?" He winked at me, and I stifled a laugh.

"Bachelorette parties full of them, all waiting to make bad

decisions. You should probably find your shirt before you head out," I quipped. "I hear they're pretty strict with those no shirt, no shoes, no service policies in case you were planning on losing those too." I gestured at his shoes.

"I *really* like her." Luca raised his brow in Jax's direction. He began digging through one of the gym bags on the counter as Jax moved his arm to my shoulders, pulling me closer. It felt like a protective move, but I had no idea why.

"Are you guys headed out?" Derek looked up from his phone as he entered the room. With his tan skin and messy blond hair, he looked like a California surfer boy. It was easy to see why Grace was so infatuated with him.

"We are," Jax said.

"You sure you want to go off with this guy, Liv?" Luca smirked as he pulled a black My Chemical Romance T-shirt over his head. "All I'm saying is I think you'd have more fun with me and 'Sweet Caroline' on a pedal tavern."

"How can I possibly turn down a drunken ride on a mobile bar that smells like sweaty feet and cheap beer?" I ribbed at Jax. "Maybe I agreed to hang out with the wrong band member."

Dallas cackled. "I promise, you're in good hands."

"Beware if he's driving, though. Look out for any mail-boxes that happen to run out in the middle of the road," Derek teased. "Better yet, call an Uber." He and Dallas snickered.

My mouth twisted into a grin. "Oh?"

"It was one time." Jax laughed, his smile reaching the corners of his eyes. "You jerks will never let me live that down."

"After Jax got his first car, he was so excited to come over and show it off that he took out our mailbox as he drove by waving with that goofy-ass grin on his face." Dallas was laughing so hard he could hardly choke out the words. "He uprooted the entire mailbox."

"It was on the Fourth of July, and our entire extended family was there in the front yard." Derek howled. "We saw *everything.*"

I smirked. "That pedal tavern is looking better and better."

"We should leave." Jax shook his head, a sheepish smile on his face as Cash entered the room. "Before you guys make Liv regret agreeing to go anywhere with me." My stomach began doing some sort of complicated gymnastics floor routine at the thought of being alone with Jax.

"I had fun hanging with you guys tonight." Cash grinned. "Grace is a sweetheart, and that Ella is a pistol."

"We had fun too." I smiled. *A pistol, huh?* I made sure to add that to my mental notes for Ella tomorrow. "Do you guys get out to Nashville much?"

"All the time," Derek answered. "We love Nashville. We're here for work a lot."

"Next time you guys are in town, you'll have to stop by our bakery. Ella and I own Livvie Cakes Bakery and Cupcakery over in 12 South. We'll load y'all up with cupcakes."

Dallas' eyes were wide as he pulled his golden blonde hair back into a ponytail. "Liv, are you telling me you make delicious desserts for a living? If you are, I take back everything I said. Don't go with Jax. He's the worst. Go with me instead." He shot a joking glance at Jax, clearly trying to get a rise out of him. "*And* I'm a good driver."

"I'd love to come visit," Cash said. "I'll try to pop in before I head back to LA."

"Alright, guys." Jax placed his hands on my shoulders. "We're going to get out of here."

"I meant what I said about those cupcakes." I waved to the guys, and Cash stepped forward to give me a hug. "It was great meeting y'all. Thanks for everything."

"See you guys later. I'll be by for cupcakes soon," Dallas called out as Jax steered me out of the room.

"You need me?" The security guard that had gotten an earful earlier was propped outside the doorway.

"I don't think so, man. Where we're going, we should be okay," Jax said. Where exactly *were* we going? "By the way, Liv, this is Brady. He's part of our security team. He's usually with me."

"Nice to meet you, Liv." He grinned at me, and my embarrassment from earlier came flooding back.

"Likewise." I could feel the heat radiating off my cheeks.

"I'll see you back at the hotel," Jax called over his shoulder as he led me down the corridor toward the exit. He swung the door open, holding it for me. The cool night's breeze helped melt away my embarrassment as I followed him down the sidewalk. A few feet beyond where their tour bus was parked, he stopped in front of a vehicle that could only be described as The Batmobile. "This is us."

"When you said you wanted to make my night, I had no clue we were going to be fighting crime in Gotham City." My eyes widened. "I left my superhero cape at home."

His cheeks flushed as he looked down at the car that looked more like a movie prop than anything you could drive. "It's a little much isn't it?"

"I'm more concerned that we won't be able to fit in it at the same time." I laughed.

"I have this nerdy thing for exotic cars," he admitted. "They're way too impractical for me to ever own one, but sometimes when we have some time off, I like to rent one to see what it feels like."

"What do you feel like driving this one?"

"A little like Batman to be honest."

"Well, let's get this show on the road, Bruce Wayne. The good people of Gotham are counting on us."

He grinned at me as he clicked the key fob, causing the doors to scissor open. He gestured toward the passenger seat. "After you." I got in, and he pushed the door, sliding it closed. I glanced around inside the car as he jogged over to the driver's side.

The inside was so foreign to me that it may as well have been a spaceship taking us to the freaking moon. For as weird as the night had been, that could have been exactly what was happening, and I wouldn't have even been surprised.

"So, where are we headed, Bruce? To the Batcave?" I raised my brow at him as he set the car in motion.

"Not quite." He laughed. "I want to take you to one of my favorite places in Nashville, but we have one pitstop to make first." He easily maneuvered through downtown without the use of a GPS and navigated the spaceship to the interstate with ease.

"I love that you have a favorite spot here in town. It better not be a pedal tavern though, or so help me I will jump from this Batmobile to escape."

"I promise it's not a pedal tavern." He laughed. "As Derek said, we come here a lot, especially these last three years. Our label is here, but our contract is up next year. We haven't exactly been thrilled with the direction things are going, so we're in the process of shopping around."

"Why haven't you guys been happy?" I asked. "If that's not too personal."

"Our label wants us to start using other writers' songs." He sighed heavily. "They've been sending us some stuff to listen to, and none of it's exciting. None of it is *us,* you know? They've also been really pushing us to do collabs with some other artists whose style isn't anything like ours. No shade, but that's not something we want to do. Don't get me wrong, if the right collaboration came along, we wouldn't say no. But it needs to be organic and not forced to pump up sales."

"From what I could tell tonight, you guys are really talented in the songwriting department and every other department for that matter. Sounds like parting ways may be the right thing to do."

"This industry is weird." He glanced over at me as he changed lanes. "I hope this doesn't sound conceited, but we got to where we are because of *our* songs. Because of our writing and the way we click together. We put our souls into what we write, and that's what got us to this point. Not because we did a collab and a high budget music video with some pop star. That probably sounds really cocky."

I sat thoughtfully for a moment. "I don't think so. If anything, I think it says you guys are smart. You know what works, but more than that, you know what feels right for you, and you're staying true to yourself. It's refreshing, honestly."

"You think so?"

"Yeah. I do." I watched as the Nashville skyline disappeared from view in the side mirror. "What's it like anyway? That level of fame... is it weird?"

"Honestly? It's weird as hell." His thumb smoothed over the steering wheel, and he seemed lost in thought for a moment. "I'd give anything if I could go on stage and not have to worry that someone may try to follow me home or back to my hotel. To be able to exist without having to be

Jaxon Slade, frontman of Midnight in Dallas. Most of the time, I want a quiet, simple life, you know?"

"And a Batmobile, obviously."

"*Obviously.*" He laughed, taking my teasing in stride.

"I can't imagine what that's like." Back when I played the honky-tonk bars on Broadway, I could walk off stage and go back to my regular life. They'd probably forgotten my name by the time the next band started up if they even remembered it at all.

"I don't mean that to sound ungrateful," he added quickly as he exited the interstate. "I know we wouldn't be where we are without our fans, and I love them. I do. I love hearing how our music was there for them during a difficult time in their lives or what their favorite song means to them. It's the other stuff that goes along with it that's challenging."

"I don't think that makes you ungrateful." I shook my head. "I think you can be grateful for your success without being in love with every aspect of it." I paused a moment and glanced over at him. "So these meet and greets, where do those fall on the love it or leave it spectrum?"

"Sometimes they can be draining. But tonight… tonight, I loved it." He smiled over at me as we cruised down a road I was only vaguely familiar with. "We're almost at our pitstop."

I began looking around for any clue as to what this pitstop might be. I saw several car lots, a bank, and a thrift store. The street was lined with businesses, but none that would be open at this hour.

That's when I saw it.

The pink neon lights blinked in invitation to Lion's Den Adult Entertainment Store.

Surely not, right? I hadn't given any indication I would be down for a trip to the Lion's Den, had I? This guy was hot, but I was *definitely* not ready for him to see my Batcave. He began to slow the car as we got closer to the neon pink beacon in the night.

Shit. Shit. Shit. My palms started sweating, and my heart thudded so hard I could feel it in my ears. The one time I forgot to put my mace in my purse, I managed to find myself in the Batmobile with a rockstar going to the fucking Lion's Den to tame my hostile kitty. *Shit.*

"Um, Jax... I think maybe you got the wrong idea here," I squeaked out as the car's speed slowed more, the entrance to the Lion's Den only a few yards away. "I know you said you wanted to make my night, but I hope I didn't make you think I would be interested in..." I trailed off as we passed by the pink neon lights, and he turned right into the Krispy Kreme parking lot. The donut shop sat far back enough that I couldn't see it until that moment, and conveniently enough, the light on their road sign was out.

"Wait, what?" Jax looked over at me, confused. "I thought everyone liked donuts."

FOUR

Jax

"OH SHIT." I brought the car to a stop in the parking lot. "Are you gluten-free?" After she'd mentioned her bakery earlier, I thought for sure she'd be down for some donuts, and these were my favorite. Every time I was in a city with a Krispy Kreme, I had to have them. "Or on a low carb thing or…"

"No, it's not that." She covered her face with her hands, her shoulders shaking with laughter. "I love donuts, but I thought—" A fit of giggles ripped through her, and it was so damn cute. I found myself laughing along with her, even though I had no clue what the joke was. She removed her hands, and even in the dim lighting of the parking lot, I could see that her face had turned pink. Her eyes glistened with tears as she tried unsuccessfully to stop laughing. "I didn't think this was where we were going," she choked out. "I kind of freaked out for a minute there. Whew. Crisis averted."

I chuckled, still completely confused, as I watched her entire body vibrate with laughter.

That's when I saw it. Pink neon lights glittered in my

rearview mirror advertising the Lion's Den Adult Entertainment Store.

Oh. My. God. "Wait. You thought I was taking you to the sex shop?" Warmth rose to my cheeks, and I roared with laughter.

She nodded and pressed her lips together, unable to meet my gaze. Slowly she turned to look at me and nodded, causing us both to dissolve once again.

"It's because I heard that 'hostile kitty' comment, huh?" I raised my brow at her.

"Oh, fuck." She covered her face once more, peeking at me through her fingers. "You heard that?"

"Sure did."

She laughed so hard she snorted, and it made me laugh even harder. "I would say 'gee thanks for a fun night' and bail, but I'm already in your car. I'm kind of committed now."

"So, you're not going to make a run for it?"

"No." She paused, smirking over at me, and I felt my heart catch in my throat. "But only because I really like donuts."

"That's fair." I snickered, put the car back in drive, and proceeded to the drive-thru. I ordered a half-dozen assorted donuts and two hot chocolates. I made it through the pickup window without being recognized and turned out of the parking lot onto the main road. "Now, for the main event."

"Listen, I'm just glad you didn't turn this Batmobile back around toward the Lion's Den. I would have made a run for it, *and* you'd have been left with no donuts." She grinned over at me, clutching the box in her hands. "That would have been tragic."

"Please." I pretended to beg. "Donut run away."

"Donut do this to me," she fired back, throwing her head

back with that bouncy laugh of hers. "Donut tell terrible donut jokes."

"Hey, I thought that was pretty clever." I shrugged, winking at her.

"Okay, yeah. It was pretty good." She pressed her lips together, suppressing a laugh. "Donut go getting a big head about it."

We howled with laughter as I turned the car and began to wind my way through the familiar roads of the Berry Hill neighborhood of Nashville.

"Hey," she said bright-eyed. "I know where we are. Sort of. There's that awesome coffee place with the really good lavender lattes."

"Sam and Zoe's." I nodded. "Though I'm partial to the Davey Mabee."

"Mmmm. That's a good one," she agreed. "This seems a little off the beaten path for you. I thought most of the record companies were around Music Row?"

"They are," I explained, "but the recording studios aren't." I parked the car in an empty overflow lot, cutting off the engine.

"Wow, there's literally nobody over here." She surveyed the quiet street as she unbuckled her seatbelt. "It's completely deserted."

"It's one of the things I love most about this spot." I smiled over at her.

"This isn't about to turn into an episode of *Criminal Minds*, is it? If it is, can I at least have a donut first for my trouble?" Her eyes glittered mischievously.

"No." I stuck my tongue out at her. "It's not. Now come on. Let's walk."

"Wait, so we don't get to eat the donuts?"

"We do," I assured her. I grabbed the hot chocolates, and she carried the donuts as we started off down the desolate road. "But I'm taking you to one of my favorite spots first."

"So, the parking lot wasn't it?" She continued to tease me, and I loved every second of it. The air felt as though it were filled with an electric charge as I fell into step beside her.

The quaint tree-lined neighborhood was full of old homes that had been converted into various businesses. However, those businesses weren't generally open past six or seven in the evening, leaving this little corner of the city quiet at such a late hour. "We recorded all of our last album here and part of the one before that. Blackbird Studios is a couple of streets over, but my favorite studio is House of Blues because it's a short walk from this amazing pie diner that serves nothing but sweet and savory pies." I gestured toward The Loving Pie Company sign on our right.

"A *pie diner?*" Her eyes were wide with wonder. "That sounds like heaven."

"It is. The owner makes these personal-sized pot pies and this mac-n-cheese pie that puts all other mac-n-cheese to shame. Mac-n-cheese. *In a pie crust.*"

"Sign me *up.*"

"I'll have to bring you here one day." She eyed me curiously, but didn't say anything. It wasn't a no, so I'd take it. "Anytime we record during the day, I always try to sneak down here for pie. If we're on a late-night schedule, it's donuts." I nodded toward the box in her hands. "Speaking of donuts, let's sit down for a minute because those donuts are calling my name." I gestured toward the small cluster of picnic tables outside the pie shop that was illuminated by twinkly golden globe lights. I climbed up and sat on top of the table, placing the hot chocolates down so I could give her my hand.

"Thanks." She used my hand to steady herself. I took the donut box from her hands, opening it and placing it on the small stretch of the table she left between us. "What's your poison?" I asked, handing her one of the hot chocolates.

She chewed her bottom lip in thought before finally plucking the strawberry iced with sprinkles from the box. "Thank you." She took one perfect bite out of it. "So, donuts, pie... I'm guessing you have a major sweet tooth."

"You guessed right." I downed an original glazed in two bites for emphasis, and she laughed as she took another bite. "Tell me more about your bakery. Did you always want to bake?"

She looked down at her partially eaten donut for a moment. "I always enjoyed it," she said tentatively. "I started out baking cakes in my tiny apartment and delivering them to people long before Livvie Cakes was born. It was one of those things that kind of took on a life of its own." Her phone pinged with a text, and she set her hot chocolate down so she could extract it from her back pocket. "It's Ella."

"Making sure I'm on my best behavior?"

"Something like that." She smirked.

"You mentioned that Ella works with you?" I plucked a chocolate glazed donut from the box and scarfed it down.

She nodded. "About a year after I opened the bakery, Ella's husband passed away. Grace had just turned five, and at the time Ella was a stay at home mom." She took another bite of her donut, lost in thought for a moment. "Ella's been my best friend since our freshman year in high school. No matter what, it's always been the two of us, you know? When Craig died, I knew I had to make the business work. It had to succeed because I had to make sure she and Grace were taken care of. So, Ella joined me full-time, and now we've been named the city's top bakery six years in a row. I couldn't do it without her."

"I was really shocked to learn you guys weren't sisters," I said as she finished off her donut. "The way you guys are with each other, I assumed you were."

"We are." She smiled fondly. "In all the ways that matter. Grace and Ella are my family. My folks passed away a few years ago, and I never had any siblings. Grace and Ella are all I have left." She sighed and opened her mouth as though she were going to say something else, but she didn't.

"Does that mean there's no special someone in your life?"

"I told you about the two special someones in my life." She raised her brow at me before taking a drink of her hot chocolate.

"I meant a different type of someone." I held the box out to her again as she grabbed a maple glazed donut and took a bite. "A romantic someone."

She took another bite, not in any hurry to answer my question. "Not anymore." She glanced over at me quizzically. "Why do you want to know?"

"Because I have a sweet tooth, and you own a bakery." I nudged her playfully.

Why wouldn't I want to know? She was beautiful and freaking hilarious, but there was something else about her that drew me in. There was something in her eyes that said she was no stranger to heartbreak, and that was something we had in common.

She studied me a moment as though she were considering if she should press the question further, but didn't. "What about you?" She took another small bite of her donut. "Tell me about your family."

I plucked a cream-filled donut from the box. "Honestly, the band is my family."

"Isn't that a thing that all bands say while secretly hating each other?"

"Sometimes." I laughed. "But in our case it's true." I took a big bite and chewed thoughtfully before finally returning the partially eaten pastry to the box. "I grew up in foster care. My dad died when I was a baby, and my mom struggled with addiction her entire life. I guess the drugs kind of won out. By the time I was in foster care permanently, I was already eleven years old. A lot of people want to adopt babies, but they're not exactly lining up to adopt the kid with behavioral issues and a drug addict mom." I sucked in a breath, shocked at how easily my life story began to tumble out of me. There was something about Liv that made me want to show her the version of me most people never saw.

"Jax…" Her face softened, and her eyes met mine.

"I had two different sets of foster parents, and neither of them were exactly winning parent of the year awards. They were both content to collect their checks. In exchange, I had a roof over my head, but not *parents,* you know? The second family I was placed with, the Millers, lived across the street from Derek. We used to ride our bikes together in the neighborhood, and because of Derek, I met Dallas. That's when my life started to change. They became the brothers I never had."

"Were they the ones that got you into music?"

I nodded. "We spent most of our time at Dallas' house. His dad had this old record player and a massive record collection. After school, we'd go hang out in his garage and listen to music for hours. Everything from Bob Dylan to Fleetwood

Mac to Pink Floyd and Michael Jackson. Dal's dad got him and Derek a couple of guitars from some thrift store. He signed them up for lessons, and they started teaching me to play too. Once Dal got his drum set, he passed his guitar on to me. That's when I became obsessed with it. Music was my escape. After Derek and I graduated, he went away to the same college as Dallas, and that's when they started Dallas Knights."

"That's when it was just the two of them, right?"

"Yep. Meanwhile, I was waiting tables at two different restaurants just trying to survive. I rented this shitty studio apartment that didn't even have a kitchen, but I fucking loved it because it was the first thing besides my guitar and my car that was mine. I would go to work for fourteen to sixteen hours every day and come home and practice until my fingers were numb. By that time, I was writing songs and playing at every coffee shop or writer's night I could get to between shifts. One night when Derek and Dallas were home for the summer, I invited them to a round I was playing at some hole in the wall bar. They heard me sing some of the songs I'd written, and that's when they asked me to join their band."

"How did you guys connect with Luca?"

"For a few months, it was just the three of us. We played some shows together that summer while they were still in town, and people really liked our stuff. We started with some cover songs and slowly started doing some of my originals, but it felt like something was missing." I took a sip of my hot chocolate. "When they went back to school that fall, Dallas rented this little run-down house off campus with a garage for us to rehearse in, but he needed a room-mate. He put out an ad, and as luck would have it, Luca was the one that found it. The rest was history. From the second the four of us played together the first time, we knew we had something special. Thankfully, a lot of people agreed with us."

"Wow," she said. "I love that. You guys clearly have a strong bond."

"We definitely have our issues from time to time. Luca and I probably butt heads the most. He came from a similar background as me. He grew up in a group home in Lexington, and until he joined the band, he didn't exactly have a lot of friends. He can be a bit closed off sometimes, but we've been around him long enough to know that's how he copes. Honestly, if I hadn't found Derek and Dal all those years ago, we might have been a lot more alike."

"I never would have pegged him for being closed off," she admitted. "He seems very comfortable with attention."

I nodded. "Attention is kind of a drug for him, but actual attachment? That's not one of his strong points. I feel like we've only gotten close to him these last couple of years, and close is a relative term. He doesn't let people in easily."

"That's good that he has you, though. That you all have each other. Finding our people in life is important." She took another bite of her donut. "So, do *you* have someone special in your life?" She looked at me pointedly, tossing my own question back at me.

I looked at her as she waited for me to answer, her skin illuminated by the twinkly golden lights. "Not yet."

She nodded, her eyes fixed on mine, and I swear I'd never seen anyone more breathtaking.

"You have some icing right here," I lied. I gently reached out to touch the corner of her perfect mouth, and her cheeks blushed beneath my touch. Her skin was as soft and buttery as I'd imagined.

"Thanks," she said softly, as I forced my hand away from her.

"You up for a walk?" I asked as she chewed the last bite of her donut. She nodded, and we discarded our cups and the box in the bin outside the pie shop. I walked alongside her, shoving my hands in my pockets to keep myself from reaching for her hand.

WE WALKED AND TALKED OUR WAY THROUGH THE neighborhood, strolling past a couple of boutiques, a salon, and even a tattoo shop. As we circled back around, we found ourselves near the House of Blues taking in the hand-painted murals on the picket fence that lined the street of artists like Minnie Pearl, Dolly Parton, Stevie Wonder, Prince, and Johnny Cash. Set against bold, colorful patterns their like-nesses appeared almost alive beneath the flickering glow of the street lamps. Finally, she stopped in front of the Johnny Cash painting, studying his face for a moment before turning to look at me.

"I did have someone," she blurted suddenly. "I was married. I got married when I was really young. He was in the music industry on the business side of things."

"Liv…"

"I wanted to put that out there. It's something I'm still getting used to." She looked down at her feet. "Our divorce was finalized six months ago."

"I'm sorry," I murmured, afraid if I pushed too much this would be the last piece I would receive to the puzzle that was Olivia Sinclair.

"It's okay. I may not have been the one that filed the papers, but I can't say I didn't see it coming."

"Regardless, I can't imagine how much that hurt you."

"It did," she admitted. "Yesterday, I saw a picture of him with this young supermodel looking girl, and honestly, it fucking sucked. It's not even that I miss him anymore." She chewed her bottom lip, deep in thought for a moment, and I waited patiently. I wanted whatever pieces of herself she was willing to reveal to me. "Anyway, I saw this picture of them together and the way he leaned into her, looking so proud to have her on his arm. I recognized it all too well because that's exactly the way he used to be with me. Back then, he loved to have me all dolled up and perched on his arm at all of these industry galas and parties. But as time went on, the invitations stopped coming." She laughed then, though I sensed she didn't think any part of what she said was funny. "He'd say he needed to go alone, or he was going to pop by the party and wouldn't be late. Needless to say, he always was." She ground her boot into the asphalt, still not meeting my gaze. "It's not like I didn't suspect there was someone else. Or maybe even more than one someone. I guess I didn't want to know. I didn't want to know I wasn't enough for him."

My heart twisted inside my chest. Not enough? This guy was a fucking idiot. She fell silent, and her face turned downward. At that moment, all I wanted to do was hold her like she deserved to be held.

I took a step toward her, placing my hand on her arm. "Any man would be lucky to have you."

"I'm sorry." She shook her head as a flush crept across her cheeks. "I wasn't fishing for compliments or anything. You don't have to—"

"I know I don't have to say it." I interrupted her. "I said it because I meant it. I don't think you realize how rare you are, Liv."

She sighed, looking at me from beneath her long black lashes. "You hardly know me, Jax."

"But I want to know you," I said softly. "Listen, Liv, I'm not going to mince words here. You're ridiculously funny. You're clearly driven and talented, and I don't have to know you well to see how sweet and kind you are. That's obvious from the way you are with Ella and Grace and how you were with the guys and me." My chest tightened, already afraid I'd said too much. "And you're beautiful. Disarmingly so. I don't know if you've noticed or not, but I can't take my eyes off you." She pressed her lips together, and I pressed forward. "So, what do you say? Will you let me know you?"

"Why?" She asked bluntly, her eyes narrowing on me.

"Look, I know we just met, and you probably think I'm crazy." I scrubbed my hands over my face. "I feel a little crazy right now, to be honest with you, but I'm drawn to you. Don't you feel it too?"

The faintest smile crossed her lips before her gaze shifted to the pavement. *Fuck.* She really was going to head for the hills. Finally, her eyes returned to mine. "Can I ask you a question?"

"Sure," I said hopefully.

She peered up into my eyes, and the cool breeze whirled around us, sending a hint of sweet citrus and champagne in my direction. "How old are you?"

FIVE

Liv

————

TWENTY-NINE. My head was spinning. I suspected he was younger than me, but I didn't think he was *twenty-nine* younger.

"Yeah, I turned twenty-nine on August 13th," Jax continued, not helping. "When's your birthday?"

"October 17th," I said flatly.

"That's soon. I'd love to help you celebrate." He was trying to distract me.

"You're twenty-nine."

"Exactly. That means I've had twenty-nine years of experience celebrating birthdays, and I don't mean to brag, but I'm kind of an expert now." He laughed nervously while I stood there unable to form actual words. Finally, he asked the necessary question. "How old are you?"

"Not twenty-nine," I fired back.

"I gathered that." I narrowed my eyes at him. "Not because I think you don't look it, but because you keep saying the word 'twenty-nine' like it's poisonous or something."

"I'll be thirty-seven," I said finally.

"Okay." He shrugged.

"When I was thirty, you were twenty-two."

"Believe it or not, I can do basic math." He held up his hands and wiggled them. "Without even using my fingers."

"When I was twenty, you were twelve."

"Way to make it weird," he teased.

I stared back at him blankly. "I think it's time for me to go home." I started to brush past him, but he grabbed me gently by my arm.

"Whoa, wait a minute," he pleaded. "I was messing with you. There's nothing about this that's weird."

"Jax, I'm eight years older than you." I wasn't sure what part of that he wasn't getting.

"Yeah, and I don't care." Jax's hand slid down my arm until he held my hand. He looked at my delicate hand in his strong one for a moment before focusing his intense eyes back on me. "I like you, Liv. I don't give a fuck about your age."

"You may not think so now, but—"

"But nothing," he said emphatically. Visions of Jessica Rabbit the supermodel danced in my head. You never think it matters until it does. He looked at me earnestly as if I'd spoken my thoughts out loud. My gaze fell to my feet, but he hooked his finger beneath my chin, bringing my eyes back to his. "I don't pretend to know everything you went through with your ex, but I can tell you one damn thing for sure. I'm not him."

I don't know if it was the way his spicy, woodsy scent mixed with the crisp autumn air, the sugar rush from the donuts, or if it was the way he looked at me like I was something special, but something inside me wanted to believe him.

"I know this sounds crazy, but I've felt a connection between us ever since I saw you standing outside that dressing room, and I think you feel it too." He took a step closer to me, my hand still enclosed in his. "So, I'm going to ask you again. Will you let me know you?'

"I don't know, Jax." I shook my head.

"Please." His mouth stretched into an adorable grin. "I promise I'll grow on you."

"Like a fungus?" I asked, my lips curling into a smile against my will.

"Exactly like that," he murmured, reaching for my other hand. I relished in the feeling of his calloused fingers against my skin.

"Okay," I agreed. I withdrew my hands from his, and a flash of disappointment flickered across his face. "Friends. We can be friends."

He raised an eyebrow at me. "Uh-huh."

"Friends," I insisted.

"You drive a hard bargain, Olivia Sinclair." He nodded slowly, pressing his lips together. "Alright. Fine. Whatever I have to agree to for you not to shut us down."

"There is no *us*," I reminded him, tilting my head in warning.

"Not yet." He grinned at me playfully. "How can you be so sure you won't find me irresistible?" That was exactly the problem. I already found him irresistible, but I just couldn't let myself go there.

"It really is getting late," I said. "I've got to work in a few short hours." He gazed at me intently as though he could figure me out and unravel me with his eyes. I averted my gaze, afraid that if he looked at me like that long enough, he probably could.

"Alright." He nodded. "Let's get you home. To the Batmobile!"

We walked back to the car in comfortable silence, close enough that our arms touched every few steps. I caught Jax gazing over at me a few times, his hand at his side and his fingers so close to my own that I could have easily taken his hand in mine. I dug my own hands deep in my pockets to keep from doing exactly that. When we reached the car, he hit the fob and opened the door, tucking me safely inside before jogging around to the driver's side.

Our conversation on the short drive to my house was light, though the way he kept looking over at me was anything but. I helped him navigate the backroads leading from Berry Hill to 12 South. A few moments later, he pulled the Batmobile to a stop in front of my house.

"Thank you for coming out with me tonight," he said softly. "I had a good time."

"Me too." I smiled over at him. "Thanks for the donuts."

"Donut mention it." He laughed and waggled his eyebrows, clearly proud of himself.

I shook my head and giggled, reaching for the door.

"Wait." Before I could protest, he hopped out and met me on the other side, helping me out of the car. "Let me walk you to your door."

"Absolutely not," I said adamantly.

"And why not?"

"Because that's too date-y."

"Is that a real word?"

"It is now," I answered.

"Because, to be clear, this wasn't a date?" His tone was joking, but his face told me he believed this was a date.

"Correct," I replied.

"Right. I guess I'm going to have to watch you walk to your door like a creeper."

"*Or* you could get back in your car and drive away."

"I can't do that. What if an actual creeper comes along and you need me to save you?"

"Fine." I rolled my eyes and chuckled. "Good night, Jax."

His eyes settled on me. All traces of laughter left his face, and in their place was a look that could only be described as tender. "Good night, Liv."

I fished for my keys and phone as I started up the stone walkway. By the time I reached the door and had my key in the lock, my phone was ringing in my hand. Worry flashed through my mind for a split second until I saw the number that flickered across. "Hello, Jax," I said, laughing to myself.

"Turn around." I turned to see him leaned against the Batmobile like a modern-day James Dean, his phone to his ear. He looked like he belonged in a Lamborghini ad and not standing outside my house.

"Yeah?"

"Will you have dinner with me tomorrow?"

"Jax, I don't—"

"Please."

"Alright," I conceded. I turned back to fiddle with the door, balancing the phone between my ear and shoulder.

"It's a non-date-y date." I could hear his smile through the phone. "And Liv?"

"Yeah?" I asked. I opened the door, looking back at him over my shoulder.

"Donut miss me too much." The line went dead, but his hearty laugh danced all the way to the door as he strolled back to the driver's side of the Batmobile. With one last wave, he was gone.

THE ALARM ON MY PHONE BLARED RUDELY, STARTLING ME awake. According to my phone, it was 8:30 a.m. I laid there for a moment and rubbed my eyes, my body already begging for coffee. By the time I'd texted Ella to let her know I'd made it home safely and willed my brain to shut down, it was after 4 a.m.

I groaned as I rolled out of bed, my feet reluctantly hitting the floor. I'd only had one glass of champagne, so why did I feel hungover? My stomach was jittery thinking about Jax and how much we'd connected the night before. My insides were a jumble of nerves. Was it possible to have an emotional hangover? Or perhaps it was because I was almost thirty-seven years old, and I'd stayed out all night like a teenager.

My phone pinged with a text before I could even make it out of the bedroom.

Ella: You have exactly one hour to get your adorable rock-star loving ass over here to tell me about last night, or I'm coming over.

I chuckled as I typed out my response.

Liv: Be there soon. Brew more coffee, and set up the IV, please.

I padded into the kitchen and turned on the Keurig before I started back down the hall to the bathroom. I flicked the light on and turned the handle on the shower, letting steam fill the room. I caught a glimpse of my tired reflection in the mirror, my mind still reeling from the night before.

Will you let me know you?

Jax's words echoed through my mind as I recalled how persistent he'd been the night before. My mind drifted to how handsome he'd looked leaned against the Batmobile when he dropped me off. The more I thought about it, the more I wondered if it had all been a dream.

Whether it had happened or not didn't really matter. What mattered was that it was back to work, and back to reality, now. There was no way in hell this dinner thing was happening.

After a quick shower, I covered the dark circles under my eyes with some concealer so as not to frighten any customers I might have to see. I sprayed my scalp with a steady stream of dry shampoo in an attempt to make my hair look presentable. I slipped a hair tie around my wrist and tousled my hair on my way to the closet to throw on some clothes.

I shoved my feet into my boots and went back to the kitchen to feed Mama who was nowhere to be seen and grabbed a cup of coffee on my way out the door. The walk to work was cool and drizzly, but I didn't mind. The contrast of the chilly air and the warm coffee helped wake me up a bit. When I walked through the back door of the kitchen at 9:23 a.m., I already felt more alert. Ella stood waiting to interrogate me with the pot of coffee in her hand.

"You had exactly seven more minutes before I came to beat down your door." She refilled my coffee as I pulled my apron off the hook, tying it around me. I tossed my bag on the hook, and she handed my mug back to me. "Tell me everything."

"Okay. Let's start with how Cash sure loved him some Ella."

"What?" She tilted her head quizzically, as though she had no clue what I was talking about. "No way."

"Girl, he made sure he was next to you all night," I reminded her. "After you left, he said you were a pistol. He's *cute* too."

She grabbed her own mug off the counter and filled it. "Yeah, he's hot, but I hardly think a guy like him would be interested in some mom with a teenage daughter. Besides, I've only got this year before Grace goes off to college, so I'm not trying to find any distractions."

I raised my brow at her, but decided to drop it. "Where's Katie?" I asked, surveying the kitchen and all of the cupcakes and tarts she'd already made. Damn, that girl was always on top of it.

"Stocking the cases out front," she responded impatiently, returning the coffee pot to its place on the counter. "So? Spill it. What happened? Did you guys make out?"

"No." I snorted, choking on my coffee. "Of course not."

"What do you mean, *of course not?* He's a hot rockstar. Why *wouldn't* you make out with him?"

"It wasn't like that." I brushed her off. I pulled the binder that contained our orders off the counter, but before I could even open it, she'd snatched it out of my hands.

"Okay then, what *was* it like?" She plopped the binder back down for effect.

"He took me to get donuts." I sighed and leaned against the counter, taking another glorious sip of my coffee. "Then, we went for a walk over in Berry Hill. He showed me one of the studios the band records at and this pie shop he really likes."

She narrowed her eyes. "So, you just went for a walk?"

I shrugged. "Yeah. Pretty much."

"There's something you're not telling me." She raised her brow at me accusatorily.

My eyes shifted to the inside of my coffee cup. "I don't know what you're talking about."

"You little turkey." She rounded on me, pointing her perfectly manicured nail in my direction. "Tell me. What happened? What did he say?"

Ella hung on my every word as I recounted the events from the night before, complete with the Batmobile, the donut jokes, and how much we'd confided in each other. She grabbed my hand, a gasp escaping her lips, when I finally told her the question Jax asked me.

"Will you let me know you?" Ella squealed. She took my face in her hands, causing me to narrowly avoid spilling my coffee. "That's so fucking romantic. Oh my God. You're gonna marry him. I can feel it in my bones."

"That is not happening." I threw back the rest of my coffee and turned to wash my mug in the sink. "That's honestly the furthest thing from my mind. It's too soon."

I could see her out of the corner of my eye, watching my every movement as I washed my hands. "Okay. *And?* We don't get to choose when we meet the right person, babe. Sometimes it happens when we least expect it."

"I love you," I said, "but you're out of your mind. You've seen one too many romcoms."

"Okay," she conceded. "I'm not suggesting you marry him tomorrow, but he *likes* you. This very sweet, very charming, *very hot* guy is clearly smitten with you. And I know you, Liv. I can tell you like him too."

"How?" I dried my hands off and grabbed a pastry bag from the counter, loading it with the milk chocolate frosting Katie had already made. Avoiding her gaze, I moved to the large island in the center of the room where we did all of our decorating. "How can you tell?"

"Gee, I don't know," she said sarcastically. "Maybe because you can't even look at me when you talk about him?"

"Because I'm *trying* to get to work." I scoffed and began to swirl the frosting over the bare dark chocolate cupcakes.

"Okay," she said. She waited until I'd decorated the first

cupcake before taking me by the shoulders, turning me to face her. "Look me in the eyes, and tell me you don't like him."

"Ella." I sighed, still looking at the undecorated cupcakes. "I don't have time for this."

"Tell. Me."

"Fine. I don't *not* like him, okay?"

"I *knew* it."

"And he did ask me to have dinner with him tonight," I confessed. "But I can't. Honestly, he's probably going to cancel anyway because *that,* what happened last night, is not real life."

"There's a zero percent chance he's going to cancel on you," Ella said flatly. "Zero, because *he likes you.*"

"Then I'll have to cancel." I shrugged. "I *cannot* go out with him again."

"Why the fuck not?"

"Because he's twenty-nine."

"Okay? So?"

"*So,* he's way too young for me," I declared.

"Oh my God, Olivia." She shook me gently by the shoulders. "He is *not.*"

"Yes, he is." I threw my hands up. "Because as you keep pointing out, this guy is a freaking gorgeous rockstar, Ella. I'm an almost thirty-seven-year-old woman with a hostile kitty guarding an even more hostile uterus. I've already been traded in for a newer, younger model, and I'm not real anxious to go through that again with *anyone.*"

"Honey, what Benton did to you was pure shit." Her eyes softened toward me as she gave my arm a comforting squeeze. "But you can't hold that against Jax. You can't judge him based on what Benton did. You need to give Jax a chance to show you who he is. Let him know you, Liv."

"This is crazy. This whole Jax thing is not real life." I turned my attention back to the cupcakes. "It's a thing that happened, and now it's done. Can we please move on?"

"I hate to tell you, but this *is* real life," she countered. "Yes, I know I keep pointing out that he's this hot rockstar, but *so what?* That's only a part of his life. That's not who he is. From what I can tell, based on last night and what you've told me, he's also a really sweet guy who tells *terrible* jokes, and he *sees* you, Liv. I know that's got to be scary after what happened with Benton, but you deserve to be seen, babe. You *deserve* someone who will treat you like the fucking goddess you are. You're having dinner with him. Even if I have to drag you by that annoyingly perfect hair of yours. You're go—"

"Sorry to interrupt." Katie's voice came tentatively from the kitchen door. "The door is open, and there's already a couple of customers up there. I'd take care of them, but we got a last-minute order I need to get started on."

"That's okay." I looked pointedly at Ella.

"I'll take care of them, Katie Bug." Ella smiled at Katie as she moved toward the door. She tossed a knowing glance back in my direction. "But this conversation is *not* over."

I let out an exasperated sigh as I continued piping the frosting on top of the cupcakes. I tried to shift my focus to creating the perfect icing swirls, to Katie as she ticked off the details of the new order—to anywhere but Jaxon Slade.

SIX

Jax

"WHAT THE HECK happened last night, Jax?" Dallas dug his fork into the giant omelet in front of him. "I've never seen you get all googly-eyed like that before, but the second Liv walked in you turned into a giant weirdo."

I sat across from him and Cash in the cafe on the ground floor of the hotel. Our server seated us in the rear corner, while Brady and a couple of the other security guys stood guard a few feet away in case any curious eyes tried to interrupt us. Luca was still in his room, no doubt having entertained a guest, and Derek had rented a Harley and set off on an early morning ride through some Tennessee hills.

"I'm not gonna lie, you shocked the hell out of me." Cash glanced over at me curiously before cutting into the fluffy stack of pancakes on his plate.

"If I'm being completely honest, I shocked the hell out of myself." I took a drink of my latte, savoring the feeling of the caffeine rushing through my system. I only managed to get about an hour of sleep. Even after I got back to the hotel, I couldn't get my brain to shut off. Liv's beautiful face was already etched in my mind as if I'd known her forever. I knew I was acting damn near crazy, but I couldn't help it. I felt like I was being pulled into a current, and I wasn't sure if she was going to let me sink or help me swim.

"So? What happened?" Dallas prodded me.

I filled them in on the night before, beginning with how captivated I'd been when I first saw Liv, to taking her home and asking her to have dinner with me. They listened intently, and when I finally fell quiet, they both studied me for a moment. "You think I'm crazy, don't you?"

Dallas shook his head and chuckled. "Man, I've known you're nuts. That's not news." I wadded up my napkin, throwing it at his head, and Cash laughed.

"I don't think it's crazy," Cash said tentatively. "I guess my question is, do you think she'd even consider letting this be anything more than a friendship?"

"I honestly don't know," I admitted. "I know there's a connection there. I know she feels it too, but the age thing really freaked her out."

"I don't think the age thing is a big deal." Dallas shrugged. "I think she could get over that with a little time." He pressed his lips together, hesitating.

"What is it?" I narrowed my eyes at him.

He chewed the inside of his lip. I got the distinct feeling he was trying to choose his words carefully. "I don't want to be a downer, but let's say she does get past the age difference. Man, this life isn't for everybody. That's one of the reasons so many of us are single, or we end up dating people in the industry. Not everyone likes having their entire lives under a fucking microscope. Not to mention having to choose between being apart or living on the road. It's a lot."

"It is," Cash agreed. "But don't let that stop you. When

it's right, it's right. Somehow you find a way to make it work."

"I'm really not trying to discourage you, man." Dallas' face softened. "I don't want to see you get hurt, and I can tell you're already crazy about this girl. I've never seen you like this, so it worries me a little. I don't want you to get attached and things not work out."

"I agree." Cash nodded. "I think you have to go into this knowing she may never let it go beyond friendship."

"Even if she does, you could still face a completely different set of challenges," Dallas added.

"I know." I sighed. "I do know that. I can't explain it, but I think she could be worth the risk of getting hurt."

"Where are you taking her?" Cash asked.

"That's a good question," I said. "I was thinking I might go over to her bakery in a bit and surprise her. Maybe I can get her to have lunch with me too."

"Mind if I tag along?" Cash asked quickly.

"You want to see Ella?" I raised an eyebrow at him.

"I wouldn't mind seeing her," he replied casually, averting his gaze. "I'll have Brady take us."

"I can drive," I offered.

"Negative, Ghost Rider." Cash smirked. "That Lamborghini isn't exactly inconspicuous. We'll need to be a little more incognito at this hour. I'm dropping the car at the rental place on my way to the airport, remember? My flight is at seven, and I don't want you to lose track of time."

"Where are you headed? I don't think you said."

"I'm going to spend some time with the in-laws, but I'll be back in a couple of days." His face fell a bit. Part of me wanted to reach across the table and hug him.

"No way are you two jerks leaving me here." Dallas

leaned back in his chair and crossed his arms. "I want some of these cupcakes. Are you guys ready?"

"Actually, there's something else I need to talk to you guys about," Cash said.

I groaned inwardly, already anticipating what he was going to say.

"Have you guys listened to any more of those songs the label sent over?" Cash looked at me expectantly.

"Yes." I sighed. "They were all terrible."

"Look, I know most of that stuff is shit." Cash leaned forward, resting his elbows on the table. "I also know nobody writes a better song than Jaxon Slade, but the label is breathing down my neck for a new single. I can't put them off much longer. Yes, your contract is up next year, but the reality is, this is going to be a problem no matter what label we go with."

I shifted uncomfortably in my chair, and Dallas shot me a sympathetic glance. Though our songwriting process was collaborative, I wrote almost every single lyric of our songs. The guys and I had come up with some promising new beats and melodies, but for the past six months, I'd not been able to write anything worth listening to.

I knew it, and the guys knew it. What they didn't know was *why*, and I wasn't ready to tell them. They thought I was merely suffering from a massive case of writer's block. At that moment, that was all I wanted them to know.

"We've been working on a couple of good hooks," Dallas lied. "We're not quite there yet, but we're getting close." His eyes flickered over to mine. I knew he was stalling for me, and I was grateful.

I felt the muscles in my neck stiffen. The band was my family, and I hated disappointing them. I knew what it was like to be let down by the people you were supposed to be able to count on the most.

"That's great." Cash nodded. "I can't wait to hear them."

"Soon," Dallas promised. "We've still got some work to do, but we should have them in the next couple of weeks."

My mouth went dry as I considered whether or not I thought that was a promise we could keep. "For sure."

Dallas expertly changed the subject. "I know we just had breakfast, but ever since you guys mentioned going over to Liv's bakery, all I can think about are those cupcakes."

"I'm ready." I gulped down the last of my coffee. "I've *been* ready."

"I need to make a couple of calls before we go," Cash said, rising from his chair. "I'll go tell Brady the plan and make my calls, then we'll head out."

"Hurry up," Dallas called as Cash left the table. "I want cupcakes."

"Thanks for saving me," I said softly.

"I've got you, brother." He reached out to fist bump me. "Now, we just have to come up with those hooks."

"I know." I ran my fingers through my hair. "I've been trying."

"I know you have," he assured me. "The inspiration will come. Try not to put so much pressure on yourself. It happens."

"Thanks, Dal."

"So," he said. "You ready to see her again?"

I smiled and nodded. My heart lurched into my throat, and my mind drifted to her beautiful face illuminated by the twinkly lights outside the pie shop. Dallas' cautious words still echoed in my mind, but I knew that sink or swim, I had to see what we could be.

SEVEN

Liv

I FELL INTO A COMFORTABLE GROOVE, working alongside Katie. Though I enjoyed the company of the other girls that worked with us, I loved the days where it was just the two of us and Ella the most.

Within a little over an hour, we'd gotten mostly caught up on our orders while dancing to Katie's favorite playlist. She loved bouncing around the kitchen to Taylor Swift, Beyonce, and Billie Eilish. Her honey-colored ponytail bobbed as she moved and softly sang along to the words of the songs. I caught her glancing at me curiously over the cake she was icing a few times, though she never asked questions.

Katie took a step back, eyeing her handiwork approvingly. "I'm going to step out front and check on the cases."

"Thanks, girl." I smiled at her and took a moment to stretch my arms when she disappeared through the door. I pulled my phone out of my back pocket and checked our business email before scrolling to my recent calls. Jax's phone number stared back at me. I knew, in reality, I needed to cancel this dinner thing, but I had to admit there was a part of me that was curious. *He sees you, Liv.* I ruminated on Ella's words.

I chewed my lip as I looked at his number. This was crazy. I was being a crazy person. I needed to call him and get this over with, or perhaps a text was better. At least I wouldn't have to hear the heat of his voice that could easily melt me through the phone. Yes, a text was a much better idea.

"Ummm, Liv." Katie reappeared in the doorway, closing it behind her before continuing. "Jaxon Slade and Dallas Stone from Midnight in Dallas are here. Right now. In our store." *Shit.* Her eyes were wide with shock, and her voice squeaked. "And Jaxon asked to see you."

Shit. Shit. Shit.

"Okay." I took my apron off and hung it back on the hook. I ran my fingers through my hair, smoothing my hands over my jeans. "Do you mind locking the door and flipping the sign to 'closed' while they're here?"

"Ella already did it," she replied, still looking stunned.

I took a deep breath and started toward the door. "How do I look? Do I look okay?"

"You look great." I knew she'd have said that regardless of if it were true, and I loved her for it. She stepped aside to let me through the door, following close behind me.

"Look who came to visit us." Ella beamed at me from where she stood talking to Cash. Brady hung out near the door and waved in my direction.

"Hey, fellas," I greeted them with a casualness I did not feel. "Did you guys come to load up on some cupcakes?"

"You bet your ass I did." Dallas smiled broadly as he moved to hug me. "Long time no see, Liv."

"Good to see you again, Dallas." I returned his hug, and Jax caught my eye as I did. "By the way, this is Katie. She's a dear friend and one of our top pastry chefs." I gestured toward Katie, whose smile was plastered on her face in a way that told me she was internally freaking out.

"Katie, I'm Dallas." He introduced himself and sauntered over to her. "Clearly we need to be friends, Miss Top Pastry Chef."

"Liv." Jax's voice was soft as he approached me. "Donut look so surprised to see me." His lips curled into a smile.

"Jax." I pressed my lips together, laughter threatening to escape me. "Donut come in here with your cheesy donut jokes." We both burst into a fit of giggles as he closed the distance between us, pulling me into his arms. I inhaled his delicious scent, and my heart fluttered inside my chest. "What are you guys doing here?"

"Dallas wasn't going to rest until he got his hands on some cupcakes," he joked.

"It's true." Dallas looked up from his conversation with Katie.

"Then cupcakes you shall have, my friend." I stepped behind the counter. I began to pluck cupcakes and a few pastries from the cases, placing them in our signature Tiffany Blue colored boxes. "What else are you guys getting into today?"

"I'm meeting with a realtor this afternoon," Dallas answered.

"Really?" Ella asked with her hand on her hip. "Wait, does that mean you're considering moving here?"

Dallas nodded. "Most of us are. Well, all of us except Luca, because he's a stubborn ass. We're all here so much, and the city is great. Derek is out exploring right now, in fact. I really wanted to get the ball rolling, maybe look at a few places while I'm here with time to kill."

"What about you, Cash?" I asked as I closed the boxes, sealing them with our logo stickers. "Are you making the move too?"

"I've thought about it," he admitted, crossing his arms. "My work has me here a lot, and it's such a great town. Nashville has a much slower pace than LA. I could get used to that."

"It's a pretty great place." I scooted the boxes across the counter. "I've loaded y'all down, so there's plenty for the other guys too. Would y'all like a drink or something to have now?"

"This is more than enough," Dallas said. "What do we owe you?"

"It's on the house." I smiled.

"I love this woman." Dallas gestured at me with his thumb before scooping the boxes off the counter, returning to his conversation with Katie.

"Is there a good coffee shop over here?" Cash asked. "We've been here a lot, but not to this neighborhood."

"Frothy Monkey," I answered quickly and moved around the counter. "If you make a right out of our store, it's across the street a few yards down. They have a full menu too. It's a great place for lunch."

Ella nodded in agreement. "We order from there at least a couple times a week."

"Speaking of lunch," Jax said, stepping closer to me. "I know we have plans for dinner, but any chance I could steal you away for lunch too?"

"It's so crazy you should ask," Ella spoke up before I could even respond. "Liv was *just* saying she was about to take off early since we're a little slow today." I shot her a warning look before turning my attention back to Jax.

"Then I guess it's my lucky day." Jax grinned.

"I was, uh, saying how tired I was." I pulled the sleeves of my sweater down over my hands. "I was going to, uh, go home and get some rest."

"You should go with Liv," Ella carried on, knowing full well what she was doing. "Order up some delivery and relax. You've both got to be exhausted." In true Ella fashion, she wasn't going to let this go.

"Now *that* is a great idea." Jax looked over at me expectantly. "What do you say, Liv?"

Ella gave me an encouraging smile, and I couldn't help but notice Cash looked thoroughly charmed by her antics.

I gazed up into Jax's eager eyes, and my resolve completely broke. "Yeah, let's do that." The relief that spread across his face was so cute, I almost forgot why I was thinking about canceling our plans in the first place.

"To the Batmobile," Jax joked

"Sorry, Bruce Wayne." I chuckled. "I live down the street, so I walk to work."

"It looks like it might rain," Brady mentioned as he peered out the door. "I could drop you guys off. It's no trouble."

"I think we'll be okay," Jax said, his eyes not leaving mine. "Thank you, though."

"We should probably head on out," Cash said regretfully to Ella. "I've still got a few things to do, and I know Dal needs to get to his meeting with the realtor. I was going to go grab a coffee first, though. Can I bring you back anything?"

"No, but you're so sweet to offer," Ella replied.

"Well, ladies, it was good seeing you both again. Tell Grace we said hello." Cash hugged both me and Ella. He waved over in Katie's direction. Dallas squeezed her with one arm, balancing the cupcake boxes in the other. She gaped at me over Dallas' shoulder.

"It was nice meeting you, Top Chef Katie. I hope I get to see you again sometime." Dallas said, turning to embrace Ella. "Tell Grace we may be neighbors soon."

"She will be thrilled." Ella laughed. "I know she'll be sad she missed you guys."

"I'm sure we'll be back *plenty*." Dallas winked at me, pulling me into another hug. "And I'm sure I'll be seeing you soon, Liv. Thanks for all the goodies."

"Anytime," I replied. "If you need any insight into the neighborhoods around here or anything, we're born and raised Nashvillians." I plucked a couple of our business cards from the holder on the counter and handed them to Dallas. "Now y'all have both me and Ella, and you can stop in any time you're in the neighborhood."

"Thanks, Liv," Dallas said, before fist-bumping Jax. "And we'll see *you* later."

"If you guys get any songs written before I see you again, send me some audio." Cash's eyes settled on Jax.

I noticed Jax's jaw tense and his body stiffen slightly. It was clear he was uncomfortable, though I wasn't entirely sure why.

"See ya, ladies." Dallas waved, and Brady unlocked the door, flipping the sign back to 'open.' Brady nodded at us, and Cash threw one last smile over his shoulder at Ella.

"Bye, y'all," Ella called cheerfully, as the door closed behind them. She turned her attention to me with a shit-eating grin. "Now, you two skedaddle on out of here. Katie and I have everything under control here." She turned to Jax, leaning in to hug him. "Take care of my girl."

"You know I will," Jax replied. "Tell my favorite accomplice, Grace, I said hi. It was nice meeting you, Katie."

"It was nice meeting you guys too," she said, still starry-eyed.

"Text me later," Ella sang, and I started back through the kitchen with Jax on my heels.

"Ready?" I asked over my shoulder, grabbing my purse off the hook by the door.

"You donut even have to ask." He waggled his brow as he moved to open the door for me. "After you."

As we set off on the short walk to my house, I noted that Brady had been right. It looked like we were about to get an autumn thunderstorm. We walked for a couple of moments before I finally spoke. "So, you're really thinking of moving here?"

"It's something I've been considering." Jax smiled at me as we strolled down the sidewalk. "The idea is getting more attractive by the second."

I averted my gaze, looking down at my boots as I walked. "How long are you in town for?"

"At least for a few days. We're on a break for a couple of weeks." I caught him looking at me out of the corner of my eye. "I guess it all depends on if you get sick of seeing me or not."

"What about Cash? It sounded like he was leaving."

"He is," he replied. "He's going to Charleston, but he'll be back in a couple of days."

I nodded. "What's in Charleston? Does he have family there?"

"He's going to spend some time with his in-laws."

"Wait. What?" I snapped my head in his direction. "Cash

is *married?* Wow. I thought he kinda had a thing for Ella. I misjudged the heck out of that."

"You didn't," he said gently. "Cash's wife, Carrie, died almost a year ago. It was the week after Thanksgiving. Brain cancer."

"I'm so sorry."

He gazed at the houses we passed for a moment, lost in thought. "Cash is like our brother, and Carrie was kind of like our protective big sister. We called her our den mother. She was the one who made sure we had enough time off. She was always reminding us of that Dolly Parton quote, *'don't get so busy making a living that you forget to make a life.'* She was the one who made sure we didn't exist solely on fast food and ramen. She made sure we took time to see the sights on some of our concert stops, where ordinarily, we wouldn't have seen anything outside the venue or the hotel."

"Well, any woman that quotes Dolly is good in my book," I said. "It sounds like she was a really special person."

"She was." He nodded. "Cash still tries to go visit his in-laws as often as he can because, besides us, he doesn't really have anyone else. Carrie's parents really accepted him. He has a few other clients on his roster, but he's with us most of the time, so we've sort of become his family."

"It's sweet how much you guys care about each other."

"I can tell he digs Ella, but I think he's honestly still a little lost," he admitted. "He and Carrie were married for twelve years. I think he's still trying to figure out how to live without her." Thunder rumbled, causing the ground to tremble beneath our feet. A few raindrops announced their presence, splatting against the pavement. "It's *definitely* going to rain."

"We're almost there." I could see my white bungalow with the navy-blue shutters a few yards away.

"That's your place up there, right?" Jax asked, gesturing toward my house. "It's nice. I love the navy shu—" Before he could finish his sentence, the rain launched a monsoon level assault on us all at once. "Shit."

"Run for it!" I screeched as we splashed down the sidewalk. We barreled up the stone walkway, not stopping until we were finally under the safety of the porch covering. "Oh my God." I didn't even have to see my reflection to know I looked like a drowned rat. I looked up at Jax, his long-sleeved black T-shirt clinging to every curve of his muscles.

"Wow." He raked his fingers through his now sopping wet hair and looked down at his clothes. "The jeans didn't fare too bad, but I think the shirt was a total loss."

"I'm so sorry." I fished my key out of my bag, shoving it in the lock and opening the door. "Let me throw your shirt in the dryer for you. I have some old concert T-shirts, and I bet one of them will fit you." I trudged into the house, kicking my boots off by the door. He followed me inside, discarding his wet Chuck Taylors.

"I don't think we're exactly the same size." He chuckled, following behind me as I padded my way down the hall.

"I know." I laughed. "I used to have a thing for oversized concert T-shirts. It was a phase. Anyway, I'm pretty sure I still have a couple." He followed me into my room, and my stomach lurched into my chest. I realized this was the first time I'd been in a bedroom, let alone a bedroom that belonged to *me,* with any man besides Ben. My heart began to race, and I was suddenly thankful I'd read that article a couple of months ago about the benefits of making your bed every day.

I tossed my purse on the bed and strode over to the closet, stepping inside. My mouth went dry as I rifled through the clothes, trying to focus on the shirt-seeking mission at hand

and not the fact that Jaxon Slade was in my bedroom. I squatted down, sifting through the folded clothes in the organizing cubes.

"Is that... is that a guitar case?" Jax's voice interrupted my search.

"Huh?" I asked absentmindedly. "Oh. Yeah. It is."

"You play? Why didn't you tell me?" I could hear the enthusiasm in his voice.

"I used to," I replied nonchalantly. "As in past tense."

"Whatever. You never forget how. It's like riding a bike."

My fingers finally landed on what I'd been looking for. I pulled the worn charcoal-grey Aerosmith shirt from its pile, checking the label inside the T-shirt before turning toward him. "Found it. It's oversized on me, but it will probably fit y —" Before I could finish my sentence, he ripped his shirt over his head, and I stood face to face with a very gorgeous, very shirtless, Jax. His chest was smooth, a perfect crease leading down his center, dividing an impressive six-pack that narrowed in a v at the waistline of his jeans. His entire body glistened, damp with the rain that soaked through his shirt. "Uh. Um. Here." I felt the heat rise to my cheeks as I shoved the shirt toward him. I quickly turned my head to prevent myself from staring, or worse still, drooling. I waited until I saw him pull the other shirt over his head out of the corner of my eye before I allowed my gaze to return to him, looking unfairly sexy in my shirt. I cleared my throat as he placed the wet garment in my waiting hand.

"I had my doubts, but you were right." Jax looked down at the shirt. "This is exactly the size I would buy. At least now I know how cute you're gonna look if you borrow my T-shirts." He said it so casually that if I hadn't already been hanging on to his every word, I might have missed it.

The laugh that escaped my mouth was so high pitched, it didn't even sound like it belonged to me. My fingers and toes tingled as I looked down at my feet, unable to maintain eye contact with him. "Told you," I mumbled almost unintelligibly.

"Aerosmith is one of my favorites."

"Mine, too. I love anything Steven Tyler does." I stepped forward to make my way out of the closet, but he didn't move. "I should go put your shirt in the dryer and change."

"Can I see your guitar?"

"What?"

"Your guitar. Can I see it?"

"Uh, sure." I turned to grab the case and handed it to him. He backed out of the closet, the case in his hand. "Come on. I'll show you back to the living room, and then I'll go change and take care of your shirt. Can I get you anything?"

"I'm good," he answered. "Why don't I go ahead and order us some food while you're doing all that? What sounds good to you?"

"You like Thai food?"

"I love Thai food."

"There's this great place called Bow Thai."

"Consider it done." He grinned. "What will you have?"

"Soy sauce noodles with tofu," I answered. "Spicy level four."

"That sounds amazing. May have to make that two."

"Make yourself comfortable." I gestured at the navy-blue sofa as Mama came out from her hiding place, hissing in Jax's direction.

He looked taken aback for a moment before his mouth stretched into a big grin. "Hostile kitty?"

I laughed. "Yep. That's Mama. I've had her for two

months, and I'm pretty sure she's been plotting my death the entire time."

"Hi, Mama," he said, as she scampered off toward the kitchen.

"Don't take it personally." I snorted. "She's an equal opportunity hater." Our eyes locked for a moment, and I suddenly remembered I was standing there looking like I'd showered with my clothes on. "I'm going to go and... take care of all of this." I gestured at myself with his wet shirt in my hand. His shirt that I noticed still smelled deliciously like him.

"I'm going to order the food," he said, settling in on the couch and opening the guitar case. "Take your time."

I heard the faint strumming of my guitar as I proceeded down the hall, through the kitchen, and to the laundry room. When I reached my bedroom, I paused for a moment in the doorframe. I could hear Jax's sweet, emotive voice singing a song off Steven Tyler's solo country record from a few years ago. It was one of my favorites off the album, a song called "Love Is Your Name."

EIGHT

Jax

I ORDERED the food and settled in on Liv's sofa. My fingers absentmindedly strummed her old Taylor guitar to the sounds of the thunderstorm outside. Occasionally, Mama would make her way into the living room and peek at me suspiciously. I leaned my hand down to pet her once, but she hissed at me before darting down the hallway.

My mind wandered to Liv looking at me, her chestnut hair drenched. Her sweater had soaked through so that it hugged every soft curve of her gorgeous body. Every moment, I found myself more and more drawn to her.

Finding out she had this guitar made me feel like I'd been handed a huge piece to the mysterious puzzle that was Olivia Sinclair, though I wasn't entirely sure why. She seemed so indifferent about it, but I felt like there was more to the story.

"Sorry. My hair felt disgusting, so I took a quick shower. You want anything to drink? I was thinking about opening a bottle of wine." Liv's voice startled me out of my thoughts. I found myself staring at her, completely speechless. Her hair was damp from the shower, and she wore a pair of grey leggings with an oversized T-shirt that fell casually off her shoulder. If she had any makeup on, I couldn't tell. I'd never seen a woman look more beautiful than she did at that moment. "Jax? You okay?" She eyed me curiously.

"Yeah. Sorry." I raked my hand through my hair. "Wine sounds great. The food should be here soon."

"Is red okay?" She turned and started toward the kitchen.

"Perfect." I returned the guitar to its case. A couple of moments later, she returned with two wine glasses filled nearly to the brim and handed one to me.

"I'm a generous bartender," she warned. She sat next to me, leaving enough space that a whole other person could have fit between us.

"My favorite kind." I smiled and held my glass out toward her. "To donuts and chance encounters."

"I'll drink to that." She gently clinked her glass with mine.

"I love your house." I took a drink and settled into the sofa so that I was facing her. "It's really cozy."

"Thank you." She took a sip of her wine. "I've only been here a few months, but it's finally starting to feel like home. Honestly, the best thing is living so close to the shop. I love walking to work, and this neighborhood is really nice. Ella and Grace live close by too, so I've got everything I need here." There was a knock on the door, and she started to get up. "That must be the food."

"Let me get it," I offered, setting my glass down on the rustic white coffee table. I answered the door, snagged our food, and tipped the driver. "This smells amazing." I returned to the couch with the bag, extracting the two containers and the plastic flatware. Liv grabbed one of the containers, lifting the lid. Balancing the food with one hand, she grabbed the remote off the coffee table with the other and flicked the television on.

"I have a very important question for you," she said with mock seriousness. "Not to be dramatic, but your answer does determine whether we'll make it through to dinner."

"So, no pressure, right?" I shrugged. I could hear the sounds of the rain and the storm rumbling outside.

"*So* much pressure." She pulled up her Netflix account on the television. "What are your feelings on *The Office?*"

"You mean the greatest show of all time?" I took a drink of my wine. "You know, as much as I loved 'The Dinner Party,' I really am partial to Jim and Pam's wedding. Did I pass the test?"

"With flying colors." She grinned and hit play. We ate our lunch and watched the show, simultaneously talking about our favorite scenes. We'd made it through a couple of episodes and glasses of wine when a loud clap of thunder rattled the house, leaving us in the dark. "Shit." She laughed. "So much for a Netflix binge."

I peeked through the blinds of the window behind the sofa. "It's really coming down out there."

"I'll be right back." She padded out of the room, quickly returning with the opened bottle of wine and one large candle that flickered in the dim light of the room. She placed it on the coffee table, her beautiful face illuminated by its golden glow as she sat next to me.

"Can I ask you a question?" I scooted closer to her as she topped off our wine glasses.

"Hmm?"

"The guitar," I said tentatively. "You said you *used to* play. What happened?"

She took a heavy drink of her wine and settled into the

sofa, facing me with her legs crossed beneath her. "My whole life I wanted to be a singer and write songs."

"Are you serious?" My eyes widened.

"Yeah, but that was a long time ago." She took another sip from her glass. "I got my first guitar when I was thirteen. I think my folks liked it because they always knew where I was. I wasn't out getting into trouble. I was in my room writing songs about boys who had no idea I existed."

"That seems unlikely," I said softly. "It'd be impossible not to notice you." Even in the flickering glow of the candle, I could see her blush.

"My parents got me this guitar as a graduation present, and I opted not to go to college. Instead, I had a fake ID made and started playing in bars when I wasn't even old enough to drink."

"Wow. I am completely floored."

"Ella and I got an apartment together. She was working retail at the time, and I was playing in every honky-tonk that would let me on stage. During the day, I started a side business baking cakes and cupcakes for people to help pay the rent. Baking wasn't my passion, but it's what I was good at." She sighed heavily, looking down at her glass. "Anyway, I met my hus... my ex, Ben, when I was twenty. In the beginning, he was okay with my music, but after we got married, things started really taking off for him. The further he got in his career, the less comfortable he became with mine. The last thing he wanted was to be courting potential clients downtown and see his wife playing for cheap beer and tips at Tootsie's. So, I stopped."

"You just stopped?" Her eyes fell, and I wanted to reach out and hold her hand.

"Yep." She took another long drink from her glass. "Ben

was right anyway. At that point, it would have been embarrassing for him. Honestly, it was probably equally as embarrassing for me to be chasing a dream that was never going to happen. I guess I didn't have that elusive *it* factor."

"Says who?" I asked the question, but she didn't answer, which was all the answer I needed. I wanted to know more. I wanted every single detail about who Olivia Sinclair was, but I feared she would shut down if I tried to push any further. "Well, I know what's got to happen now." I took her wine glass from her hand, placing it on the table along with my own. I pulled her guitar from its case and handed it over to her. "I'm going to need to hear you sing."

"Jax, really. It's been forever."

"No better time to change that than now," I insisted. "Please. I want to hear you."

She reluctantly took the guitar and settled it in her lap, her fingers gliding over the frets. "I don't normally give private concerts. Especially not to bonafide rockstars sitting in my living room." She narrowed her eyes at me. "I want to make it clear that I'm only doing this because I'm two glasses of wine in."

I raised my brow at her and leaned forward, waiting. "Noted."

She took a deep breath, closing her eyes. Finally, she began to play. I immediately recognized the opening notes to a slowed-down version of "Ring of Fire" by Johnny Cash.

Her voice started off soft, gravelly, and haunting, but slowly it began to build. By the time she reached the chorus, her vocals became more powerful with a bluesy twang. Her voice cracked, raw with emotion, in all the right places. Trained vocalists took lessons for years to learn how to do what Liv was doing effortlessly. I'd never envied a musical instrument before, but as I watched her fingers move smoothly over the fretboard, I knew I'd let this woman play me any way she wanted to. When she finished the song, she opened her eyes to find me gazing intently at her.

"What?" She grimaced, reaching out to take a sip of her wine. "Why are you looking at me like that?"

"Liv, that was the most beautiful thing I've ever heard," I said. "For the record, can I just say that your ex was a fucking idiot? Anyone that would discourage you from doing what you just did is a complete moron."

"I'm really not—"

"Nope." I stopped her. "I'm not even going to let you say it. Liv, you're amazing. If I were your husband, I never would have let you stop, but then again, I never would have let you go."

She chewed her lip and looked down at her fingers that still fluttered along the strings.

"You have a gift, and you sing from a place that you can't fake. I can hear every emotion in your voice, and frankly, it's exquisite. You can't give this up. You could start again."

"No way." She shook her head. "That ship has sailed."

"It most definitely has not," I argued. "The ship has docked, and we are now boarding the USS Olivia. You can't let this go, Liv. Music is where your heart is. It's all over your face. You have to keep singing."

"You're crazy. I can't go back to that whole bar scene now. They'll laugh me off the stage."

"*You're* crazy if you seriously let this go," I retorted. "Besides, who said you had to go to a bar? Write with me."

"What?" She looked at me incredulously. "Get out of here." She set the guitar down, propping it against the sofa.

"I'm serious," I said softly. "Write with me."

NINE

Liv

———

"WRITE WITH YOU? I think you've had a little too much wine." I laughed. "Is it time to cut you off?"

"I'm serious, Liv." Jax looked at me with such sincerity that it caused my heart to soften around the edges. He leaned closer to me and placed his hand on my knee, taking a deep breath. "I told you our label wants us to sing other writers' songs, but I didn't tell you *why*. It's not because they're trying to change us. It's because of me. I've been struggling to write any new material. I'm the one who writes our lyrics, and for the last six months, I haven't been able to write anything. Not even a single decent hook."

"But… why?" The reasons he'd seemed so uncomfortable earlier, when Cash mentioned him writing, began to come into focus.

"I haven't told anybody about this yet, but it started after Carrie passed away."

"I'm sorry, Jax," I said softly. "A loss like that would make it difficult for anyone to write."

"Well, it's not only because of Carrie." He chewed his lip

thoughtfully. "I told you last night that I lived in the foster care system. My mom signed me over to the state. She didn't even put up a fight, Liv. She disappeared, and I've spent the better part of my life being angry and bitter. After Carrie got sick and found out she didn't have long left to live, we spent a lot of time talking. We talked about life and how fucking unfair it all is. All Carrie and Cash ever wanted was a family, but Carrie got sick, and that was no longer a possibility. It made me angry that two people so deserving of love, so deserving of every dream to come true, were being denied the chance, you know? Meanwhile, my mom chose drugs over her own damn kid."

"Jax…" I covered his hand with my own.

He looked down at our hands, his hair falling into his pensive eyes. "One of the last times I saw Carrie, I was just so pissed at the world. I was mad that one of the only people who understood me was dying." His eyes shined in the soft glow of the room. "Carrie told me I had to let go of the anger. She said it was like I was beating my own head against a wall, but expecting my mom to feel the pain. She understood because when she was first diagnosed, she was angry too. But if she'd stayed angry, she'd have missed out on so much love." He frowned, his head hung low. "After she died, I couldn't stop thinking about what she said. All I've ever wanted was a family, and I started thinking that maybe my mom was somewhere out there. I thought maybe we could have some sort of relationship. So, six months ago, I started trying to find her. I started searching for her online, and that got me nowhere. I talked to the state, and there was no record of her after she turned me over to their custody."

I wanted to comfort him. I wanted to say something that would make him feel better, but I knew there were no words to ease his pain. Instead, I squeezed his hand, waiting for him to continue when he was ready.

"I finally hired a private investigator, but he still hasn't been able to find her. For six months this has been going on, and I don't know why, but it's like I'm broken. I'm afraid I may never find my mom, and I might not ever have a person in this world I belong to. Now, the one thing I'm good at, the one thing that was mine, I can't seem to do anymore. If we don't get something new for the label soon, they're going to force our hand and make us record something we don't want to. I feel like I'm letting the band down, and they're all I've got."

"I'm sure they'd understand if you told them what you've been going through," I tried to reassure him. "I know you can trust them."

"It's not that I don't trust them, but it doesn't come as easily with them as it seems to with you." His eyes pleaded with mine. "We have this crazy connection, and I feel comfortable telling you things about me nobody else knows. Maybe you can help pull the words out of me."

"Jax, I haven't written a song in ages." I sighed. "I don't even know if I can anymore."

"I'm asking you to try," he murmured. "For me."

He looked at me so hopefully, there was no way I could tell him no. I didn't know if I could help him, but what did I have to lose in trying? "I'll go get a notebook and a pen."

He threw his arms around me, and the butterflies took flight in my chest. "Thank you."

I was amazed at how easily it all came back to me. Maybe it was the wine that allowed my guard to come down, or maybe Jax was right, and it really was like riding a bike. Somehow, the words and melodies began to pour out of me.

Jax and I worked well together, bouncing ideas off each other as if we'd always written together. For hours, he opened up about life without his mom, while we passed the guitar back and forth. I loved watching him work. I loved the way his brow furrowed as he softly sang the words, trying to perfect the melody. I loved how excited he got when it started to come together and the way his eyes constantly found mine in the flickering candlelight.

I had to shift my gaze downward for fear that the lightning in his stormy eyes would strike me dead right on the spot. I grabbed my phone off the coffee table to check the time only to see a text from Ella.

Ella: Soooooo??????

I stifled a laugh as I tapped out my answer.

Liv: Soooooo far soooooo good. ;)

"I take it that's Ella checking in to make sure she doesn't need to come rescue you," Jax joked, taking another drink and emptying the contents of his glass.

"Something like that." I chuckled.

He placed the glass on the table. "I believe I promised you dinner. What sounds good to you?"

"You know what? The weather is still pretty crummy. Let me take a raincheck, and *I'll* take care of dinner tonight." I stood, placing my guitar back in its case.

"Are you sure? With the power out, that might be a little difficult. I could at least order a pizza or something."

"I'm positive. Besides, isn't necessity the mother of invention?" I grabbed our empty wine glasses and my phone, unlocking it so that it illuminated the space around me. "Grab the candle and come with me." He followed me into the kitchen curiously, setting the candle on the counter. I placed our glasses beside it before plucking another bottle of red wine from the rack on the counter. "Will you do the honors?" I passed him the bottle and a corkscrew.

"Of course," he said, setting to work on opening the wine.

I slid open the patio door and pulled the screen door closed, allowing the sound of rain to fill the room. Standing on my tiptoes, I pulled the wooden cheese board from one of the top cabinets. As I began putting together my hodgepodge charcuterie board, I became aware of his thoughtful eyes following me, watching me work with intrigue. I moved through the kitchen, cloaked in darkness, pulling items from the cabinets and a couple from the fridge, placing them artfully on the board.

"Okay," I said, carrying the board to the small rustic grey dining table next to the patio door. "Dinner is served."

I moved the candle to the table and he followed, grabbing the wine and glasses, placing them on the table and taking his seat beside me. "I don't think I've ever seen Pop-Tarts on a charcuterie board before."

"They're strawberry." I grinned, plucking one from the board and taking a bite. I'd piled together a smorgasbord of snacks including almonds, grapes, pretzels, string cheese, Goldfish crackers, some cookies from the bakery, some left-over pepperonis from pizza night with Ella and Grace, and iced strawberry Pop-Tarts.

"This might be the best dinner I've ever had." His lips curled into a smile as he grabbed a Pop-Tart.

"You might need to raise your standards a little bit." I

smirked, taking a sip of my wine. My hair blew lightly around me as the breeze flowed through the screen door.

"I think my standards are just right." Thunder rumbled and we fell quiet for a moment, taking in the sounds of the autumn storm.

I glanced over at him to find him already looking at me. I quickly looked away, taking another sip of my wine.

"What do you say we play a little game?"

I narrowed my eyes at him. "What did you have in mind?"

"Well, we have some wine. How about a little getting-to-know-you drinking game?" He raised his brow at me. "Maybe Never Have I Ever?"

"Sure," I said cautiously. "What are the rules?"

"You've never played before?"

I shook my head.

"We each take turns saying something we've never done. If the other *has* done that thing, they take a drink."

I shrugged. "Sounds simple enough."

"Ladies first." He smiled over at me, taking another bite of his Pop-Tart.

"Okay." I pressed my lips together, suppressing a laugh. "Never have I ever played Never Have I Ever until today."

"You dirty cheater." He clutched his hand to his chest, feigning shock.

"Drink up," I teased.

"Alright." He took a drink of his wine. "I see how this is going to be. Never have I ever baked a cake."

"Jaxon Slade," I said with mock surprise. "The audacity." I took a long sip of my wine. "Fine. Never have I ever been arrested."

"Me either." He took a handful of almonds off the board.

"Now, if we had been playing this game with Luca, he would have had to drink."

"Oh really?"

"Yep. He got mouthy with a bodyguard once when he was acting like an idiot at an afterparty a couple of years ago." He tossed a couple of the almonds in his mouth. "Disorderly conduct. Cash convinced the guy to drop the charges, though." He paused thoughtfully for a moment. "Never have I ever gotten a tattoo."

I took a long swallow of my wine.

"You have a tattoo?" His eyes widened with surprise.

"One." I pulled my T-shirt down and brushed my hair to the side, exposing the back of my left shoulder to him. "I got it for my birthday last year."

"It's beautiful." He leaned in, the roughness of his fingertips sending chills down my spine as he lightly traced the outline of the rose that was drawn in a crisp black line. "Does it have a special meaning?"

"It was kind of my gift to myself after Ben left," I admitted. "He gave me the divorce papers a month before my birthday, and I felt lost. I guess I still feel lost sometimes." My eyes met his over my shoulder. "Anyway, he hated tattoos and never wanted me to have one. He always said they were unattractive on a woman. So, this was one of the first things I did for me. It symbolizes my new beginning. The thorns represent the hurt I've been through, and the three leaves represent the constants in my life: myself, Ella, and Grace. The rose itself is the new beginning. It's where I hope I end up, and they're my favorite flower."

"But not the red ones," he said matter-of-factly.

"How did you know that?" I analyzed him.

"I don't know." He shrugged and popped a grape in his

mouth, chewing thoughtfully. "Red roses seem too basic. You're different."

"You're not wrong." I grinned. "I love tequila sunrise roses. They're a lot harder to find, though. They're yellow at the center, and they fade out into shades of peach and orange and fiery red."

"A lot like a sunrise."

"A lot like that." I picked up a pretzel from the board. "Never have I ever lived outside my hometown."

"Really?" He took a pull from his glass.

"True story. I mean, I do enjoy traveling when I've had the chance to do so. Ella, Grace, and I take a yearly girls trip and that sort of thing, but I've never really seen myself living outside of Nashville or at least not outside of Tennessee. I love it here."

"I feel like I've done nothing but live on the road," he replied. "I've still got a place in Louisville, but I'm hardly ever there. I would love to settle down and stay somewhere for longer than a couple of weeks at a time."

"I can't imagine how hard that is."

"It's not like I have much to go back to. Louisville is the place I live," he said, "but it's not home."

"Where is home?" I looked at him thoughtfully.

"That's to be determined." A solemn expression settled on his face before he grabbed a cookie, taking a bite. "Snickerdoodles are my favorite. Did you make these?"

I couldn't help but notice how swiftly he changed the subject, but I didn't want to press the issue. "Of course."

"Damn, Liv," He took in a deep breath. "Is there anything you can't do?"

"Change a flat tire," I answered flatly. "There was an incident this past spring. You can ask Ella. It ended with both of us covered in dirt on the side of the interstate, and we still had to call AAA. Almost put my eye out with that wrenchy thing."

He choked out a laugh. "Could you mean a tire iron?"

"All I know is it looks like some sort of medieval torture device."

"Don't worry. I can change all your tires," he said easily. "Okay. Never have I ever had a surprise party."

"Me either." I shook my head, taking a cracker from the board. "I've never really done a lot for my birthday."

"Because you don't want to?"

"I don't know. I guess I don't feel real comfortable being the center of attention. Besides, I've always been the one that enjoys planning stuff for the people I love. Like this year, for Ella's birthday, I threw a hair metal party complete with leather skirts and a KISS cover band."

"Please tell me there are pictures because this is something I will need proof of." He took another bite of his cookie.

"Oh, there are. Ella dressed up like Bret Michaels, and my hair was teased up to the heavens. The higher the hair, the closer to God." I giggled. "It was a good time."

"You said you don't feel comfortable being the center of attention. Why not?"

"I guess Ben was the one who was always in the spotlight." I ran my finger along the rim of my glass. "I got used to being in the background, you know?"

"No, I don't." He shook his head, and his eyes met mine. "Liv, you deserve to be so much more than in the background of someone else's story. You deserve to be center stage."

My cheeks blushed, and I shifted my eyes to the darkness that extended beyond the patio door. "Never have I ever played on stage at The Ryman."

"Cheap shot," he teased. He threw back the remainder of

his wine before pouring himself another glass and topping off mine.

"Yes it was, but I just have to know what that feels like." I picked apart a pretzel, gazing at him thoughtfully. "The Ryman is kind of the dream for a lot of musicians or at least it was for me back in the day. Patsy Cline, Johnny Cash, Elvis, all of the greats have played there. So, what's it like? Had you played there before the show last night?"

"One other time." He polished off the rest of his cookie. "It's pretty incredible. The sound in that place is unreal, and there's something intimate about it. You can look out and see the faces in the crowd, unlike so many other venues where they all sort of bleed into this backlit blur. There's an energy there that's indescribable. It's almost…"

"Spiritual?"

"Yeah." He smiled. "That's exactly it. There's a connection that happens on that stage that's unlike any other venue."

I sighed. "It sounds magical."

He looked over at me sincerely. "You deserve to be on that stage, Liv, and I believe it will happen one day."

"I wish," I said incredulously. I popped a grape in my mouth, eager to change the subject. "Your turn."

"Hmmm…" He sipped his wine contemplatively for a moment. "Never have I ever been in love."

I raised my eyebrows and picked up my glass, swirling it in my hand a moment before taking a long drink. "Really?"

"Nope." He shook his head. "I've dated a couple of girls over the years. They were nice and all, but none of them were serious girlfriends. It's never been high on my priority list before. I guess part of me has been scared."

"Scared of love?"

"Scared of losing it."

I nodded. "It is scary."

"But is it worth it?"

"I'm probably not the right person to ask." I placed my elbow on the table, resting my chin in my hand. "I'd probably do things differently if I knew then what I know now."

"Because your feelings for him changed?"

I sighed and picked up my glass, studying the way the wine lightly sloshed in the flickering light. "Because how I felt about him changed how I felt about me." I threw back the rest of my wine and poured myself another glass.

"Liv... I—" He started, but I shrugged him off.

"It's okay," I assured him. "I made my choices, and they were the wrong ones. That's the way it is sometimes."

"But you get to make new choices now." Jax reached out, gently touching my arm. "You get to rise from the dirt and thorns and become your own tequila sunrise."

"You're sweet, Jax." I gave him a small smile before clearing my throat. "What do you say we take the rest of this back in the living room and pick up where we left off? I really think we were onto something." I rose to my feet, feeling his eyes on me as I tucked the wine bottle under my arm, grabbing the board and my glass. "Do you mind grabbing the candle?"

He peered at me as though he wanted to say something more, but decided against it. Instead, he gathered his glass and the candle. "Lead the way."

TEN

Jax

WE CONTINUED WORKING through the evening and that second bottle of wine. I found myself seduced by the way she ran her fingers through her hair when it fell in her eyes and how she chewed her lip when she was deep in thought. Her voice cut right through my soul, breaking me wide open.

I couldn't get enough. I wanted to know all of her stories, and I wanted to tell her mine.

Hours later, I placed the guitar back in its case, and we settled into a contented silence. She curled into the couch facing me, her feet tucked beneath her. I'd managed to sit close enough to her that I could easily reach out and hold her hand. I didn't, but God did I want to. I looked into her eyes, which were hazy with exhaustion and wine. Maybe it was the alcohol or maybe she was getting more comfortable with me, but she didn't try to look away. "Thank you for doing this with me, Liv. I don't know what it is about you, but you seem to get me. I know I've got a ways to go, but today felt good."

"I should be thanking you." She bit her lip, resting her head on the back of the couch.

"You're the one who did me the favor," I reminded her.

"Maybe it started out that way, but writing with you tonight was like finding a piece of myself that's been missing." She looked at me through her dark eyelashes. "It's been so long since I played or even tried to write a song. Short of the occasional karaoke night with Ella, I stopped singing altogether."

"But why?"

She stared at her hands for a moment. When she looked back at me, tears were shining in her eyes. "Because it hurt too much. I gave it all up for Ben, but it's not *his* fault. I chose that path, and I chose wrong because the day I let go of my music, I let go of myself too. I let go of every dream I ever had."

Her voice broke, and my heart clenched in my chest. I reached out, carefully wiping away a tear that had spilled onto her cheek. "Liv," I whispered. I leaned into her slowly, stopping halfway. I cupped her cheek, my hand trembling slightly. Her lips parted, and my pulse felt as though it might beat out of my fingertips. My entire body flooded with warmth as she erased the distance between us. Her lips brushed against mine, soft like cotton candy. She moved her hands behind my neck and gently tugged me closer, our kiss deepening. Waves of desire nipped at my heart, threatening to pull me under when she suddenly pulled away.

Her face flushed, and she wiped her cheek with the back of her hand. "I think I've had too much wine." She shook her head, laughing softly. "I'm really sorry."

I winced. "I'm not." I wasn't sorry at all. I wanted to kiss her again, and again, and again. It stung a little that she blamed our kiss on the wine, but I had a feeling that wasn't entirely true. The wine may have lowered her defenses, but

I'd felt this connection growing between us from the moment I met her.

"I shouldn't have done that." She looked down at her hands, chewing her bottom lip.

"You don't need to apologize," I murmured, pulling her into my arms. My fingers lightly stroked the silky strands of hair that spilled down her back. She relaxed in my embrace, and I held her quietly for a few moments, feeling the gentle rise and fall of her breath. "You don't have to put up any fronts with me. I *want* you to open up to me. You don't have to give up on your dreams, and you shouldn't. You're so fucking talented. I wish you could see what I see. Your voice is unlike anything I've heard before. People hire voice coaches and train for years and don't ever come close to the voice you've got. You've got a way with words. You write from a place you can't fake." I paused, inhaling her sweet scent. "I'm a little in awe of you, to be honest. You're real, you're funny, and your heart is genuine. God, you're so beautiful, and you don't even realize it. I know you think we couldn't work, and I know you're scared, but Liv, I want this. I want *you*. You're—"

A soft snore escaped her, and I realized she'd fallen asleep. I suppressed a laugh as I leaned back into the sofa with her still folded in my arms. "You're perfect," I whispered. I couldn't stop myself from placing a soft kiss on top of her head before settling in and drifting off to sleep.

I WAS STARTLED AWAKE BY THE BUZZING OF THE POWER BEING restored and the lights flickering back on. When I opened my eyes, I could see the morning sun already beginning to filter through the room. Liv raised her head from my chest, squinty-eyed and confused. The fact that she'd fallen asleep on me seemed to register, and her sleepiness was replaced with a look of sheepishness.

"Sorry about that." She sat back, rubbing her eyes. "I didn't mean to use you as a human pillow."

"Don't be sorry," I replied. "I'm not." Now that I knew what it felt like to hold her in my arms, I never wanted to stop. My lips still ached to touch hers again.

"Please tell me I didn't snore."

"Not at all," I lied, a soft smile playing across my mouth.

She grabbed her phone off the table, illuminating the screen to check the time. "It's already after seven. I need to get ready for work." She stretched and yawned, seeming reluctant to move yet. "I'm going to text Ella to let her know I'm running a little behind. You want some coffee?"

"I'd love some." I was determined to soak up every second I could with her.

"Come on." She motioned with her head as she gathered the empty wine glasses. I followed with the remnants of the charcuterie board and the empty wine bottle. The sound of birds chirping their morning song filtered through the screen door we'd left open the night before. She placed the glasses in the sink and fired up the Keurig, busying herself with cleaning the dishes. "How about a latte? I think I still have some muffins from the shop if you're hungry."

"That sounds great." She went to work brewing the espresso and steaming the milk for each of our drinks before finally handing me an oversized mug. She placed some blueberry muffins on a small plate, moving to sit at the kitchen table. I reclaimed my spot next to her, looking out beyond the patio and into the backyard, finally able to see it in the light of day. "Wow. Your patio is gorgeous. Is that a firepit back there?" I noticed the wrought iron table and chairs set, along with a large umbrella in the center on the distressed wood patio. A stone walkway led from the patio out into the yard where the firepit was surrounded by cozy outdoor couches. I could see the posts that surrounded the walkway and the entertaining area that held strings of globe lights. I imagined it looked stunning lit up at night.

"That's one of the reasons I bought this place," she explained. "I told myself I was going to start having people over to the house more. So far, it's just been Ella and Grace. Katie has been here a few times too and now you."

"I feel honored." And I did. Knowing I was one of the few she'd let into her personal space made my heart do somersaults inside my chest. "Don't let me forget to give you your shirt back before I leave, by the way."

"Keep it." She waved me off. "It looks better on you than it ever did on me. That reminds me, I need to go get yours out of the dryer."

"You should keep it. In case you miss me." I waggled my eyebrows, and she rolled her eyes, a smile creeping onto her face.

"In order for me to miss you, you'll have to leave first." She cracked a smile. "Speaking of, do you need me to drive you back to the hotel?" She sipped her latte, closing her eyes for a second from the sheer bliss of that first sip.

"I'm good." I shook my head. "I'll text Brady to come get me." I pulled my phone out of my pocket and tapped out a quick text.

"What are your plans for the day?"

I took a bite from my muffin. Naturally, it was heavenly. "That depends."

"On?"

"If you'll let me see you again."

She laughed softly, a blush rising to her cheeks. Her hair was still messy from sleeping, and I had truly never seen anyone more beautiful. "You're not tired of hanging out with me yet, huh?"

I grinned. "Not a chance."

She chewed her lip thoughtfully for a moment, and I glanced away to stop myself from thinking about what it would be like to kiss her again. "Last night, you said you've never made a cake before." She took another sip of her coffee, her hands wrapped around her mug. "Come to the shop later, and I'll teach you."

"I'd love to, but you have to let me take you out for that dinner tonight." I knew asking was a risk, but something felt different this morning. Something about our energy had shifted since the night before, and it felt as though she might be slowly letting her guard down.

She sat thoughtfully for a moment, gazing into the back-yard. Finally, she turned her eyes back to mine. "Okay."

"It's a date." I smiled. This time, she didn't try to deny it. Maybe she hadn't quite caught up with me yet, but I was willing to wait.

"WAIT." LIV LAUGHED, HOLDING OUT HER HAND TO STOP ME from dumping the cup of powdered sugar I held into the bowl of the electric mixer. "Remember, you have to sift it first." I'd spent the afternoon at the bakery, and she'd been teaching me how to bake while Ella and Katie looked on in amusement. We'd managed to make a chocolate cake and some plain white cupcakes before Liv began teaching me how to make a simple vanilla buttercream.

"Just dump it in there," Ella said with a dismissive wave of her hand. "It's fine."

Katie snickered, elbowing Ella playfully in the side. "Don't listen to her. There's a reason she's our business manager."

"And it's the same reason I make all of Grace's birthday cakes." Liv stuck her tongue out at Ella before turning her attention back to me. "Sift the sugar into the bowl with the butter."

"Like this?" I asked, slowly pouring the sugar through the sifter and into the bowl. The paddles on the mixer whipped in a slow circle.

"Exactly." Liv beamed at me, and I found my gaze falling to her soft lips. "We're going to add some vanilla extract, and a little almond extract." I watched intently as she measured out the ingredients, pouring them into the bowl. "Now, we turn up the speed and whip it into submission."

We both reached for the switch at the same time, and my hand covered hers for one blissful second.

"Sorry." Liv quickly withdrew her hand, the faintest hint of pink creeping onto her cheeks. "You do the honors."

I noticed Ella give Liv a pointed look, raising her brow. "Whip it into submission, honey." Ella sassed. "Whip it good."

This time, Liv was the one narrowing her eyes in Ella's direction.

"You got it." I laughed, sliding the switch so the paddles whirred inside the bowl.

"You're doing good, and you've got the best teacher,"

Katie said, squeezing Liv's shoulder as she walked past her. "I'm going to go clean the cases out front."

"Thanks, Katie Bug." Ella hunched over the island in the center of the kitchen, resting her head on her elbows as Katie disappeared through the door. "So, what are you two doing tonight?"

"I'm taking Liv to dinner." I smiled at Liv, and the pink in her cheeks turned a rosy red. "In exchange for this baking lesson."

Ella tilted her head slightly, a dreamy smile spreading across her face. "You guys are so cute." Liv exchanged another look with her in a seemingly wordless conversation I couldn't decode. "What? You are." She sighed heavily. "I guess I'll go and start closing things down since Jax clearly isn't setting the kitchen on fire today."

"You mean like you did when I tried to teach you how to make crème brûlée?" A mischievous grin spread across Liv's face.

Ella snorted. "Those torches should really come with a warning label."

"She set our old order notebook on fire and almost singed my eyebrows off," Liv said with a laugh.

"She's over-exaggerating." Ella grinned. "It was only one eyebrow."

"Get out of here." Liv picked up a dish-towel off the counter and swatted her with it.

Ella giggled and started toward the door. "I'm going," she said, leaving Liv and I alone for the first time since we'd been there.

Liv flicked the switch on the mixer, and it slowed to a stop. "Now, we're going to load up a pastry bag with the buttercream and decorate the cupcakes with it." I watched as she filled the pastry bag with the thick frosting before handing it to me. She placed two of the cupcakes in front of me. "You're going to squeeze a small dollop in the center first, and then slowly swirl the icing over the cupcake."

"Swirl," I repeated. "Is that a technical term?"

"In fact, it is." She laughed, placing her hands over mine. "Try to apply even pressure to the bag so the icing doesn't go everywhere." My fingers tingled as she gently guided my hands over one of the cupcakes, resulting in a beautiful mountain of frosting. "Awesome. Now, you try."

She removed her hands from mine, and I tried to emulate what we'd just done on the next cupcake. This time, the frosting leaned heavily to the right.

I laughed. "That didn't turn out so good."

"That's not bad for your first one," she said, placing another cupcake in front of me. "This time, use that little dollop in the middle as your guide. Imagine you're placing circles around it, even as you build the icing up."

I nodded and tried again. This time, it looked damn near perfect.

"See?" Her eyes sparkled up at me. "You did great." She held her hand out. "Here, I'll finish these up real quick so we can go to dinner."

I handed her the bag and leaned against the counter, watching her work. She quickly moved the bag over the remaining cupcakes, covering them with a perfect mound of white buttercream.

"You really are good at this." I watched as she leaned down so that she was eye level with the cupcakes, inspecting them. Once she was satisfied, she stood and wiped her hands on her apron. "And you seem to really enjoy it."

"I do enjoy it." She untied her apron, hanging it on the

hook beside the door. "It just isn't really what I wanted to do for a living. I'm good at it, but it's never been what I was passionate about. Baking was supposed to help afford me the ability to do what I loved. It was supposed to be more of a means to an end, but that's the way it is sometimes, right? What we're good at and what we're passionate about aren't always the same things." Her tone was light, but her wistful smile betrayed her. She turned away from me, busying herself by putting a few bowls in the sink. "I'm thankful for the bakery. I don't mean to sound like I'm not. It's just not what I saw myself doing for the rest of my life."

I knew she thought her dream had passed her by, but I felt strongly she could still pursue a career in music. We wrote so well together. I knew she was doing it to help me, but what if it could be something much, much more? I opened my mouth to say something, but before I could she'd turned back toward me expectantly.

She smiled. "You ready to go get that pie?"

"Definitely," I said.

"We're heading out," she called to Ella and Katie.

Ella peeked her head in the kitchen. "You two have fun." Once again, Liv's face appeared to have a silent conversation with Ella's.

"I drove the Jeep to work so we could leave straight from here." Liv grabbed her purse off the hook and dug her keys out. "You get to play DJ."

I opened the door for her, following her out into the night. We weren't even on the road yet, but my mind was already going ninety miles an hour.

The night air enveloped us in a cool autumn blanket as we drove with the top off the Jeep, Liv's hair blowing wildly around her. We passed houses and businesses with Halloween decorations out front, which meant I had to play "Thriller" as my first selection. I laughed as Liv danced in place at a red light, complete with ridiculous zombie faces. Then of course, I joined her.

We sang "I Don't Wanna Miss A Thing" by Aerosmith at the tops of our lungs, trading off vocals and harmonizing with each other. Our voices blended together smoother than the butter and sugar in the buttercream we'd just made. With each song I picked to play, it was as though we'd previously rehearsed them. There wasn't one sour note between us, and we played off each other easily, the way you do when you've been in a band with someone for a long time.

A band... I thought about how easy it had been to write with her, how comfortable it was to be with her. The songs we'd started were good, and I knew the band would love Liv's style. I had no doubt we'd be able to write some material for Midnight in Dallas, but the more I thought about it, something felt off. Part of the reason the songs we'd started felt so right was because of *her.* Because of us, together.

An idea started forming at the corners of my mind. Music was Liv's dream. Sure, she could be a successful songwriter, but she belonged on the stage. Her presence radiated magic. What if we could do something together? We could have our own duo and...

"Earth to Jax." Liv laughed, nudging my arm. "I lost you somewhere around that last Lumineers song. You okay?"

I turned to face her only to realize we'd already arrived at the pie shop. "Yeah, I'm good. Let's go."

"WELCOME TO THE LOVING PIE COMPANY. OH, HEY, Jaxon," the owner of the pie shop greeted me with a wide smile. "It's been a minute. Are you guys recording tonight?"

"Not tonight," I replied. "We're in town on a break. This is my… this is Liv Sinclair."

"Suzanne Loving. Wait, you own Livvie Cakes, right?" Suzanne's eyes lit up.

"Yes, I do." Liv blushed. "How did you know?"

"My best friend lives over in 12 South, and we were at your bakery a couple of weeks ago. You were out front talking to a customer, and I heard you introduce yourself as the owner. You have the best cupcakes in town. Seriously. That Pumpkin Praline should have songs written about it."

"That's high praise coming from the woman with the best mac-n-cheese in town." Liv smiled. "Jax told me all about it, and I can't wait to have some."

"Have a seat anywhere you like." Suzanne gestured to the mostly empty dining room. "We're kind of slow on week-nights. You guys are getting the works. You have to try our Red Velvet Hot Chocolate. It'll change your life."

"That sounds amazing." Liv beamed. "Thank you."

"Thanks, Suzanne," I said, leading Liv to my favorite table in the back by the window. "Look at you being recognized."

Liv laughed and took off her jacket, slinging it over the back of the chair. "I can assure you, that's the first time it's ever happened." She looked around the dining room, taking in the bright walls and the framed photos of various slices of pie and coffee drinks. Her eyes settled on a movie poster on the wall opposite us, featuring a piece of Red Velvet Chess Pie. "This place is fun."

It was so cozy in the converted house, it was easy to forget you weren't in someone's dining room. That was one of the things I loved most about the pie shop.

"Two Red Velvet Hot Chocolates." Suzanne placed two giant mugs in front of us, complete with toasted mini marshmallows.

"This smells delicious," Liv said, scooping up the mug with both of her hands.

"So, two mac-n-cheese pies?" Suzanne asked. "I can also add some jalapeños to that if you're feeling spicy."

"Yes, please." Liv nodded.

"That sounds great," I said.

"Coming right up." Suzanne nodded before disappearing back through the kitchen.

I took a sip of my hot chocolate. "You're feeling spicy, huh?"

She raised her brow, giving me a little shrug. "Maybe a little." She took a sip of her hot chocolate, closing her eyes. "Life-changing, as advertised. I'm going to want to come here all the time now."

I smiled. "I could see us in here, coming up with song ideas over coffee."

"We need to get to work on those songs we started," she said. "I know you have to get some ideas over to Cash soon."

I chewed my lip a moment, my eyes settling on the mug in front of me.

"There you go again."

I brought my eyes back to hers. "What?"

"You had that same far off look in your eye in the car a few minutes ago." She peered at me curiously. "Are you stressed about the songs? We can go back and work on them tonight if you want."

I shook my head. "It's not that."

"What is it then?"

My gaze shifted for a moment, my foot lightly bouncing with nervous energy. "I started thinking about something today…"

Liv's face fell. "Were the songs not quite what you were hoping for? I told you I'm rusty, but I'll—"

"No, no." I interrupted her. "It's not that at all. You're a phenomenal songwriter. It's just… it's gotten me thinking I may not want to use all of these ideas for the band."

"Oh." She tilted her head and pursed her lips slightly. "What did you have in mind? Maybe a solo side project?"

I leaned in, focused on her. "What if *we* had a project together? Our own duo."

"What?" she blurted, startling herself with how loud her voice was. "No way. You're joking."

"Not at all. I think we work well together, Liv. I love writing with you, and it comes so easily. It's like we've performed together for years. Do you know how rare that is?"

"Yeah, but I'm no performer."

"I call bullshit." I looked at her pointedly. "Maybe you haven't been on a stage in a while, but you belong on one. Look, I know you think it's too late for you, but it's not. You could still do this. *We* could do this—together."

"I don't know, Jax." She shook her head. "I was a different person back then. That was ages ago. I don't even know if that woman still exists."

"Then who have I spent the last couple of days with?" I challenged her. "Because *that* woman is still passionate about music. That woman belongs on stage, singing her stories for the world to hear."

Her expression softened, and she stared out the window

wordlessly for a moment. Finally, she turned back toward me. "You really think that?"

"I *know* that."

"And you really want to do this? With me?"

"Yeah," I said. "I do. I know it's a lot to think about, but will you promise me you'll at least consider it? We'll keep writing over the next couple of weeks, and you can decide if and when you're ready."

"I wouldn't want it to come between you and the band, though." She frowned.

"It doesn't have to," I said. "Lots of people do side projects or even join other bands while maintaining their original projects. Look at people like Miranda Lambert, Brandi Carlile, and Steven Tyler. Even the Jonas Brothers made it work."

She eyed me momentarily as if trying to decide if I would suddenly tell her this was all part of some elaborate joke. "Okay. I'll think about it."

My smile stretched to my ears. "Thank you." At least I knew I'd have the next couple of weeks to hopefully convince her that we could have a future together, both on and off the stage.

"Two jalapeño mac-n-cheese pies." Suzanne appeared at our side, placing our plates in front of us. "Can I get you guys anything else right now?"

"No, thank you." I smiled, looking over at Liv. "I think we've got everything we need."

ELEVEN

Liv

MY MIND FELT like it had been on a Tilt-A-Whirl ride. First, I'd kissed Jax, and then he'd suggested we start our own musical act. My head kept telling me what a bad idea this was. I was far too old, and I could never be good enough for a man like him. He was a handsome, successful, and much younger rockstar. Yet I felt my heart being pulled more and more in his direction. I loved the way his eyes always seemed to find mine and how easily we fit into each other's lives. I found I was having to remind myself about the age difference and the fact that he'd be back on a tour bus soon, but I'd still be here.

Writing songs with him was one thing, but becoming a bonafide performer? That was entirely different. I was still grappling with the idea of even being *with* a rockstar, let alone becoming one myself. Part of me wanted to say yes on the spot. This had been my dream for so long, but I was a different person back then. Now, I had the bakery and Ella and Grace. I had different responsibilities than I did all those years ago. Add to that the potential complications of us having feelings for each other, and you had a recipe for disaster.

Though I'd told Ella I was helping Jax write some songs, I hadn't been able to bring myself to tell her about the kiss or his crazy business proposal. I could tell she suspected something was up by her knowing glances, and I already knew what she would say. But could I really risk going all-in with someone only to be replaced again?

Despite how much I tried to deny my feelings for Jax, I wanted to soak up as much time with him as I could. We spent every day that week together. He hung out with me in the kitchen at work for more baking lessons, and we went to the pie shop a couple more times.

Nearly a week after we first met, Jax and I were at a fall festival at the local botanical gardens with Ella, Grace, Cash, and Dallas. Jax and Dallas sported beanies and sunglasses in an effort to disguise themselves, but Brady came along too, just in case they got recognized by any crazed fans. It was a sunny but chilly day and that meant it was even busier than usual. People were scattered everywhere, taking in the beautiful fall flowers, pumpkin houses, and live bluegrass music. Families picked out pumpkins to paint, and carts were staggered along the gardens serving delicious and overpriced fall fare.

"What do you ladies want to do first?" Cash directed his question to Ella, Grace, and me.

Grace beamed. "Let's go watch the band."

"I like the way you think, Grace." Dallas sniffled, tugging his beanie further over his ears. We moved to the stage area and found an empty space in the grass to sit. Jax sat just behind me, close enough that I could almost lean into him. I noticed Brady sat a little off to the side, presumably to give us some privacy.

"Brady, come sit with us." I waved him over.

"Yeah, man," Jax agreed. "I know you're here to help us in case anything crazy happens, but we want you to hang with us too."

Brady scooted over closer. "I just didn't want to intrude on your date."

Despite the chill in the air, a simmering heat rose to my cheeks. Ella raised her brow at me.

"You're not intruding on anything," I assured him.

"So, Grace, tell me about school." Cash cleared his throat, changing the subject.

Grace shrugged. "School is fine, I guess, I'm just ready to graduate."

"Hey." Ella reached out and squeezed her arm. "Don't rush it."

Dallas laughed. "Sounds like you've got a case of senioritis."

"It doesn't seem possible." Ella shook her head. "My little girl is all grown up, and now she's going to leave me all alone with an empty nest."

"You won't be all alone." Grace laughed and rolled her eyes. "You'll still have Aunt Liv."

"But that's not the same as having my little baby bird." Ella wrapped her arms around Grace, covering her head in kisses.

"Mom!" Grace tried to wriggle free from her mother's grasp. "You'll be fine."

I smirked. "We can always get you a cat like Mama."

Ella snorted. "Don't you think we've got enough hostile kitties around here?" She mimed a cat scratch. "Me-ow."

Cash choked on a laugh, turning his attention back to Grace. "What are your plans after graduation?"

"I'm not really sure." Grace shrugged. "I kind of want to study abroad, maybe somewhere like London. It'd be nice to have a change of scenery."

I grinned. "And I'm sure the boys with British accents are an added bonus."

Ella grimaced before turning to Grace. "I don't even want to *think* about it. You're not allowed to date till you're fifty."

Grace giggled. "I thought it was till I was thirty?"

Cash chuckled, clearly amused.

"If you keep on, I won't let you date till your next life." Ella ruffled Grace's hair.

The wind picked up, causing a chill to rip through me. I tugged the sleeves of my sweater over my hands.

"Are you cold?" Jax slid closer, wrapping his arms around me.

I noticed Ella watching with a goofy smile plastered on her face.

"Actually, I think I'd like a coffee or something." I started to get up, but Jax stopped me.

"I'll go get it," he said.

"What about you two?" Cash asked Ella and Grace, rising to his feet.

"I'd love a hot chocolate." Grace grinned.

Ella flashed him a dazzling smile. "I'd love a hot chocolate with alcohol in it."

Cash chuckled. "I'll see what I can do."

Brady and Dallas both stood.

"You guys have got the right idea." Dallas nodded with a sniffle. "I'm going to go get something too. I can't seem to shake this cold feeling."

"We'll be right back." Jax grinned down at me before they disappeared into the crowd.

"I love that you're dating a rockstar." Ella sighed. "I could get used to hot men waiting on me and bringing me boozy cocoa."

"We're not dating," I insisted. "We're friends."

"Friends." Ella rolled her eyes, a slight smile playing across her lips. "Right."

"What?" I narrowed my eyes at her.

"You keep telling yourself that," Ella sang, turning to watch the band. I opened my mouth to say something to try to refute her, but every reason I could up with seemed weak, even to me.

The band was playing bluegrass covers of popular songs. They'd covered The Beatles, Lady Gaga, and The Backstreet Boys by the time the guys returned with the drinks.

"I've got hot cocoa for Grace and a Monster Smashed for you, Ella." Cash handed Ella her cup, and Brady gave Grace hers as they returned to their seats.

"A Monster Smashed?" Ella laughed.

Cash cocked his head. "Let's just say, I'm glad you took an Uber here."

Dallas sat and took a long pull from his cup. He grimaced. "I got a Hot Toddy, and it tastes more like whiskey that's been set on fire." He coughed into his elbow.

Jax settled next to me, handing me my drink. "And Jack-O-Lattes for us, which is their fancy term for an Irish Coffee."

"Yum." I took a sip, savoring the warmth of the styrofoam cup in my hands.

"We should see if we can get the band to sing an early birthday song for Aunt Livvie." Grace grinned mischievously.

"Absolutely not," I laughed. "I'm perfectly content with

bluegrass Backstreet Boys. It's the version of 'I Want It That Way' I never knew I needed."

"Wait a minute," Cash said. "It's almost your birthday?"

I nodded, but Jax answered for me. "On the 17th."

Dallas beamed. "We need to—"

"Excuse me," a voice said from above us, "but are you Jaxon Slade and Dallas Stone?"

We looked up to see two girls, who couldn't have been much older than Grace, staring eagerly down at the guys. One had colorful mermaid hair, and the other could have easily been Jessica Rabbit's sister.

Brady's posture hardened immediately, his arms crossing over his chest as though he were ready to jump into bouncer mode.

Jax laughed but stiffened slightly. "Yeah, we are."

"Are Luca and Derek here too?" The mermaid girl's eyes widened.

"No," Dallas said. "It's just us, I'm afraid. They had something else going on today."

"Can we take a picture with you guys?" Jessica Rabbit's sister asked.

"Sure," Jax said, giving me a sympathetic smile as he and Dallas stood to take a picture with their waiting fans.

I felt my body tense as I watched Dallas and Jax interact with the two girls. Jax's idea to start our own duo ping-ponged in my mind. As much as I wanted a career in music, I wasn't sure this was something I could get used to.

"Thank you so much," the mermaid girl gushed as Jax and Dallas sat.

"Are you guys famous too?" Jessica Rabbit's sister looked at me, Grace, and Ella expectantly.

A feeling of unease bloomed in my chest. A meet and

greet was one thing, but I wasn't so sure I was ready for people to approach me out in the wild. I liked my privacy and being able to do something as simple as enjoying a day out with friends without being scrutinized. Ella furrowed her brows with concern in my direction, clearly in tune with my nervousness.

"We're a new punk rock girl group," Ella said without missing a beat. "Josie and The Hostile Pussycats."

I snorted, and Cash nearly choked on his coffee.

"Oh my God!" the mermaid squealed. "I'll look you guys up on Spotify."

"Thanks, ladies." Dallas laughed as the two girls scampered off into the crowd.

"Josie and the Hostile Pussycats? Really?" I swatted Ella's arm.

"Ow!" Ella recoiled. "Fine, you can be Josie."

Dallas sneezed, narrowly avoiding spilling his drink.

"You okay, Dal?" I asked. I started digging through my purse until I found my mini-pack of tissues, passing them to him.

"Yeah, I'm okay. Thanks," he said. "I think I'm just a little run down from the tour. I'm sure I'll be good as new in a few days."

Jax put his arm around me, rubbing my arms to warm me. Ella flashed me a knowing smile, and I took a deep breath, Jax's delicious scent mixing with the sweet smell of the coffee. I allowed myself to rest my head on his shoulder, vaguely aware of the conversation the others were having beside us. The band began to play a slow melody, a twangy version of an Ed Sheeran song.

Jax kissed the top of my head and softly sang the words in my ear, causing my insides to turn to mush.

Without thinking, I covered his hand with my own, our fingers intertwining for one sweet moment. Maybe Jax and I were a bad idea, but I had to admit, I loved this song.

"OKAY, HOW DOES THIS FEEL FOR THE SECOND VERSE?" I looked down at the notebook I'd been writing in as I strummed the guitar in a slow, melancholy rhythm and began to sing. "*I wonder if you ever wonder about the man that I've become. If you ever think about the dreams I dreamed or the battles that I've won.*"

Jax nodded his approval. "Perfect."

"I was thinking something like this for the chorus." I changed keys, my eyes closing as I half-spoke, half-sang the words. "*Do you think we ever look up at the same midnight sky? Do you ever think about the guy...*" I pursed my lips in thought, trying to find the right words. "*...do you ever miss the man...*"

"*You let become a stranger.*" Jax finished for me, the emotion in his eyes illuminated in the soft glow of my living room. "Damn, Liv. It's like you're inside my head. You're taking all these feelings I've had about my mom for so long and turning them into something beautiful."

He looked at me with such intensity, I felt as though my insides might catch fire.

"I can't explain how or why, but you understand me in a way nobody has before." He gently brushed away a piece of hair that fell into my eyes. "It feels good to get all this out... cathartic, even. Like I can finally let go of some of this anger and hurt I've been holding on to for so long."

Goosebumps rushed over my body. "I'm glad." His eyes

locked with mine, and my heart began to race, pulsating so hard I could hear it thudding in my ears. I focused on placing the guitar in its case in order to stop myself from kissing him like I had the first night we'd written together.

"What do you say we break for dinner?" I stood, motioning for him to follow me to the kitchen.

"Let me take you out," he said, falling into step behind me.

I laughed. "We've existed on going out and take out all week. Let me cook for you."

"How can I turn down an offer like that?"

"You can't." I tossed a smile at him over my shoulder.

"I think we should turn this into a little game," he said as I flicked on the kitchen light. "Make it a little more interesting."

"Uh-oh." I started rummaging through the cabinets, plucking out everything I needed to make a pot of spaghetti. "Another round of Never Have I Ever?"

A mischievous grin spread across his face. "I had something else in mind."

I paused for a moment and crossed my arms, leaning against the counter. "Like what?"

He pulled his phone out of his back pocket and started scrolling. "We take turns picking a song with the sole purpose of trying to make the other person dance. The first to dance to three songs loses."

"I can take you down *and* make dinner at the same time. I'll even let you go first."

"Bold move," Jax said. "Head and shoulder movements count as dancing too, so you can't be doing any of this." He swayed his shoulders and bobbed his head from side to side.

"Quit making up these bullshit rules so I can beat you at

your own made-up game." I stepped closer to him, my hand on my hip.

"*And* she's a trash-talker. I like it." He closed the space between us in one stride, standing so close that his warmth could have melted me like a forgotten ice cube on the floor. "We'll see if you're still this cocky after I make you dance to three songs in a row. First, we need to determine a prize."

I raised my brows at him. "Besides bragging rights?"

"Obviously. I'm going to need something to show off my victory."

"Fine. What do you want?"

"I want what every man wants." He leaned into me, lightly pushing me against the counter.

My breath caught in my throat and every nerve in my body tingled.

He placed one hand beside me, bracing himself as the other reached behind me and grabbed the clear canister off the counter containing one cookie. "The last snickerdoodle."

"Deal." I squared my shoulders, tilting my face up to his in what I hoped was a challenging stare and *not* like I wanted to devour him like a snickerdoodle. Because that thought *definitely* hadn't crossed my mind more than half a dozen times.

I moved around him to start chopping the onions and garlic as his first pick began to play. He danced beside me, bouncing his head wildly like he was in *Night At The Roxbury*.

I shook my head. "Your first choice is 'Party In The U.S.A.?' Really?"

"What?" Jax started doing the sprinkler, and I choked on a giggle. "This is a classic."

I added some olive oil to the skillet on the stove and

leaned against the counter, overjoyed to have a front-row seat to this show.

He pouted as the song ended, handing me his phone. "Your turn."

I quickly searched for my selection as I started sautéing the fragrant vegetables. The opening notes to "Ice Ice Baby" began to play, and I spun around, rapping into my spatula. He gritted his teeth and gripped the counter trying to keep himself from dancing, but by the time I got to the chorus his shoulders had started to rock.

"Shit." He laughed. "Beginner's luck." He took his phone back while I added the tomato sauce and my signature blend of spices to the skillet. I filled a pot with water, placing it on the stove to boil as the opening notes to "Thriller" began to play.

"That's cold. You already know I love this song." I poked him in the chest. "No one can resist the siren call of the King of Pop."

Jax howled along to the creepy background sounds of werewolves, and once the music began, I shimmied to the left, clapping my hands above my head. When I repeated the motion to the right, he joined in. I paused long enough to set the pasta sauce to simmer, but I bounced right back into place when the chorus started.

"You want to play dirty?" I asked, snatching the phone from his grasp. "We can do that." I smirked and hit play on "Can't Touch This." I started doing a terrible rendition of the running man, and Jax couldn't stop himself from dancing with me.

"Dammit." Jax laughed while I dropped the noodles into the boiling pot of water. "I've got to make this next one count."

"Do your worst," I said, checking on the sauce.

"Oh, I will." He grabbed the phone, making his selection, and "Walk This Way" started to play.

I groaned. "You're onto me and my love for Steven Tyler." I was dancing before the first verse kicked in. "Dinner's almost done, and I still need to give you my last pick since you're going to lose and all."

"I could still win this." He grinned wildly.

"Best you can hope for is a tie, but that's not going to happen." He handed me the phone, and I located my last song. "I'm about to pull out the big guns. Are you ready?"

"I was born ready."

I made a dramatic show of pressing play, and the sounds of "(I've Had) The Time Of My Life" filled the air.

Jax threw his hands up in defeat. "Are you kidding me? I wanted to *be* Patrick Swayze when I was a kid." He rolled his hips, giving me his best Swayze impression.

"Victory!" I shouted, taking a triumphant lap around the kitchen and back to the stove. I drained the spaghetti and combined it with the sauce. When I turned to face Jax, he was dancing up to me as though he were reeling me in on a fishing pole. I laughed so hard my sides hurt when he pulled me into him and twirled me around. "Come on. Dinner's ready." I attempted to pry myself out of his grasp, but he spun me back into his arms.

"Not yet." His grin spread so wide it reached the corners of his eyes. "It's time for the big finish."

"Absolutely not." I giggled, trying to wriggle out of his arms, but he was much stronger than I was. I shrieked his name as he picked me up around my waist, spinning us around. I threw my head back with laughter, feeling lighter and more liberated than I had in ages.

When he returned me to the ground, he pulled me close and pointed to the top of the refrigerator where Mama sat looking at us as though we'd lost our damn minds. She meowed with disgust, narrowing her golden eyes.

"I'm so glad Mama was here to witness your defeat," I teased. "How does it feel to lose at your own game?"

"I don't know." He pulled me closer, his laughter fading to a contented smile. "Because it kinda feels like I won."

I felt all the boundaries I'd tried to put up softening as I allowed him to wrap me in his arms. I sighed, breathing in his calming warmth. He rested his head on mine, and I began to question the game I'd been playing with myself, trying to deny my feelings for Jax. I sensed a crack in the foundation of the walls I'd built around me, but somehow that felt a lot like winning too.

TWELVE

Jax

"You really don't have to do all this," I said, watching Liv flit about the kitchen, rummaging through her kitchen cabinets. She stacked ingredients alongside pots and pans, preparing to make a recipe she appeared to have memorized by heart. The countertops were already adorned with the muffins, pumpkin bread, cupcakes, and snickerdoodles she'd made.

"I want to," Liv assured me. "Poor Dallas. He seemed a little sniffly a couple of days ago at the festival."

"He said he thought it was probably just a cold."

"And my great grandmother's chicken and dumplings are perfect for fighting off the common cold." She tossed a smile over her shoulder at me as she pulled some chicken from the refrigerator.

Mama trotted past us and started meowing wildly at the back door, her paws clawing at the glass.

I shook my head and chuckled at Mama. "What's got her riled up?"

"Who knows?" Liv shook her head and turned her attention to whatever she was searching for in the pantry. "Sometimes she gets a wild hair and wants to go exploring out by the firepit. Do you mind letting her out?"

I moved to the back door, opening it for Mama, and she darted off the back deck. I leaned against the counter, watching Liv work. "I know Dallas has quite the appetite, but you're making enough to feed a small army." I gestured to the plethora of treats.

"I can't very well take Dal a care package and leave the rest of the guys out." She set to work on the chicken. "Now they'll all have dinner and plenty of snacks. I also picked up some vitamin C and Gatorade for Dallas. Don't let me forget to grab those before we leave later."

I nodded and flashed her a coy grin. "Do I get to benefit from any of this care package?"

"Who do you think the snickerdoodles are for, silly?" She raised her brow at me. "And I'm keeping a small pot of the dumplings here for us." She suddenly seemed self-conscious. "If you want to come back with me, of course."

"You know I do." I thought my heart might jump right out of my chest and into her hands. Not only had she made my favorite cookies just for me, but she'd assumed we were eating dinner together. Things between us felt like they'd been progressing, especially since the festival, and I was beginning to think she could see the potential in us that I saw.

"Dallas is going to love this. The rest of the guys will too."

"I'm happy to do it. The guys are your people, and you're one of my people, so now they're my people too." She shrugged. "I like to take care of my people."

"I love that about you."

Her creamy skin turned slightly pink. "When I was growing up, my mom was always cooking for people. Food was her love language."

"So that's where you get it." I grinned. I felt a small tug at the corners of my heart, reminding me of those moments lost with my own mother.

"My mom was the type of person who showed up with food for every occasion. It didn't matter if someone just had a baby or a death in the family or if they were sick. She had a dish for all of that. I used to help her in the kitchen, making chicken and dumplings, casseroles, and cakes all the time. I remember standing on a stool to help her cook when I was too small to reach the counter. She was always patient with me, letting me taste the cake batter or take half the day rolling out dumplings. Those are my favorite memories of her."

A smile spread across my face as I imagined a mini Liv standing beside her mother, one finger dipped into a mixing bowl.

"What?"

"I was just picturing little Liv. I bet you were cute. You still are." She chewed her lip, and I couldn't help but think about what it felt like to kiss her the other night.

Suddenly, Mama's loud meow interrupted my thoughts.

"I've got it,' Liv said, wiping her hands on a dish-towel on the counter. She crossed to the back door and opened it, letting out a shrill scream before taking off out the back door. "Oh my God! Mama!"

"What's wrong?" I rushed outside to find her chasing Mama around in an attempt to get her to drop the very stunned, or very dead, chipmunk she held in her jaw.

"Drop it, Mama!" Liv shrieked. "Bad cat! No!" Mama dropped the chipmunk who, much to my surprise, was alive. Seeing it attempt to scurry away, Mama went into attack mode again. I dove for Mama as Liv lunged for the chipmunk.

Liv's face crumpled with horror when she realized she'd grabbed the rodent with her bare hands. "Oh my God! What do I do? What do I do with it, Jax?" I howled with laughter because I didn't know who looked more terrified: Liv or the chipmunk. "If I put it down here, Mama *will* find it, and I cannot be finding dead baby chipmunks."

Mama hissed as I tossed her inside, closing the door. I could barely form words, my body shaking with laughter as I rushed back to Liv's side and took the tiny rodent out of her hand. "I'm going to go put him over the fence. He'll at least have a fighting chance out of Mama's line of sight." I took the little guy to the farthest point of the backyard and gently set him over the fence, watching as he scampered away probably terrified out of his little chipmunk mind.

By the time I got back to the deck, Liv was giggling uncontrollably. "I can't believe I just did that."

"You're a hero." I chuckled, pulling her into my arms. "You should have seen yourself. You were like Snow White, if she were a fearless ninja."

"Fearless, or just plain stupid," she said, shaking her head. "That crazy cat."

"I think that was her way of bringing you a gift." I snickered. "I remember Dallas had a cat back when we were in school that used to do that. It's their way of showing they love you."

"I guess it's the thought that counts." She grinned. "Come on. I need to finish these dumplings for Dallas."

LATER THAT EVENING, WE WALKED THROUGH THE ENTRANCE of the hotel with Brady on our heels. He'd met us out front to ward off anyone who may try to approach, but the hotel lobby was mostly empty, except for Antoni, Cash, and Derek, who were talking just outside the elevator.

"Oooh, look who it is," Antoni purred. "How are you, Miss Thing? What's all this?" He made a sweeping gesture at the crockpot in my hands and the pile of baked goods that Liv carried.

"Just a little care package I made for you guys." Liv expertly balanced the goods in one hand, hugging Antoni with the other. "I wanted to make something for Dallas to help him feel better, and I wanted y'all to have plenty to share."

"You made all this?" Cash's eyes gaped open. He looked at me questioningly, and I nodded. His face seemed to soften as he watched Liv.

Derek peered into the container at the top of Liv's stack with a clear lid. "Are those cupcakes?"

"They sure are." Liv beamed.

"Can I please steal one?" Derek asked. "I'm headed out for a bit, but I can't walk out of here without one of those."

"I'm not going anywhere, but can I take one too?" Brady grinned.

Liv laughed. "Sure."

"I'm gonna take one for the road too," Antoni said, helping to ease the lid off the container, pulling out two cupcakes and handing one to Derek. Brady reached in, grabbing one before pressing the lid closed and immediately taking a bite.

Antoni bit into his cupcake, closing his eyes. "Girl, I'm gonna have to go to confession. These are positively sinful!"

Derek took a bite of his cupcake and sighed. "Your cupcakes are the best." He reached out and squeezed Liv's arm. "I hate to grab and go, but I'm meeting with a friend who's in town. Save me some of whatever is in that crockpot because it smells delicious."

"Drive safe." Liv smiled at him.

"I'll be right back," Brady said. "I'm going to walk Derek out."

"Later, Derek." I waved as he disappeared through the entrance with Brady on his heels.

"Well, that's my cue too, boo-boo." Antoni air-kissed Liv. "I'm going home to Texas for a few days to see the fam, but I'll see you boys in LA. And I hope to see you again soon, pretty lady." He gave me a pointed look as he rolled his suitcase behind him into the night.

"I'll go up with you guys." Cash hit the button on the elevator. Liv, Cash, and I made the ascent to the twelfth floor, where our rooms were. "This was really nice of you, Liv."

"It can't be fun being sick in a hotel room." Liv scrunched up her nose.

I led her down the hall toward Dallas' room. "It definitely isn't."

Liv smiled. "Besides, y'all need a home-cooked meal every now and then."

"Thank you," Cash said. "Really, this means a lot."

We stopped in front of Dallas' room, and I knocked on the door. After a few seconds, Dallas emerged, looking miserable in sweats and a hoodie. His eyes were puffy, and he looked exhausted. "Hey, guys. What's going on?" He rubbed at his throat, trying to soothe his hoarse voice. His eyes settled on the crockpot, then bounced over to Liv and the mountain of goodies she held. "No way. What's all this?"

"Chicken and dumplings." Liv nodded. "And lots of other goodies. I brought enough for all of you and then some."

The door across from Dallas' room opened, and Luca stepped out, his head cocked as he looked at us.

I chuckled. "Seriously. We could probably feed the entire hotel staff."

"You're a fucking angel." Dallas sniffled.

Luca gestured at me and Liv. "Something smells good out here."

Dallas beamed. "Liv made us food."

"Damn," Luca said. "You made all this for us?"

Liv nodded, then twisted back toward me. "Shoot. I left the bag with the other stuff in the Jeep."

"Other stuff?" Luca asked. "There's more?"

"I brought some paper bowls and plates, that kind of stuff. Dal, I got you some Gatorade and Vitamin C. Oh, and some green tea."

"I can go grab it," I offered.

"I'll run down and get it," Liv said. "You go plug in the crockpot."

"Let me at least take these off your hands." Luca held out his arms, and Liv unloaded the treats on him.

She dug her keys out of the tiny purse that was slung across her body. "I'll be right back." She touched my arm before heading back down the hall toward the elevator. My eyes lingered on her as she walked away, my chest swelling with admiration.

"I can't believe she did all this for us." Dallas shook his head, opening the door further to let us in.

I found a spot on a table near the door to plug in the crockpot, and Luca placed the other food beside it. Dallas immediately started rifling through the containers. He inhaled deeply. "Wait, is this pumpkin bread? Damn, that woman is amazing."

Luca grabbed a blueberry muffin and took a bite. "This is delicious. Cash, you want one?" He held the container out toward him.

"Thanks." Cash plucked one of the muffins from the tin. "That Liv is something else, and damn can she bake."

"Wait till you try the dumplings." I crossed the room to one of the chairs, sitting on the arm.

"You better lock that shit down, Jax," Luca warned.

Dallas rolled his eyes. "Sage words of wisdom from the guy who can't even get a girlfriend."

"I can get one," Luca said. "I just don't *want* one, but if I did, I'd want one like Liv."

I smiled, looking down at my hands. "Trust me, I want her. She's… incredible."

Dallas took a bite of his pumpkin bread, chewing thoughtfully for a moment. A sad smile spread across his face. "She reminds me of Carrie." His eyes widened as though he were shocked by the words that escaped his mouth.

For a second, it felt as though the air had been sucked out of the room. Luca's eyes darted over to Cash, and I looked over at him tentatively.

"Cash, I'm sorry, brother." Dallas frowned.

"Don't be." Cash waved him off. "You're right. I was thinking the same thing. This is the kind of thing Carrie would have done." His gaze fell to the floor, a mournful expression tugging at the corners of his mouth.

"Yeah, it is." Luca's voice was solemn. "She always made sure we were taken care of."

"I miss her." Cash sighed. "Every single day."

"Me too," I echoed. We sat quietly for a couple of moments before I gently changed the subject. "I've been meaning to tell you, I've got some new music in the works. I'll send it to you later." I gave Cash a hopeful smile. "I think you're going to be surprised."

"That's great news," Cash said. I could tell he was genuinely happy, but his smile didn't quite reach his eyes. "I can't wait to hear it."

Before I could say anything else, Liv was knocking at the door. Luca let her in, and she busied herself by unpacking the bag, placing everything neatly out on the table.

"Who wants the first bowl?" Liv asked, lifting the lid off the crockpot. She turned to face us, ladle in hand, a big smile on her face. She looked to each of us, noticing the shift in the atmosphere. "Are y'all okay?"

Dallas rambled over to Liv and threw his arms around her in a bear hug. "Thank you, Liv."

"You're welcome." Liv returned his embrace. "Can I make you some tea or anything?"

"Right now, I need some of these dumplings in my life." Dallas rubbed his hands together, taking the ladle from her hand.

Cash rose to his feet. "So do I."

"We better get on that before Dallas eats it all." Luca moved in behind Dallas, patting Liv on the back when he passed her.

Liv's eyes found mine, and she smiled. I ambled my way to her, pulling her into my arms. She yelped slightly as I lifted her off the ground, holding her close. Her arms tightened around me, and I savored the way she felt in my embrace.

When I finally set her back on her feet, she turned her face upward curiously. "What was that for?"

I reached out and squeezed her hand. "I'm just glad you're here."

THIRTEEN

Liv

—————

A COUPLE of days before my birthday, Dallas asked if Jax and I would go with him to look at a place he was strongly considering buying. It was a gorgeous penthouse apartment in Midtown with an incredible view of the city. We cruised through town in my Jeep with the top off, soaking in the warmth of the sun and the slight nip of the autumn breeze. Occasionally, I noticed Jax watching me as the wind whipped my hair around, and I squirmed beneath his gaze. I'd felt a tension building the entire week we'd spent together, no matter how much I tried to deny it.

After we pulled into the garage at the condo complex, Dallas guided us to the top floor penthouse where we were to meet the realtor. Dallas knocked on the door and we were greeted by a lady who had to be in her mid-to-late sixties with bright red hair teased up to the sky and cherry red lips. When she gestured us in with her hand, I noticed her long oval nails painted the perfect matching shade of crimson.

"Dallas," she drawled. "So good to see you again, hun. These must be your friends." She turned to me, extending her hand. "Hi, doll. I'm Darcey Dubois, realtor extraordinaire. Pleasure to meet you."

"Liv." I smiled, shaking her hand. "Nice to meet you."

"And who is this strapping young man?" Darcey turned her attention to Jax.

"Jaxon," he replied with a nod. "Nice to meet you, ma'am."

"Goodness gracious, seeing how gorgeous you three are makes me miss my youth," Darcey said with a flourish, turning on her red-bottomed heels and leading us through the foyer into the expansive apartment. "It may be hard to believe, but when I was your age, I was quite the looker too. But age came a-knockin' and honey, there simply ain't enough Oil of Olay this side of the Mississippi to fix these wrinkles." She turned to face us as we wandered into the fully furnished living room overlooking the city. "Not that y'all have to worry about that anytime soon. Y'all don't look a day over twenty-nine."

I snorted and felt Jax's hands grip my shoulders as Darcey barreled on. "Listen to me rattlin' on. What y'all really came to see is this gorgeous penthouse. Like I've told Dallas, I know y'all are musicians, as are many of our residents, so it's important to note all of our units have been completely sound-proofed. Our homes can also come fully furnished if you like what's here. There's this phenomenal interior designer who handpicked every single item in this house, down to the brass fixtures." She began leading us through the apartment. She rattled off various details as she wound us through the kitchen complete with a bar, the spare bedrooms, an office, a game room, another separate den that would make the perfect music room, and finally, she took us upstairs to the master suite. "Now this, my dears, is the showstopper. We have an ensuite gas fireplace, a minibar, and that master bathroom may as well be a damn day spa. The closet alone is the size of my first apartment. Then, of course, there's that magnificent view. You can see for miles from up here."

"This is amazing," Jax said from beside me.

"Wow." I sighed, taking in the view of the city.

"Right?" Dallas asked. "What do you think?"

"You'd be crazy not to take it." Jax crossed his arms over his chest, appraising the scenery.

"I think it's stunning, Dal," I replied. "That kitchen is pretty rad too."

"I'm gonna need you to come over and help me break it in." He poked me with his elbow. "Maybe you can teach me how to cook."

I grinned. "Deal."

"Alright." He chuckled, placing a hand on my shoulder. "Well, Miss Darcey, I think you have yourself a deal. I'd like to put in an offer."

"That's what I like to hear," she sang as Dallas walked around, inspecting some of the fixtures. She turned her attention to me and Jax. "Now, when can I get you two in a new home?"

"Huh?" I asked.

"You'll need room to grow, I'm sure," she continued on. "Do y'all prefer to be in the city, or do you want a place with a little land?"

"Oh." My face flushed as I realized what she was saying. "I have a place over in 12 South. We're not, um, together, but Jax is considering moving here."

"Hmm," she said as though she didn't really believe me. She studied us a moment, pursing her red lips. "I'm sorry, darlin.' I just assumed because y'all look so darn cute together." She smoothed her hands over her black pantsuit. "Let me get this offer together. Dallas, hun, you want to follow me down to the kitchen, and we'll get these papers started?"

"Yes ma'am." Dallas flashed us a thumbs up as he followed Darcey back down the stairs. "Let's do this."

"Did you hear that?" Jax nudged me with his hip as I focused my eyes on the Nashville sky. "She said we look cute together. I *donut* believe it."

"You're silly." I laughed and shook my head, turning back toward the stairs.

"And you love that about me." Without even looking at him I could hear the grin that stretched across his face. "That's how I know I'm wearing you down." I turned to face him as he stepped closer to me.

"I donut know what you're talking about," I teased. This time he didn't laugh.

"She's not wrong, Liv." His thoughtful eyes held mine, and he tucked a strand of hair behind my ear. "You know she's not. We're good together in every possible way."

I felt my breath catch in my throat. I knew he was right, but his being right didn't change my fears. My insecurities came bubbling back to the surface in an overwhelming wave. I hadn't been good enough for Ben. Some days, I wasn't even sure I was good enough for me, and I was afraid there may come a day I would no longer be good enough for Jaxon Slade.

"You guys coming?" Dallas called.

"We should… we should go downstairs," I mumbled half-heartedly. Before Jax could say another word, I all but fled down the stairs.

"What do you think of this one?" Ella held up a bottle of navy-blue nail polish, inspecting it in the light.

"You know I think that color looks great on you." I picked up a deep oxblood color and handed it to one of the nail technicians who waited to lead us to our pedicure stations. It was my birthday, and Ella had managed to get full coverage for the bakery and booked a full afternoon of beauty at a salon down the street. We were scheduled to get blowouts and makeup applications, but we were beginning our afternoon of pampering with manicures and pedicures.

After we selected our colors, the technicians guided us to our adjacent pedicure chairs.

"Where do you want to go for dinner tonight?" Ella asked, kicking off her heels as I pulled off my suede knee-high boots. She busied herself with rolling up her jeans while I dunked my feet into the water, pulling the sleeves of my chunky black sweater dress over my hands. "Adele's was booked already since it's Saturday, but what about that fancy sushi place we went to for Katie's birthday before she became a vegetarian?"

"Sure," I said halfheartedly. "That sounds good."

She fixed her eyes, studying me. "Talk to me. What's going on in that beautiful head of yours?"

I picked at my cuticle as I looked over at her. "It's Jax. It's just that—"

"He's head over heels for you?" She raised her brow at me.

"He's not—"

"Olivia," she cut me off. "Do you really think I haven't noticed? I've *seen* the way you look at each other. I've seen the way he is around you, all squishy and adorable."

I looked down at my hands, avoiding her watchful gaze.

"Jax and I have been writing music together. He wants us to start our own musical act, just the two of us."

Ella's eyes gaped open. "Are you serious? That's amazing, Liv. So, when is this happening? Are you guys signing a deal or something?"

"God, no." I shook my head. "I don't even know if I'm going to do it."

"What do you mean you don't know if you're going to do it? Obviously you're going to do it."

I sighed. "It's a huge decision, Ella. This would change my entire life."

"Yeah," Ella said. "For the better."

"Not necessarily. I love making music, and writing with him is easy. It's like we've always written together, but there's so much more to it than that. The predictability of my schedule would be gone. I'd be on the road a lot, which means I would be away from you and Grace. And privacy? That would be out the window, and I don't know, but there's something comforting about being able to fuck up without the entire world knowing about it."

"You are not going to fuck anything up," Ella assured me. "This is an amazing opportunity. One that you deserve. You need to do this. You owe it to yourself to go after this dream."

"What about the bakery?"

"What about it?" Ella asked. "We will make this work. Katie is a rockstar, and we can always hire more help."

I chewed my lip. "What about Jax? What if we start this whole thing and he ends up hating me?"

"I hardly think you have to worry about that. That man is falling in love with you, Liv, and you clearly have feelings for him too. Why are you fighting this so hard?"

I sighed and rested my head against the back of the pedicure chair. "I'm scared, Ella. I'm so fucking scared."

"Of what?"

"What if history repeats itself and—"

"I'm going to stop you right there," she interjected. "The last week and a half, I feel like I finally have *you* back. Ever since Jax came into the picture, you've been more *you* than you've been in years. For fuck's sake, you're singing again. You're writing songs and actually considering giving this music thing a go. This is *huge,* Olivia. Jax isn't Benton. You know how I know that?" I looked over at her. "He encourages you to do the things you love instead of shoving them out of sight like they're something to be ashamed of. Benton wanted you to suppress so many of the beautiful things that make you who you are. Jax doesn't want to change a single thing about you."

"Maybe not now, but what if that changes?"

She reached over and grabbed my hand. "Honey, love is a risk no matter how you slice it. There will always be a chance you could get hurt, one way or another. Love isn't about choosing who you think won't hurt you. It's about choosing who's worth hurting for. Look at me and Craig. I loved that man more than anything in the world. You know how good he was to me, and you know the hurt I've felt every day since we lost him. Even knowing the way it would end up, I'd choose him all over again. That's what love is." Tears glistened in her eyes, and I covered her hand with mine. "You're getting another chance to live the life you always wanted, Liv."

"What if I'm not good enough?" I whispered.

"You are more than good enough." She squeezed my hand. "Besides, you know I don't hang out with losers." A smile twitched on her lips. "I mean it. You're good enough, and honestly, I think if anyone can help you see that, it's Jax. I think he could love you the way you deserve, but more importantly, I think he can help you love yourself the way you deserve. You're getting a second chance here, babe. You should take it."

I saw the sadness gloss over her eyes again, and I laced my fingers through hers. "You're going to get your second chance too."

"Maybe one day." She smiled softly. "For now, I get to live vicariously through you. Promise me you'll think about it, okay?" I sat thoughtfully for a moment until she nudged me with her elbow. "Okay?"

I knew Ella was right. I owed it to myself to think about what she'd said and about what Jax had been showing me since the night we met. I looked back over at Ella and nodded. "Okay."

FOURTEEN

Jax

"Let's set up the snack table over here." Grace pointed to a vacant part of Liv's back patio. Luca and Derek followed her directives and moved the folding table accordingly. "Katie and Dallas will be back with the decorations any minute now."

"Perfect." I surveyed the backyard and envisioned how everything would come together. Ella had taken Liv out for a spa day so that we could spend the afternoon getting everything ready. "The caterers confirmed they'll be here at six to get set up, and Brady texted to let me know he just picked up Cash from the airport. They're going to stop by the florist and pick up everything there for me. I think we've got it all covered."

"All that's left is to start the cake," I said, following Grace inside through the patio door. I started unpacking the grocery sacks I'd placed on the kitchen counters.

"You sure you can do this?"

I placed my hand over my heart as if she'd wounded me. "You think I can't bake this cake?"

She wrinkled her nose, looking over at me. "I'd be lying if I said I didn't have my doubts."

"My own coconspirator doubts me," I scoffed. "I'm hurt, but since you're worried, you can stick around and be my sous chef."

"You better stay close," Luca teased, maneuvering around us to grab a beer out of the fridge. "We want Liv to have a kitchen to come back to." I laughed and picked up the dishtowel from the counter, slapping him on the arm with it. "You think we got enough alcohol?" Luca twisted the top off his beer.

"Yes, I do." I narrowed my eyes at him. "This isn't one of your ragers. This is a Liv party, and I'm going to need you to act accordingly please."

"Fine." Luca pretended to grimace. "I *guess* I'll be on my best behavior. What can I do to help?"

Mama sauntered into the kitchen, turning her golden eyes upward at Luca before hissing disapprovingly and scampering off down the hall toward Liv's bedroom.

"Weird cat," Luca mused.

"That's Mama." Grace shrugged. "She hates everyone."

"We're back," Dallas sang as he and Katie bustled inside, popping their heads through the doorframe of the kitchen.

"Perfect timing." I clapped my hands together, turning my attention back to Luca. "Go help them unload everything, and you guys can start setting up. I'll come help once I get this cake in the oven. We'll have even more to do once Brady and Cash get here with everything from the florist."

"On it." He took a swig from his beer and followed Dallas and Katie toward the front door.

"You ready to bake this cake, Chef?" Grace started pulling

bowls, pans, spatulas, measuring cups, and spoons out from their respective homes.

"I was born ready!" I exclaimed, examining the recipe for the dark chocolate cake with raspberry buttercream icing. Grace helped me decide on a cake, but I was going to use some of the tricks Liv had taught me to jazz it up a bit. At least, I hoped that's what I was going to do. "You sure know your way around this kitchen." I watched her find everything we needed with ease as I stepped over to the oven, setting it to 350 degrees as the recipe instructed.

"I'm here a *lot.*" Grace placed a large mixing bowl in front of me, and I began measuring out the flour. "Aunt Liv and I love to try out these crazy Pinterest baking projects together. The three of us are together a lot. Always have been. During the holidays we like to stay up all night, baking Christmas cookies and fudge, and listening to crooner Christmas music. It used to make Benton crazy. He hated it."

I raised my brow at her as I sifted together the flour, sugar, and cocoa. "Really? Why?"

Grace shrugged as she walked around to the other side of the counter, facing me. She propped her elbows on the smooth marble, resting her head in her hands. "Benton never really liked mom and me all that much. We were kind of the family he never wanted. Mom and Aunt Liv were always best friends, but after my dad died they became even closer. When they started working together, the three of us became pretty much inseparable. Benton worked late a lot, and he went to events most weekends, so the three of us would hang out together. It's always been us."

"I know that had to be hard for you and your mom." I looked up at her sympathetically. "I'm sorry about your dad."

"It was tough, but mom and Aunt Liv made sure I never

felt like I was missing out on anything, you know? They've been to every school play and parent night. They even took me to the father-daughter dance at my school a few years ago. Honestly, I don't know where mom and I would be without Aunt Liv." She opened the package of chocolate pieces and measured them out so I could begin melting them for the batter. "I think she likes you."

"You do?" I peeked at her over my shoulder. "Did she say anything?"

"She didn't have to."

"I like her too."

"I know," she said simply. "Promise me you won't hurt her, okay?"

I turned around and met her sincere eyes with mine. "I never want to hurt her. I only ever want to make her happy."

"And you gotta know we're a package deal." Her voice was laced with worry. "You get Aunt Liv, and you get me and mom too."

"I wouldn't have it any other way," I assured her. "I promise."

"Good." She nodded. "Then you have my blessing. Now, stir your chocolate before it burns."

My heart was in my throat as I turned my attention back to the stovetop. I knew what a big deal this was. Grace was a huge part of Liv's world, and her approval was important to me.

"Knock, knock," I heard Cash's voice call as he and Brady made their way to the kitchen. "I come bearing the entire florist shop. I was afraid we wouldn't be able to get it all in the car." His eyes lit up when he saw Grace. "Hey, Grace." She moved around the counter to hug him. "It's good to see you again. How's your week been? How's your mom?"

"We've been good," she answered. "Mom took Liv to the salon to get her out of the house for a while so we could get ready for the party."

"How much longer do we have?" He looked over at me, rolling up the sleeves of his white dress shirt.

"About three hours," I replied. "Ella texted to let me know they finished their pedicures. She said if she had to she could probably stall a little longer by stopping to get coffee before they head back here."

"We've got this," Cash said. "We can pull this surprise party together in three hours."

"Speaking of surprises," I started. "Did you guys park in the driveway?"

"Two steps ahead of you," Brady spoke up. "I parked across the street, and as we were coming in Katie was moving her car so there are no cars left in the driveway except for Liv's and Ella's. That's surprise party 101."

"You guys are on it." I swirled the spatula through the chocolate, which was now shiny and melted. "I'm about finished with the cake. I need to clean up real quick, but I can help decorate before I make the frosting."

"Take your time. Grace and I've got this." Cash winked over at her. "Jax, I wanted to tell you, those songs you've been working on are brilliant. I listened to them this morning. They're fantastic. You said Liv helped you write them?"

"She sure did." I nodded. "I'd never have been able to write them without her."

"She's incredibly talented," he said. "We need to get her writing with you for the next Midnight in Dallas album."

"Wait till you hear her sing." A smile stretched over my face at the thought of her beautiful voice.

"She can sing too?" Cash raised his eyebrows at me.

"You have no idea," Grace piped up. "She's seriously the best singer I've ever heard, and I'm not saying that because she's my aunt. No offense, Jax. You're a close second." She beamed over at me and laughed.

"No offense taken." I chuckled. "I know when I'm out of my league."

"Well, I can't wait to hear her." Cash clasped his hands together. "Miss Grace, what do you say we get going on those decorations?"

"Are you good here?" She watched me gently stir the batter.

"I'm good, *and* I haven't even burned the house down." I stuck out my tongue at her.

"Yet," she emphasized.

"Go ahead." I laughed as I started to pour the batter into the three cake pans on the counter. "I'll be right behind you guys."

"After you," Cash said to Grace, gesturing to the back patio door. With one last glance over her shoulder, Grace let him guide her outside.

I put the cake pans in the oven and said a silent prayer that those baking lessons with Liv had paid off. I scrubbed my hands over my face, a nervous tension building inside me. I'd decided I was going to try to get her to sing some of the material we'd been working on together for the guys. I knew the second they heard us, they'd see what I'd seen this entire time —that she was destined to be on stage, and that together, we were magical. I hoped their excitement would help her realize she wanted to give this a shot.

Then, there was the matter of my gift for her. In the little time I hadn't been with Liv, I'd written a song for her. I had every intention of singing it to her for her birthday, but after our encounter a couple of days ago at the penthouse, I'd grown increasingly worried she'd never let go and give me a chance, musically or otherwise.

I'd spent months being uninspired, but when she came along, the floodgates opened up. I knew the second I sang this song for her, there was no turning back. She'd have no doubts about my feelings for her.

I knew I had to share it with her. I had to tell her how I felt.

My heart raced, and my palms began to sweat. I was scared she would shut me down, and I could lose her forever.

But I knew deep down, she was a risk worth taking.

FIFTEEN

Liv
___

"ARE you sure you left your keys in here?" I asked, shoving my key in the front door. "I could have sworn you got your sweater out of your car before we left."

"Ummmm, yeah. I'm positive," Ella replied, sounding completely unsure. "I must have left my car unlocked. I think I left them on the kitchen table." I flicked the switch next to the door.

"I could have driven, you know. We don't want to be late picking up Grace." I started down the hall, and Ella closed the door behind us.

"It'll take two seconds," she promised, her heels clicking behind me. I entered the kitchen, but before I could even slide my hand over the light switch, the room was suddenly illuminated.

"Surprise!" A chorus of voices shouted, and I shrieked, one hand flying to my mouth as the other reached for Ella's arm. My eyes adjusted, and the faces of everyone around me came into a twinkly-lit view.

"What the…" There stood Brady, Derek, Luca, Dallas,

Katie, Cash, and Grace. Finally, my eyes settled on Jax at the center of them all. I turned to Ella. "Did you... "

Ella shook her head gently, turning her gaze to Jax. "It was all Jax's idea."

"You did this?" I could feel tears forming behind my eyes as I turned to face him.

"I had a *lot* of help." He stepped toward me. "I know we haven't known each other long. Many of the people in this room haven't known you long, but I... *we* wanted you to know how special you are, today and every day. Grace, will you do the honors?"

Grace proceeded to the back door, flinging it open to reveal a twinkly-lit dreamworld. I gasped and moved forward, not stopping until I was outside on the patio. Gorgeous white archways led out into the yard, and a beautiful bohemian style table had been set up, complete with plush pillows for seating. Tequila sunrise roses and rose petals had been scattered around like confetti. I could smell the warm spiciness of Thai food that I instinctively knew was from Bow Thai. I could recognize the smell of those soy sauce noodles anywhere.

To my right, there was a snack table filled with goldfish crackers, an assortment of donuts, and Pop-Tarts—all call-backs to our first couple of days spent together. Soft music played through speakers I couldn't see while the bonfire roared, waiting for people to surround it for warmth. I felt Jax's presence next to me, and my eyes found his in the soft glow of the lights around us. Tears streamed down my cheeks as I threw my arms around him.

"Happy Birthday, Liv." His voice was soft and low as he folded me into his arms.

"I donut believe you did this," I said through my tears.

"Happy Birthday, honey." Ella wrapped her arms around

my shoulders, kissing me on the cheek. I pulled Grace into my arms, and everyone filed out onto the patio to give me hugs and birthday wishes.

"I don't know about you, but I'm *starving!*" Dallas pulled me into a hug and kissed my cheek.

I chuckled. "How are you feeling, Dal?"

"Much better, thanks to you." Dallas made a beeline for the Thai food that Katie was beginning to uncover. "Food line starts behind me."

I turned my gaze back to Jax, his eyes filled with warmth as he placed an arm around me. "After you, birthday girl."

———

AFTER DINNER, WE LINGERED AT THE TABLE, ENJOYING THE light breeze of the night air. We laughed as Luca shared stories of their lives on the road and felt Dallas' excitement when he talked about his new penthouse. Derek told us about the areas he'd been exploring the past few days. He asked Ella and I questions about cities like Leiper's Fork, Franklin, and Spring Hill. Grace bubbled over about the Homecoming Dance she was looking forward to the following weekend. As I took in the faces around me, I couldn't deny how beautifully we all blended together.

"I believe I heard there was some cake here." Dallas looked pointedly at Jax.

"I believe I heard that rumor too." Jax winked before jogging into the house. A couple of moments later, he returned carrying a beautiful cake with rich pink frosting, illuminated by the candles that flickered on top of it. He placed it in front of me. "Make a wish, birthday girl."

I gasped, taking in the gorgeous confection and the perfect waves of the icing. "Did you make this?"

"He did." Grace spoke up before he could even begin to discredit what he'd done. "It was all Jax."

"Dark chocolate with raspberry buttercream." He beamed. "I learned from the best. Now make a wish."

As I looked at the faces around me, my wish was simple. I blew out the candles, and everyone cheered.

Jax began to expertly cut and serve the cake, giving me the first slice. I dug my fork into the decadent cake, moist with melted chocolate and the perfect amount of raspberry frosting, and took a bite. "Jax, this is divine."

"Damn, Jax." Derek took his first bite. "I didn't know you had it in you."

"Seriously," Brady echoed.

"Yeah, man," Luca agreed. "If this whole music thing doesn't work out, I think you could have a future as a baker. This shit is amazing."

"So Liv, I was shocked to learn you'd been holding out on us," Cash said from across the table where he sat next to Ella.

"What's that?" I asked.

"Jax sent me some clips of the songs you two have been working on together." He grinned. "I had no idea you were a songwriter." I looked over at Jax, and he gave me an encouraging nod.

"She sings too." Ella chimed in. "She's only got the most beautiful voice on the planet."

"That's what I heard." Cash nodded.

"Well, that settles that." Luca threw his napkin down on the table. "We're going to need a private concert."

"Yes," Grace chimed in. "Come on, Aunt Liv!"

"You guys—" I started, but Dallas cut me off.

"Please, Liv." He looked over at me with what could only be described as a sad puppy dog face. "Sing for us!"

I looked at the pleading, smiling faces around me, before turning to Jax, who gazed at me with anticipation. "I already have my guitar over by the fire."

"What the hell." I shrugged. "Let's do it."

We moved out to the bonfire with our beverages in tow. Katie stopped by the drink table and snagged one of the open bottles of wine, bringing it with her to top off our drinks.

I sat next to Jax and watched as he carefully pulled his guitar from its case, handing it to me.

"Y'all have got to hear this girl sing some Johnny Cash," Ella said.

"That's the truth," Jax echoed from beside me.

I gazed at the expectant faces around me for a moment, and then I closed my eyes and began to play. I sang "Ring Of Fire" to overwhelming praise before Jax and I played a couple of the new songs we'd been working on together. When we finished, everyone applauded as Jax returned his guitar back to its case.

"Damn, Liv." Dallas took in a deep breath. "You really were holding out on us."

"Watch out, Jax," Luca teased. "We'll be replacing you with Liv if you're not careful."

Derek took a sip of his wine and leaned back into the sofa. "Seriously, your voice is incredible. You should be making records."

"I agree," Cash said, looking at me and Jax. "Have you guys considered starting your own project separate from Midnight in Dallas?"

Grace beamed. "That would be awesome."

"Actually, I mentioned the idea to Liv a few days ago."

Jax looked over at me hopefully. "I've been trying to convince her it's a good idea."

Luca nodded approvingly. "That's a fucking brilliant idea."

"I told you so." Ella grinned.

"It's not that I think it's a bad idea," I said. "It's just a big commitment, and I wouldn't want to get in the way of the band."

Cash shook his head. "It wouldn't. Artists have side projects all the time. It's absolutely possible for Jax to do both without it taking away from the band."

"And it's not like the two wouldn't have some crossover," Dallas mentioned. "The music would be complimentary enough that Jax & Liv could easily be the opener for Midnight in Dallas, especially while you guys are starting out."

Ella squealed. "I can hear it now—and the Best New Artist Grammy award goes to… Jax & Liv!"

"Jax & Liv need to be a thing," Luca agreed with a nod.

"You guys have something special." Derek gave me an encouraging smile. "Something that's completely separate from Midnight in Dallas."

Jax nudged me with his elbow. "That's what I've been trying to tell her."

"You've written some great material that could absolutely be used for the band's next album, but there are some songs I think need to belong to Jax & Liv," Cash said simply.

Dallas leaned forward, focusing on me. "I think I speak for everyone when I say we want you involved on the next Midnight in Dallas record."

"Damn right, we do," Luca echoed as Cash and Derek nodded in agreement.

"And if you'd be willing, it'd be nice to have your voice

on a song or two." Dallas looked at me hopefully. "But more than that, Jax & Liv need to be a reality."

"Come on, honey." Ella cheered me on. "Do it."

"The important thing to remember is you guys aren't on any sort of timeline," Cash said. "You and Jax are in the driver's seat. Right now, you can focus on writing songs for a record. We don't have to make any announcements or have you performing in the public arena anytime soon."

"Cash is right." Jax placed his hand on my knee. "There's no rush. We'll take our time, and we won't take our music to the public until you're ready."

As afraid as I was, I knew I wanted this. I wanted to give this a shot, and I had to admit, the excitement on the faces surrounding me was contagious. "Okay." I turned to face Jax. "Let's do this."

His eyes widened. "Are you serious?"

"Yes." I smiled. "Let's make Jax & Liv a thing."

He wrapped me in an excited hug as everyone around us burst into cheers and applause.

"We need to toast the birthday girl." Ella hoisted her glass up high. "To my best friend and sister from another mister." Everyone joined her, holding their beers and wine glasses high.

Katie looked over at me sweetly. "To the best boss and a wonderful friend."

"To the best aunt in the world." Grace held up her glass of sparkling water.

"With the incredible voice." Cash lifted his glass in my direction.

"To Jax & Liv." Dallas smiled over at me.

"Jax & Liv," everyone echoed, clinking their glasses.

Finally, Jax held his glass to mine. He leaned in so only I

could hear his voice, soft and low in my ear. "To the most incredible woman I'll ever meet."

A LITTLE BEFORE MIDNIGHT, EVERYONE FILTERED OUT EXCEPT for Jax.

"I'll call you tomorrow." Ella gave me a knowing glance, leaning in to hug me.

"Okay." I nodded, wrapping Grace in a hug. "I love y'all."

"Love you too, Aunt Liv." Grace's smile lit up her face as she bounded after her mom.

"I'll lock up," Ella called before closing the patio door behind her, leaving me and Jax alone for the first time that day. We stood beneath one of the archways, and I gazed into his stormy blue eyes, which seemed to glow beneath the twinkle lights.

"I have one more gift for you," Jax said softly. Offering me his arm, he led me back to the bonfire.

"Jax, you've done so much for me already." He gestured for me to sit and withdrew the guitar from its case once more, sitting beside me. "I can never thank you enough for what you've done."

"I wrote something for you." His eyes found mine, and my heart thundered inside my chest. He began to strum a soft, slow melody with his eyes trained on mine. His voice was raw with feeling, and it became clear he was telling the story of how we met. By the time he reached the chorus, tears filled my eyes. *"Can I hold your hand? Will you let me walk you to your door? I know we just met, and it's 3 am, but all I want is more."*

I wiped at the tears that fell unchecked down my cheeks as he continued to sing.

"I want to be the man who is better than every other man that came before. So, give me a chance. May I have this dance? Baby, will you let me love you more?"

I couldn't take my eyes off him as he strummed the last note. He returned the guitar to its case and pulled me to my feet, wrapping me in his arms.

"Jax, that was beautiful." I pulled back so I could look into his soulful eyes. I could have burst into flames from the heat of his gaze.

"What do you say, Liv?"

"I don't know what I did to deserve how truly wonderful you are." I placed my hands on his firm chest, gripping his sweater. He wiped away the tears that spilled down my cheeks with the pads of his thumbs. "But I'm so scared, Jax."

"Olivia." He said my name softly, taking my face in his hands. "I'm falling in love with you."

"Jax… I'm..." I trailed off, and he leaned in so close I could feel the warmth of his breath on my lips. For a second, I swear my heart forgot to beat.

"Fresh out of excuses?" He finished for me, leaning in closer, waiting. Waiting for my answer. Waiting for my permission.

For the first time in as long as I could remember, I didn't think. I didn't question if I deserved it or if I was good enough.

"I'm falling in love with you too," I whispered, tugging his shirt, pulling him closer.

"Yeah?"

I nodded, and I felt him sigh with relief.

He kissed me tenderly at first, his soft lips grazing mine.

My hands slid up his chest and behind his neck, and as I gently pulled him closer, his kiss grew more and more fervent.

When I finally broke our kiss, we were both breathless. He kissed the top of my head, wrapping me in his arms. "I can't tell you how bad I've been wanting to do that."

SIXTEEN

Jax

THE NEXT MORNING, the sound of a soft rain tapping against Liv's bedroom window caused me to stir. I'd fallen asleep with her in my arms and woke with her body still folded into mine.

After we'd put out the bonfire and turned off the lights outside, we'd kissed our way back to her bedroom where I'd kissed her over and over and over again.

I didn't try to push it further, though I definitely wanted to. I wanted *her*. I wanted to be close to her, but I also knew that her allowing herself to feel what she felt for me was a huge step—one I didn't take for granted. I knew she was still fighting with feelings of not being good enough, though it killed me that she ever felt anything less than perfect.

She'd been with her ex for nearly half her life. I knew it would take a while for all her walls to come down, and I was okay with that because I was in it for the long haul. I just had to show her.

I heard her soft sigh, and she shifted slightly, causing the covers to fall so her shoulder was exposed. The strap on her tank top had slipped down, so I returned it to where it belonged. I tightened my arms around her, kissing her shoulder blade. "Good morning," I murmured in her ear. I felt her body respond as she turned toward me, kissing me lightly.

"It's really unfair you know." Her voice was still raspy with sleep.

"What is?" I asked, playing with a piece of her silky hair.

"That you actually wake up looking like this." She laughed, wrapping herself around me and nestling her head into my chest.

"Speak for yourself." I gently rubbed my fingertips along her bare arm and kissed her forehead. "You're beautiful, Liv. You're breathtaking."

Her fingers traced circles along my bare chest sending shivers all throughout my body. "I want to lay here with you all day."

"That sounds like the perfect rainy Sunday to me."

"How much longer do you have before you have to go back out on the road?"

"We leave Tuesday morning." I groaned at the thought of having to leave her. "It's only for a month, and then we're off for the holidays. We may end up with a couple of appearances we have to make, but nothing crazy. I don't want to leave you."

"I know," she said softly, "but I'll still be here when you get back."

"Promise?"

"I promise." She lifted her head off my shoulder, planting a kiss firmly on my lips. "And I can come to visit you in Louisville too."

"There's nothing for me back in Louisville but an apartment that, for the most part, collects dust," I insisted. "What I want is right here in Nashville. I'll be coming back here, but I don't have to stay here if that's too much too soon. I can always get a hotel room."

"I want you here." Her hand found mine, and she intertwined our fingers.

My heart caught in my throat. *I want you here.* "I've got to say, I love hearing you say that."

"Yeah?"

"Yeah," I replied. "I was so nervous last night, Liv. When I told you how I felt, I thought it might push you away."

"I'm sorry," she whispered. "I know I haven't made this easy on you."

I rolled over so that I hovered over her. "You have *nothing* to apologize for. Nothing. I get why you've been scared, but I want to show you I think you're fucking perfect, Olivia Sinclair."

"Speak for yourself." She pulled my face down to hers and kissed me slow and deep. "How about I make us some breakfast?"

"How about you let me do the cooking since it's technically still your birthday weekend?" I trailed a string of kisses along her jawline before my lips found hers again.

"You're spoiling me already." Her emerald green eyes glowed as she chewed on her bottom lip. I felt myself coming undone.

"For the record, every time you bite your lip…" I brought my face so close to hers, I could feel her breath catch beneath me when her lips parted. Her lips were pillowy like little rose-colored clouds. "It drives me crazy in the best of ways."

"Is that so?" A flirtatious smile spread across her face, and she bit her lip once more.

Damn, she had me. She had me wrapped around her little

finger already. "Oh, is that how you're gonna play this?" I brushed her lips with mine before plunging my hands into her sides, tickling her. She squealed and wriggled beneath me as I continued my tickle attack. Finally, I gave in to her giggling pleas for me to stop, and I kissed her hard. "Come on, I'm making waffles."

WE LAZED ABOUT TOGETHER ALL DAY SUNDAY, COVERING each other in kisses. The only moments we'd been apart were the few she'd spent on the back patio that afternoon talking to Ella on the phone. I'd come into the kitchen for another cup of coffee when I saw Liv leaning up against the railing outside with a soft blush on her cheeks and a smile on her face. She was the most beautiful woman I'd ever seen. Everything about her drew me in like the first sunny day after a cold, dark winter. All I wanted to do was bask in her rays.

The next day, I joined Liv at work. The rest of the guys came to the store to visit and say goodbye to Liv, Ella, Katie, and Grace, who showed up after school.

I loved how easily she fit in with the guys. I watched while Liv attempted to show Dallas how to make a cherry pie. They erupted into a fit of giggles when he somehow managed to get the red goo all over his hands, looking like he'd committed a heinous crime. He'd chased Katie around the room, acting like he was going to wipe the evidence all over her. Even Luca, who didn't really warm up to new people, seemed to have a certain affection for Liv.

Cash loved the girls. It was evident in the way he never stopped smiling when he was around them. It was the happiest I'd seen him in a long time. He was also ready and willing to do anything he could to make Jax & Liv a thing, but he didn't push. He wanted it to be on Liv's terms.

After the guys left and we closed up the shop, we walked back to Liv's bungalow hand in hand. Mama hissed her hellos to us as we bounded through the door. She watched with annoyed curiosity as we cooked dinner together, clearly put out that I was still invading her home territory.

I wrapped my arms around Liv's waist, nuzzling my face in her hair while she chopped the vegetables for the soup she was making. I inhaled her sweet citrusy scent, knowing I could never get enough of moments like these. We continued our new tradition of picking songs to play that would make the other dance. I loved the way she threw her head back with laughter when I made a complete fool of myself, which I did often just to make her smile.

"Okay." I rubbed my hands together as she passed me to put the pot of soup on the stove. "It's my turn to pick a song."

"Lay it on me," she said. "I'm ready."

I scrolled through the music on my phone until I landed on the song I was looking for. "Can't Help Falling In Love" began to play as she turned to face me. "May I have this dance?" I extended my hand to her, and she took it, letting me pull her close. She smiled up at me, sliding her arms around my neck. "I'm going to miss you so much, Liv." I leaned into her, placing a soft kiss on her forehead.

"I'm going to miss you too." She pulled my face down to meet hers, brushing her lips against mine.

I leaned in so that our foreheads touched as we danced together in the kitchen. I soaked up every second of feeling her in my arms, becoming more and more aware that after tonight I wouldn't be able to hold her like this for so many days. Too many. Finally, I said the words I hadn't planned on saying. "Come with me."

"What?" Her face was veiled with shock as though there was no way she could have heard me correctly.

"Come with me," I murmured. "We could work on some new music, and we'd be together."

"I can't do that." She shook her head. "I'd love to be with you. You know I would, but I can't just leave."

"Consider it a Jax & Liv trial run," I tried to persuade her.

"I can't leave the business right now, and Grace's homecoming dance is this weekend. I have to be here to see her off."

I thought back to my conversation with Grace from Liv's birthday, and I knew what I was asking of her was crazy. "I know. I'm sorry. I'm just going to miss you so damn much."

"I know. I am too, but this is something we're going to have to figure out how to deal with. At least, until our own music takes off."

"I know," I admitted. I didn't love it, but I knew she was right. I also knew I would do whatever I had to in order to make it work. "How about this? I could fly you out sometime after Grace's dance for a few days. A long weekend even."

She sighed. "I want to, but I don't know if I can get away from work. It's close to Halloween, and we get so busy with orders."

"You don't have to answer me now." I held her face in my hands and kissed her gently. "Just think about it."

She smiled up at me. "I will. I promise."

I hoped she would because the thought of being without her for the next month hurt like hell.

SEVENTEEN

Liv

"I DON'T WANT to leave you," Jax whispered early the next morning, pulling me into his arms on the steps of my front porch. The sun was barely up. Brady had arrived to get Jax so he'd have time to pack his things at the hotel before their bus pulled out of Nashville.

"I know. It's going to be okay," I said with a little more confidence than I felt. I had no doubt my feelings for Jax were real, that *our* feelings were real, but I also knew this was still very new. It was fragile, and we were trying to figure it all out together. A month apart right off the bat was a hurdle, but not one I thought we couldn't handle. At least, I hoped we could handle it.

In many ways, my mind was still trying to play catch up with my heart. Jax was something I never saw coming. It was crazy to think that a few days ago we'd been strangers, but now the idea of having to be apart for a month crushed me. Regardless of what happened with our own music, I knew I would support his career ambitions because I never wanted him to be in the position I'd been in all those years ago. I never wanted him to feel he had to choose between me or his dreams.

"Liv, I need you to promise me something." His eyes were partly cloudy with a chance of thunderstorms. "Promise me you'll still be here for me to come back to. Please."

"Jax, I promise. I'm going to still be here." I cupped his face in my hands and brought his lips to mine.

"Yeah?" His voice was low and husky as he intertwined his fingers with mine.

"Yeah," I said softly, standing on my tiptoes to kiss him. "But you better go before Brady kills us both." I waved to Brady who was waiting in the car to give us privacy. He dipped his head in greeting before turning his attention elsewhere.

"I know." Jax sighed, enveloping me in his embrace.

"Let me know when you guys get to Louisiana? And tell the guys we'll miss them."

"What about me?" A playful expression spread across his face. "Will you miss me?"

I grinned up at him, my arms encircled around his neck. "Mmm-hmm."

"How much?"

"I donut think I can put it into words." I smiled and bit my lip.

"Now you're *trying* to kill me, huh?" He laughed and lifted me off the ground, bringing us nose to nose. "I'm going to miss you so much." He set me back on my feet and kissed me. It was one of those kisses that was a thousand kisses wrapped in one. It was soft and sweet, full of desire and longing. It was a hello and a goodbye all at once.

"I'll miss you too." He released me and trailed his hand

down my arm, his fingers mingling with mine. He bounded toward Brady's waiting SUV parked on the street.

I turned to go inside, afraid I would dissolve into tears if I watched his car pull away, but Jax's voice caught my attention. "Turn around!" When I did, he was leaning out the passenger side window, making a heart shape with his hands. "You're perfect, Olivia Sinclair!"

I blew him a kiss that he pretended to catch as Brady pulled the car away from the curb. Though I was sad to see him leave, I realized for the first time in a long time my heart was nothing but happy.

———

"WHAT DO YOU *MEAN* YOU DIDN'T HAVE SEX WITH HIM?" Ella asked incredulously later that morning, leaning against the counter at the bakery. She watched intently while I drizzled ganache over the top of some mint chocolate cupcakes. Katie was out front, loading the cases for the day, which left Ella to interrogate me. "Jax stayed with you for *three nights,* and you didn't have sex with him? Did you at least *want* to?"

"Of course I wanted to," I cried. "Have you *seen* him? He's gorgeous. I'm just not there yet."

"Honey, I feel like he could get you there." She crossed her arms across her chest. "The man's abs have abs for crying out loud."

"That is *not* what I meant." I rolled my eyes.

"What is it then?" She moved so that she stood next to me, watching my every move. "He literally told you he's falling in love with you, and I *know* you're falling for him."

"I know, but I'm not ready." I sighed. "Ella, I was with

Ben for seventeen years of my life. He's the only person I've ever *been* with."

"I know, and what a snoozefest that was." She snorted before looking up, catching the pained expression on my face. "Well, he *was*, but that's all the more reason you should have done it. You deserve to experience what it feels like to be absolutely worshipped."

"Look, I want all of these things. I do," I said. "but I'm not ready. There's so much that goes into... *that*... I want to be ready."

"Ohhhh... did you not have a bikini wax? I told you, you really have to keep that up. Otherwise, it turns into the swamp thing down there."

I burst into laughter, placing the remainder of the ganache on the counter. "My affairs are in order down there," I joked. "I don't know. I'm just nervous. No other man has seen me naked in my entire life but Ben. It's scary. Then there's the age difference and the fact that he looks like *that*. You should see him with his shirt off. His chest is so firm and smooth and..."

"And you want to lick that ganache right off of it?" Ella squealed.

"Pretty much," I admitted. "I'm scared he's going to be... disappointed. I don't exactly have a rock hard body like he does."

"And?" She propped her hand on her hip. "Don't you dare forget that he's the lucky one here, Liv. That's the truth."

"You are the ultimate hype woman." I chuckled as I crossed to the sink to wash my hands.

"Damn right I am." She nodded. "Which means I'm going to have to take you shopping for lingerie before you go visit him on the road. When do you leave? We could go this afternoon."

"I don't know if I'll go."

"Did you hit your head?" She placed her hands on the sides of my face, smushing my cheeks together. "What do you mean you don't know if you'll go?"

"He's going to be gone for a month," I said, prying my head from her grasp. "I can't leave for that long right now."

"The hell you can't. Katie and I can hold down the fort here. I'm serious, Liv." She crossed her arms over her chest. "You need to go. If you don't want to go for the whole month, fine, but at least go for a week or two. Look at it as a test drive for your future career as a rockstar." Her eyes lit up with excitement. "I think you should surprise him."

"How?"

"It's simple. We get the guys in on it. You have to be adamant in telling him you're not able to go, though. He needs to not be expecting it at all. We get the boys to sneak you into their show and stick you in the front row. He looks out and sees you and *ta daaaa!*" She turned her fingers inward, admiring her navy-blue polish.

I considered her suggestion for a moment. "It's not a bad idea."

Before I could say anything else, Katie burst through the kitchen door with a big smile on her face. "You've got a delivery out front, Liv."

"A delivery?" I questioned. Ella and I glanced at each other then back at Katie who nodded cheerfully. Ella and I followed her back through the door and gasped. On the counter was a beautiful arrangement of tequila sunrise roses. There had to be at least four dozen.

"Open the card!" Ella shrieked, shaking me by the shoulders. "What does it say?"

"Hold on." I waved her off as I plucked the card from its holder in the bouquet. My heart felt like it was about to take flight out of my chest when I opened the small yellow envelope with Ella and Katie reading over my shoulder.

DEAR LIV,
  I can't wait to come back home
  to my sweet tequila sunrise.
  Miss you already.
  Love,
  Jax

"YOU ARE *SO* GOING!" ELLA SQUEALED AS SHE AND KATIE bounced excitedly together. "If we have to fold you up, put you in a suitcase, and take you ourselves, you are *going* to see that man."

I turned to face my friends. "Do you really think I could take a couple of weeks off?"

"Hell yeah, I do!" Ella threw her arms around me.

"We'll take care of everything here." Katie reached out and squeezed my arm. "You always take such good care of us. Let us take care of you."

"Okay. I'll go." I held up a finger to Ella. "But not until I see Grace in her Homecoming dress."

Ella grinned. "Deal."

I pictured Jax and my heart disappearing out of sight earlier that morning in Brady's SUV, and I knew there was no way I could wait another month to see him again.

THE WEEK JAX WAS GONE PASSED BY EXCRUCIATINGLY SLOW. The evening before my flight to Los Angeles, I was packing while I waited for Ella to arrive. Grace had rehearsals for her part in her school play, so Ella was coming over for dinner.

My phone rang from beneath a pile of clothes on the bed, and I dove for it.

"Hey, Dal," I said, cradling the phone between my ear and shoulder.

He chuckled. "We've been over this. My code name is Agent Sprinkles."

"My bad." I snorted. *"Agent Sprinkles."*

"You're gonna blow this entire operation, Officer Cupcake." His laughter was infectious and boisterous, and it was one of the things I liked most about him. "I've got everything worked out. Brady will sneak away to pick you up at LAX when your flight lands at 8:15 tomorrow evening. He's going to bring you right to Microsoft Theater, and Jax will be none the wiser until he looks down and sees your beautiful face in the front row."

"You sure he doesn't suspect anything?" I asked, folding a pair of jeans and placing them in my suitcase.

"Not a thing." He assured me. "In fact, he's been moping around extra hard today. I feel kinda bad for him, but a lot less so now that he'll be seeing you tomorrow. We're all excited!"

"I owe you a million cupcakes, Agent Sprinkles."

"Affirmative, Officer Cupcake." He cleared his throat. "Well, the eagle has landed, so I better run." I heard Jax's confused voice in the background asking who he was talking to.

"Thank you so much, Dal. You're the best," I said.

"I love you too, Mom. Talk to you tomorrow."

I giggled as Dallas disconnected the call.

"Pizza delivery!" Ella's voice called down the hall when she bustled through the front door. I heard Mama hiss her greeting as the door closed. "Mama, you're gonna have to get over yourself since I'll be the one feeding your hostile-kitty ass for the next two weeks."

"In here!" I yelled, placing a folded T-shirt in the suitcase.

"I come bearing gifts." She appeared in the doorway with a Victoria's Secret bag in one hand and a pizza box in the other. She placed the pizza box on the dresser and tossed the bag in my direction. "Also, your cat is an actual psycho."

"What is this?" I asked suspiciously, peering into the bag as though a bomb might go off inside it at any moment. I withdrew a sheet of the hot-pink tissue paper before extracting a black balconette lace bra and matching panties that didn't look like they would cover much. I shot her a look and wadded up the lacy unmentionables, throwing them at her head. "Seriously?"

"Uh, yeah, I'm serious." She laughed, catching the panties and throwing them back at me. "There's more where that came from inside that bag. You can't be heading off to LA with granny panties in your suitcase or, God forbid, on your actual body."

"I don't wear Granny panties," I scoffed.

"Oh yeah?" She walked over to my suitcase, pulling out a modest pair of full-coverage underwear. "What do you call this little number that you picked up from Costco?"

"Don't you dare take Costco's name in vain." I laughed, snatching the underwear from her hand.

"Costco is where you buy toilet paper in bulk, *not* sexy underwear." She flopped down on the bed and began sifting through my suitcase. "Wow, you are prepared for all climates. Sweaters, tank tops, dresses, *sexy lingerie,* thanks to your best friend."

"Thank you." I raised my brow at her. "And yes, from what Dallas told me, we'll be making our way across the country over the next couple of weeks."

"If it were me, I'd have three suitcases for that two-week trip. Are you excited?"

"I am." I nodded. "And nervous."

"Because you're gonna *do* it?" She grinned at me mischievously.

I shook my head. "I don't know if we will or we won't. All I know is I feel all twirly and like my heart is going to fall out of my butt."

"That's love, my friend." She stifled a giggle. "Honestly, I'm really proud of you."

"For what?"

"For taking this chance. Not just on Jax, but on yourself. I know this has been a lot for you, and I know how scared you were."

"Correction. Still am. What if I do this? What if I go all in, and it doesn't work out?"

"What if it does?" She smiled and grabbed the sweater I was folding, tossing it back on the bed. "Come take a break. Let's eat and catch up on last week's *Grey's Anatomy* before you jet off to see McLoverBoy. I'll grab the pizza."

I followed her down the hall. "I'll get the wine." My stomach began doing flips because I knew that this tomorrow night, I would be back in Jax's arms.

I LANDED IN LOS ANGELES RIGHT ON TIME, AND THOUGH I
had every reason to try to relax on the plane, I'd been far too
jittery to rest. I watched a movie, wrote down a few ideas I
had for some songs, and stared out the window as I willed the
time to go by faster.

After we landed, I found the nearest restroom so I could
change into something far cuter than the sweats I'd worn on
the plane. I rolled on some deodorant to hopefully prevent the
onslaught of sweat that threatened to form before changing
into a silky black camisole. I wriggled into a pair of jeans and
my jacket before exiting the stall.

Ella insisted on some impossibly high heels that I
regretted wearing the instant I put them on. I touched up my
makeup in the mirror and fluffed my hair. Once I was certain
no one was looking, I adjusted my boobs, making sure my
lacy black bra was in perfect position. I appraised my reflection in the mirror, and I had to admit, Ella was right about the
bra. With one last deep breath, I set out to retrieve my
luggage, and then I was off to find Brady outside the lower-
level baggage claim.

I wove through crowds of people scattered in confused
clusters while they tried to figure out where they were going. I
started looking for Brady, my suitcase rattling behind me and
my carry on bag thudding against my hip. Finally, my eyes
zeroed in on him. He stood off to the side holding up a sign
that said 'Officer Cupcake.' I burst into laughter and walked
as fast as I could in the ridiculously high heels.

"Hey, Liv!" Brady greeted me. Before I even thought
about what I was doing, I flung my arms around him.

"Brady, thank you for doing this." I smiled up at him. "I
really appreciate you helping me."

"Anything for you and Jax," he replied. "Let me help you

with your bags." He took my carry on and suitcase with ease, and I set off behind him. "Jax is going to be so glad to see you."

Once we got to the car, Brady opened the door to the SUV, and I climbed inside while he loaded my luggage into the trunk. I felt myself start to relax as Brady pulled the car away from the curb.

We made it to Microsoft Theater, and by the time I got inside, the band would be nearing the end of their set.

Brady pulled the car to a stop outside a side entrance. "The hotel is across the street. I'm going to run your luggage over so it's waiting for you there in the room. I always have extra keys for everybody's room in case one of these knuckleheads gets locked out, or I need to come to their rescue. You go on with Cash, and I'll be back to get you guys in a few."

I looked out the window to see Cash waving at me from the door, beckoning me toward him.

"Thanks, Brady." I squeezed his arm, slung my tiny purse across my body, and bounded out of the car.

"It's good to see you, Liv." Cash pulled me into a quick hug before putting a lanyard around my neck that read 'all access.' He quickly led me through the underbelly of the venue. "You got here just in time. They've only got a couple of songs left. I'm going to take you up to Antoni, and he'll show you to your seat. He'll stay with you and bring you straight back after the show's over." He looked back at me with his kind, hazel eyes. "He's going to be so happy to see you."

My stomach started doing somersaults as he wound me through the corridors lined with various crew members and security. I recognized a few of the same faces from the show in Nashville as we passed by. When we reached the main floor, I saw Antoni waiting with his headset on. His face broke into a wide grin when he saw us approaching. "How are you, Miss Thing?" He gave me a quick hug, then turned his attention to Cash. "I'll take it from here, boss."

"I'll see you in a few." Cash squeezed my shoulder and jogged back in the direction we'd come.

Antoni offered me his arm. "You ready to go see your man?" He did a little shimmy, and I took a deep breath, letting him lead me through the crowd.

The audience erupted into screams of approval as Midnight in Dallas finished up "Fortress."

That's when I heard Jax's voice. "This last song is a new one. I wrote it for a very special woman in my life. We've never played it in front of an audience. In fact, the only person I've ever played it for is her, and I... I miss her a lot. It's called 'Love You More.'"

Antoni turned toward me with wide eyes as Jax began to play. "Girl, this is your song, ain't it?"

Jax's eyes were closed as he started to sing. The crowd held up their phones with their screens illuminated, swaying along to the slow rhythm of the song.

As promised, Antoni guided me to the front of the stage where there were two empty spaces. I gazed up at Jax, and for a moment, I forgot to breathe. He looked so handsome and perfect up there. His eyes were still closed, but to his left, Derek caught my eye and smiled.

Antoni squeezed my arm and leaned into my ear. "He's got it bad for you, girl." I looked over at him with tears in my eyes. The song ripped me wide open again just as it had the first time.

As Jax neared the end of the song, he still hadn't opened his eyes. To his right, Luca looked at me, and his face brightened. He glanced at Jax, realizing his eyes were closed. He winked at me, and I watched as he crossed over to Jax, saying something in his ear. Jax's eyes looked like a storm on the horizon when they sprang open, and he frantically scanned the crowd.

Finally, his gaze landed on me, and his smile was so big it made the corners of his eyes crinkle. When he sang the last words of the song, his eyes locked on mine.

"Thank you, LA!" Luca said, and the band continued to play the melody of the song. The curtain began to slowly fall as the crowd screamed their praise. "We are Midnight in Dallas! Good night!"

"That's our cue, baby girl." Antoni grabbed my hand, and we were off, weaving through the crowd. He expertly sliced through throngs of people until we were back in the long corridors Cash had led me through. He guided me down an unfamiliar hall that said 'stage entrance.'

That's when I saw him running toward me. Jax's face glistened, and his white T-shirt was damp with sweat causing it to cling to every perfect curve of his muscles.

I ran as fast as my heels allowed until I could jump into his arms, right where I belonged.

EIGHTEEN

Jax

LIV'S CHESTNUT hair flowed behind her as she jumped into my arms, her legs wrapping around my waist. She took my face in her hands and kissed me hard on the mouth. I buried my face in her neck, and I was surrounded by her sweet citrus scent once more.

"Hell yeah!" Dallas whooped as he ran to where Liv and I were still locked in each other's arms. He started to applaud, and soon he was joined by Luca, Derek, Cash, Antoni, Brady, and the entire team backstage.

"I can't believe you're here." I gently placed her on her feet, but kept my arms around her.

"Surprise!" I beamed at him.

"Alright, alright. You've had your greeting. It's our turn," Dallas teased, moving in to hug Liv. "It's good to see you, Cupcake."

I looked at them curiously. "Cupcake?"

"You did good work, Agent Sprinkles." She patted Dallas on the back.

"Agent Sprinkles? Wait, you knew?" I asked incredulously. "*And* you had code names?"

Dallas grinned. "Well, obviously.".

"We *all* knew," Luca said, swooping in to give Liv a quick hug and a kiss on the cheek.

"It was hard keeping it from you," Derek admitted, taking his turn to embrace Liv. "Especially seeing how down you were when you thought she wasn't coming."

"But we knew she'd be here soon, and you'd be okay." Cash winked.

"I am more than okay." I reached for Liv's hand and pulled her to me.

"Thank God for that," Derek ribbed at me. "You've become insufferable without her."

"Seriously," Dallas agreed. "Sir Mopes-A-Lot over here."

"Lies. All lies." I laughed. "Gentleman, if you'll excuse us, I want to spend some quality time with my beautiful girlfriend who flew across the country to see me."

Liv looked at me with wide eyes at the mention of the word 'girlfriend.' I mentally kicked myself for not having that talk with her before now.

"Are you two ready?" Brady asked, reading my mind. "I've got the car parked outside."

"Yes. Yes, we are," I curled my arm around Liv's shoulders and steered her away from the group.

"See you guys tomorrow," Derek called. They all waved their goodbyes, and we followed Brady out into the balmy California night.

"So, about the 'girlfriend' thing," I said. "I'm sorry. I know we haven't talked about it, but I just... I want to be whatever says we belong to each other. Was that okay?"

She smiled. "It's more than okay. It's perfect."

I couldn't stop myself from kissing Liv once we were

tucked inside the back of the SUV en route to the hotel. "I'm so glad I get to do that again."

"And you can for the next two weeks." She smiled flirtatiously up at me, pulling my face back down to hers. "As long as that's still okay with you."

My mouth fell open. "Are you serious?"

"I donut believe I would make this up." She grinned. "Ella and Katie are holding things together at the shop while I'm gone, so I'm yours for the next couple of weeks." She placed her dainty hand on the side of my face, and I covered it with my own. I stared into her eyes that sparkled beneath the passing lamplight. She bit her lower lip, and my heart rate picked up speed, thudding in my ears. I had never wanted anyone, or anything, more than I wanted her.

"There you go biting that lip." I touched my thumb to her pillowy mouth. "You know that drives me crazy."

"I know," she whispered. It was as though a match had been lit and was being dangled over a barrel of gasoline, waiting to catch fire.

The second Brady pulled the SUV to a stop, I lurched from the car with her hand in mine and sprinted through the side entrance of the hotel. I barely even nodded to the doorman that let us in. I pulled her onto the passcode-protected elevator reserved for VIP guests, and it began its excruciatingly slow ascent to the top floor. I stood behind her, brushing her hair to the side so I could kiss her neck, my hands trailing down her shoulders. Finally, the elevator doors opened, and we barreled down the hall, hand in hand. Once we reached the room, I fumbled for the room key with shaky hands.

The door clicked open, and once we were safely inside, the flame was ignited. I tossed the card to the ground and took her in my arms, pressing her gently against the back of the door. She kicked off her heels as she took my face in her hands and kissed me.

"I missed you so much," I whispered between kisses as she yanked her jacket off, tossing it to the ground.

She tugged my shirt over my head, running her hands over my bare chest.

"I missed you too," she murmured. She took my hands into hers and slid them beneath her camisole before ripping the silky garment over her head.

"Holy shit." She was breathtaking. Her hair spilled over her shoulders and down her breasts that peeked out from her lacy black bra.

"What?" She looked up at me with concern.

"You're stunning, Liv." I tucked a piece of hair behind her ear, my breathing ragged. I pressed a kiss onto her forehead, trying to quell the desire that threatened to take over me. With trembling hands, she fumbled with the buckle on my belt, and I felt my self-control begin to unravel.

"I want you, Jax." Her voice was low and sultry as she slid her arms around me.

"Yeah?" I whispered, leaning into her.

"Yeah." With her answer, I scooped her in my arms and carried her to the bed. I kicked off my jeans and moved over her, trailing feather light kisses from her jawline to her collarbone and all the way down her belly. My hands shook slightly as I unfastened the button on her jeans, helping her out of them.

"You're perfect," I said softly. Her creamy skin was wrapped in lace, and she was breathtaking. As I gazed into her emerald eyes, I knew I could search the world over and never find a woman more perfect for me than her.

She covered my cheek with her hand. "I'm sorry I've made you wait so long."

I leaned into her touch, pressing a kiss into her palm. "Don't ever apologize for that. I want you to be sure."

"I'm sure now." Her fingers slid beneath the waistband of my boxer-briefs, and I moaned, my shaft straining against the cotton so hard I thought I might burst through the fabric.

Shit. I don't have a condom.

I scrubbed my hand down my face. "The thing is… I didn't know this would be happening, so I wasn't actually, um, prepared."

Her brow creased as she read between the lines, and then her mouth formed a perfect o. "That's okay. I don't care, and I'm on the pill anyway."

"Are you sure?" I asked.

She nodded. "I need you, Jax."

Yet, I didn't move. I couldn't stop looking at her—couldn't believe she was finally mine. But there was something else too.

A shadow passed over her face, a flash of insecurity. "Is something wrong?"

"God, no. I just…" I began, my voice hoarse. "I've imagined this so many times in my mind…"

Her lips curled into a blinding smile. "I hope I can live up to your expectations."

"Oh you do." I said it so quickly and emphatically it caused her to giggle. "You *really, really* do. And let me be clear, I have a pretty damn good imagination, but nothing could have prepared me for just how perfect you are."

Her lashes fluttered, and her cheeks flushed. She was truly the most beautiful woman I'd ever seen. What if *I* didn't meet *her* expectations?

"I guess I'm just..." I pushed my fingers through my hair. Sweat beaded along my brow, and my nerves sent Mayday signals shooting through my limbs as I blew out a breath. "Fuck me. I guess I'm nervous."

"Well, I'm trying to fuck you, but you won't stop talking." She crushed her lips to mine with a kiss so hot it could have branded me, letting the whole world know she owned my ass.

And just like that, all of my fears and worries melted away. I raised up, and she arched her back, granting me access to the clasp of her bra. My fingers fumbled until the lacy fabric released, and I tossed it aside. I nipped at the supple skin at the base of her neck and swept kisses along the swell of her breasts, stopping only to take the tip of her pink bud gently between my teeth.

She murmured my name, threading her fingers through my hair, giving it a gentle tug.

I moved to her other breast, flicking its rosy peak with my tongue until it perked. She writhed beneath me as I took her in my mouth.

"How do you taste so good?" I asked, licking and kissing my way back down her abdomen.

"Maybe... it's because... I'm a baker," she said between pants. "What do I taste like?"

"Sweet." I licked her inner thigh. "Like a vanilla cupcake," I slipped my fingers between the lace of her panties. "You're so wet." Suddenly, I was starved—completely ravenous for her. I grinned and arched my brow. "I think I need to have a taste."

She wriggled as I took my time sliding the lace down the length of her long, lithe legs. I held her foot in my hand and placed a kiss on her ankle.

"Please," she begged.

I licked and nibbled my way up her calf and then her thigh, until I reached her folds. "I'm going to enjoy every delicious bite."

She whimpered as I swirled my tongue along her flesh in slow circles.

Her hips rose to meet my mouth, greedy for my warmth, so I applied more pressure, stroking her faster and faster. She twisted her hands in my hair, and her breathing came in ragged gasps.

She bucked beneath me. "I want to come with you inside me, Jax."

Good God, that was the sexiest thing I'd ever heard. With one last lick, I moved back up the mattress and got to my knees. She gripped the elastic on my boxer briefs and pushed them down my thighs, freeing my erection.

My tongue flicked over my lips as she took me in her hand, sliding it slowly up and down my length.

"Fuck," I groaned, throbbing against the smooth skin of her palm. "That feels so good."

A wild look burned in her eyes. "Does it meet expectations?"

"You have no idea," I said, lowering myself over her. She guided me to her entrance, and I slipped inside her, burying myself deep within her walls.

I rocked against her, slowly moving in and out, and I could already tell I wouldn't be able to last long.

"You feel like heaven." My heart pounded as our pace quickened.

She pulled my face down to meet hers and kissed me hungrily, wrapping her legs around my waist. Overwhelmed with desire, each thrust came harder and more fervently as she tightened her grip and bit her lip. I nuzzled her neck, desperately trying to hang onto our rhythm without sending myself over the edge.

"Jax…" She sighed my name, and her breaths came in soft, shallow waves, until I felt her crumble around me. It was a matter of seconds before she took me down with her, and we were basking in the afterglow of our ecstasy.

I pressed a kiss to her forehead as we tried to catch our breath, her bodies melded together. "You really are perfect."

"You said that already," she whispered into my shoulder.

"And I hope you never get tired of hearing it," I said, taking a piece of her tousled hair between my fingers. "Because I plan on saying it for a very long time."

For as long as she would let me.

Her eyes met mine, a soft smile spreading across her face. "Yeah?"

I kissed her beautiful lips once more. "Yeah."

NINETEEN

Liv

THE NEXT MORNING, I woke to the sound of my phone chirping. The morning light was beginning to cause a soft glow around the window. Bleary-eyed, I plucked the phone off the nightstand, and a text from Ella appeared on the screen, complete with an onslaught of suggestive emojis.

Ella: So… how did he like your new lingerie?

I laughed softly so as not to wake up Jax as I typed out my response.

Liv: He loved it!

I added a winking smiley face for good measure. Before I could even put the phone down, I saw the little bubbles appear that signaled she was typing.

Ella: OMG!!! You did it! Girl, go get you some of that morning delight. You've earned it.

I chuckled as I gently returned the phone back to the nightstand. I rolled over, nestling myself into Jax's chest.

Jax didn't seem the least bit phased by the fact that I didn't have the body of a twenty-five-year-old supermodel. He didn't care about my cellulite or that my stomach wasn't flat. Instead, he'd been completely turned on by every dip and curve. He took his time, savoring me as though I were a decadent dessert he may never get to have again, only to turn around and devour me once more. I'd never felt sexier than I did under his ravishing gaze.

I knew one thing for damn sure. Sex with Benton Wyatt had never been *anything* like this.

He stirred, pulling me tighter against him. "Good morning, beautiful."

I pressed a kiss into his shoulder blade. "Did you sleep okay?"

"Mmm, did I ever." He moved so that he hovered over me and kissed the tip of my nose. "I love waking up beside you."

"Really?" I asked, already breathless as his eyes found mine. He started a trail of kisses along my jawline before he landed one right on my mouth. He gently nipped at my bottom lip before kissing me slowly, deeply. Like he was trying to stir my soul from the inside.

"I can't get enough of you." His voice was a low, raspy growl as he began to leave kisses along my collarbone. "As it happens, we have this hotel room for a couple more hours before we have to get on that cramped bus with the rest of the guys."

"What exactly do you suggest we do with that time?" I purred, my body responding to his touch as his hands gingerly explored my body.

"I could think of a thing or two…" His seductive eyes flickered over me.

He brought his mouth back to mine, and I gently shoved him over, rolling with him so that I straddled him. "Yeah?" I leaned down and grazed his mouth with mine.

"Yeah," he whispered. He stared into my eyes so

intensely, I wasn't sure whether I was going to melt into a puddle or burst into flames. His eyes were filled with longing as he cupped my face in his hands. "You wreck me, Olivia Sinclair." He crashed his lips into mine. "You absolutely wreck me."

The truth was, he wrecked me too.

———

THE NEXT FEW DAYS PASSED IN A BLUR. WE WERE IN SAN Diego for a night before heading back up to San Francisco and Sacramento. We didn't get to do much in the way of sightseeing, but I did get to see the Golden Gate Bridge for the first time from the window of the bus.

While the band was busy doing press and soundcheck, I hung out a lot with Antoni and Cash. I learned that Antoni traveled with the guys as an assistant, taking care of their every need and helping Cash with any additional tasks he didn't have time for. Basically, Antoni worked his ass off twenty-four/seven.

On the bus after their shows, we'd either watch movies together, or Jax and I would work on some new music before retreating to his bunk, falling asleep in each other's arms. It was a tight fit, but we didn't mind the extra excuse to be close to one another. I found I didn't mind bus life at all if it meant I got to be next to Jax, though I missed Ella and Grace fiercely.

We traveled through the night to Las Vegas where we would be staying in a suite for two whole days before heading back on the road. It was Halloween, and though it was only a little after lunchtime, the casino floor was already filled with a wild array of ghouls, goblins, and women wearing lingerie with some sort of mask or animal ears. When we walked through the door to our suite, Jax had barely tipped the bellman before I collapsed on the sofa.

"Comfy?" Jax asked with a laugh. He plopped down beside me, pulling my legs onto his lap.

"This is glorious," I replied, sinking deeper into the cushions. Though I didn't mind snuggling up with him in his bunk every night, it had been murder on my thirty-seven-year-old back. "I am one with this couch. I live here now."

"I wish we didn't have to go to that party tonight." Jax flopped his head against the back of the couch. Midnight in Dallas had been invited to a Halloween party being thrown by some big wig in the industry at the Omnia Nightclub inside Caesars Palace where we were staying. The hotel was going to be packed to the brim with Hollywood A-listers and the music industry's finest. Admittedly, I'd never been one to get star-struck, but I did get a bit of a thrill when I found out we were going to be at the same party as Steven Tyler. It was still impossible for me to believe I could ever fit in this world as anything but a bystander.

"Why not? It's going to be fun. Besides, I get to wear a pretty dress." I smiled up at him flirtatiously. I was excited about the prospect of getting all dressed up together and going out. Due to the genius that was Antoni, I still got to maintain my anonymity. He was in charge of the costume selection and had decided on a masquerade theme for our entire group.

Jax and I had talked my first day on the road about how we'd handle my privacy. I still wasn't ready to have my life on display. That was one of the reasons I wanted to take things slow with our music. Traipsing around Nashville together had been one thing. With the exception of the girls recognizing him at the fall festival, Jax had flown under the radar with ease. I knew things would be different on the road, though. There would be lots of press, paparazzi, and overzealous fans waiting to catch a glimpse of the band and anyone who may be associated with them. Jax agreed it was best to keep my identity a secret until I was ready to put our music, and our relationship, out into the world.

The guys knew how we felt, and they'd been equally as protective of my privacy. To anyone not in our little group, I was an assistant like Antoni, and so far, no one had even batted an eye.

"I can't wait to see you in that dress," he assured me. "We've barely had a moment alone since we left LA. All I want is to stay in this room and make good use of that king-size bed and the jacuzzi."

"We still have a little while before we have to get ready to go." I bit my lip suggestively. "I was thinking a bubble bath would be nice." I rose to my feet and reached my hands out to him, pulling him up with me.

His lips curled into a seductive smile as I ran my hands up his chiseled chest. "Yeah? And then what?"

"And then you could carry me to the bed," I purred as he leaned down, trailing soft kisses along my neck.

"And then?"

"And then..." I continued, putting on the breathiest, sexiest voice I could muster. "And then you could lay me down... and then we could..."

His lips traveled up to my jawline. "Yeah?"

"Take a nap," I whispered directly in his ear, unable to contain my giggles. He pulled back to look at me, his head cocked to the side.

"You think you're funny, don't you?" He tried unsuccessfully to keep a straight face, a sly smile playing across his lips.

"I *know* I'm funny." I grinned. He regained his composure, and the smolder in his eyes returned. He leaned in so close, I could feel the warmth of his breath on my lips.

"I think you left out one minor detail of this plan of yours." His voice was a soft murmur in my ear.

"What's that?" I asked, my body leaning into his involuntarily.

"This." His fingers found my sides like heat-seeking missiles, and he ambushed me with tickles. I shrieked and laughed, attempting to wriggle my way out of his grasp. "Oh no, you don't." In one swift motion, he scooped me up and threw me over his shoulder. He didn't release me until he pushed his way into the bedroom, gently tossing me down on the bed. He climbed in with me, hovering over my body. "Still tired?"

I pulled him into me and kissed him tenderly. "Not even a little bit."

"I'VE GOT TO SAY, I'M USUALLY MORE OF A CHANGE FROM MY daytime pajamas into my nighttime pajamas type of girl, but I could get used to this." I twirled my way down the hall. Jax turned toward me, his mouth falling open. "What do you think?"

"Wow," Jax whispered, closing the distance between us. "You're breathtaking."

"And you look so handsome in your tux." I smiled, smoothing my hands over the jacket of his navy satin tuxedo. The paisley detailing inscribed in the tux stood out against his black dress shirt. His blue-grey eyes were framed by a simple matte-black mask.

"I'm sorry. I can't get over how stunning you look." He took my hand in his and twirled me around, admiring the dress. I had to admit, Antoni had knocked it out of the park. The strapless sweetheart gown hugged my body as if it had been made for me. It fanned out into a train that could only be described as a work of art. The merlot-colored satin was adorned with beautiful black lace detailing that got more intricate toward the bottom fan. The mask I wore matched the dress exactly, the burgundy color popping against my fair skin. Antoni had wanted to bring in a hairstylist and makeup artist for me. He said that was something I'd have to get used to eventually, but I really wanted to do it myself. There was something oddly comforting about going through the ritual of styling my hair and meticulously applying some makeup after a long, luxurious soak in the jacuzzi. I felt completely out of my element, but I had to admit, the dress was gorgeous. I felt like a movie star standing next to Jax.

There was a knock at the door and Jax groaned, reluctantly releasing me from his grasp so I could answer it.

"Holy shit, Liv," Dallas said, pulling me into a hug. "You look gorgeous."

"Look at you guys!" I let my gaze travel to each of them in their masks and tuxedos, identical to the one Jax wore. The only difference was that Dallas wore classic black, Derek a gunmetal grey, Luca was in deep emerald green, while Cash had donned the same ensemble in white. Brady wore his signature all-black, only this time it was a suit instead of his usual pants and T-shirts. Antoni kept with the theme, but his tux was made entirely of purple sequins with a matching purple satin mask. "You all look so debonair. Antoni, you look fantastic."

"You are a vision, Liv." Antoni kissed me on the cheek. "I

don't know about you fools, but I'm ready to shake and quake what my mama gave me on that dance floor."

Together, we made our way to the Omnia Nightclub. By the time we reached the front doors, a few more bodyguards in suits had joined us. Flashbulbs popped as the paparazzi took an endless amount of photos of the costume-clad guests entering the club.

One particularly aggressive photographer continued to yell Jax's name until he zeroed in on me. "Hey, pretty girl! Let me get your picture! Look at me, gorgeous!" He pushed forward, shoving his camera closer to my face. Before he could get a good shot, Luca stepped in front of me, taunting him.

"Are you saying *I* don't look pretty? I'm offended." I heard him say as Cash and Antoni swooped their arms around me, guiding me inside. Jax and the rest of the guys were still stuck in the throngs of photographers while Brady played defense, fending off the crowd.

"Are you okay?" Derek asked after he'd broken free of the mob of photographers. "Those guys can be assholes sometimes."

"I am." I smiled gratefully at Luca as he approached. "Thanks to this guy."

"Those guys piss me off. You good?" He put an arm around me. "You're shaking, babe."

I hadn't even realized my hands were trembling. It's not like I didn't know this type of thing happened, but I'd never experienced it before now. If that's what happens when I'm just a nobody on the arm of a rockstar, what would it be like if I actually *became* a rockstar?

"I'm okay." I forced a smile as Jax and Dallas filed inside with Brady and the rest of security rounding up the rear. Jax squeezed through the crowd until he was by my side, lacing his fingers with mine.

We stopped by the bar before Antoni led us onto the dance floor, the sequins on his tux a sparkling beacon for us to follow. The occasional flashbulb went off as a couple of chosen photographers, who likely paid an obscene amount to be there, took pictures of guests.

Jax took me by the hand and spun me around, pulling me back to him. Scantily clad waitstaff expertly wove their way through the crowd, passing out champagne. We danced together for a while until everyone started going their own way. Luca disappeared into the crowd while Derek and Dallas joined the guy I recognized to be Sam Corbyn, their opening act on the tour, at his table. Cash had migrated to the bar, no doubt talking business with someone. I glanced around the dance floor and spotted Antoni shaking his hips with a nice-looking guy dressed as a firefighter, who wore his jacket open to reveal a set of washboard abs. *Go, Antoni!*

Even though the song playing was upbeat, Jax pulled me into his arms, slowly moving me around the dance floor. He leaned in, pressing a kiss to my cheek as a flashbulb went off beside us. I flinched, startled by the streak of light in my face. Before we could see who the flash belonged to, they'd already disappeared into the crowd. I could feel Jax's body stiffen as he glared out into the sea of people.

"It's okay," I reassured him, feeling that same unease from earlier set in. "I've got a mask on anyway. It's alright."

"I know." He sighed. "I just want to make sure you're protected. I don't want your identity getting out there before you're ready." He wrapped his arms around my waist, leaning in so his mouth hovered at my ear. "I know we haven't been here long, but all I want is to be alone with you. We could go back to the suite. I bet there are some pajamas there with your name on them, or you don't have to wear anything at all." He flashed me a seductive grin, and my knees went weak.

"Yeah, let's get out of here." I beamed up at him. "But we should probably let the guys know we're leaving, and I really need to find a restroom."

"I'll ask Brady to escort us back to be safe, and I'll find Cash and tell him we're leaving. You go find the bathroom. I'll meet you at the entrance where we came in." I pecked him on the cheek and set off into the club.

I was winding my way through the throngs of people, picking up my dress as I went, when I felt a gentle hand grab my wrist. "I love your dress," a dainty voice said.

I turned to see who the voice belonged to, and I blinked hard, certain my eyes were playing tricks on me. The girl looked *exactly* like Jessica Rabbit, aka Shelby Kirkland, dressed as a flapper or a shimmery chandelier. I wasn't sure which.

Wait… could that really be her? Shit.

"Uh, thank you so much." I looked up to see Benton Wyatt walking straight toward me, carrying two martini glasses. *What the hell is he doing here? We're not in Nashville anymore.* Of course, he wasn't wearing a costume. He took himself far too seriously for things like that. I withdrew my wrist from Jessica Rabbit's grasp and pressed forward. If she knew who I was, she didn't let on.

Shit. Shit. Shit. I kept my face neutral as Ben's eyes connected with mine. A flicker of something passed across his face as he looked at me. Recognition? Approval? Dare I say, attraction? I wasn't sure what it was, but he walked right past me without incident. I kept walking and never looked back.

I finally found the bathroom and ducked inside for a

moment, grateful to not be sandwiched between a sea of sweaty bodies. It was hard to believe it had only been a month since I saw that photo of Ben with Jessica Rabbit and felt all the hurt come rushing back. But now? I felt grateful. If all of that hadn't happened, I never would have met Jaxon Slade. I hadn't wanted Ben to recognize me because I truly had nothing left to say to him. Except perhaps, thank you for ending a relationship I should have ended a long time ago. I couldn't wait to get back to Jax, so I started my trek back through the club to get to the entrance.

As I shouldered through the horde of people, I caught a glimpse of Luca's deep-green tux. He was off to the side, alone, standing by a small circular table with some sort of mixed drink in front of him. Though he was looking in my direction, he didn't seem to see me. When I approached, I saw him reach inside his jacket pocket and pull out what looked to be some sort of small bottle. He popped the top off and poured more than a couple of pills into his hand before knocking it back with whatever concoction was in his glass.

"Luca?" I touched him lightly on the arm. For a moment, it was as though he was looking right through me. When his eyes finally focused, I could see they were hazy and blood-shot, even through the mask. "Are you alright?"

"Yeah, I'm good." His words came a little slow and slurred. "Just letting off some steam." He took another drink, draining the glass in one last pull.

"Are you sure you're feeling okay? I thought I saw you taking something on my way over here. Are you sick?"

He shrugged me off. "Had a little headache is all."

I held up his now empty glass. "Maybe lay off of this for the rest of the night. Whatever was in this little glass certainly won't help that headache. You want me to get you some water? I can run over to the bar for you."

"Nah, I'm good." He shook his head and turned his attention to a beautiful blonde a few feet away, wearing something lacy and see-through who seemed to have set her sights on him. She beckoned him over with the curve of her finger, and Luca practically salivated. "And I think I'm about to be even better." He turned to me with a wink before grabbing my hand and placing a kiss on top of it. "You really do look gorgeous tonight, Liv."

Before I could say another word, I watched him stumble in the direction of the blonde and whisper something in her ear. She grinned slyly before letting him escort her away. I stared after him a moment, unsure what exactly I'd witnessed. Something felt off, though I had no reason to believe Luca would lie to me either. I was probably just being paranoid.

I sighed and set out for the entrance where Jax and Brady were already waiting for me.

"Everything okay?" Jax asked as I approached. I considered telling him about seeing Ben, but decided against it. Running into him had been a little jarring. It was like finding a photograph of someone from your past buried at the bottom of a shoebox of memories, but what it showed me was that Benton Wyatt was my past. My future was with Jax.

"I had kind of a weird interaction with Luca on my way out here," I said.

"Sounds like typical Luca." Brady rolled his eyes. "He has a tendency to get a little out of hand at parties. I'll keep an eye on him when I get back. Don't you worry about it."

I nodded thoughtfully and decided to drop the issue as Jax laced his fingers through mine, and we made the trek back to the suite under Brady's watchful eye.

TWENTY

Jax

THE DAY AFTER THE PARTY, Liv and I took advantage of room service as we lazed about in bed, watching movies and talking. I wondered if it was possible we'd ever run out of things to say to each other. I loved her easy laugh and the ways she took care of me without even knowing. I loved the way she drew little circles on my chest with her fingertips as we drifted off to sleep each night, and how she was always waiting for me with a bottle of water and a kiss when I came off stage. She made me feel like I finally belonged to someone.

We broke out the guitar and worked on one of the songs we'd started from the comfort of the king-sized bed, dressed in our matching white robes from the hotel bathroom. These were the moments that reignited my passion for songwriting. For months, I'd been in a drought, but ever since Liv had come into my life, I'd had an abundance of creativity. We wrote song after song together, and I knew when it came time for us to cut a record, the hardest part would be deciding which songs to put on it.

Liv's phone dinged from the nightstand, and she set the guitar down on the bed before reaching for it. She burst out laughing as she looked down at the screen. "Look at this." She turned her phone to show me a picture of Ella and Grace making silly frowning faces in Liv's kitchen. Ella held her arm high above her head, capturing Mama on the floor giving them the side-eye. Grace held up a piece of paper with the words 'we miss you' printed in big bubble letters.

I shook my head and chuckled. "I kind of miss that hostile kitty."

A soft smile lit up her face as she pulled the phone back, gazing at the screen again. "God, me too. This is one thing I don't know that I'll ever get used to."

"What do you mean?"

She sighed. "I'm used to seeing Ella and Grace all the time. And Katie and Mama. I miss them."

"I know they miss you too."

"This is one part of the whole music thing I don't really know how to navigate," she admitted. "I know tours and events get scheduled months, and even years, in advance sometimes. I hate the idea that Grace or Ella might need me, and I'm somewhere across the country. Or even across the world. I don't want them to ever feel like they can't count on me."

I looked down at my hands and thought about how I'd felt the week I'd been on the road without Liv. Until her, I didn't know what it really felt like to have someone to miss or someone waiting for me at home. I was always with the people I considered family, so I never had to worry about whether or not I'd be able to be there for them if they needed me.

"Hey," she said, reaching out and touching my arm. "What is it?"

"I was just thinking about how foreign the idea of missing someone was until I met you. The guys and I are always together. Honestly, sometimes I wish I could have a chance to miss Dallas." I snorted out a laugh. "Even when it comes to my mom, it's not like I miss *her*, you know? I don't have a catalog of fond memories from my childhood. I guess I miss the idea of who she could have been."

"I'm sorry, Jax." She placed her hand on the side of my face, her thumb stroking my cheek.

"I'm not." I shook my head. "You've given me something worth missing." I placed my hand on top of hers, cupping her hand with mine. "I feel lucky that I have you and that you decided to give this music thing a shot. Even though I have someone worth missing, maybe I won't have to very often because we'll be together."

"I feel lucky too." She leaned in, kissing me deeply.

My heart swelled, overcome with gratitude. I took her hands in mine. "Look, I know how important Ella and Grace are to you. No matter what our commitments are for the band, you come first, and that means the people you care about come first. If they need you, no matter where we are, I promise to get you home to them."

She smiled.

"I never want to take you away from Ella, Grace, and Katie. We'll fly them out to visit. I'll do anything I can to make sure you guys always feel connected."

"Thank you. That means a lot to me."

"And whenever we start touring, we'll just have to bring Mama with us." I winked at her.

"Can you imagine Mama on a tour bus?" She snorted. "That's one way to ward off any nosy fans."

"With Mama around, we wouldn't even need security." I laughed, but the wheels in my mind had already started turning. "I have an idea." I grabbed the guitar and started strumming a soft, sorrowful melody.

She studied me while I played the tune over and over, working out the words in my mind.

Finally, I started to sing. *"What's it like to have half your heart on the other side of the world? Thousands of red lights, nothing but long nights, keeping a boy from his girl."* I continued to play the melody as I looked over at her. "What do you think?"

"I love it. I'm going to write it down." She grabbed the notebook we'd been working out of and started scribbling the words.

"I feel like that could be a verse, but it needs something more."

She nodded and jotted something else in the notebook. "Okay, what about this?" She swayed slowly, and her voice filled the air. *"What's it like to always wanna go home? Because you know every city you're in is the wrong one when you have someone worth missing."*

"That's it. This is why I love writing with you. It's like you read my mind." With one last strum of the guitar, I placed the instrument on the bed, leaning over to kiss her. I grabbed the notebook and tossed it aside. "I think it's time for a break. What do you say we make use of that Jacuzzi before we have to get back on the bus tomorrow?"

Her eyes shimmered up at me in the warm light of the room. "I like that idea."

I held my hands out to her and pulled her from the bed,

guiding her into the bathroom. I turned the faucet, and she sat on the edge of the tub as the water began to fill.

"Thank you," she said, her voice low and sweet. "For being so understanding and for caring about what makes me happy."

I sat beside her, my fingers grazing her cheek. It occurred to me that this wasn't something she was used to. She hadn't really known what it was like to be supported in a relationship. I remembered my conversation with Grace on Liv's birthday. She'd told me that Benton never really approved of her closeness with Ella and Grace. I thought about how her ex had let her believe she was somehow not good enough. He'd been the reason she'd ultimately let go of her dream of a music career.

"All I want is for you to be happy." And I did. I silently vowed to never let her feel stifled or unimportant another day in her life. Liv had given me the greatest gift of all. She'd given me a person to belong to, something worth missing. The least I could do was spend my life making her happy.

TWENTY-ONE

Liv

———

OVER THE NEXT couple of days, we traveled through Phoenix and Salt Lake City. By the time we made it to Denver, I could tell the guys were exhausted. It was easy to see how road life could take its toll on you. We'd been eating a steady diet of takeout and gas station snacks. The room service menu was the closest any of us had gotten to anything home-cooked and, truth be told, I was fairly certain home-cooked meals were rare for the guys. While watching the band start their show that evening, Cash and Antoni inadvertently gave me an idea.

"Honey, I'm so hungry I might eat you if you stand still long enough." Antoni pursed his lips, crossing his arms across his chest. "If I have to eat another Filet-O-Fish, I'm gonna turn into Nemo."

I scrunched up my nose. "You actually eat those things?"

"You know what sounds so good?" Cash asked. "Some spicy chili."

"Oh, yes," Antoni purred, "and some piping hot cornbread. Honey, all this food talk is like soft porn for me."

"Hmm." I turned toward Cash. "What are the chances we could sneak out unnoticed right now?"

He eyed me curiously. "Pretty good, I'd say. What do you have in mind?"

"I'm going to cook dinner for everybody," I said. "I could use some help since we're on a bit of time crunch."

"You're gonna cook *on the bus?*" Antoni asked incredulously.

I nodded. "Homemade chili and cornbread."

"You know all that's on there is a hot plate and a toaster oven, right?" Cash questioned me with his eyes. "Is that even possible?"

"I didn't say it would be easy." I laughed. "I think it can be done, but I'll need some help."

"This girl is about to feed beans to a bunch of grown men trapped in a tin can with one bathroom. You know what that is?" Antoni raised his perfectly arched brow at me. "Bravery, honey."

Cash rubbed along the stubble on his chin. "Antoni, can you hold down the fort tonight?"

"In my sleep, boss." Antoni waved him off.

"Let's do this," Cash said to me. "Why not?"

"Y'all have fun," Antoni called after us. "I'll see you in time for dinner."

I pulled out my phone and searched for a store nearby as we wound our way through the venue to the side entrance where the bus was parked. "There's a Target a couple of miles away. Want me to call an Uber?"

"Why do that when we can take the bus? We'll need all the time we can get to prepare. Might as well get started on the drive back." Cash grinned, unlocking the door of the bus. He gave a wave to the driver, an older gentleman with grey hair, who sat working on a crossword puzzle. "Hey, man. You mind giving us a lift to the store?" He took my phone from my hands and showed him the address of our destination.

"Sure thing," the driver said. "Hop in."

I pulled up the notes app on my phone and made a list of everything we'd need as we made the short drive to the store. The driver dropped us off at the front, instructing us to text him when we were finished so he could pick us up at the door. We walked through the automatic doors, and Cash grabbed a cart.

I took in a deep breath through my nose. "I love the smell of Target. Smells like everything I never knew I needed."

Cash laughed as he pushed the cart beyond the dollar section and the cash registers.

"Let's start over in housewares," I said as he steered the cart down the aisle, past the greeting cards and office supplies. "We need a few things to cook with, starting with something to actually put the chili in."

Cash looked around as we strolled through the store. "This was Carrie's favorite thing to do on date night. We'd go out to dinner, and she didn't care about going to the movies or to a concert or anything. She wanted to come to Target."

I smiled over at him. "Sounds like my kind of girl."

"I'm sorry." He cleared his throat, and I noticed his eyes looked misty. "I just realized this is the first time I've even been inside a Target since she died."

"I didn't realize…" I placed a hand on his arm. "We can leave. I'll find another store."

He shook his head and laughed softly. "No, it's okay. Really. Grief is just weird like that. It sneaks up on you and makes you do weird stuff, like cry in the middle of Target."

"That's not weird," I assured him.

He followed me down an aisle with cookware, and I started putting the few items I needed into the cart. "You're too sweet to tell me the truth."

I laughed softly. "No, I mean it. After Ella's husband Craig died, she couldn't go into a grocery store for six months. That was their thing. They went to the store together every Sunday morning. Then when Grace was born, she went with them too. But after Craig passed, she couldn't do it. She tried a couple of times, but the closest she got was the parking lot. So, I took over her grocery shopping for a while. I told her that when she was ready, we'd go together. It was about six months later when she decided she was ready to give it a try. She ended up breaking down in the middle of the frozen food aisle over a DiGiorno pizza because those were Craig's favorite."

Cash furrowed his brow. "Poor Ella."

"I've never lost a spouse, but I lost my parents. The thing I remember being so painful about grief was that for so long, it felt like my entire world stopped, but everyone around me kept going on as though nothing even happened. Holidays still came and went, and the days passed like normal when it was anything but."

He pushed the cart around the corner toward the grocery portion of the store. "I know that feeling well. I've tried to stay busy because if I keep going, I won't have time to feel it. Now, I'm coming up on the one year anniversary, and the holidays and Thanksgiving were her favorite. I could go back home to her family's house because that's what we always did for Thanksgiving, but the idea of being there without Carrie on her favorite holiday makes me feel... overwhelmingly sad." He swallowed hard. "But the idea of being alone makes me even sadder."

"So, don't be alone." I grabbed his arm and stopped in the middle of the canned goods aisle. "Come to Thanksgiving at my house this year."

He looked down at his feet a moment, his cheeks flushed. "You really don't have to do that."

"I know, but I want to. I was already planning to invite all of y'all. And listen, there's no pressure. It doesn't have to be the start of a new tradition. It can just be a day with people who care about you. Jax will be there, and Ella and Grace will be there because we always spend Thanksgiving together. I know they'd love to see you too. Grace adores you, you know."

A smile spread across his face. "I really like her too. And Ella... she's great."

"Good. Then it's settled. You'll be spending Thanksgiving with us." I nodded emphatically before moving down the aisle and plucking a few cans of chili beans from the shelf.

"Jax is lucky to have you, Liv." Cash said, catching my eye as I dropped the cans into the cart. "Hell, we all are. I mean, who else would make these jokers dinner on a tour bus?"

I nudged him as we fell into step beside each other and continued toward the produce section. "I'm not here alone, am I? Besides, somebody had to do something. We could not let Antoni eat another Filet-O-Fish."

Cash grimaced. "Truly, it was our civic duty to make this dinner."

I laughed as I pulled some pre-cut onions from one of the refrigerated shelves.

"And Antoni was right. Beans and onions on a tiny bus with a bunch of dudes? Brave."

I laughed. "Maybe we should swing by the pharmacy for some Pepto on the way out."

"I *know* we should. And some Beano and Imodium. There's a reason Dallas isn't allowed to eat at Taco Bell when we're on the road. I'm just saying."

We giggled as we forged ahead through the paper products, retrieving some bowls, flatware, and napkins. "Okay, I think we've got just about everything. Let's hit up the pharmacy on the way out."

"Roger that," Cash said, stopping with one finger held up. "Actually, maybe I should go grab a plunger. You know, just as an insurance policy." He broke into a big grin, and even hundreds of miles away from Nashville, I felt at home.

THE NEXT DAY WE WERE IN KANSAS CITY, AND AFTER THE show, we drove through the night to Chicago where the guys went straight into a full day of press. We were at the last interview of the day for a nationally syndicated talk show. Cash, Antoni, and I waited in a separate greenroom where we could watch the interview on a big, flat-screen television.

"So Liv, have you and Jax thought about when you may want to get in the studio to record some tracks? I could even set up a few showcase gigs for you guys." Cash said, pouring himself a cup of coffee from the expansive refreshment table. "Before long, you guys will be doing shows like these together."

"Trash tv." Antoni pursed his lips disapprovingly. "The American dream, honey."

"Yeah, it pretty much sucks." Cash chuckled. "Unfortunately, it's a necessary part of the machine."

"I don't know." I laughed awkwardly. "It's been years since I've been on an actual stage."

"Well, you're a natural. That much is for sure." Cash sat beside me on the plush sofa. "The songs you and Jax have been working on are some of the best he's ever brought to me. You've got a real gift."

"If Cash Montgomery says you have a gift, girl, you've got *it,*" Antoni informed me. "That means you are the whole enchilada and nacho bar, baby."

I shook my head and laughed, shifting my focus to the television as the interview continued. The pretty blonde host set her sights on Jax. "Let's start with you, Jaxon. There's been some reports floating around from the show you did a few nights ago at Microsoft Theater about a new song you sang for a special lady in your life. Can you tell us more about this mystery woman?"

Jax blushed, a smile sweeping across his face. The live studio audience cheered their approval. "She's... well, she's the best thing that's ever happened to me."

"By the looks of this photo floating around the internet today, you've even had your first public appearance with her," she said as a grainy photo of the two of us appeared on the screen. It was the photo that had been taken while we were dancing at the Halloween party. I noticed Jax's jaw clench as he saw the photo in question, but thanks to the mask Antoni selected, my identity remained concealed.

The host continued to press for more information. "Can you tell us who she is? Is she a singer too?"

"She's a talented woman, but you wouldn't know who she is just yet." He grinned, and I found myself smiling too. "I'm going to protect her privacy until she's ready to have her name out in the world. Right now, I'm pretty happy keeping her all to myself."

"That's so exciting! It sounds like things are getting pretty serious," the blonde continued. "Do you see yourself settling down and starting a family?"

"I'd love that." A look of surprise flashed across his face as though he'd been caught off guard by the question. "Honestly, I'd love to get married and have a house full of kids. That would make me pretty damn happy."

I felt my heart sink right into the floor.

Before the host could probe him any further, Luca spoke up and redirected her attention. "In case you're interested, I'm still single." The crowd cheered as the host shifted her focus to Luca.

I felt my stomach churn and the color drain from my face. Of course, he wanted kids. Why wouldn't he? Why hadn't I thought of this before? I knew how important family was to him.

"Liv?" Cash's brows knitted together, and he placed a gentle hand on my shoulder. "Are you alright?"

"You need me to get you something to drink?" Antoni asked. "You look like you're about to toss your cookies, girl."

I mumbled something about not feeling well and stumbled out into the hallway in search of the bathroom.

I pushed through the door to the ladies' room and into a vacant stall, shutting the door behind me. Tears threatened to form in my eyes. I didn't know if I could ever give him the family he wanted, and above everything else, didn't Jax deserve that? I'd been unable to give Ben the family he wanted, and look how that turned out. What would happen if I couldn't give Jax his dream either?

I heard the bathroom door open and close, followed by Antoni's voice. "Liv? You okay in there?"

"Yeah. One second." I took a deep breath, bracing myself before I exited the stall.

"You sure? Honey, you look like you've seen a ghost." He patted my back as I moved to the sink, splashing some cold water on my face. He grabbed some paper towels out of the dispenser and handed them to me.

"I'm okay. I think I'm just tired," I lied.

Antoni eyed me suspiciously, and I got the feeling he didn't believe me one bit. "Sweetheart, if you need somebody to talk to, you've got a friend in me, okay? I know you got kinda dropped into this life, and it's a whole lot to process. I've been working for these guys for three years now, and it's *still* a lot. Don't feel like you're swimming out there all alone."

"Thanks." I gave him a small smile. "I appreciate it, but I'm alright. Really."

Antoni studied me a moment as though he could sniff the truth right out of me. "Okay." He nodded, gesturing toward the door. "After you."

I pushed through the door, and when I turned the corner, I walked smack into Jax, who gripped me by the shoulders. "Hey, are you okay? Cash said you were sick."

"I'm fine." I forced a smile. "I think I'm just exhausted. Really, I'll be fine."

"Let's get you to the bus." He pulled me to him, kissing the top of my head. "You need to rest. Come on."

I felt a pang in my heart as I wrapped my arm around his waist. What if I couldn't give him what he wanted? What he deserved?

What if I wasn't good enough?

A couple of moments later, we boarded the bus along with the rest of the guys, who all shared their concern over me. I tried to wave them off, but they fawned over me as though I was an injured animal.

After I managed to shake them off, Jax took me back to his bunk. "Do you mind if I lay down with you? I just want to hold you."

I nodded. "I'd like that." In fact, that was all I wanted. To wrap up in his arms for as long as possible because there may come a time when I no longer could.

We curled up in his bunk together, and I buried my face in his chest, his arms wrapped tightly around me. Jax's words from the interview reverberated through my mind as he gently stroked my hair. I thought about the family he dreamed of having and wondered if I was selfish for holding on to him when I may never be able to give him what he deserved.

TWENTY-TWO

Jax

WE FELL asleep in Chicago and woke up in Louisville, our last stop before we'd drop Liv off in Nashville a couple of days later on our way to Atlanta. The band had some local press lined up at one of the big radio stations in the city before we were to head to soundcheck. I looked out from the booth to where Cash, Antoni, and Liv stood in the hall waiting. The DJs had already attempted to ask me about my 'mystery girl.' Once again, Luca jumped in and deflected the attention back to him, and I was grateful.

I'd barely said a word the entire interview, too distracted by the far off look in Liv's eyes. She'd clung to me a little longer than usual in my bunk that morning. I asked her if she felt better, and she'd said she did, but I could tell she was lying by the way she smiled. It didn't quite reach her eyes, as though she'd forced it for my benefit.

Cash had pulled me aside and asked if there was anything he could do to help cheer her up. Even he'd noticed something was off with her. She'd seemed to be enjoying her time on the road with me just days before. I knew she missed Ella and Grace, but she'd seemed happy. At least, I thought she had.

I asked if she was sure she was okay, and she'd said she was just tired and that sleeping on the bus was starting to get to her.

The band would be staying in their respective homes while we were in Louisville, which meant I would finally get to take Liv back to my apartment. I was a little nervous for her to see how empty it was, much like my life had been without her in it, but I'd been anxious to bring her here for some alone time. I was hoping that once we had a little time to ourselves, I could get her to open up about what was bothering her.

We stopped at The Palace for an early soundcheck, and then we were planning to take the afternoon to relax before heading back for the show. Sam Corbyn was wrapping up his soundcheck while we, minus Cash and Antoni, waited in the dressing room.

"How does it feel to be back knowing you're about to move to Nashville?" Liv asked Dallas, taking a sip from her water bottle.

"It feels good," he said. "Louisville will always be home, but Nashville has kinda captured my heart."

"It's captured mine too," I said, leaning over to kiss Liv on the cheek.

Her eyes sparkled with warmth as she gazed up at me for one blissful second. But once the moment passed, the despondent look on her face returned.

There was a knock on the door, and Antoni entered with a flourish.

"Hey, Antoni. What's up?" Luca asked.

"I'm here for Liv." Antoni strolled into the dressing room

and reached out his hand to her. "You and I have a date at the spa, honey." He gave a little shimmy, and I furrowed my brow in confusion. "Courtesy of Cash Montgomery and the dashing gentlemen of Midnight in Dallas." That's when I realized this must have been Cash's doing, and I made a mental note to thank him later. "You need an afternoon of relaxation and beautification, and God knows I need less of *this*." He looked back at me apologetically and made a sweeping gesture at us. "No offense to you boys. You're great and all, but the bullshit is strong with y'all."

"Antoni's right," I assured Liv as she looked back at me, her head tilted slightly in confusion. "You deserve some pampering." The guys backed me up, encouraging her to go enjoy herself.

"Okay," she said, letting Antoni take her hand. "Thank you, guys. This is very sweet of you."

"Now, kiss lover boy goodbye because I'm not bringing you back till we're all decked out for the show tonight." Antoni propped a hand on his hip. "I took the liberty of calling up a couple of boutiques in town, and we're getting something cute to wear for the hometown show."

I stood and gave Liv one last lingering kiss.

"Alright. Save it for later, Romeo." Antoni waved me off, pulling Liv toward the door. "She's gonna look like the queen she is, and so will I."

"Have fun," I called, and Antoni pushed her out into the hallway. My heart sank as the door closed behind them. Our talk would have to wait.

After soundcheck, I was walking out the back door of The Palace with Brady when Cash jogged out to catch up with me.

"Hey, Jax," he called. "Can I talk to you for a second?"

"Sure." I stopped walking and waited for him to catch up.

"I'll be waiting in the car." Brady gave us a respectful nod and continued to the SUV.

"What's up?" I asked, shoving my hands in my pockets.

"I'm sorry I didn't clear the spa thing with you first," Cash said. "It was a spur of the moment thing. Liv seems like she's feeling really down, and I was talking about it with Antoni earlier. I remembered Ella took her to a spa for her birthday, so I thought maybe that might help cheer her up. Antoni wanted to go with her because he thought maybe she might need someone to talk to since Ella's not around. You know he loves her to death. We all do."

"There's nothing to apologize for. I appreciate you doing that for her, and honestly, I wish I'd thought of it. I don't know, man." I shook my head and ground the toe of my Chuck Taylors into the pavement. "Something's off. Maybe she realized the touring thing is too much for her?"

Cash folded his arms across his chest. "Something happened yesterday when we were in the greenroom, Jax. We were watching your interview back there, and she bolted."

"Fuck." I scrubbed my hands over my face. "Maybe she's not ready for this... for *us.*"

"I don't think that's it." Cash sighed. "I really don't. I know she cares about you. Seeing the way she looks at you..." He trailed off, and his eyes fell to the ground. "It reminds me of the way Carrie used to look at me. It's something special, Jax."

I knew Cash deserved to know the real reason I hadn't

been able to write. He deserved to know the impact Carrie had on my life and everything leading up to now. "I need to tell you something, Cash." I cleared my throat. "I didn't tell you the truth about why I wasn't able to write for so long." I told him about the numerous conversations I'd had with Carrie leading up to her death. I filled him in on beginning the search for my mom and what Carrie told me. *If I'd stayed angry, I would have missed out on so much love,* she'd said. "But more than that, I realized if I kept living the way I was living, I may never get to have what you and Carrie had. I was so damn mad at the world. I was going through the motions, and now that I've found Liv..."

"You're not angry anymore." He squeezed my shoulder and gave me a faint smile.

I sucked in a deep breath. "Not even a little."

"That's love, man." He ran his hand through his hair. "It has this weird way of driving all the anger out of your heart. It's like it takes up so much space that there's no room for it anymore."

"But... how do you live without her?" I hated myself for asking the question because I knew it wasn't the same. Carrie was gone, and even if I lost Liv, I'd still get to live in a world where she existed.

"I don't know that I'd call what I've been doing living so much as existing," he admitted. "I was so angry when Carrie died, or at least I thought I was. Really I just had all this love that had nowhere to go anymore. The truth is, I'll never stop loving her. But listen, you're not going to lose Liv. I truly believe that."

"I hope you're right." I looked down at the asphalt and blinked back the tears that threatened to form in the corners of my eyes.

"And Jax?" I lifted my gaze to look at him. "Carrie would have loved her. She would have been so proud of you."

"Fuck, man. I miss her."

"I miss her too," Cash confessed. "Every day of my life. Though I have to admit, things have felt... lighter since Liv came into our lives. And Ella and Grace. They've brought a lot of happiness to my life too."

"I can't lose her, Cash." I shook my head adamantly. "I can't."

"I know." He clapped me on the back. "I'll see you back here this evening."

"Thanks, man." I nodded as he turned and started back toward the door. I steeled myself and walked to the car where Brady waited.

I wasn't sure what was going on in Liv's mind. I just knew I had to let her know, that no matter how much she tried to push me away, I wasn't going anywhere.

TWENTY-THREE

Liv

IT TURNED out that a spa day with Antoni was exactly what I needed. We got massages and facials first, which gave me some time to decompress. I hadn't been able to tell Ella about the interview or how I was feeling because there wasn't much privacy on the bus. I was careful not to let her think anything was wrong. I knew how much she'd worry, but I longed for her advice.

Antoni and I drank champagne as we got manicures and pedicures, and the next thing I knew, I'd pretty much spilled not only all the details about how Jax and I got together but everything that happened in the seventeen years before that.

After a refill on our champagne, we were escorted to the sauna to wait until our stylists came to get us for our final stop of the day in the hair and makeup chairs.

"Okay, missy. What happened in the greenroom yesterday?" Antoni asked, his hand stroking the stubble on his face. "And you better not even try to give me that 'I'm tired' bullshit again, or I will smack you upside your unfairly beautiful face."

I sighed and leaned my back against the wall, taking a sip of my champagne. "Remember when they asked Jax what his hopes were for the future? If he saw himself settling down and having a family?"

"Oh my God." Antoni gasped, placing his hand on my shoulder. "You don't know if you'll ever want that?"

"No, it's not that at all," I assured him. "I care about him so much. Honestly, after Ben and I split, I didn't really know if this was a thing that would ever happen for me. I didn't know that I'd ever find someone, but then Jax came along. He's everything I could have hoped for."

"And he's head over heels in love with you," he added, "so what's the problem?"

I ran my fingers through my hair, drawing in a deep breath. "I was diagnosed with endometriosis when I was twenty-nine. At the time, my doctor told me it was possible that pregnancy wouldn't ever be in the cards for me, but Ben and I kept trying because we both wanted a baby so badly. When I turned thirty-two, those two little lines finally appeared on the pregnancy test." I looked down at the bubbles in my champagne, watching them rise to the surface before bursting into nothing. "For eleven weeks, it was like the wind had been put back in our sails, and I thought maybe there was hope for me and Ben. We were shopping for baby clothes and making plans for the nursery. Then, one night I woke up with these intense cramps and..." I wiped away a tear that had escaped down my cheek. "We lost it. After that, talks of a family came to a screeching halt. My relationship with Ben became transactional at best. He seemed to blame me for what happened. I've gone over it again and again in my head for years, and I can't figure out what I did wrong. I took the vitamins and ate all the right things. I did fucking yoga. I thought I did everything right."

"Liv, honey." Antoni held my hand between his. "That wasn't your fault. You have to know that. Sometimes these things happen. There's no reason, and it isn't fucking fair. I'm so sorry you went through that, and I'm doubly sorry that prick you were married to didn't love you the way you deserved. For what it's worth, I really do believe Jax loves you. I've certainly never seen him like this. That boy would go to the moon and back for you."

"I know." I sighed. "I know he would, but he said he wanted a family. I don't know if I'll ever be able to give him that, Antoni. He deserves to have everything he could ever want."

"Sweetheart." He squeezed my hand. "I think you're forgetting one important detail."

"What?" I asked.

"He wants *you*."

"What if I'm not enough for him?"

"Hot damn, no ma'am." He shook his head. "Don't even let your pretty head go there. You're worrying yourself sick, and that man, who is very much in love with you, has no idea what's going on."

"But isn't it wrong for me to stay with him knowing I may not be able to give him what he deserves?"

"What would be wrong is if you didn't let *him* decide what he deserves, honey," he said softly. "You've got to let him know what's eating at you."

The door to the sauna opened, and a salon coordinator wearing all black appeared. "Olivia and Antoni, we're ready for you."

We followed the young woman through the spa and into the salon area where people were milling about, chattering over the sounds of hair dryers. Before she delivered me to my assigned stylist, Antoni grabbed my hand and whispered in my ear. "You've got to talk to him, honey."

"I know." I forced a smile and nodded.

I knew he was right, but I also knew I was terrified that once Jax knew the truth, he would realize I wasn't enough for him.

ANTONI AND I ARRIVED AT THE PALACE RIGHT BEFORE THE meet and greet. We wove our way through the backstage area until we found the dressing room where Cash was standing just outside.

"Hey, Liv," he greeted as Antoni stopped to talk to Brady. "You look fantastic."

"Thanks." I smiled. "That was really nice of you, by the way. Thank you so much for sending us."

"How are you feeling now?" He leaned against the wall to the side of the doorframe.

"A lot more relaxed," I said. "Thanks to you."

"Good." He nodded. "You know if you need anything, anything at all, I'm here for you, right? I'll do anything I can to help you."

"I know," I replied. "I appreciate you, Cash, more than you know."

He gazed at me quietly for a moment as though he wanted to say something else, but decided against it. "Jax is in there. I know he'll be excited to see you." He gestured toward the dressing room behind him, and I knocked on the door.

"Yes?" I heard Dallas call.

"Are you guys decent?" I asked through the door.

Luca grinned wildly as he opened the door. "When have you ever known us to be decent?"

"That's fair." I laughed and entered the dressing room.

"You look great," Luca appraised me. "Jax, your girlfriend is gorgeous. Why don't I have a gorgeous girlfriend?"

"Maybe because there's not a woman alive who'd be willing to put up with your shit," Dallas challenged, raising his brow.

Luca paused thoughtfully and shrugged. "Yeah, that might be it."

"Hey, beautiful." Jax greeted me by pulling me into his arms. "He's right, you know. I do have the most gorgeous girlfriend in the world." He gazed down at me, and I saw a flicker of worry flash across his face.

"Brady has the first group here now." Antoni stuck his head in the door as Cash slipped into the room and stood near the far wall.

"You guys good?" Derek glanced around at everyone before settling his eyes on me and Jax.

"Yeah," I answered. Jax reluctantly released me from his grasp, and I crossed the room to stand with Cash.

I'd watched the meet and greets several times since being on the road with the band, and I loved watching the guys interact with their fans. Derek was always the more mellow one, but he still had quite an effect on the ladies. Luca ate up every ounce of attention that came his way, flirting with all the women. Meanwhile, Dallas was the one who made everybody feel at ease, joking and laughing with each person that came in.

Jax's smile lit up the room and the heart of every woman

who walked through the door of the dressing room. People often seemed completely disarmed by the fact that his warm disposition matched the genuineness of his smile.

Small groups of fans filtered in and out, much like Ella, Grace, and I had the first night we met the guys. I noticed Jax's eyes search for mine as people filed in and out of the room. Finally, the last group entered. It was a young couple with their daughter who looked to be no more than about five or six years old.

"Who do we have here?" Jax smiled at the bright-eyed young girl.

"Cora." She gave him a bashful smile, and he crouched down so that he was at her eye-level. She tugged at the hem of her ruffly pink dress.

"Cora," he repeated. "That's such a pretty name. A pretty name for a pretty girl." She grinned again, hiding her face in her mom's side.

"Thank you." The mom smiled, ruffling Cora's hair. "We love your music, but Jaxon, you are Cora's *favorite*. When we found out you guys would be here, we knew we had to bring her to meet you."

"Thank you so much for coming to see us," Jax said, his eyes fixed on Cora. "May I have a hug?"

Cora looked up at her mom as though asking for her approval, to which she nodded. "Go ahead, honey. It's okay." She ran into his arms, and he expertly scooped her up, holding her on his hip. He took his time talking with Cora and her parents while the rest of the guys made over her. Dallas made silly faces at her, causing her to burst into a fit of giggles.

Antoni grabbed my hand and leaned into my ear. "You okay, honey?"

I nodded. I noticed Cash watching me, and I wondered if he could see right through me.

Jax was a natural with Cora. Seeing him interact with her caused sharp bolts of shame and guilt to shoot through me. How could I deprive him of having his own Cora one day?

After the guys took pictures with Cora and her family, one of the other guards showed them out, and Brady let us know it was showtime.

Jax put his arm around me wordlessly, and we walked to the side stage area, listening as Sam Corbyn finished his set. He stood with his arms around me until it was time for him to get plugged in and hit the stage.

"I'll meet you here after the show." He leaned in to kiss me on the forehead before disappearing backstage. I stood with Antoni and Cash as I had many nights before, watching the guys play their hearts out.

By the time the band began to play the melody to "Love You More," a deep sadness had settled into my heart. Jax deserved someone that could give him the family he longed for. He deserved the whole world, and I knew that no matter how much I wanted to, I couldn't promise him that. He deserved someone that loved him enough to let him go so he could still have that dream.

Tears blurred my vision as he sang the chorus. His eyes met mine once more, and I couldn't control the sob that escaped me. Tears streamed down my face as I turned on my heel and backed away from the stage. I heard Cash call after me and Antoni's voice telling him to give me a moment. I tore through the backstage area with my head down, running down the hall, and I didn't stop running until I was outside the back entrance of The Palace. I gulped in the chilly night air, leaning against the wall outside with my hands clutched to my chest.

The pain felt as though it might drown me. I knew that tonight, I had to break my own heart. I had to let Jaxon Slade go.

TWENTY-FOUR

Jax

"Liv!" I breathed a sigh of relief when I found her outside the backdoor of the venue. Under the lamplight, I could see her face was damp with tears. My mind whirled as I tried to figure out what could have happened to make her this upset. "What's wrong?"

"I—" She started to speak as Brady came barreling out after me. "I just needed some fresh air."

"Brady, can you take us to my apartment now?" I asked, not taking my eyes off Liv. "I'll text Cash and ask him to grab the rest of my stuff."

"Of course." He nodded, his eyes awash with concern. We walked to the car, and even with her hand in mine, she felt a million miles away. The ride to my apartment was painfully silent as I stole glances of her grief-stricken face.

Brady pulled up to the kiosk outside my complex, and I flashed my card out of my window, opening the gate. We pulled to a stop outside my building, and I exited the car, helping Liv out behind me. Brady gave me a sympathetic nod before pulling away.

I led her to the door and slid my key in the lock, letting us inside. She stepped through the threshold as I closed the door, locking it behind us.

"So, this is it." I flicked on the light, illuminating my spacious, but very empty apartment. The walls were stark white and completely bare. The sleek black couch and television looked comically small in the expansive space.

"I think someone stole the rest of your furniture," she joked half-heartedly, stepping further into the living room.

I studied her as she walked around, her eyes on everything but me. So many questions tugged at the corners of my mind. Did she regret coming to see me? Had she realized being with a touring musician wasn't what she wanted? Worse still, that *I* wasn't what she wanted?

The sheer curtain was already pulled open when she walked over to the window and stared wordlessly out into the night sky. Liv was right in front of me, but I felt like I was losing her. I'd racked my brain all day trying to figure out what changed. My mind kept coming back to the interview we'd done in LA, and after what Cash told me earlier, I suspected I was right.

I steeled myself as I approached her, gently placing my hands on her shoulders. "Can we talk?" I felt her muscles tense beneath my fingers, and she cast her gaze downward. "Baby," I pleaded, "please talk to me. What's going on? You haven't been yourself since yesterday." I hooked my finger under her chin, gently bringing her eyes back to mine. "Please, Liv."

She pressed her lips together and shook her head.

"I've been going over and over this in my mind. To figure out what changed. It was the interview we did yesterday. It's because of what I said, isn't it?" I scrubbed my hands over my face. "That you're the best thing that's ever happened to me and that I wanted to get married one day. It was too much for you, wasn't it?" Her gaze fell to the floor, but I pressed on, taking her hands in mine. "I'm sorry. I didn't say those things to rush you or push you into anything. You *are* the best thing that's happened to me, and I do see a future with you, but I'll be patient. I will wait as long as you ask—"

"It's not that." She wrenched herself from my grasp, turning away from me.

"But it *is* something." My mouth went dry. "What is it?"

"I'm afraid I won't be enough for you." Her voice broke, her shoulders shaking as she wept into her hands.

"Where is this coming from?" I closed the distance between us and took her in my arms. "You're more than enough for me. You're everything to me."

"I can't give you everything you want," she choked out.

"Liv, *you* are what I want." I searched her eyes, trying to understand.

"You want a house full of kids. You want children." She looked at me wistfully. "And you should be able to have them."

"So you don't want kids." My entire body felt heavy. "Okay. I get it, but that doesn't change how I—"

"It's not that. I've been down this road before. I've tried to have a family, but my body made it impossible, and I don't think I can handle another miscarriage, Jax. I can't take having my heart broken like that again."

Finally, the words she'd said hit me. She wasn't saying she didn't *want* a family with me. She didn't know if she'd be able to *give* me one. I felt a pang of disappointment deep in my gut. Admittedly, this wasn't something I'd ever considered.

Crazy as it was, I'd pictured our future together a lot over the past couple of weeks, and in those visions, I'd seen myself carrying Liv over the threshold of a home of our own. I'd thought about the kind of parents we might be together. I wondered what our lives would look like many years from now when those children were grown, and I'd imagined we'd sit on our front porch, old and grey, reminiscing about the beautiful life we'd created together.

But what was most important to me about that future was her. The rest of it was nothing without *her*.

"Liv, look at me. I don't think you understand. I want *you.*"

"But you want a family, Jax. You deserve that, and I'm being selfish holding onto you knowing I may never be able to give you that."

"There are a million ways to make a family. There are a million ways to make a *home*." I took her beautiful face in my hands. "The only thing I've ever had to my name was that shitty apartment. Then, after things started to go well for the band, this slightly less shitty, but still empty apartment. I never had a person I belonged to. Don't get me wrong, the guys are like family, but I never had a *home*. Home is where you are, Liv." I wiped at the tears that had fallen down her cheeks. "I want to build a family with you. I want a future with *you*. Whether that means we adopt, foster, or just rescue a bunch of furry brothers and sisters for Mama. No matter what it is, I want it all with you."

"You do?" Her voice was a hoarse whisper, and her face softened.

"I understand if you're not there yet. I meant what I said. I'll be patient." I wrapped my arms around her. "I'll wait as long as you need me to because *you* are what's been missing from my life. You're home to me. I love you, Liv."

She looked at me through her tears, pulling my face down so that my forehead rested against hers. "I love you too, Jax."

"Yeah?" I whispered.

"Yeah." I kissed her soundly, my hands tangling in her hair. I smiled down at her. "I donut want to live without you."

She laughed softly, falling into my arms. At that moment, I held my entire world in my hands.

I GROANED AS THE BUS PULLED TO A STOP IN FRONT OF LIV'S house. Her two weeks with me had drawn to a close, and we were dropping her off before we finished the last few dates on the tour. I wanted nothing more than to get off this bus and stay with her, but I knew that in a few more days, I'd be home with her for the holidays. *Home.* After all this time, I finally had someone to call home.

"Girl, what am I going to do without you?" Antoni asked, throwing his arms around Liv. "Are you sure you can't stay? I'm going to miss you so much."

"I'm going to miss you too," she replied. "*All* of you." The guys each took turns hugging her and saying their good-byes. "And I'll see y'all at Thanksgiving?"

"You know I'll be there, Cupcake." Dallas smiled.

Antoni propped a hand on his hip. "I'll bring the yams, honey."

"Count me in," Derek added.

Luca pretended to be thinking hard about her invitation before breaking into a genuine smile. "I'll be there."

"It's not going to be the same without you here," Cash placed a hand on her shoulder, giving it a squeeze. "Tell Ella and Grace we said hello, and I'll be seeing you all for Thanksgiving."

"Thanks for everything, Cash." Liv wrapped him in a hug. Finally, her eyes settled on me.

"I'm going to walk you to your door." I grabbed her suitcase and duffle bag. "I'll be right back," I said to the guys.

"Take your time," Cash said. "Bye, Liv."

We quietly walked hand in hand up the walkway to her front door. She clicked the key in the lock, shoving the door open. I rolled her suitcase inside, placing the duffle beside it. Mama peered at us down the hallway before hissing and scampering off toward Liv's bedroom.

"I think she missed us," Liv joked, circling her arms around my neck.

"I don't want to get back on that bus without you," I murmured, pressing a kiss into her forehead. My entire body already ached knowing I wouldn't get to hold her at night or wake up next to her.

"I wish I could have stayed longer," she admitted. "I'm sorry about… everything. For freaking out like that and for not telling you what I was feeling sooner."

I tucked a loose strand of her hair behind her ear. "I'm sorry too. That wasn't something we'd talked about yet. Honestly, hearing it on some TV interview wasn't the way you should have heard it for the first time either."

She nestled herself in my embrace. "You better get going. You don't want to be late getting to Atlanta. Traffic will be nuts." I knew she was right, but it was the last thing I wanted to do. I longed for the day we would never have to part ways again.

"I know." I sighed. She walked back outside with me, and I pulled her into my arms, inhaling her citrusy scent one more time. "I'll call you and FaceTime you every day."

"Shit or get off the pot, man! Kiss her already, for fuck's sake!" Luca's voice called out. I could hear Cash, Dallas, and Derek laughing in the background as we turned to see the guys crowded around the cracked bus windows.

"Seriously," Antoni yelled. "Kiss that girl, dammit. *Kiss her!*"

"You heard them. Are you gonna kiss me or not?" She raised her brow at me and bit her lip. My fingers were in her hair and my hand on the back of her neck as I pulled her to me. I grazed her lips lightly at first, tasting the warmth of her breath. I kissed her slow and deep, savoring every second. I'd have forgotten all about the guys on the bus if they hadn't burst into cheers and applause, causing us both to laugh.

She turned toward the bus with a little curtsey, making them cheer even more. When she turned back to me, she pulled my face down to hers for another kiss. "Let me know when you make it to Atlanta."

"I will," I promised.

With one last squeeze of her hand, I started down the walk. When I reached the door of the bus, I heard her call out to me. "Turn around!" A grin spread across my face as I turned to see her running toward me. She didn't stop until she jumped into my arms, planting a kiss firmly on my mouth. "I love you, Jaxon Slade."

"I love you, Olivia Sinclair."

TWENTY-FIVE

Liv

AFTER I RETURNED and debriefed Ella over lattes, I was thrown right back into my normal life. The bakery was in full swing with holiday orders, which made the time fly by. I loved being back with Ella, Grace, and Katie, but I also felt like a large piece of me was missing.

I missed Jax fiercely, and I was surprised to realize how much I also missed the rest of the guys. I missed precious Dallas and his goofy sense of humor, though he made sure to send me a 'Hey Cupcake' or 'Miss you, Cupcake' text every day. I missed Derek's calming presence and Cash's steady friendship. I even missed Luca's wildcard charm and sweet Antoni, whom I now exchanged calls and texts with all the time.

I missed being on the road, or maybe it was that I missed what that meant: being with Jax and writing music. Being around Jax was like getting drunk on inspiration. Even back when I wrote music all those years ago, I'd never been as inspired as I was now.

While I was at work, my fingers longed to have my guitar

back in my hands again. Finally, a couple of nights before Jax was scheduled to return, I had some time to sit on the couch and pick up my guitar. I sat with the notebook Jax and I had been writing in splayed out on the coffee table and started playing around with a melody that had been buzzing in my mind all day. I tried to get in my groove, but I was unsettled and distracted. Something was missing or more accurately —someone.

Mama perched herself on top of the sofa, silently judging me through squinted eyes.

"I know it sucks, Mama. You don't even have to tell me."

She meowed disapprovingly as I ran my fingers through my hair.

I turned out all the lights and lit the candle we'd been burning the day the power went out. Then, I rummaged through the kitchen and found one last package of strawberry Pop-Tarts lingering in the pantry. I opened a bottle of wine and poured myself a glass, bringing it back to the living room along with my Pop-Tarts.

Finally, I trudged to the closet and found exactly what I was looking for. I ripped my shirt over my head, discarding it on the floor. I pulled Jax's shirt on. It was the one he'd insisted I keep the day we got caught in the rain. It hung a bit off my shoulder, and it still smelled like him. I inhaled deeply, taking in his scent, smiling to myself as I padded back into the living room and returned to the couch.

Mama side-eyed me when I picked the guitar up again and began to play. I sang through some of the lyrics that had been dying to pour out of me for days.

My phone rang from the coffee table with a FaceTime call from Jax. I swiped to answer the call, and his face illuminated the screen. "Hi." He smiled, but it didn't quite reach his eyes. He looked tired and a little dejected.

"Hey, handsome," I said softly. "Are you okay? You look exhausted."

"Yeah. I can't seem to remember how to sleep without you anymore."

"Aw, babe." I frowned. "I'm sorry. I miss you."

He sighed. "I miss you too. It's killing me." He squinted at me as though he was inspecting something, then broke into a wide grin. "Are you wearing my shirt?"

"Yeah." I smiled sheepishly and nodded. "I wanted to write tonight, but it wasn't the same without you, so I decided to try to channel you." I flipped the camera around so he could see the candle along with the wine and Pop-Tarts on the table. I panned over to Mama who stood from her perch, turning so her butt faced the camera. I giggled and flipped the phone back to my face.

"She clearly misses me too." Jax laughed. "And it would appear that great minds think alike." He pulled the phone away from his face and panned down a little so I could see that he was wearing the shirt I'd given him. "When we stopped to fuel up, I went into the gas station and got some Pop-Tarts. Now all I need is you."

"You've got me," I promised. "Always." His gaze flickered downward. "Is everything else okay? You seem a little down."

"I heard from the private investigator earlier today." He sighed. "Still no leads on my mom."

"I'm so sorry, honey." I longed to reach out and comfort him.

"The more time that passes, the more I think I may never find her." He shook his head. "I don't even know her, but I can't stop thinking that I may never *get* to know her. We're strangers to each other. I know she did what she had to do, and everything turned out the way it was supposed to, but it's a hard truth to swallow."

"I wish I could hold you, Jax." I knew there was nothing I could say that would take his hurt away, and it crushed me.

"Me too." His eyes softened as he gazed at me through the screen. "I swear, I'm never going to let you go." I sank back into the couch and wished I could crawl into the screen with him, curl up against his chest, and listen to his heartbeat whisper to me promises of a beautiful future together. He scrubbed down his face with his hand and gazed at me through sleepy eyes. "Will you play what you were working on for me? Hearing you sing always makes me feel better."

"Sure, but it's nowhere near finished yet." I propped the phone on the coffee table and settled the guitar in my lap. I closed my eyes as I began to strum the soft, sweet melody. *"Sun peeks through the window. Baby, please don't let me go. Cause it turns out I was living half a life, but with your love I'm whole."* I changed chords as I shifted into what would be the chorus. *"I thought home was a place, till I found you. Getting drunk by candlelight..."*

A loving smile crept onto his face. "Is that about us?"

I nodded and chewed my lip.

"It's beautiful, Liv. Hold on a second. Play that chorus again." I started the song from the chorus, singing the first two lines when Jax jumped in with his voice full of feeling. *"Getting drunk by candlelight, with a hell of a view."* I felt a flush sweep across my face, and I smiled. "Well, you are a hell of a view."

"So are you," I murmured.

"Start from the top again," he urged. "I've had something

in my head ever since you left, and I think it could be perfect for the other verse."

"Okay." Just like that, we were making music together thousands of miles apart.

WE STAYED ON THE PHONE UNTIL WELL AFTER MIDNIGHT. THE guys filtered in and out of the front of the bus, joining in on our call. Jax had propped the phone on the small dining table, and it was almost as though I was sitting there at the end of the booth with them.

"Okay," Luca said, swirling the amber liquid in his tumbler. "It's time for a rematch."

"Rematch?" I asked.

"Here we go again," Antoni said, not looking up from the magazine he'd been leafing through.

"Luca thinks he can beat me at poker." Dallas snorted and disappeared out of the frame for a moment.

Derek gave an amused grin. "He lost to the tune of a thousand bucks last night."

"I was a little rusty," Luca said defensively. "But I'm ready. I'm on my third drink, and three is my lucky number."

Jax shook his head and chuckled.

Derek took a sip of his beer and raised his brow. "Last night you said your lucky number was four."

Luca took a swig of his drink. "Because that's how many drinks I'd had."

"And clearly it wasn't so lucky." Dallas returned with a deck of cards. "Well, not for you, anyway."

Luca smirked. "Which is precisely why my lucky number is now three."

Antoni shook his head. "I cannot believe I put up with you fools."

Cash leaned back and crossed his arms over his chest. "Luca, as your friend and manager, I just want it on the record that I think this is a terrible idea."

"Want me to deal you in, Cupcake?" Dallas' face filled the screen.

"We can hold your cards up for you. I promise not to peek." Luca winked.

"Jax?" Dallas asked, shuffling the deck.

"Nope," he answered, rising to his feet and picking up the phone. "You've stolen my girlfriend's attention long enough. I'm going back to my bunk." He turned the screen so I could see Cash, Antoni, Derek, Dallas, and Luca. "Say goodnight, gentleman."

I waved as they sang their chorus of goodbyes, and Jax's face came back into view. The light around him dimmed as he moved toward the bunks.

He grinned. "I would say I'm sorry about those guys, but at this point you kind of know what you signed up for."

I laughed. "I do, and I wouldn't change a thing."

There was a rustling on his end as he crawled into his bunk, closed the curtain, and slipped in his AirPods. "Can you still hear me?"

"Loud and clear," I answered, downing the last of my wine.

"Hi," he said. In the pale light of the bunk, Jax's eyes were a dark, piercing navy.

I smiled. "Hi."

He pressed his head into the pillow emphatically. "God, I miss you."

"I miss you too." I rose to my feet and stretched. "I think you've got the right idea. Time to move to the bed."

He raked his teeth over his bottom lip. "Damn, I wish I could get in that bed with you."

I grabbed the candle from the coffee table and padded through the house, turning the lights off as I went. "I know it's hard to get any sleep in that bunk."

"Who said anything about sleeping?" His voice was gravelly and hushed, causing my core to blaze.

My cheeks burned, a side effect of the wine and being in love with Jaxon Slade.

"And what would we be doing if you were here?" I asked with a flirtatious tilt of my head.

"Well, I would start by lighting a few candles," he began. "Ambient lighting is a must."

I brought the candle into the frame. "Check."

His laugh was a low rumble. "Don't tease me."

"Oh okay," I said as I entered my dark bedroom, placing the candle on the dresser. I propped the phone against a picture frame beside it. "So, I take it you don't want me to do this."

I turned and took a couple of steps away from the screen, the soft glow of the candle casting a veil of confidence over me.

"Liv… What are you doing?" he asked as I grabbed the hem of Jax's T-shirt that I wore and slowly pulled it over my head, discarding it on the floor.

"Oh…" he said as I glanced back at him from over my shoulder. "Oh my."

I pulled my hair out of its messy bun and shook it so that it cascaded loose over my shoulders.

"Oh *fuck.*"

"Something wrong?" I turned to face him and raised my brow, thankful for the way the dim light disguised how not cute my bra was. I hadn't planned on giving my handsome boyfriend an impromptu striptease, so I wasn't exactly prepared, nor did I have a clue what I was doing.

"Definitely not," he said, licking his lips.

I curled my lips into a seductive grin, buoyed by his response. "Good." I pushed my leggings over my hips and stepped out of them. Luckily, I'd ditched the Costco panties in favor of a cute pair of boy shorts that morning when I'd gotten dressed.

I picked up the phone and the candle and sauntered over to the bed, placing both on the nightstand. "There. We have our mood lighting." I leaned my head on my hand and adjusted the phone so he had the perfect view of me from my thighs up. "What would you do next?"

His breath shuddered. "I would slip your bra strap over your shoulder…"

I grazed my fingertips along my clavicle, pushing the fabric so that it hung loose on my arm. "Would you kiss me here?" I touched the spot where the strap had been, and he nodded. "How about here?" I brought my fingers to the curve of my breast. "And here?"

"Yes," he said, almost inaudibly.

Goosebumps pebbled my skin as I trailed my fingers along all the places his lips would go. "Then what would you do?"

Watching him watch me made my core tighten and caused a delicious heat to rise through my body.

"I'd take off your bra," he answered, so I slipped one hand behind my back and fiddled with the clasp until it broke free, sending it falling to the mattress. I shifted to my back, taking the phone in my hand and holding it over me, giving him an aerial view.

"Fuck." He brought his clenched fist to his mouth.

The growl in his voice caused the buds of my breasts to perk, and I started to move my fingers along my skin, pretending my hand was his.

"I want you so bad, Liv. You're killing me."

"If you were here, I'd take your shirt off, and rub my hands along your chest." I trailed my fingertips down my stomach, teasing the elastic of my panties.

A flash of dark covered the screen as he ripped off his shirt and settled back on the pillow.

"Then I'd take off your belt and unzip your jeans."

There was movement on the other end that let me know he was following my directives.

"And I would slide those cute fucking boyshorts down your thighs," he murmured, as my fingers hooked in the elastic and pushed them down.

"I would touch the perfect v of your waist," I said. "Then, I would take you in my hand... and I'd move slowly up and down."

He let out a moan, his eyes rolling back slightly. "I... would rub my thumb along your..."

I whimpered as I let my fingers slip into my folds, moving in small circles.

"And then I would slip inside you."

I dipped my fingers inside my warmth and sighed as I slid them along my skin in a rhythmic motion.

"Jax..." His name tumbled off my lips. "I love you."

"I love you too," he said.

We continued to climb higher and higher, sounds of pleasure spilling out of us. Jax covered his mouth to stifle the noise, but I couldn't have stopped myself if I'd wanted to.

I moved my hand faster over my slickness, bringing myself close to the brink, and with one last stroke, I broke free. "Oh God." I arched my back and covered my sensitive skin with my palm as my aftershocks sent shivers racing through my limbs.

"Fuck," he panted. He pressed his head back into the pillow and cried out his release, his eyes rolling back slightly. "That was… the hottest thing… I've ever seen."

"Wow," I said. "That was—"

I stopped mid-sentence when I heard something that sounded like a shower curtain being ripped open.

"Dude, are you oka—" I heard Luca's voice, and saw Jax's face crumple in horror before the screen went black. "*What the fuck!*"

"What the hell are you doing?" Jax hissed.

I gasped, instinctively pulling the sheet over me, even though Jax had dropped the phone, and neither of them could see me. Jax cursed, and I heard the curtain close before he came back into the frame.

"You sounded like a fucking wounded animal, man," Luca whispered loudly. "How was I supposed to know you were in here letting the snake out of the fucking cage?"

"Shit." Jax raked his hand over his face, and I fought the urge to laugh. "What are you even doing back here? Aren't you supposed to be playing poker?"

"I lost," Luca replied.

"Already?" Jax asked.

"Guess you're not the only minute man around here." I could practically hear the smirk on Luca's face.

"I hate you," Jax said, but there was a hint of a smile on his lips. "I really do."

"This never happened," Luca said through the curtain. "I was never here."

"Thank you." Jax shrank into the mattress as though he hoped it might open up and swallow him.

"And, uh, Liv?" Luca's voice was softer this time. "Don't worry. I didn't, uh, see anything except Jax's junk. Okay bye."

Jax cringed into the pillow, and I pulled the sheet up to my chin and sputtered out a laugh. "Better your junk than mine."

TWENTY-SIX

Jax

THE LAST DAYS of the tour were impossibly long. Anytime I wasn't on stage or doing press, all I wanted to do was talk to Liv. Talking to the private investigator hadn't helped my mood, but it did have me thinking more about the future. I'd spent so much of my life being angry that I didn't have someone I belonged to. As disappointed as I was that there was still no information on my mom, I couldn't find room in my heart for anything but happiness for my future with Liv.

A little after dark, Brady dropped me off in front of Liv's house with my suitcases and a dozen tequila sunrise roses, and I could barely contain myself when she ran down the walk to greet me. I dropped my bag as she jumped into my arms, and I was enveloped in a cloud of orange blossoms. I kissed her soundly, wrapping her in my arms. I handed her the bouquet and returned her to her feet. "For my sweet tequila sunrise."

She closed her eyes and breathed in their fragrance, her creamy skin glowing in the night sky.

Liv had cleared out some space in her closet and dresser so I wouldn't be living out of suitcases for the next several weeks. Her house already felt like home, but I knew anywhere with her would feel that way.

We spent our first night back together in her living room working on the song we'd started a couple nights before. Mama jumped on top of the coffee table and watched us. I wondered if she would be annoyed that I'd encroached on her territory again until I saw that she'd drifted off to sleep to the sound of our voices.

"I think we have an amazing song here," Liv said, setting down the guitar so we could take a break. "This one feels extra special for some reason."

"This is your song," I reminded her. "You were the one that started it."

"This is *our* song." She raised her brow at me. "I couldn't have written it without you."

"I think we should sing it for everybody on Thanksgiving and update them on what we've been working on."

"You think so?"

"I do." I nodded. "It's damn near perfect, and I know Cash is chomping at the bit to hear some more of our stuff."

She shrugged. "Sure. We can do that."

I glanced over at Mama who still slept soundly on the table. "You know, I think I'm growing on her."

"You're good at that," Liv whispered, crawling onto my lap and kissing the tip of my nose. "Welcome home, Jax."

Home. My heart felt like it was going to beat out of my chest as I crushed my lips to hers. With Liv, I no longer felt I was missing something. Instead, I felt like I'd found the place my heart belonged. I was finally home.

THE DAYS LEADING UP TO THANKSGIVING FLEW BY. I HELPED Liv at the bakery as much as I could. I watched as she and Katie fulfilled order after order, and I became an expert at boxing up their creations. I never went to the front of the store, though, unless there were no customers. The last thing we wanted was to cause a scene and have paparazzi hanging out.

Dallas got moved into his new place, and he spent the last couple of days before the holiday at the store with us. He helped me box up the cakes, and he even answered the phone from the back when Ella and Liv were busy out front with customers.

"Livvie Cakes Bakery and Cupcakery, this is Dallas speaking," he'd chirped into the phone. "How may I help you?" Katie snorted in the background, bursting into a fit of giggles. He slid next to her and bumped her hip with his. "Yes, ma'am. Like Dallas, Texas. No, it's not too early to place an order for Christmas. What can we do for you?"

After we wrapped up at the store each night, Liv and I worked on new music and resumed our kitchen dance parties as we made dinner. I always picked at least one slow song so I had an excuse to hold her close.

On Thanksgiving, Liv got up early and set to work preparing what we'd need to make the big dinner later. "Okay, I need to make the dressing, the green bean casserole, and the macaroni and cheese. I've got to get the turkey put in the oven in about an hour." She ticked off her mental list, running her hands through her hair. "Ella and Grace are bringing the rolls. I already made the cranberry sauce last night." I sidled up behind her and slid her hair to the side so I could kiss her neck. "I feel like I'm forgetting to do something."

"The dessert," I whispered between kisses.

"That's not it." She waved me off. "We brought that home yesterday, remember?"

"I donut believe that's the dessert I was referring to," I murmured in her ear.

"Oh?" She turned to look up at me, biting her bottom lip. "What dessert were you referring to exactly?"

"The kind where we have dessert for breakfast in bed." I waggled my eyebrows at her.

"I only have a few minutes to make myself look presentable before I have to get the turkey in the oven and get started on this stuff before everyone gets here. And I still have to take a shower."

"As it happens, I need a shower too." I gently pressed her against the kitchen counter. "You ever heard the saying 'two birds one stone?'"

That afternoon, the house was alight with laughter as everyone crowded between the living room and kitchen. Cash was talking to Grace about her school play and answering questions she asked him about his experience in the music business. Luca and Derek were watching a football game on tv while Dallas and Katie chatted animatedly. Antoni and Ella talked circles around each other as they helped me and Liv in the kitchen.

Dinner was perfect, and I could see many Thanksgivings in the future with all of us together much like this one, laughing and telling stories. After dinner, I started a fire in the firepit, and we all moved the party outside with our drinks and Liv's guitar.

"Everything was amazing." Dallas sighed, stretching out on one of the couches between Derek and Katie. "I'm properly stuffed."

"Until ten minutes pass and you're ready for more pie."
Katie poked him in the side.

"Constantly with the food," Luca shook his head as he
warmed his hands by the fire.

"What's with the guitar?" Antoni asked excitedly, taking
his seat on the other side of Liv. "Are we going to have a little
campfire sing-a-long? If so, I request some Backstreet Boys."

"I hope this means what I think it means," Cash spoke up
as Ella and Grace joined him on one of the couches.

"We want to show you guys something we've been
working on and get your thoughts." I cleared my throat as Liv
took the guitar in her hands.

"Oooh," Antoni purred. "A private concert? Yes, please."

Liv looked over at me with bright eyes. "Ready?"

I leaned over and kissed her softly. "Ready."

TWENTY-SEVEN

Liv

"SHUT UP!" Antoni cried, dabbing at the corners of his eyes. "How dare you make me cry on Thanksgiving."

Ella sighed, hugging her knees to her chest. "That was beautiful."

"_So_ romantic," Grace agreed.

"Wow." Cash looked over at us with wide eyes. "That was incredible."

"I think we just heard Jax & Liv's first single." Dallas nodded, settling back into his seat.

"I think so too." Derek took a swig of his beer. "Seriously, that was incredible."

"And I don't want to put a bunch of pressure on you…" Cash trailed off.

"Why do I feel like the next words out of your mouth are going to be nothing but pressure?" I laughed.

Cash chuckled as he stood and paced before us. "Well, I haven't even had the chance to tell you guys yet, but the band has been asked to headline the big New Year's Eve show here in Nashville. The press got wind of Dallas moving here, and I guess that makes the band local enough for them. Anyway, it's a pretty big deal, and it's televised nationally. What if we use that as an opportunity to show the world Jax & Liv for the first time?"

"I'm sorry." I shook my head in disbelief. "It sounds like you're saying we should perform this song on a *national* stage."

"That's exactly what I'm saying," Cash said, stopping in front of me. "It's kind of the perfect opportunity, and nothing gains hype like a big reveal on a national stage. You're a Nashville girl, and the band is at least partially local now, so there would already be major local interest."

"It *is* worth mentioning that this puts your relationship in the public eye." Dallas folded his arms across his chest. "That's something you have to really be ready for."

"I think it's something we can handle." Jax squeezed my hand. "But I don't want to do anything you're not ready for."

I took a deep breath and looked around at the expectant faces around me. Finally, my eyes settled on Jax who gazed back at me with a hopeful expression.

This was a big deal, and Dallas was right. Was this something I was ready for?

I loved Jax, and I knew I saw a future with him in it. I knew there was nobody I would rather do this with than him, but I also wasn't sure I was ready for everything that came along with this choice.

Sensing my hesitation, Ella spoke up. "People are going to love you, Liv, and I think they're going to really respond to your love for each other. It comes across in your music, and people will *feel* it. You guys have a story that deserves to be heard. You're ready for this."

My stomach felt like it was doing backflips as I looked

from Ella to Jax. The way his smile reached his eyes, I knew without even asking that he was ready for this. Finally, I turned my gaze to Cash who was waiting patiently for my answer. "Can I think about it?"

"Sure," he replied. "Take the weekend to think it over. I'll need to let them know so we can start building some hype. That is, if you want to go through with it."

"I'll think about it. We'll talk it over and let you know first thing next week."

This could be a dream come true.

It could be everything I ever wanted, but what if I wasn't good enough? What if Benton Wyatt had been right all along?

"You've been tossing and turning all night. What's going on?" I felt Jax wrap his arms around me, pulling me into him. He gently kissed my shoulder, and I felt myself relax, my entire body melting beneath his touch.

"I've been thinking about this whole thing." I sighed. "You really think we should do this?"

"I do," he said softly.

I rolled over so that I was facing him, his skin veiled by the moonlight that filtered in through the blinds. "You really think we're ready? Not even musically, but our relationship?"

"Liv, I'm ready for anything as long as you're by my side." He tucked a piece of hair behind my ear. "Tell me what's worrying you."

"Bands break up over differences all the time, right?" I asked softly. "What if you start to hate me after working with me for a while?"

"You don't actually think that's a possibility, do you?" He

chuckled and placed a tender kiss on my forehead. "We work well together no matter what we're doing. It's as easy as breathing for us."

"You're right," I admitted, "but do you think it will put too much of a strain on us? I don't want it to have a negative impact on our relationship."

"I think that's where we have to set some boundaries." He traced light circles down my arm. "Work has to stay at work, and we come first. No matter what. If it ever feels like it's causing tension, we take a step back and reevaluate, but I don't think it's going to be like that."

"What if people hate it?" I groaned. "What if they hate *me*? What if people think I'm too old to be doing this? What if I'm not good enough?"

"Is that what *you* really think, or is that a belief someone else put in your head years ago?"

I chewed my lip, lost in thought. He had a good point. I closed my eyes for a moment and imagined what nineteen-year-old Liv would do. I thought about how that Liv felt about herself before other people told her how she *should* feel. That Liv knew what she was capable of. She knew exactly who she was and what she deserved, and I knew what her answer would be. For her, this wouldn't even be a question.

"You really want to do this?" I asked, opening my eyes to look into his.

"I really want to do this," he whispered.

Once again, I didn't think. I let my heart do the talking. "Me too. I think I'm ready to show Jax & Liv to the world."

"Yeah?" His smile stretched across his mouth.

I took his face in my hands, kissing him soundly. "Yeah."

THE DAYS BETWEEN THANKSGIVING AND CHRISTMAS PASSED
in a twinkly lit blur. Jax and I put up our first Christmas tree
together as Mama watched disapprovingly from the sofa. She
quickly forgave us when she realized she could knock all the
ornaments off the tree in the middle of the night, one at a
time. Jax also got to participate when Grace and I had our
holiday baking pajama parties. I loved the tenderness he
showed her as he carefully cut out the dough for our ginger-
bread men. I could tell by the way Ella gazed at them over her
glass of wine that she loved it too.

Things were extra busy at the bakery for the holidays, but
Jax and I still found time to rehearse and work on new material. Cash continued to speed things along, even managing to
set up a mini photoshoot in my backyard on a chilly Sunday
afternoon so I wouldn't have to miss any time at the store.
Cash had done everything he could to make this as easy on
me as possible, and I was grateful. He'd even brought the
final images by the bakery one evening later that week while
Jax was there so we could see them together for the first time.
Grace and the rest of the guys came, and we locked the doors
and had our own mini viewing party, complete with cupcakes
and champagne. Cash set up his laptop on the counter, and we
all crowded around to see the final selections.

My hands flew to my mouth when Cash enlarged the
images on the screen. Through the magic of the editing
process, the photographer had managed to extract us from my
backyard and put us up against the backdrop of a stunning
sunrise. They'd taken my fence and made it look even more
distressed than it was in real life. Then, there we were with
our bodies turned toward one another. Jax looked down at me,
his eyes smoldering, with one hand behind my head as though
he were about to pull me in for a kiss. He had on a simple

white button-up, dark pants, and a tie. I had one hand on his waist as the other pulled him toward me by his tie. I wore a long, silky sleeveless dress with a beaded bodice in the most beautiful shade of peach. Between the hair and makeup team and the miracle that was photoshop, I looked almost ethereal as I gave the camera a coquettish stare. 'Jax & Liv' had been inscribed above our heads in a beautiful script. Ella and Grace shrieked with delight, pulling me and Jax into a series of hugs while the guys whooped and hollered.

Jax hadn't been able to spend as much time at the bakery as usual because he, along with the rest of the guys and Cash, had been taking meetings with various record labels who were all in something of a bidding war for who would get to work with Midnight in Dallas. Several labels were interested, and the guys would soon be faced with a pretty big decision as to what label they would ultimately go with. Their current label had stepped up their offerings, should they choose to resign with them, making it an even tougher choice.

One weekend, Jax paid for us to go into the studio, and with the help of the rest of the guys, we recorded the song we would be playing for the New Year's Eve special. Cash had everything prepared for the song to be released to the masses at midnight on January 1st. He felt certain that after the world heard our song, Midnight in Dallas wouldn't be the only ones the record labels were fighting over.

Cash was already in talks with a couple of directors about a music video for our song, and everything was moving at warped speed. I was both terrified and thrilled by the fact that when the clock struck midnight on New Year's Eve, my life would never be the same.

By the time Christmas Eve rolled around, I was thankful for a couple days of rest. Ella and Grace were spending time with Ella's mom, and the guys had other plans, which left me and Jax alone for our first Christmas together. We watched movies, lazed about in bed, drank wine, and savored every second together.

On Christmas Day, we snuggled on the couch by the light of the Christmas tree, never even making it out of our pajamas. We exchanged gifts and reveled in the luxuriousness of having nowhere to be but with each other. We were slow-dancing in the kitchen, waiting for our lasagna to bake, when I found myself overcome with gratitude for the beautiful man in front of me.

"I have something for you," he whispered in my ear as he held me in his arms. We stopped swaying, and he pulled a small wrapped box out of his back pocket.

I smiled up at him. "But you've given me so much already."

"Open it," he urged.

I gingerly unwrapped the small package revealing a black velvet box. I gently pried it open to find a beautiful, dainty rose-gold necklace with a shining round disc pendant. 'Liv' had been inscribed on the front in the same beautiful font from the images Cash had shown us.

"It's beautiful, Jax." He took the box from my hands, carefully extracting the necklace and unfastening the clasp. He moved behind me as I swept my hair to one side so that he could secure the chain around my neck. Once he'd done so, he turned me to face him, and I glanced down to see my name shimmering up at me.

"Liv, you mean everything to me. You're so special, and I've had the distinct honor of having you to myself these last several weeks. Now, it's time for the whole world to see how amazing you are, and I have no doubt they're going to love you too." He slid his finger beneath the charm, lightly caressing the surface with his thumb. "I want you to share with the world who Liv is, but this part I want you to keep close to your heart." With that, he flipped the tiny disc over to reveal 'Jax' inscribed in the same script on the other side.

"Jax," I clutched the pendant gently against my chest, and tears filled my eyes. "I love you." I threw my arms around his neck, pulling him down to me so I could kiss his perfect mouth. "I love you so much."

He placed a gentle kiss on my forehead, and I'd never felt more safe or loved. "I love you, Liv."

TWENTY-EIGHT

Jax

NEW YEAR'S EVE ARRIVED, and the energy of Nashville was electric. It was a cold but clear day, and fans had already started lining the streets early in the morning in anticipation of the evening's festivities. Liv had been a bundle of nerves most of the day until she finally set off with Ella, Grace, Katie, and Antoni for an afternoon of getting glammed-up for the show.

Brady and the guys picked me up from Liv's house, and we traveled downtown for all of the press Cash had lined up before the big show. We stopped by the bakery for a box of treats on the way because Dallas had a craving for cupcakes. Cash had masterfully leaked information about Jax & Liv in the days leading up to the show, and the media was in a frenzy. Social media was buzzing with #Jax&Liv and #Who-IsLiv. We teased the unveiling of the new project during our interviews, but the world wouldn't get a look at us until we finally took the stage together in front of millions of people, live on national television just before midnight.

People had started to piece together that Liv was most likely the woman I'd been photographed with at the

Halloween party in Las Vegas, and the internet had been trying desperately to identify her. There were rumors about it being some up-and-coming pop star and even a famous actress. Of course, no one had even gotten close to the real thing.

Cash had also lined up a meeting with another record label executive, some guy who was anxious to meet us and throw his hat in the ring. According to Cash, the guy was adamant he could offer us something none of the other labels could, so he'd agreed to let him have his fifteen minutes after we finished up with press for the day.

After we wrapped up, we were sitting in our trailer relaxing for a moment when there was a knock on the door.

"Come in," Cash called. The door opened to reveal a dark-haired guy in a smart-looking suit. "You must be from 6th & 15th Records. I'm Cash Montgomery, and this is the band. That's Dallas, Derek, Luca, and Jaxon." He pointed to each of us, and we gave a nod of acknowledgment.

"I'm the *owner* of 6th & 15th," he said. "The name is Benton Wyatt. It's a pleasure to meet you, gentlemen."

"Nice to meet you, Benton. Please have a seat." Cash gestured to the vacant lounge chair beside me. "I hear you have quite the proposal for us."

"Jaxon." Benton said my name like he was trying it on, completely ignoring Cash's question. "I heard you have a new project you're launching tonight."

I smiled. "I do, with my girlfriend Liv."

"Is that right?" Benton wore a look of amusement on his face.

"Would you like a cupcake, Benton?" Dallas asked as he opened the Tiffany Blue box on the small coffee table, grabbing one for himself.

Benton's eyes lingered on the box, and though he looked like he was practically salivating, he declined. "No, thank you."

"Liv is an amazing baker. She owns Livvie Cakes Bakery and Cupcakery," Dallas gushed, taking a bite of his cupcake. I shot him an annoyed glance. "What? The cat will be out of the bag soon anyway. You can keep a secret for the next couple of hours, can't you, Benton?"

"Of course I can." Benton nodded, eyeing me. "It sounds like you'll be looking for another contract soon."

"We will, but we're taking it one step at a time," I said.

Benton looked like he wanted to say something else, but Cash spoke up before he could. "If memory serves me correctly, 6th & 15th houses strictly country artists right now." Cash folded his arms and leaned back in his chair. "Why the interest in Midnight in Dallas?"

"It's simple really," Benton replied, shifting his focus to Cash. "I'm looking to expand the brand. Nashville is growing, gentlemen. It's not all country music anymore, as I'm sure you know. I want 6th & 15th to represent a more diverse roster."

"Starting with Midnight in Dallas?" Derek asked curiously.

"That's right," Benton agreed.

Luca eyed Benton suspiciously. "Okay, but why us?"

"You guys are one of the hottest acts on the scene." Benton leaned forward, his attention back on me. "I want to be part of your evolution, and I think Nashville is the perfect home for your band."

"As I'm sure you can imagine, we're fielding a lot of interest," Cash said. "What can you give us that no other label can?"

"How does a ten million dollar sign-on bonus sound?" Benton asked casually, settling back into his chair.

"It sounds not real," Dallas commented, taking another bite of his cupcake.

Derek laughed. "It sounds like sign me the hell up."

"That's what I like to hear,' Benton said with a nod, glancing over at me. "If I can also secure your side project, I think we could make that number go up."

"How much?" Luca asked.

"Significantly." Benton's gaze settled back on me. "But I move fast."

"I think I could move fast for ten million," Derek joked.

"We don't move quite that fast." Cash's eyes flickered over to me. This was going unlike any other label meeting we'd had. Benton had barely acknowledged the rest of the guys, focusing most of his attention on me.

"We definitely don't." Dallas shot Benton a look.

"And I won't even consider a label for Jax & Liv without Liv present," I added firmly.

"When will she be here?" Benton countered, a challenging look in his eye. "I'd love to meet her. I could stick around."

My fists clenched involuntarily, and I folded my arms across my chest, determined not to let this big-shot asshole get under my skin. "We can set up another time to talk, but Liv and I won't be making any decisions tonight."

"In fact, we should probably let you get on with your evening so the guys can get focused for the show tonight." Cash said, moving to open the door. "If we're interested, we'll make sure to give you a call."

"Hmmm." Benton nodded and rose to his feet, handing me a business card. "Well, that's a shame. Here's my card in case you should change your mind."

"We won't," I said under my breath.

"Thanks for stopping by." Dallas made a face as Benton straightened his tie and exited the bus without so much as a backward glance. "What the fuck was that about?"

"I don't know." Cash returned to his chair. "I think we can all agree we won't be calling him back. We don't work with assholes."

Dallas snorted, a smirk tugging at the corners of his mouth. "We work with Luca."

"That's fair." Luca shrugged.

"What was his deal with you?" Dallas asked, turning toward me. "He seemed zeroed in on you the whole time. It was weird."

"Tell me about it." I looked down at the sleek black business card in my hands with the gold typeface.

"Don't worry about that jerk," Cash said dismissively with a wave of his hand. "The Benton Wyatts of the world are a dime a dozen. I just got a text from Antoni. He and the girls are on their way over. It's time for you guys to get ready for the show."

"Showtime!" Dallas clapped his hands together. "I call dibs on the bathroom." He disappeared to the far end of the trailer.

"Dallas needs to do his hair," Luca teased, propping his feet up on the table. "Good thing some of us woke up like this." He gestured across his body.

I chuckled softly, my eyes still focused on the business card, when I felt Cash's hand on my shoulder. "Forget about it. Tonight is about you and Liv. Here, let me file that away for you." With that, he took the card out of my hands and threw it in the garbage.

"Cash, why don't you start your own label?" I asked,

attempting to put Benton Wyatt out of my mind. "You know more about the business than all of these jokers combined."

"I'd be lying if I said I hadn't thought about it." Cash scratched the back of his neck. "Carrie was always telling me I should. She loved the idea of us having our own business and growing it together. I thought about it a lot before Carrie passed, but since then I... I don't know."

"It's never too late," Derek said, "and you know we'd help you."

"Fuck yeah, we would," Luca added.

"I think it's still worth considering." I nodded at Cash. "I think she'd want you to carry on."

Cash's face grew pensive as he looked over me. Before he could say anything else, Dallas bounded down the hall and struck a pose. "How do I look?"

"Literally the same." Luca snorted, and we all dissolved into laughter, except for Cash who was lost in thought.

TWENTY-NINE

Liv

My stomach twisted with nerves as we pulled up to the venue. Even from inside the SUV, the sound of the crowd was deafening. I'd watched the New Year's Eve celebration from the couch for several years with Ella and Grace, but I'd never imagined performing there.

This didn't seem possible, even in my wildest dreams. Yet here I was about to perform in front of the masses with the man I loved and everyone who mattered most to me by my side.

After receiving the Cinderella treatment from the stylists, I looked like a woman who performed for millions, but on the inside my blood had run ice cold. I was shivering with fear. What if I choked? What if I got on that stage and couldn't sing a single note?

Grace grabbed my hand as Antoni pulled the car to a stop. "You've got this, Aunt Liv."

"I feel like I'm going to puke," I admitted.

"Hot damn, no ma'am!" Antoni interjected. "There will be no hurling in that gorgeous dress or in my car."

"You look amazing, Liv!" Katie exclaimed, turning to face me from the passenger seat.

"Look at me." Ella gently grabbed my face between her hands. "You are brilliant, and you are beautiful."

"And you are *fierce.*" Antoni reached his hand back, placing it on my knee.

I took a deep breath, my entire body trembling.

"You can do this," Ella assured me. "Now, let's get you in there to see Jax."

Ella and Grace guided me out of the car, and I somehow made it inside the trailer. I felt like I was floating overhead, watching everything unfold beneath me.

I entered to the unanimous approval of the guys as they got a look at my transformation. Every hair on my head, plus some clip-in extensions, had been styled into glamorous loose waves. The makeup artist had my skin looking glowy and my eyes sparkly, framed by thick lashes. My eyes popped against the fabric of the floor-length emerald gown I wore that hugged me in all the right places. It draped off my shoulders and came up in a sexy high slit, shimmering anytime the light hit it.

"Wow," Jax said, pulling me into his arms. "You're breathtaking, Liv."

I laughed nervously. "Scared out of my mind is more like it."

"You're going to be perfect." He kissed me on the forehead. "I promise."

"Guys, it's almost time. The golf carts will be here in a moment to take us up to the staging area," Cash announced. "You look fantastic, Liv. You all do." His gaze flickered from me to the guys who were wearing some rocked-out suits and then settled on Ella and Grace who were decked out in their own sparkly dresses.

My eyes widened as I looked back at Jax. He enveloped me in his arms one more time and placed a tender kiss on my lips. "After the band's set, I'll be announcing us, and you come on out just like we rehearsed. Donut worry, okay? I got you a little something to help make today extra special. I didn't have time to wrap it, though." He quickly reached beside the sofa where a guitar case was standing upright.

"Are you serious?" I asked in disbelief.

"Open it," he urged. I took the case from him, laying it gently on the floor so that I could prop it open. I gasped as I peered inside at the gorgeous Gibson Hummingbird Acoustic-Electric guitar in a rich shade of mahogany. "Pick it up." He watched me excitedly as I gingerly picked up the guitar by the neck. "I already got it all tuned up for you."

The light flickered across the sides of the instrument, drawing my attention to an intricate etching along its neck. Tears welled in my eyes as I realized he'd had 'Sweet Tequila Sunrise' engraved on it in a shimmering gold script. "Jax... it's beautiful."

"I love you," he whispered.

"I love you too." I kissed him tenderly, breathing in his comforting scent.

"Alright, everyone." Cash clapped his hands together. "They're here. It's showtime."

"Are you ready?" Jax asked, his stormy eyes filled with admiration.

With one last kiss, I took his hand in mine. "Ready."

I watched Midnight in Dallas from the side of the stage with Ella and Grace at my side. The band's energy was explosive, and the sea of people practically roared around them. Antoni talked animatedly with Cash and Katie while Brady kept watch nearby. The further the guys got into their set, the more anxious I became.

My hands trembled as I gazed out into the seemingly endless crowd. A crowd that loved Midnight in Dallas, but would they love *me*? Doubt rose like bile in the back of my throat, hot and acidic, threatening to eat away at any shred of confidence I'd built up. My mouth went dry, and my entire body shivered as the opening notes of "Fortress," the last song of their set, began to play.

"What if I mess this up?" I turned to Ella, my eyes huge with worry.

"You won't," she assured me, wrapping an arm around my shoulders.

"How do you know?"

"Because you were always meant to be here, Liv." She leaned her head against mine. "You're going to go out there and slay the shit out of that song."

"You really think so?" I asked, curling my arm around her.

"You were made for this, Olivia." Tears formed in Ella's eyes, and her voice wavered slightly. "I've known it since we were nineteen, and you used to sneak me in to watch you play at the honky-tonks. I knew this moment would happen one day, but you had to believe it too, babe. You were always meant to be here, and I'm going to be right by your side every step of the way. Always have been, always will be."

"Are you ready, Liv?" Cash asked, placing a hand on my shoulder. I could hear the band drawing to a close. "You're almost up."

"Damn right she's ready," Ella spoke for me, and I nodded wrapping her in a hug. "She was born ready."

"I feel like we need a group hug up in this bitch!" Antoni pulled me and Ella into his embrace as Grace, Cash, and Katie piled in. "You're gonna kill it, honey."

Cash smiled. "Let's get you plugged in."

Luca and Derek exited the stage, each giving me a hug as Jax's voice filled the air.

"As you all know, tonight is a special night. New Year's Eve has always been known for new beginnings, and tonight is a big one for me. I'm about to bring someone out that's very important to me. She's kind of my whole world. With the help of Dallas on the drums, I want to show you something dear to me that I've been working on. Tonight, I want to introduce all of you to Jax & Liv." The crowd's screams were ear-piercing as Jax's grin flickered over to where I stood off-stage. "Please join me in giving a warm welcome to the other half of Jax & Liv, Nashville's own, Olivia Sinclair!"

With one last deep breath, I stepped out to the roar of deafening cheers and applause and waved to the crowd. I was afraid my knees might buckle beneath me as I crossed the stage to the mic stationed beside Jax, my dress billowing behind me. He reached for my hand, and as I looked into his eyes, I felt my worries begin to melt away.

"How are y'all doing tonight?" I asked the crowd, my voice shaking slightly. Their response thundered all around me. I gulped in a shallow breath as their uproarious excitement continued, their energy bolstering my spirit. I looked over at Jax who gave my hand an encouraging squeeze. "I'm Liv, and you already know this beautiful man beside me, Mr. Jaxon Slade, and together we are Jax & Liv!" My voice continued to tremble, but the audience didn't seem to notice as they erupted into a frenzy. Behind us, the giant screen in the middle of the stage illuminated with one of the finalized photos we'd seen at the store a few nights before. Our names were emblazoned at the top in our signature swirly script. To our left and right sides were two other jumbo-sized screens that showed us in real-time. I felt tears threatening to form behind my eyes as a flurry of emotions coursed through me. "We want to thank you for being a part of this special moment with us, and I truly can't imagine having our debut anywhere but this magical city I've called home all my life."

"Now, I get to call it home too." Jax grinned over at me. "The song we're going to sing for you tonight is all about what it means to be home. Sometimes home isn't a place. It's a someone."

"And sometimes that someone comes along when we least expect it," I said as Dallas counted us off, and with quivering hands, I began to strum the melody to the sound of the blaring approval of the crowd. I closed my eyes, desperately trying to center myself so I wouldn't mess this up.

"This song is called 'Sweet Tequila Sunrise,'" Jax said, "and it'll be available for download at midnight tonight."

"We hope you enjoy it." I looked over at Jax, and suddenly, it was just the two of us. In my mind, we were back in my living room with an open bottle of wine and the soft glow of a candle dancing across our faces.

"*Rain taps on the window, and baby, I don't want to go. I'd been living my life a lost boy, but in your arms, I'm home,*" Jax sang as he gazed over at me. Our voices intertwined in sweet harmony as we reached the chorus.

"*I thought home was a place, till I found you. Getting drunk by candlelight, with a hell of a view. I found home looking in your eyes. My love, my life, in your sweet tequila sunrise."*

Jax and I stumbled through the front door sometime after 3 a.m. when Brady dropped us off at my house. We plopped the guitars down in the foyer with two loud thuds.

After the show, there were several reporters waiting to talk to us about the single, and then we all spent the rest of the night celebrating back at Dallas' new place. The champagne was flowing, and it felt so good to have all us all together again.

Our single had broken into the Top Five on iTunes within ten minutes of being released and reached number one within the hour. The performance had gone beautifully, and I practically floated off stage to the sounds of the cheering crowd. From the show and the interviews to our single making it onto the charts, the entire night still felt unreal, but nothing felt as unreal as the perfect man beside me.

I giggled while Jax kissed my neck as I fiddled with the lock, bolting it shut. Mama meowed her distaste at us from down the hall for rolling in at this ungodly hour.

"I've been waiting to get you alone all night," Jax whispered between kisses, pressing me lightly against the door. Finally, he pulled back slightly so that he could take me in with his eyes. "You were amazing tonight, Liv."

"*We* were," I reminded him, placing a tender kiss on his lips. "I'm not going to lie, I was scared out of my mind when I first walked out on that stage."

"No one would have ever known." He slid his hands around my waist, pulling me closer. "You were right at home." The butterflies whirled around in my stomach like they had the first night we met. "What's going on in that beautiful mind of yours?"

"Everything. The last three months. Tonight. You. You're more than I could have ever hoped for. This all feels like a dream." I smoothed my hands over his chest and around his neck. "A dream I never want to wake up from."

"I've felt like that a lot these last few weeks," he said softly, "but you're better than any dream I ever had for myself. Besides, if this was a dream, could you feel this?" His voice was low and sultry as he leaned in so close that his lips grazed mine. "Or this?" He kissed his way down to my collarbone, and my skin felt like it was on fire everywhere his lips touched.

I slid my hands beneath his shirt, trailing my fingertips along his firm chest. I traced along his v lines and slipped my fingers into his belt loops, tugging him closer. His hands traveled slowly up my body, tangling in my hair as he kissed me deeply. Breathless, we finally broke apart, and he leaned his head against mine. I pressed one last kiss to his lips before I moved past him down the hall toward the bedroom.

I heard his seductive voice call after me. "Turn around." Slowly, I turned to face him, a soft smile playing on my lips. "Damn, I'm the luckiest guy in the world." He closed the distance between us, crashing his lips to mine, and we tore at each other's clothes to the soundtrack of Mama knocking the ornaments off the tree one by one.

JAX AND I SPENT NEW YEAR'S DAY BASKING IN THE afterglow of the show the night before. The internet was going crazy for Jax & Liv. Meanwhile, Cash was already fielding requests from record labels and media outlets left and right. We took this last opportunity to shut out the rest of the world and enjoy the last little bit of calm before the year started off in a full-blown storm of press, recording, label meetings, and so many more things I had yet to wrap my mind around. I still had a few things to finish up at the bakery before I could fully dive into the world of Jax & Liv, but decided they could wait one more day. Instead of thinking for one second about work, we snuggled the day away on the couch under Mama's contented gaze.

Jax wasn't in bed when I woke the next morning. I stretched leisurely as the light bathed me in a soft golden glow, figuring he would be returning with coffee soon. I mentally started running down the list of things I needed to finish at the shop, both excited and nervous about the prospect of taking some extended time away.

While I waited, I fumbled my hand over the nightstand to retrieve my phone off the charger.

I rubbed my eyes as I illuminated the screen. My heart immediately plummeted to my stomach when I saw seventeen missed calls, the majority of them from Ella, and twice as many unread text messages. My social media notifications were in the thousands. I slid my finger across the screen to access my messages, but before I could, Ella's name flashed with an incoming call.

"Ella, are you okay?" I answered, my voice panicked.

"Oh, thank God." Ella sighed into the phone. "Liv, don't come to the store. Katie and I have this under control. We've already called the police on these damn paparazzi assholes, but right now it's a freaking zoo."

"What?" I gasped. "What are you talking about?" Suddenly, the line went quiet. "Ella, what is going on?"

"You haven't seen it yet?" Her voice was soft with concern.

"Seen what?" I asked, my mind confused and severely under-caffeinated.

"Liv, whatever you do, don't look at the news. Don't get on social media, and don't turn on the tv. I'm begging you. Please don't. Just wait a few minutes, and I'll be there," she pleaded.

"What?" I asked, my blood turning to ice. I pulled the phone away from my ear, flicked it to speaker and immediately pulled up my newsfeed.

"Liv, *please,* " Ella begged. "Please don't."

My mouth went dry, and beads of cold sweat started to form over my entire body as I was assaulted by headline after headline:

Jaxon Slade debuts new project with middle-aged divorcée.

Why Jaxon Slade's cougar mystery woman wanted to remain a secret.

Failing bakery owner, Olivia Sinclair, latches on to Midnight in Dallas Frontman, Jaxon Slade.

Benton Wyatt's gold-digger ex-wife, Liv Sinclair, and her boy toy mid-life crisis.

My eyes flickered over the articles as phrases jumped out, slapping me hard across the face:

Washed up, wannabe country singer

Liv Sinclair's plan to save her failing business, with the help of Jaxon Slade

Benton Wyatt's barren ex-wife, Olivia Sinclair

"Oh my God," I whispered. My eyes traveled down to the comments section:

She hasn't even been divorced long. Bet she cheated on her ex to further her career.

Yuck. This woman needs a plastic surgeon. She looks OLD.

Ugh. I hate women like that. Opportunistic bitch. Jaxon deserves better. Like me. LOL

Let's say for a second they ARE in love, which I doubt. But I know I saw an interview recently where Jaxon Slade said he wants kids. Has she not thought about this?

I felt bile rising to my throat, and I choked out a sob.

"Fuck," Ella said quietly. "Liv, are you okay? Where is Jax?"

I looked up, and Jax had appeared in the doorway, his eyes red-rimmed and filled with concern. "I'm right here, Ella."

THIRTY

Jax

"LIV, WE WILL FIGURE THIS OUT," I said, my chest tightening with fear.

She shook her head vehemently. "No, we won't. Don't you see? There *is* no figuring it out for me. I have to try to salvage what's left of my life."

"Liv, I know who did this," I admitted through gritted teeth. "That asshole ex of yours came to see us the night of the show. He's trying to break us up."

"What?" Shock washed over her face. "Why didn't you tell me?"

"I didn't know it was him until I saw this shit today," I explained. "He booked a meeting with us, but the entire time he was focused on me and what was happening with Jax & Liv. Now I know he was clearly up to something. He must have gone to the press to get to you."

"That can't be," she cried. "He's not the best guy, but he wouldn't do that. At least, I don't think he would." She buried her face in her hands, and I wrapped my arms around her. She let herself relax for a moment before prying herself from my grasp. "I can't believe this is happening."

"Liv, we will get through this." I rubbed the back of my neck, feeling a cold sweat begin to form.

"No," she spat. "*You* will get through this, Jax. It isn't *your* life that's been completely turned upside down."

She might as well have slapped me across the face for as much as her words stung. "You *are* my life. If your life is turned upside down, so is mine."

"I was crazy to think this could ever work." She rose to her feet and started pacing the floor beside the bed. "I don't know what I was thinking."

"Baby, we will get past this," I insisted, and she whirled on me.

"We can't," she sobbed. "You don't understand, Jax."

"Then *help* me understand."

"I can't just exist in someone else's shadow again, okay? I lived in Ben's shadow, and now here I am in yours." She paused her pacing long enough to gaze at me wistfully. "Nobody cares how I got here. All they see is me latching onto your coattail."

"That's not how it happened."

"Don't you see? It doesn't matter." She threw her hands up. "People don't give a shit what the truth is."

I stood, grabbing her arms though holding on to her would prevent her from slipping away from me. "I'll put my music on hold. I'll quit altogether. You could be a solo artist. I'll quit the band if I have to. Whatever I have to do, Liv. I'll do it. I'm not losing you. None of it matters without you."

She looked up at me with sad eyes. "If you did that you'd be no better than me, and if I *let* you, I'd be no better than

Benton. Music is a part of you, Jax. It's in your soul. You can't stop. I won't let you."

"So, you want to quit?" I steeled myself, the tears in my eyes causing her to look out of focus. "You want to just give up? Liv, I love you. I can't let you go. I won't."

"I can't allow my identity to be swallowed up by another man," she said softly.

"Is that all I am to you?" My heart twisted, and I felt as though the wind had been knocked right out of me. "Some other man?"

"No." She shook her head vehemently. "I love you, Jax, but sometimes love isn't enough."

"Not enough? Liv, it's everything."

"I used to believe that," she admitted. "Love is enough until it isn't. You think it's enough right now because maybe *right now* it is. But what happens when this starts to affect *your* career? The *band's* career? What happens when you realize you want a child of your own, Jax? You say adoption will be enough for you, but what if it isn't? What if you realize it isn't enough for you?"

"Liv, I—"

"I fought too hard to get here, Jax." Her voice sounded small and defeated. "To have what semblance of a life I have on my own with the bakery."

"The bakery isn't your passion, Liv!" I shouted. "It isn't even what you want to be doing!"

"But it's *mine*," she countered. "Maybe it isn't what I most wanted to do in life, but it belongs to me, and nobody but Ella and I made it what it is. Now, that's being threatened. That's been my livelihood, and it's the livelihood of a lot of other people too, people who count on me. I can't... I can't do this, Jax. It's too much."

"You don't mean that. You don't." I clenched my fists at my sides, digging the tips of my fingers into my palms. I'd have taken a punch to the face or a kick in the stomach, anything to distract from the pain that settled into my chest. "You're scared. Somehow you *still* think you're not good enough. You still think you don't deserve to be loved."

"I'm so sorry." She pulled herself from my grasp, and I felt her warmth leave me all at once. Her mouth fell into a hard line as she crossed her arms protectively over her body.

"Please," I begged. "Don't do this. I love you."

"I know," she whispered, walking past me toward the bedroom door.

"Turn around." I was pleading, desperate for any last shred of connection with her. She paused in the door frame but didn't turn. "Liv, please. Turn around."

She braced herself against the door frame, but still didn't face me. "I'm going for a drive, Jax. When I get back I need you to not be here." She started down the hall, and I went after her.

"Please turn around." My voice and my heart broke. "That's all you have to do. Turn around, and we can fix this." By the time I caught up to her, she'd grabbed her purse and keys. She had one hand on the door, and I had one hand on her. "Please, Liv. I love you."

"If you love me, you'll be gone when I get back." She didn't look back as she sprinted down the walk—the same walkway where she'd jumped into my arms many times before. I watched as she jumped in her Jeep, and in seconds, she was gone. I closed the front door, and it felt like the walls were caving in as I slid to the floor.

Liv, the only home I'd ever known, was gone.

I FINISHED PACKING MY THINGS IN A FOG OF DESPAIR. MY stomach felt sick when I realized I was about to leave Liv's for the last time.

Every moment leading up to this one replayed in my head, an excruciatingly painful montage of everything I'd lost in a matter of moments. I folded her Aerosmith shirt and held it for a moment, picturing how she'd looked the day she'd given it to me... how beautiful she'd looked, even soaked from the rain.

I laid the folded shirt on the bed and dug her house key out of my pocket, laying it on top of the shirt. I took one last look around before rolling my suitcase into the foyer, placing it beside the large duffle I'd already set there. Mama watched with curious eyes from her spot on top of the couch. I moved to sit on the sofa, and she perked up, unsure what to think about my emotional display. I had about five minutes left until Dallas would arrive to get me. I hadn't even told him what was happening yet. I couldn't bring myself to say the words. That would make it feel too real.

I closed my eyes a moment and took in her orange blossom scent one more time.

When I opened my eyes, I found that Mama had inched closer to me, her golden eyes gazing at me intently.

"I know you didn't like me much, Mama," I said to her, "but I guess I came to love you and your ornery ways. I need you to look after Liv, okay? I love her so much, Mama. She's my whole world, and I don't know what I'm supposed to do. I don't know how I'm supposed to live without her." Mama tilted her head as though she was considering what I was saying. I dropped my head into my hands, my shoulders shaking.

I felt a soft thud beside me followed by the touch of a tentative paw on my leg. I looked up to see Mama's knowing eyes searching mine. I reached my hand out to her, and for the first time, she didn't run. She didn't flinch. Instead, she leaned her face into my hand, rubbing against my fingers.

I stroked my hand down her back softly, and without warning, she put her front paws on my arm and reached up to nudge my face with hers.

"I'm gonna miss you too," I whispered. She purred her reply as my phone pinged with a text signaling that Dallas was here. The pit in my stomach grew because I knew that meant it was time for me to leave. I placed a soft kiss on Mama's head. "Take care of her, Mama."

I stood, and Mama watched as I gathered my bags and gulped back a deep breath. I opened the door, turning the bottom lock. With one last look inside, I closed the door, leaving behind everything that mattered most to me in the world.

THIRTY-ONE

Liv

I PULLED into the driveway of my bungalow and cut the engine of the Jeep, gripping the steering wheel until my knuckles turned white. Part of me hoped he hadn't listened to a word I said. That I would walk into the house and he'd be there, but I knew that wasn't what was best—for me or for him.

I caught a glimpse of my reflection in the rearview mirror, my eyes swollen and red from crying. I'd only driven down to the park a few blocks away from my house because I could hardly see through my tears. I'd sat there for the better part of two hours. Ella called, and I was so hysterical I could barely tell her what happened. She wanted to come to me, but I needed to be alone.

Part of me wanted to get Benton Wyatt on the phone and call him every name under the sun, but I knew that wouldn't help. I couldn't believe he would do this to me. He'd moved on with Jessica Rabbit. Why did he get off on ruining my life and hurting me?

The more I thought about it, the more I realized it didn't matter. If it hadn't been Ben, it would have been someone else. Journalists dig up dirt on people all the time. I'd been living on borrowed time, and I knew it.

Jax made me feel things I'd never felt before. I was more alive in his presence than I had been for nearly two decades, and that caused me to stop thinking clearly. My past was like a grenade, and now that it had exploded all over the internet, all I could do was try to minimize the fallout.

The last thing I wanted was to ruin Jax's career, but if I'd stuck around that's exactly what would have happened. People would stop looking at him for his talent and start remembering him as the guy who took on the middle-aged charity case. Anything that reflected badly on Jax also had the potential to affect Dallas, Luca, Derek, and even Cash and Antoni.

Then, there was the bakery. There was Ella, Grace, Katie, and everyone employed by Livvie Cakes. My name had been something I'd grown to be proud of, but now it tarnished the entire business.

I spent so long trying to find even the tiniest amount of happiness in my life, any shred of normalcy. I'd been trying to find my footing now that I no longer resided in Ben's shadow, only to find myself in Jax's. I could have been happy there, but not at the cost of everything else. Not at the expense of Jax's success and happiness. I knew he was devastated. Knowing how much I hurt him crushed me, but I knew that in the long run, I was doing him a favor. He would meet someone else. Someone who didn't complicate his life. Someone who could give him everything he ever wanted and everything he deserved. He would fall in love again, and he would be happy.

Sometimes love just wasn't enough. I was selfish to have held onto Jax as long as I did, but dammit, being loved by him felt so good.

Tears streamed down my face as I heard Jax's voice in my mind.

Turn around.

I couldn't turn around because if I had, my resolve would have broken. I'd have run back into his arms, and where would that have gotten us?

Jax would have settled for a barren, middle-aged mess of a woman who would have undoubtedly ruined his entire life. I would have been the selfish bitch who placed her own happiness above so many others' wellbeing. It was better for everyone if I disappeared from sight for a while. I'd let the media circus die down, and then I'd go back to my quiet existence. It wasn't a bad life. I had Ella, Grace, and Katie. And Mama, of course. I'd be happy.

Well, happy enough.

The thought of going inside that empty house made my stomach churn. I contemplated grabbing Mama and burning the entire place to the ground. Every corner of that house was now littered with memories of Jax, but the last thing I needed was the paparazzi showing up because I'd gone nuts. Besides, no matter how painful it would be to see Jax everywhere, I couldn't imagine *not* seeing him everywhere.

With trembling hands, I gathered my keys and purse and made the short trek to the front door. Before I'd even reached the porch, I heard a yowling noise that sounded like an injured animal, crying out in pain. I paused a moment and looked around, trying to discern where it was coming from, only to realize it was coming from inside the house.

I shoved the key in the lock and sprinted inside to find

Mama howling on the other side. "Mama!" I tossed my bag and keys on the floor as I crouched down to her. She paced wildly in front of me, meowing frantically as I inspected her. There was no blood. She was moving freely and nothing appeared to be broken. "Mama, what is it?" Jax's guitar was gone from the foyer, leaving mine looking lonely.

She wove her little body between my feet as I stood. I looked over at the Christmas tree. Surprisingly, all of the ornaments were still intact. My old guitar was leaned against the wall near the sofa as though it were waiting for me and Jax to return to our living room writing sanctuary. I went to the kitchen to make sure she had food and water, careful to avoid stepping on her as she tried her best to entangle herself in my feet with each step I took. I looked down to see her bowls completely full, untouched even. "What's going on, girl?" She continued her yowling as my feet carried me unwillingly to the bedroom.

I had to see it. I had to see for myself that he was gone. Better still, I *deserved* to see it.

Mama trailed my every move, her paws inches from my feet as we passed through the door. The bed was made as though we hadn't been laying together just hours before, blissfully unaware that our world was imploding while we slept.

My eyes immediately settled on the foot of the bed. The Aerosmith shirt I had given him was folded neatly on the comforter with my house key laying on top.

There was no note, though it wasn't like there was anything left to say. I'd broken his heart right here in this room only a couple of hours before. I picked up the shirt and clutched it to my chest, causing the key to fall onto the bed.

I brought the soft cotton to my nose and breathed it in. It

still smelled like him. His scent had been ingrained in the fibers of the fabric, and that was all it took to bring me to my knees. I collapsed on the floor beside a yowling Mama, sobbing with the shirt clutched to my chest.

I almost wished the universe had never put him in my path. That I'd gone on unaware love like the kind Jax showed me existed. I almost wished I never knew what it felt like to be held by him. To be loved by him.

Almost.

Mama's yowling subsided, and much to my surprise, she crawled onto my lap. She gently climbed her two front paws onto my chest, pressing her tiny head to mine. "Mama..." I brought my hand to her back, stroking her soft fur. She pulled her face away from mine and peered up at me. "You miss him too, don't you?" She nudged my chin with her head, her unspoken answer. She curled up in my lap, and I felt the soft vibration of her purr on my legs. "I miss him too, Mama. I miss him so much."

I didn't know how I was ever going to be okay again without Jax.

All I knew was, I had to be.

Somehow, I had to be.

I don't even know how long I'd been sitting there when I heard the front door slam shut.

"Liv!" Ella called frantically, but I was weeping so hard I couldn't answer her.

"Aunt Liv!" Grace's panicked voice shouted. I felt their footsteps vibrate beneath me as they ran into the room to find me and Mama in a heap on the floor. Their faces fell as they took in what a mess I was. My body trembled, physically aching to feel Jax's arms around me again.

Without a single word, Ella and Grace sat beside me on the wood floor. Ella had tears in her eyes as she kissed the side of my head. They bookended me and held me tight, leaning their faces into mine. I felt like I was splitting in two, and for several moments, they were the only things keeping me from falling apart. We'd all taken our turns holding each other together over the years, and I knew I'd never be able to get through this without them.

"Have you eaten anything today?" Ella asked softly, and I shook my head in response. "Grace, would you go make something for your Aunt Liv? And pour her a glass of water. We need a minute."

Grace nodded and hugged me hard. "I love you, Aunt Liv." She gave Mama a gentle scratch on the head before disappearing out of the room.

"Guess Mama isn't a hostile kitty after all. A standoffish little shit maybe." Ella chuckled softly, but I couldn't even bring myself to smile. She smoothed her hand over my hair. "I'm so sorry, sweetheart. Can you tell me what happened?"

Ella wrapped me in her embrace as I wept and explained every soul-crushing detail, down to Jax begging me to turn around. I heard her sniffle as I cried in her arms. "I love him so much, Ella. I love him so much it hurts."

"I know, honey. I know."

"I don't know what to do," I cried. For several moments, Ella held me and let me cry. She didn't try to fix it. She didn't push me to talk anymore. She just sat with me and let me cry until I felt like I couldn't cry anymore. When my breathing slowed and she felt my shoulders start to sag, she stood and extended her hand to me.

"Come on." She pulled me to my feet and wrapped an arm around my waist. "You don't have to have it all figured out today. First things first, we get some food in you and maybe a few glasses of wine. We watch some horror movies because love is dead. Grace and I will make some cookies that won't ever make it into the oven because we'll eat the dough out of the bowl with spoons like the heathens we are. And I'm not going to leave your side. Not now, not ever. No matter what you do, you'll never have to do it alone. Now. Food."

She guided me to the kitchen where Grace was making grilled cheeses. I leaned against the counter as Ella busied herself opening a bottle of wine.

Then, I caught a glimpse of a box of Strawberry Pop-Tarts on the counter, and I felt the hot tears spill down my cheeks once again.

I FORGOT HE WAS GONE AS THE LIGHT FILTERED THROUGH THE blinds early the next morning, my eyes still hazy with sleep. I forgot for one blissful second that my entire life had gone up in flames. I thought I would open my eyes to see him as I'd done so many times before.

Only when I opened my eyes, it wasn't Jax's face I saw.

Ella, Grace, and I had fallen asleep, all of us piled in my bed along with Mama sometime after the fifth *Halloween* movie. Thankfully, the wine had allowed me to fall into a dreamless sleep, my body finally giving in to the exhaustion. As I laid there in the early morning light, I replayed the previous day over and over in my mind.

I leaned over Mama, pulling my phone off the nightstand. I illuminated the screen to see no missed calls or messages from Jax.

My heart sank, even though I knew he had no reason to

ever talk to me again. I knew I'd done the right thing for him. But knowing I'd never hear his laugh or look into his stormcloud eyes again was enough to make me feel like my chest was caving in.

My inbox and social media platforms were thousands deep with messages, probably about the dozens of press pieces I'd seen the day before. I couldn't bring myself to look at any of them. Instead, I locked my phone and placed it back on the nightstand.

"Hey," Ella said, turning over to me.

"I should go to the bakery today and try to start sorting through this mess." I wiped at my cheeks with the back of my hand.

"Nope," Ella said flatly. "I've got it under control. You're going to stay here. Sleep, take a bubble bath, watch more Michael Myers, whatever you need to do, but you're not coming to the store. Grace and I are going to go home and change for work. We'll take care of things there, and then we'll come back over tonight, or you can come to our place if you need to get out of here. Whatever you want to do."

I knew she was right. Truthfully, I was of no use to anyone like this. The last thing I needed was for the paparazzi to be camped outside the store only to get a glimpse of me looking like a mess. I needed to lay low right now and let Ella handle things at the store. "I think that's a good idea. I'll stay with you guys tonight. I'll need to get out of this house."

Grace had stirred from Ella's other side. "We can have a pizza night. We can bring home some cupcakes from the bakery."

"That sounds good." I nodded.

"On that note, we better get going so we can get to the

store." Ella yawned and rubbed her eyes. "But we'll both be checking on you. Do you need anything before we head out?"

"I'm okay." I forced a smile. "Thank you both for being here. I don't know what I'd do without you."

"We love you, Aunt Liv," Grace said sweetly. "We'll always be here."

I followed them to the door, but Mama lingered lazily in the bed. Ella pulled me into a hug before grabbing her purse off the floor, and Grace wrapped her arms around me.

"We'll see you this evening," Ella said. "Let us know if you need anything at all, okay?"

"Okay," I agreed.

Ella started out the door, but Grace stopped and turned back toward me. "Aunt Liv?"

"Yeah?"

"For what it's worth, I know Jax loves you. He wanted to make you happy," she said sadly. "He told me so."

"What?" I asked, taken aback.

"The day we were getting ready for your party," she said. "He told me then, and I believed him." Tears spilled out onto my cheeks. "I may not know everything that's going on, but I think he really does want you to be happy, even if that means he doesn't get to be." She gave me a wistful smile and embraced me once more. I watched as she and Ella pulled away, and I closed the front door, leaning up against it for a moment.

I looked down at the guitar on the floor of the foyer, and my heart sank. I grabbed the handle on the case, picking it up. I walked the few steps into the living room to grab my other guitar. Awkwardly, I carried both instruments down the hall to my bedroom, setting them on the floor as I flung open the closet door.

One by one, I shoved them both into the closet behind the racks of clothes and coats. I moved the hangers around until not one speck of either case was visible anymore. I buried them along with the dream I'd had since I was nineteen and any hope I'd had of a future with Jaxon Slade.

THIRTY-TWO

Jax

I LEANED my head against the sofa in Dallas' penthouse apartment, where I'd been for the last fifteen days. Fifteen days without Liv.

I hadn't been able to bring myself to make any decisions, to do anything at all that would force me to accept that Liv was no longer mine.

Dallas offered to take me back to Louisville, but the thought of going back to that apartment without her killed me. It was where we'd said we loved each other for the first time. It was where she'd been so afraid she couldn't give me everything I deserved, not realizing she was all I wanted. I pictured her standing there, the way she'd cried into her hands.

I'm afraid I won't be enough for you.

Despite what she'd said the day she asked me to leave, I couldn't help but think that was what was at the root of it all. She'd been broken down so far, she truly couldn't fathom the idea of being enough for anyone. Benton Wyatt had crushed her spirit, and it was he who'd caused the firestorm with the press. It was because of him she'd left me.

For the first several days, I'd barely spoken to anyone. I broke down and texted Ella an excruciating three days after Liv left me. I couldn't stand not knowing how she was doing.

Jax: I have to know how she is. Please.

Ella: She's not great, Jax. All of this sucks. How are you holding up?

Jax: I don't know what to do. I miss her so much.

Ella: I'm so sorry. I know she misses you too.

It took Dallas threatening to call Liv before I'd told him everything. I finally told him about what Carrie had said to me all those months ago, my mom, and what happened with Liv. Saying it out loud tore my heart apart all over again.

Then, there was the anger.

The anger I'd felt for so many years had returned with a vengeance, bubbling up inside me like a pot of water on the verge of boiling over.

For the last two weeks, I'd communicated with the rest of the guys through Dallas. He'd fielded their questions for me because he knew I wasn't in the mental state to talk about it. I couldn't answer questions that I barely understood the answers to myself.

Midnight in Dallas was on a touring break until early March. Derek ended up finding an apartment in the same building as Dallas, so he'd headed back to Louisville to pack. Luca had gone back home, having always preferred his solitude. Both had tried to reach out to me, but I couldn't talk. Antoni called, and I didn't answer. Cash rented an AirBnB nearby, and he'd sent me a text every single day that, for the most part, I'd avoided. I knew he cared, but I also knew he needed answers about what was happening with Jax & Liv. He asked if he should call Liv, but I told him to wait, hoping against all hope we'd hear from her. Really, I hoped she'd change her mind.

I'd put Cash off long enough, and he'd finally come to Dallas' penthouse to check up on me. The three of us sat in silence in Dallas' living room a while before Cash finally spoke.

"You still haven't heard anything?" Cash asked, and I shook my head.

"I'm sorry, man." Dallas reached over and squeezed my shoulder.

"Are you sure you don't want me to call her?" Cash questioned. "Maybe she'd talk to me and—"

"And what?" I snapped. "She made it clear she didn't want me around, Cash. She doesn't want me. She doesn't want anything to do with me."

Dallas sat thoughtfully for a moment. "I know you're hurting, Jax. I do. I understand you've not wanted to talk about it much, but man you *need* to talk about it. I see this anger building in you, and it's not healthy. Look, I can't begin to imagine how you're feeling right now. I also can't imagine what it was like for her to wake up to this bullshit. She wasn't entirely wrong either. We've seen what a shitstorm like this can do to people. It can ruin people's lives."

"I would have done anything to make it work," I insisted. "Anything."

"I get that," Dallas said softly, "but you have to realize what that's asking of *her.* You weren't the one they made out to be a fucking gold-digger. They talked about her miscarriage, man. The most personal details of her life were on display for everyone. You were the prince charming who saved her, but by my calculations, *this* princess saved herself. She built that fucking business. She was the one who made the choice to put herself out there, but nobody saw that. Nobody saw *her.*"

"I did," I whispered.

"We know." Cash nodded. "We know you did. We all did, but imagine being her for a second. Imagine what it felt like for her to see her life plastered all over the internet and people saying she didn't deserve what she had. Not just professionally, Jax. They attacked her character. They attacked her entire life."

I knew he was right, and it killed me.

"I fucking hate that Benton Wyatt douche canoe." Dallas shook his head. "I don't know how he could do this to Liv. Takes a special kind of asshole to do something like that."

Anger rumbled at my core as my phone rang from the coffee table in front of me. My heart immediately sank when I recognized the number of the detective working on my mom's case. I slid my finger across the screen to answer the call. "Hello?"

"Mr. Slade, it's Detective Bryant," his gruff voice replied. "I've got some news regarding your mother, Deanna Slade. Do you have a few moments we can talk?" His voice had softened a bit from his normal business as usual tone, which caused my already raw nerves to stand at attention. So far, his updates had consisted of a few brief calls to let me know that he was sorry, but there was no new information.

"Sure," I said, getting up from the sofa and walking into the kitchen. I settled onto one of the bar stools at the island in the middle of the kitchen. "What's up?"

"Mr. Slade, I got a lead on your mother a few weeks ago that led me to St. Louis, and I started canvassing the streets and the homeless shelters. That's when I got a tip that sent me to a shelter in downtown St. Louis, and the director there was able to confirm that someone matching her description had been staying there up until about a month ago."

"Wait, what?" I asked, unsure if I'd heard him correctly. "You found her?"

"The sources I found hadn't seen her on the streets or in the shelter for several weeks, so I broadened my search to the local hospitals," Detective Bryant explained. "I did find her, Mr. Slade, but I regret to inform you that your mother passed away about a month ago due to a drug overdose. Her body is being kept in the morgue at St. Louis University Hospital."

"I'm sorry, what?"

"I'm so sorry, son." He sighed into the phone. "I wish I had better news."

"She's dead," I said, still in disbelief. "You're telling me she… she's gone?"

"Yes, son," he answered. "I'm very sorry, but there's something else. The director of the homeless shelter called me late last night. She told me she found something that belonged to your mother that had been left at the shelter. I'd like to bring it to you this afternoon, if I may. I'm back in Nashville, and I can come right to you."

"What is it?" I asked, my rage threatening to rise to the surface.

"I think you should see it for yourself," he said gently. "Text me the address of a place I can meet you, and I'll be there soon."

"Okay," I responded. "I'll see you soon." Once I ended the call, I tapped out Dallas' address in a text to Detective Bryant as my legs carried me back to the living room where Dallas and Cash waited for me.

"Jax? Are you okay?" Cash asked.

Dallas eyed me, his face awash with concern. "You look like you've seen a ghost."

I took my seat next to Dallas and sat there a moment, lost somewhere between numbness and an all-encompassing rage. "It was the detective calling about my mom. She's dead."

"What?" Dallas asked, his voice laced with shock.

"Jesus, Jax," Cash said, leaning his elbows forward on his knees. "I'm so sorry."

My eyes flickered to both of theirs. "He's on his way over here to give me something he found of hers."

"Do you know what it is?" Dallas questioned, and I shook my head.

I didn't know, and at this moment, I wasn't even sure I wanted to.

THE DETECTIVE'S VISIT WAS SO SHORT THAT YOU'D NEVER suspect he'd handed me the only thing left of my mom: a worn and beat up shoebox that contained God only knew what.

I would make sure she'd have a proper burial, but there would be no funeral. Cash, Dallas, and the guys would come out of respect and support for me, but the one person I wanted to be there wouldn't be.

If my mom had any friends, I didn't know about them. I knew nothing about the life she had, except that it was now over.

"Would you like us to step out?" Cash asked as I stared at the shoebox in my lap. "We can give you some privacy."

"No." I shook my head. "Stay."

I took a deep breath, trying to prepare myself for what I

might find in this old shoebox, the last connection I had to my
mother. Dallas and Cash watched nervously as I lifted the lid
as though I was about to attempt to defuse a bomb.

Staring back at me were yellowed and worn paper clippings. Some that had once belonged in newspapers and others
that were once part of glossy magazines. I gently lifted a piece
out, realizing it was one of the first press pieces ever done
about Midnight in Dallas from the paper in Louisville.

"Wait, is that us?" Dallas asked, peering over my shoulder.
Wordlessly, I nodded and handed it to him. The next piece my
fingers landed on was a cut out from *Rolling Stone* back when
we were interviewed about our last album. I lightly ruffled my
fingers over the cutouts. There were dozens of them.

"They're all of us," I said softly. "Of me."

Then I saw one that caught my eye. It was an article about
me and my 'mystery woman.' Tears flowed down my face as I
looked at the photo that accompanied the article. It was that
same paparazzi photo of me and Liv from the Halloween
party in Las Vegas. Liv was so beautiful she practically radiated off the page. I was kissing her cheek in that picture as
though I'd kiss her every day for the rest of our lives.

I placed the box on the coffee table, holding on to the
photo of me and Liv between my fingers. "She knew about
Liv," I choked out before finally tossing the paper back inside
the box and rising to my feet. The last string tethering me to
whatever shred of sanity I had left snapped. I rubbed my
hands over my face and paced the length of the living room.

"I'm so sorry, Jax. This isn't fair—" Cash attempted to
comfort me, but I cut him off.

"You're damn right it isn't fucking fair," I shouted,
running my hands through my hair in frustration. "My mom is
dead, and the only home I've ever fucking known doesn't

want me! What was the fucking point of me finding her? What was the point of me falling in love with her? For her to tell me that love isn't fucking enough?" The anger overflowed inside me, spilling out on everything around me. Cash and Dallas appeared frozen in place. "I've got to get out of here."

"Wait, what?" Dallas asked as he and Cash immediately stood. "Where are you going?"

"To pay Benton Wyatt a visit." I tensed my jaw and clenched my fists.

"Is that a good idea?" Dallas questioned. "I hate the bastard too, but I'm not sure you should do that."

"I don't care," I said through gritted teeth.

"Do you even have a car here?" Cash asked.

"I'll call Brady. I'll get a fucking Uber," I shouted. "I'll walk there if I have to, but it's time he and I had a talk." Cash and Dallas exchanged a look.

"Well, you're sure as shit not taking an Uber." Dallas reached into his pocket and extracted his keys. "I'll drive."

I shook my head. "I want to go alone. I have to do this by myself."

"Jax, I know you're upset. You have every reason to be, but guys like Benton are power-hungry. They're vindictive, and they'll stop at nothing. Look at what he's done already," Cash said cautiously. "Please be careful."

"Yeah, well," I said, "I've got nothing left to lose."

Dallas sighed and reluctantly handed me his keys. "Take my car. Give him hell."

Cash nodded his approval, and I snatched the keys out of Dallas' hand, storming onto the elevator.

Hell was exactly what I planned to give him.

THIRTY-THREE

Liv

IT HAD BEEN fifteen days since I'd felt his arms around me. His scent haunted me like a ghost. I'd catch it, and the tears would start flowing down my cheeks because I knew that's all it was. That's all that was left. Just a trace.

I still hadn't taken off the necklace he'd given me. I often found myself lightly caressing the tiny charm as though it were a genie in a bottle, and I could somehow make Jax magically appear.

I'd slept with his shirt and the Aerosmith shirt next to me every night. Together, they retained enough of his scent that when I'd fall asleep, I could almost imagine him there with me. Then, in the early hours of the morning as daybreak began to filter through the blinds, I'd get a glorious three seconds where I'd forget. Those glorious three seconds before I opened my eyes when I could smell him there. For those three seconds, Jax and I were still home.

It was the opening of the eyes that was the problem. That was when I was reminded that the life, the *me* that I'd come to love, was gone.

Ella and Grace were doing their best to hold me together. Katie had taken a couple of shifts with me too, bringing over some takeout that I'd picked at and turning on Netflix. When she asked if I wanted to watch *The Office,* I dissolved into a puddle of tears, causing poor Katie to feel awful. It wasn't her fault I was a mess. It was mine.

Antoni went back to LA on New Years Day, but he'd called many times after Ella reached out to let him know what happened.

I heard from all of the guys during the time I'd been apart from Jax. My chest twisted with shame each time their names showed up on my phone because I knew I didn't deserve their compassion. I wondered if he knew they'd reached out. Initially, Dallas contacted me worried out of his mind because Jax wouldn't talk to him. I didn't go into detail, but I told him we'd broken up. I told him it wasn't Jax. It was me.

I resisted the urge to ask him how Jax was doing. I knew I didn't have a right to that information any longer, but that didn't stop me from typing out the text and deleting it dozens of times. It also didn't stop Dallas from telling me anyway.

Dallas: He really misses you, Cupcake. I've never seen him like this.

Liv: I miss him too.

Dallas: Are you sure about all of this?

I wasn't sure at all. I started tapping out a reply but erased it because I knew that information didn't help anyone. It didn't change anything.

Cash checked on me, but he never asked about Jax & Liv, and I was grateful. We still had a single that was climbing the charts despite the bad press. I knew I would have to tell him it was over soon, but the idea of saying it out loud made my heart feel like it was breaking all over again.

The business had taken a hit after all the press came out. It was normally a bit slow after the holidays, but it was even slower than usual. You wouldn't think so based on the number of people coming in and out, but they weren't there to buy anything. They were bystanders craning their necks, hoping to catch a view of the train wreck that was my life. Somehow we'd managed to keep the press from finding out where I lived, which was both a blessing and a curse. It was a blessing because at least I still had my home as my refuge and a curse because it had become a mausoleum of my memories with Jax.

Ella had been a rockstar. She'd managed to terrify several of the paparazzi staking out the store. They'd been hoping to catch a glimpse of me so they could undoubtedly sell my photos to some website that would run them alongside a piece about Olivia Sinclair, the barren gold-digger bitch.

Then there was Mama. Ever since Jax left, she'd been my constant companion. She wove between my feet and no longer hissed at me. She'd taken to sleeping in the bed with me at night, curling up on one of Jax's shirts. I knew she missed him too.

I'd barely cooked the entire two weeks, opting instead for takeout or to not eat at all. Every time I went into that kitchen, all I could see was Jax dancing around the room or pulling me into his arms. Instead, I spent my time on the couch mindlessly watching Netflix, letting shows I couldn't tell you anything about play episode after episode while I stared off into nothingness.

I was staring at the television when Ella appeared before me that afternoon, turning the television off. She set a paper grocery sack on the coffee table.

"Hey, babe." She sat beside me and squeezed my arm.

"Hey," I mumbled. "Where's Grace?"

"She's at home. It's just me today," she said. "Listen, I want you to get up, and go take a shower. I'm going to make us some chamomile tea, and I brought some food. Don't worry. I didn't make it, so we won't be subjected to food poisoning."

I forced a smile.

"Come on." She patted my leg. "Go take a nice hot shower, and I'll have everything waiting for you in the kitchen."

Reluctantly, I did as she asked. I stood under the steady stream of the showerhead for several moments, soaking in the warmth. After I was done, I had to admit the simple act of just washing my hair and putting on a cozy sweater did make me feel better.

I walked into the kitchen, and Ella had a bowl of soup and some hot tea waiting for me.

"Well, look at you," Ella said. "You look almost human again. By the way, that tea is hot as the sun, so don't even try to drink it yet."

I sat at the table and ate a spoonful of the soup. "This tastes exactly like your mom's potato soup."

She gave me a sad smile. "That's because it is. Mom hasn't cooked in ages, not since her disease progressed, so I asked Katie if she would make it for me."

I reached over and squeezed her hand. We ate in comfortable silence, and by the time we were finished, the tea had reached the perfect temperature.

"Let's take the tea to the couch," Ella said, getting up and rinsing out the dishes, placing them in the dishwasher.

We finally settled on the sofa under Mama's watchful gaze. "Talk to me, Liv." Ella furrowed her brow.

I looked down at the mug in my hands. "I miss him so much." A lump formed in my throat, and tears burned behind my eyes. "I love him, Ella."

"I know you do, honey," she said softly. "I know. God, I haven't seen two people look at each other the way you two did since me and Craig." She gave me a wistful smile.

"What would you have done if you were me? Do you think I made a mistake?"

She pressed her lips together. "I believe you did what you thought was right, but at what point do you stop doing what you think is best for everyone else and start doing what's best for *you*?"

"If I'd stayed with Jax, I could have ruined his entire career." I sighed. "I couldn't let him do that."

"Don't you think that should have been his choice?" Ella asked. She took my mug from my hands and placed it on the coffee table along with her own, taking my hands in hers. "Liv, I can't tell you if you made a mistake. I can't tell you if this would have ruined anyone's career or that Jax wouldn't have wanted biological children of his own one day. I can't tell you what would happen to the bakery. All I *can* tell you is what I know for sure. And what I know for sure is that Jax loves you. He would probably give everything up to make you happy, but I also know you love him too much to ever let him. And no matter what happens with the business, we're going to be okay. We'll figure it out. I want you to be happy. If you really think that means letting Jax go, I'll support you. You know I will."

"But you think it's the wrong decision." I rested my head on hers.

"I think you found the love of a lifetime," she said gently. "Love like that is so rare, Liv. I'd set the whole world on fire to get Craig back. I think sometimes you have to say fuck it all, and do what your heart wants. I know you're trying to save him some heartache and hardship, but I think you're trying to save yourself too. I think you're scared. I know you don't want to live in his shadow, and I know what the internet has said is less than flattering. But Liv, they don't know you. They don't know the truth, nor does that sleazeball Benton Wyatt. They don't know that Jaxon Slade pulled you out of the shadows or that you were more yourself with him than you ever were with Benton. They don't know what I've always known and that's how fucking special you are. With or without Jax, or anyone else for that matter, *you* are a remarkable woman. Jax may have helped bring you out of the shadows, but you've always been the light, Liv. You've always been *my* light."

"I feel like every bit of light I had left has gone out," I whispered.

"Absolutely not," she said firmly, sitting up to look at me. "Your light has never been dependent on anyone but you. It's still there."

I sucked in a deep breath. "What do I do, Ella?"

"I wish I could tell you which path to take." She sighed. "I wish I could tell you the exact right choices to make, but the road to happiness is a bumpy one. Sometimes you have to hit a few potholes and take a few wrong turns to get to happiness. Sometimes you're cruising along happy as can be, and out of nowhere, everything goes up in flames. But those moments of happiness are worth the pain. They're worth every bit of it. So, what do I think you should do? I think you have to figure out what happiness means to you, and you have to unapologetically do that. In the words of the great philosopher, Dolly Parton, 'Find out who you are and do it on purpose.' I think you get to be a little selfish, Liv. That's what I think. I also think if I ever see Benton Wyatt again, I will kill him with my bare hands."

"If it hadn't been him, it would have been someone else. It was only a matter of time." I shook my head.

"Well, it wasn't someone else, it was *him*. I hope all of his hair falls out and he winds up in an erectile dysfunction commercial."

I snorted. "I can't say that wouldn't bring me some joy right now."

A soft smile played across her lips. "I love you, babe. I want you to be happy."

"I love you too."

"Just think about this, okay?" She pulled me into a hug. "Think about what it is *you* want."

I nodded, and we settled on the couch together, finishing our tea. When she left, I locked the door behind her and trudged back to the couch.

I pulled the sleeves of my sweatshirt over my hands, settling back into the couch. I grabbed the remote, clicking the button, and the next episode of a show that I did not care about started to play. Mama stretched out next to me, content to nap at my side, as I let the voices on the television lure me into a dreamless sleep.

THIRTY-FOUR

Jax

I ALMOST TOOK OUT A 'NO PARKING' sign as I pulled Dallas' Mercedes to a stop outside 6th & 15th Records. The record label was housed inside an old renovated home near Music Row with a banner outside congratulating one of their artists on going platinum.

I pushed through the front door to find a stunned receptionist gaping at me.

"You're Jaxon Slade." Of *course,* she recognized me.

"I need to see Benton Wyatt," I said firmly. "It's urgent."

"Mr. Slade, you have to have an appointment," the receptionist said quietly, looking terrified of me. Hell, at that moment, I was terrified of me too.

"Please," I pleaded. "I need to talk to Ben. We're old friends." The lie dripped right off my tongue. She narrowed her eyes as though trying to decide if she believed me. Maybe it was the fact that I looked like I'd lost my best friend, but she bought it hook, line, and sinker.

She pointed to a door toward the center of the building. "Go through there. It's the last door on the right."

"Thank you." I sprinted through the first door and came to a stop in front of his office. His name was engraved in the frosted glass along with the 6th & 15th logo. I could hear him talking on the other side, but from the pauses he took, I gathered he was on the phone. I stormed through the door, and Benton's mouth fell open.

"Chris, I'm going to have to call you back," he said before slamming down the phone. "How did you get back here?"

"What? I thought you wanted to meet with me, Benton?" I feigned shock. "Isn't that why you called that meeting with the band on New Year's Eve?"

Benton shook his head as he maneuvered to the other side of his desk. He leaned against it, crossing his arms over his chest. "What do you want, Jaxon?"

"To give you this." I strode over to him and threw my fist at his face, connecting with his nose.

"Shit!" Benton covered his face with his hands. "What the hell is wrong with you?"

"You fucking asshole!"

"What the hell is your problem?" He pulled his hands away to reveal the blood trickling down his face. He wiped at it with the back of his hand, managing to get some on the sleeve of his pristine white shirt. "I ought to have you fucking arrested for assault!"

"It was your fault that shit got out to the press. Are you happy now? You ruined her, and you ruined us."

"Jesus Christ." Benton sighed. "It wasn't me, Jaxon. I never talked to the press."

"A likely fucking story." I snorted.

The receptionist from out front burst through the door, a look of horror on her face as she caught a glimpse of Benton.

"I'm fine, Ali," he said. "Give me and Mr. Slade a moment, and cancel my afternoon meetings."

"Yes, sir," she said fearfully. "I'm sorry." She pulled the door closed behind her.

"It wasn't me," Benton insisted, turning his attention back to me. "I wouldn't have done that to Liv."

"Oh, I guess you *were* interested in signing us with your damn ten million dollar bonus then?"

"No," he confessed. "I wasn't. Look, I'll admit it. My intentions weren't exactly honorable. I didn't want you to be together, but I wouldn't have hurt her like that. You maybe, but not her. I didn't talk to the press, but I know who did. Will you sit down?" He gestured to one of the leather armchairs in front of his desk.

I narrowed my eyes but said nothing.

"Fine. I'm going to sit down, though." He rounded the desk to the oversized office chair, dabbing at the blood that continued to run down his face. "If the music thing doesn't work out, you could have a promising career as an MMA fighter."

"If it wasn't you, who was it, Benton?" I asked, not at all interested in hearing his stupid jokes.

"I saw you and Liv together at that Halloween party in Las Vegas."

"What?" My heart sank. "She never told me that."

"I don't think she saw me." He shook his head. "If she did, she didn't say anything. She walked right past me, and I followed her. That's when I saw her with you. My girlfriend Shelby recognized you from your stupid band, and I started doing some digging, trying to figure out what you were doing with her."

"I don't know why the fuck you cared." My jaw tightened

involuntarily. "*You* left her for someone else. Why the hell did it matter to you that she'd moved on?"

"It made me realize I missed her."

"So, you decided to come check me out?"

"Yes." He nodded. "I wanted to know who the hell you were, and then I watched the show that night. I watched *her,* and that's when I knew I was still in love with her. I told Shelby I'd made a mistake, that I realized I wanted my wife back. I realized how special Liv was, and naturally, Shelby was pretty upset."

"You're a real piece of work, you know that Benton?" I scoffed. "What was the plan? Were you going to try and break us up?"

"I wanted to," he admitted. "I'd planned to call Liv and see if I could convince her to talk to me, but before I could… well, you saw it all over the internet. Hell hath no fury like a woman scorned."

"Liv was the one who had to pay for what you did to that girl," I snapped. "*Liv* was the one who suffered, and she left me because of it."

"Really?" His eyes widened, amused.

"Fuck you!" I slung my hand across the desk, knocking the pencil cup and the various trinkets to the floor in one swift movement. "You crushed her spirit. Liv has always been special, but you snuffed out her light every chance you got."

"I know," he said quietly. "What do you want me to say? That I'm a piece of shit? That I wasn't the husband she deserved? I know that. Don't you think I know that now? I made a mess of my life and hers. I blamed her for… for things that were out of her control. All of that is true, but it doesn't change the past."

"She was happy with me. I never wanted to change a

single hair on her head. She's fucking perfect, and you never deserved her."

"Well," he chuckled flatly. "Finally, something we can agree on. But if she was so happy with you, Jaxon, why did she leave you?"

"Because she didn't want to be in someone else's shadow again. She didn't want the media circus to reflect badly on me and the band, and frankly, because she doesn't think she deserves even a shred of happiness, and that's on *you.*"

He averted his gaze to his hands folded in his lap. "I know I messed up. I know I didn't treat her right, but I want to fix it."

"If you really wanted to fix it, you should have let her go. You should have let her find some fucking happiness with someone who truly loves her."

"I do love her."

"No, *I* love her, Benton." I slammed my fists on the desk so hard that what little was left on the surface shook. "Liv was my entire fucking world and because of you, I lost her."

"I didn't—"

I shoved my finger in his face. "*You* broke her, Benton, and I hope it haunts you for the rest of your pathetic life."

I turned and walked out of Benton Wyatt's office, slamming the door. I barreled down the hall past reception, and once I was back in the Mercedes, I peeled out of the parking lot with tears streaming down my face.

I drove around for what felt like hours, lost in every way imaginable. The street signs blurred together as I drove and drove. I was barely aware of where I was until I looked up and saw the neon hot sign at Krispy Kreme.

THIRTY-FIVE

Liv

I AWOKE TO A KNOCKING SOUND. The room had darkened, and night had fallen while I was asleep.

My eyes adjusted to the darkness, squinting in the soft glow of the television. I heard the knocking again coming from the front door. It wasn't Ella or Grace because they would have used their keys. I grabbed my phone off the table, and it lit up to show that it was a few minutes after five. Maybe Katie was dropping by, though normally she would send me a text first, and I didn't have any messages.

"One second." I scrambled to the light switch and flicked it on as whoever was on the other side of the door knocked once more. I swung open the door, bringing me face to face with Benton Wyatt. "What the hell happened to you?" He had the beginnings of a black eye and bloodstains beneath his nose, on his shirt collar, and along one sleeve.

"Jaxon Slade happened," he said flatly.

"I'm sorry, *what?*" I asked. *Jax* did that? I was both shocked and slightly... amused? Proud?

"Do you mind if I come in?" He gestured toward the door with his head. "It's kind of cold out here."

"Oh," I said, taken aback. "Um, okay." I stepped aside, allowing him to walk over the threshold, closing the door behind him. "How did you find out where I live?"

"I have my ways." Benton walked past me and into the living room. "Nice place you have here."

"Thanks." I narrowed my eyes at him as Mama hissed in his direction and darted down the hall.

"You got a cat? I thought you hated cats."

"I never hated cats. You were allergic."

"You still have your Christmas decorations up," he continued. "You always had ours down before the first of the year."

"That's because *you* hated them," I reminded him. "You said Christmas was nothing more than a Hallmark marketing ploy."

He nodded. "I guess I did say that, didn't I?"

"Why are you here, Ben?" I asked, crossing my arms protectively over my chest. "If you came here to settle a score with Jax, he's—"

"I didn't." He cut me off. "I came to talk to you."

"About how you sabotaged me?"

"Can we sit?" He held his hand out toward the sofa that Mama had vacated. I eyed him suspiciously a moment, finally nodding as I sat beside him. "Liv, I didn't talk to the press. I wouldn't do that to you."

"Right," I scoffed. "There's no one else who would do something like that."

"It was Shelby," he said quietly.

Jessica Rabbit had talked to the press? She and I had never even met. "But why? I saw the two of you in Las Vegas, but—"

"Wait, you saw me too? You didn't say anything. You barely even looked at me."

"I know." I shrugged. "Why should I? You'd long since moved on, and I'd moved on too. Sorry if I didn't want to have small talk with my ex-husband and the girl he left me for."

"Well, seeing you that night... with *him*... it got to me. I realized I missed you, Liv." I gave him a blank stare as he continued on. "Shelby was the one who identified Jaxon because she's a fan of his band. Anyway, I started trying to figure out why you were hanging around this guy when I started hearing rumors about Jax & Liv and—"

"You called that bogus meeting with Midnight in Dallas to get to me," I finished for him.

"Kind of," he admitted. "Mostly, I wanted to check this guy out and figure out what he was doing with you."

"You are unbelievable, Ben." I threw my hands up. "What? Is it that hard to believe someone would actually care about me?"

"No," he said quickly. "That's not it at all. I guess I wanted to see who this guy was that had gotten your attention. I stuck around and watched the show. And..." He trailed off, rubbing his hand over his stubble. "Liv, I realized I still loved you. I saw that spark in you that I fell in love with so many years ago, and I realized I never *stopped* loving you."

A sarcastic laugh bubbled out of me. "Are you kidding me right now?"

"I know I wasn't exactly supportive." He looked down at his hands.

"By not exactly supportive, you mean you literally wanted to suppress *everything* that made me who I was until I became someone I didn't recognize, right?" I fired back. "Because *that* is what happened."

"You're right," he confessed. "I realize that now."

"You know, Ben, I never understood what was so wrong with me to begin with."

"It wasn't you," he acknowledged. "There was never anything wrong with you. It was me."

"Oh, I know that *now,*" I said firmly, realizing for the first time that I believed it. "You always had to make me smaller and smaller in order to make yourself bigger." He started to speak, but I barreled on. "I don't blame you. You may have done it, but I allowed it to happen for years until I all but disappeared."

"I'm sorry," he said simply. "I wish there was something I could say."

"So, why did she do it?" I asked. "Why did Shelby do it?"

"After the show that night, I sat her down and talked to her." He sighed. "I told her I was still in love with you and that I'd made a mistake. I told her I wanted to try to work things out with you." I shook my head in disbelief. "She was understandably upset. She threatened to ruin my life, but that's not what happened."

"Instead, she ruined mine." I pressed my lips together in a firm line, seriously contemplating blackening his other eye.

"Yes," he replied. "She took it out on you."

"Well, thanks for letting me know." My voice was dripping with sarcasm.

"I made a mistake, Liv." He looked at me sincerely, his brown eyes glistening. "I made a *lot* of mistakes. I didn't treat you the way you deserved, and I know that now, but I want to try again. I want to make it right."

I looked at him thoughtfully for a moment. Once upon a

time, this was everything I wanted to hear, but that was before I knew what it was like to live without him. That was before I figured out that maybe I wasn't so bad after all.

That was before Jax.

Hearing him say those words, I felt nothing but sorry for him.

Sorry that he'd missed out on who I could have been.

Sorry that he'd been so insecure he had to tear me down to build himself back up.

But I wasn't sorry enough to take him back. I should have left that relationship a long time ago.

"I appreciate the sentiment," I said. "I do."

"But you don't want to be with me." He shook his head, looking defeated.

"No," I answered. "I don't."

"Because you love him."

"Because I love myself." I sighed. "Ben, you did me a kindness when you asked me for a divorce because I probably never would have left. I would have lived in your shadow for the rest of my life. When you left, I found out who I was, who I *still* am."

I was *proud* of the woman I'd become. I was stronger than I'd ever given myself credit for. I was fucking capable and…

"I realized I deserve to be loved." Jax's face flashed through my mind. We were eating donuts outside that little pie shop he loved and getting drenched as we ran to my front door in the rain. We were writing songs by candlelight in the middle of a storm. I was looking at him and the faces of my friends at the surprise party he planned, eating the cake he'd made for me. We were dancing in the kitchen and curled up together on the tour bus. I was performing on stage in front of millions of people, but the person that mattered most was standing right beside me. "And I deserve to love someone even when it's not easy. *Especially* when it's not easy. Even when it feels like my world is falling apart, I deserve to love and be loved, anyway." I turned toward him and stood. "Ben, I'm sorry, but I need you to leave. I have somewhere I need to be."

"It's him, isn't it?" Benton's face fell.

"It's him," I said, "but it's also me." He stood, and I placed a hand on his arm. "I forgive you, Benton. You want to make it right? You make it right by learning from it, by becoming better. Not for me, but for you."

"You really are something special, Olivia."

"I'm finally starting to see that," I admitted.

"For what it's worth, I hope you don't give up on music," he said as we walked side by side to the door. He paused and turned back toward me. "You've got a gift, and I'm sorry I never told you that."

"Thank you, Ben." My mouth stretched into a sly grin. "Sorry about your face."

"Sorry about... everything else." He gave me a wistful smile. "Take care, Liv. Be happy."

I grinned as I let him out the door. "I plan on it." I only hoped Jax could forgive me.

I practically sprinted to my room, intent on finding something decent to throw on so I could go find Jax. But before I could even open the closet, there was another knock at my door. I groaned, figuring Benton must have left something. I ran back into the foyer and flung open the door to find Cash standing on the front stoop.

"Cash!" I exclaimed, my eyes wide.

"Hey," he said tentatively. "Sorry to drop in on you like

this, but I was wondering if you'd seen Jax." He shifted uncomfortably and shoved his hands in his pockets.

"No, I haven't. Not since..." I trailed off, and my gaze fell to my feet. "I was actually going to see if I could get him to meet up with me to talk. Is everything okay? Do you want to come in?"

He looked at me nervously. "Do you have any idea where Jax might be?"

I shook my head. "He hasn't been here. I know he went to see Benton, and he may or may not have, but definitely did, punch him in the face." I grinned.

"Is there anywhere you can think of that he might be now? Any place he might go if he was upset?"

"Cash, you're scaring me." I narrowed my eyes. "What's going on? What's wrong with Jax?"

He sucked in a deep breath and sighed. "Jax got some news earlier today about his mom."

"Did they find her?" I asked hopefully.

"They did." He frowned, his shoulders slumping forward. "She's dead, Liv. The detective brought over something they found that belonged to her."

My hands flew to my mouth, suffocating a gasp that tried to escape. "What was it?"

"It was a shoebox full of pages she'd cut out of magazines and newspapers of Jax," he said, "some as recently as the Halloween party in Vegas."

Tears pricked at the corners of my eyes. "Oh my God. Jax... I should have been there for him. I should have been with him when he found out." I shook my head. "This is all my fault, Cash. I've got to find him."

"Is there anywhere you think he might go? Dallas stayed at the penthouse in case he comes back there. Derek and Luca even went to make sure he didn't drive back to Louisville, but no such luck. I've been driving around trying to find him. He won't answer any of our calls or texts. I'm pretty sure he's turned his phone off."

That's when it hit me.

I darted back inside and slipped on my boots. I grabbed my keys, phone, and purse and sprinted back through the door, closing it behind me. I looked at Cash as I turned the key in the lock. "Call Ella and make sure he didn't end up at the bakery. I'm going to look for him." I jogged toward my Jeep, and Cash fell into step behind me.

"Do you think you know where he is?" He moved faster to catch up with me.

"I hope so."

"Shouldn't you grab a coat? I think it's supposed to snow."

"I'm fine." I waved him off, flinging the car door open and tossing my purse inside before turning back to Cash. "We're going to find him, Cash. We have to."

"We will," he assured me. "Go. Let me know if you have any luck." I jumped into the driver's seat, and he shut the door for me. I slammed the car into gear and backed out of the driveway. I tried Jax's phone, hoping maybe he'd turned it back on, but I went straight to voicemail.

I gripped the steering wheel, willing the other cars on the road to go faster. "I'm coming, Jax."

THIRTY-SIX

Jax

I WASN'T sure how long I'd been sitting in Dallas' car. I'd gotten a half-dozen donuts and driven over to the spot I'd taken Liv the first night we met. I parked in the same overflow lot and sat in the car for what felt like hours. The later it got, the more cars trickled out of the neighborhood until there was only me and the lamplight left. As advertised, the donuts had been hot when I got them, but I couldn't bring myself to eat them. I'd placed them in the passenger seat untouched.

The rage I'd felt earlier in the day, the same rage that caused me to go punch Benton Wyatt in the nose, had subsided leaving behind a sorrow so deep I could feel it in my bones. My entire body ached for Liv, and the realization that I'd lost her for good had finally begun to settle in.

Finding out about my mom hurt like hell, but I couldn't say it was surprising. I'd never be able to fully understand what happened or why, though I couldn't help but take solace in realizing she'd cared for me in her own way. Maybe I was telling myself that so I could feel better about all of this, but I believed she was proud of me. She collected those clippings because she was proud of me and the man I'd become. It comforted me to know she'd gotten to see how happy and in love I'd been, even if it was only in a photo. I hoped somehow that knowledge brought her peace in her final moments, that when all was said and done, she knew she made the best choices she could for me.

I'd spent all these years thinking she abandoned me, that I never crossed her mind. For so long, I thought that meant I wasn't worth loving. But if none of that had happened, where would I be now? I wouldn't have the band, and I never would have found Liv. Maybe love sometimes meant knowing when to let go—knowing when we weren't what that person needed.

I wished I could have reconnected with my mom. I'd had all these dreams of finding her, marrying Liv, and having a family of our own. In that vision, my mom had gotten to be a part of my life. I may never have been able to look at her as a motherly figure, but I'd hoped we could forge a friendship somehow. Those visions were all I had left of the future I'd dreamed of. My mom was gone, and Liv was too. Now, it was my turn to let go.

As angry as I was at the universe for bringing Liv into my life only for me to lose her, I knew I'd lose her a thousand times if it meant getting to love her once. I'd never love anyone like that again. I knew that people lived lifetimes and never got to experience that kind of love. I was fucking lucky I had it at all, even if it wasn't forever.

I gazed out into the night as it started to snow, which was a rare sight in the south. Big, fluffy flakes rained from the sky, dancing in the street lights. I buttoned my coat, got out of the car, and clicked the lock on the fob, tucking it inside my pocket. I started down the street toward the pie shop, the cold air stinging against my skin. My breath appeared like a cloud in front of me, and the smell of snow hung in the air.

I shoved my hands in my pockets to ward off the cold. There was a certain peacefulness in the quiet snowfall. The flakes fell all around me, gently grazing my cheeks as they continued their descent from the sky.

The twinkly golden lights were on, making the vacant pie shop look as though it lived inside a snow globe. I climbed on top of the same picnic table we'd sat on that first night in the crisp autumn air. I leaned forward, resting my elbows on my thighs, and closed my eyes. In my mind's eye, I could see Liv and I walking through these streets, talking for hours. I could hear her beautiful voice singing to me the night we got wine-drunk in her living room. I could see the way she looked in my eyes when she told me she was falling in love with me. I could almost feel her in my arms. A tear slid down my face as I let the memories of her flood my mind like a thousand perfect snowflakes falling from my heart.

I could almost smell her sweet, orange blossom scent intertwined with the snow.

"Turn around." I heard the sound of her sweet voice as though she was standing right behind me. "Jax, please turn around."

"Liv!" My eyes flew open, and I turned to find her standing there, shivering in leggings and a sweatshirt. Her face glistened as a mixture of tears and snowflakes dampened her rosy cheeks. I closed the distance between us, peering down into her emerald eyes. "What are you doing here? How did you even know I was here?"

"I didn't. Not for sure," she admitted, wiping at her eyes with the back of her hand. "But I hoped. Cash told me about your mom. I'm so sorry, Jax. I'm sorry for everything. I should have been there for you. I never should have let you walk out that door. I never should have said those things to you. I should have turned around. I wanted to, but—"

"It's okay." I tucked a piece of hair behind her ear and wiped away a snowflake that fell on her cheek with my thumb.

"It's not okay." She shook her head. "You were right about everything. I *was* scared. I was terrified of being hurt again. I was afraid I wouldn't be enough for you. The truth is, I was never lost in your shadow because *you* brought me into the light, Jax. You made me fall head over heels in love with you, but you also helped me fall in love with *me* again. You were right. Anything this life throws at us, we can get through it together. I don't care what anyone else says. They can think whatever they want about me as long as I'm the woman that gets to love you. You are the love of my life, and I would set my world on fire for you. I love you, Jaxon Slade."

"I love you so much," I cried, tears of relief slipping down my cheeks. I scooped her up in my arms, her legs wrapping around my waist as I crashed my lips to hers.

"Come home, Jax," she whispered, wrapping her arms around me tighter. "Please, come home."

I sighed, leaning my head against hers, and smiled. "I already am."

THIRTY-SEVEN

9 Months Later

LIV

"I'M JUST glad that reporter saw through the bullshit and contacted you," Ella said, taking a sip of her champagne as we stood off to the side, watching our newfound family chat animatedly. We'd started a tradition of having Sunday dinner anytime we could all be in town together. Ordinarily, we alternated houses, but this time was different. We had all gathered early at The Loving Pie Company before heading to our next stop.

I shrugged. "I guess there really is no such thing as bad press." This was something we'd talked about many times over the last few months. Sometimes it was a little hard to believe something so wonderful came out of something that had caused so much pain.

A few days after Jax and I got back together, a fearless female reporter with the Huffington Post contacted me for a piece they were working on about strong women and their 'second acts,' featuring my story. The reporter had even gotten a glowing quote from Benton Wyatt himself for the piece. I hadn't seen him since the night he showed up at my doorstep, but I'd seen pictures of him in the *Nashville Scene* with a beautiful entertainment lawyer in town. He looked happy, and truthfully, I hoped he was.

The reporter set the record straight about my business and who I was. I even opened up to her a little about my fertility struggles and my relationship with Jax. This led to an onslaught of other press, and the next thing I knew, thousands of women were reaching out to me on social media because my story resonated with them. It felt kind of weird putting my life out there on display, but then I thought about the me from months before.

I'd felt old and washed-up. At almost thirty-seven, I'd thought my life was basically over. But really, it was just beginning. If I could help other women realize they, too, were just getting started, it was all worth it.

"I'm still salty that Shelby girl never apologized for what she did. I hope she can never get her eyeliner to be even ever again." Ella snorted. "And who'd have thought Benton would come out of this smelling like a rose?" She narrowed her eyes at me. "Though I will side-eye him for the rest of his life."

Somehow word had gotten around that someone had tried to sabotage me, and the reporter asked if I knew who it was. I pretended I had no idea. At the end of the day, it didn't really matter what Shelby Kirkland had done. What mattered was that I chose not to let it define me.

"What happened definitely sucked," I said, "but it helped me see that it didn't really matter what everyone else thought. Besides, if that article hadn't been printed with the info about the foundation, who knows if we'd be opening Deanna House. Some of that, I owe to Ben."

Benton surprised us all when he became one of the first donors for The Deanna Slade Foundation, an organization Jax and I formed in memory of his mom. The foundation was started to provide mental health care and drug rehabilitation for unhoused men and women. Jax and I, along with Midnight in Dallas and the bakery, had decided to contribute twenty percent of our future revenue to the foundation. What we hadn't anticipated was the number of independent donors we would get after the Huffington Post piece ran with a blurb about the foundation. Due to the generosity of those donors, we were slated to break ground on Deanna House, our first halfway home, right here in Nashville next spring.

"You're right," Ella admitted, "but I don't have to like it."

"If you ask me, things turned out pretty good." I looked over at Jax who caught my eye and smiled. "We've got a lot of reasons to celebrate."

I grabbed Ella's hand and we joined everyone at the center of the room. "I'd like to raise a toast," I said, raising my voice and my flute of champagne. "To Cash, and to the beautiful beginnings of Carrie On Records!"

We were piled in the small lobby of the office that would now serve as headquarters for Cash's label. He started the label out of his new Nashville home, but he knew early on he needed to find a permanent space for the business. Jax and I spent a lot of time at The Loving Pie Company in Berry Hill while we recorded our album earlier in the year. During one of our visits, we noticed a 'for sale' sign at one of the renovated old houses down the street that had been zoned for commercial use. Cash loved it because it wasn't right on Music Row, and it was close to the recording studios the band loved.

"To Jax & Liv." Cash held his glass toward me. "For becoming Carrie On Records first signed act."

"What are we?" Dallas feigned offense. "Chopped liver?"

"You didn't let me finish." Cash laughed. "And to the band who started it all. You guys believed in this dream of mine, and I wouldn't be here without you. I'm proud to have Midnight in Dallas on the Carrie On Records label."

"To Carrie," Jax toasted. "She would be so proud of you, man."

By summer, Cash had signed three other artists, including Sam Corbyn. He had also found the perfect summertime assistant in the form of Grace, who'd decided she wanted to consider a career in the music business. Cash was more than happy to teach her everything he knew, and though I knew Cash loved having Grace work alongside him, I think what he enjoyed most was how much that meant he got to see Ella.

Grace beamed. "Thank you, Cash, for giving me the opportunity to learn from the best."

"Girl, you ain't got nobody fooled." Antoni pursed his lips. "I think we all know the real reason you decided you wanted to work in the music business, and he's about six feet tall with a British accent, gorgeous red curls, and he goes by the name of Sam Corbyn."

"I don't know what you're talking about." Grace grinned mischievously.

As Cash got busier, it became difficult for him to maintain his management duties for me and Jax and for the band, but luckily he knew the perfect replacement. Antoni transitioned into a management role and having him on the road when we toured made life so much more fun.

Our first self titled album came out in late September, and we were the opening act for Midnight in Dallas. It worked well to have the two groups together. I knew being on stage that long was exhausting for Jax, but he never complained. At Jax's insistence, we'd taken to me doing a couple of solo numbers during our set. He said it was because he needed a little break, but I suspected he really just wanted me to have the chance to shine all on my own.

Cash and Antoni said we'd be headlining our own tour by this time next year, but I was content taking things one day at a time. After all, a lot could happen in a year.

"I have something for you, Cash," Derek said as he grabbed a thin, but long, rectangular package propped up against a nearby wall, handing it to Cash. "I thought maybe you could hang it above the reception desk."

"What's this?" Cash asked, a curious expression creeping onto his face.

"Open it," Derek urged.

Cash tore at the wrapping to reveal a beautiful black-and-white photo collage encased in a

matte-black frame. His eyes became misty as he gazed down at it a moment before proudly turning the collection of photographs outward so we could all see. I felt my heart catch in my throat. The collage contained candid shots of all of us that Derek had taken at Sunday dinners, Thanksgiving, backstage, and even a few from when he had visited the bakery.

At the center was a gorgeous photograph of Carrie, her smile wide with laughter. I felt Ella squeeze my hand from beside me. Though it had been given to Cash, in a lot of ways, it felt like a gift for us all.

"Wow." Luca finally broke the silence.

"This label... well, it started as a family," Derek said. "I wanted to find a way to pay tribute to that."

"It's..." Cash's voice wavered slightly. "This means the world to me. Thank you." He grabbed Derek in a hug.

"Let's hang this beautiful masterpiece," Dallas said, moving behind the desk and locating a hammer. "Katie, do you mind holding the picture up so we can make sure it's centered?" She moved around the desk and held the collage until they landed on the perfect spot. After Dallas hung it securely on the wall, we stood back and admired it together in quiet reflection of the loving family we'd found in each other.

Jax made his way over to me, placing his hands on my shoulders and kissing my cheek. "We better get going if we're going to meet Darcey by three," he said softly.

Ella squealed. "Send me pictures."

"Good luck, you two." Cash smiled warmly at us. "Thank you for being here."

We said our goodbyes and made the drive to a gorgeous, sprawling home about twenty-five miles southwest of Nashville. The white house sat in the middle of ten acres, with a scalloped picket fence all the way around the perimeter. It was a lot of house for the two of us and Mama, but in the next couple of years, we hoped to fill it with a lot more love in whatever ways we could.

After inspecting the house together, we found ourselves in the kitchen with none other than self-proclaimed realtor extraordinaire, Darcey Dubois.

"Well, what do y'all think?" Darcey purred, making a sweeping gesture with her hand. "Do you love it, or do you love it?"

Jax laced his fingers with mine as we exchanged a knowing glance. "We love it," we said together.

"Fantastic," Darcey drawled. "You two are the cutest darn things. Alrighty then, I'm going to draw up the offer real quick. Y'all want to take one last peek around?"

"Sure." I smiled and led Jax onto the back deck that overlooked a small pond. The autumn breeze whipped through my hair as I turned to him, wrapping my arms around his waist. "This place is perfect. Mama is going to love it."

"I don't know." He laughed. "I think Mama has gotten used to being a tour cat."

Once Jax came home, Mama wouldn't let either of us out of her sight. Since we had our own tour bus, we decided to see how she'd do coming on the road with us. Turns out, she was made for it. She loved lounging on the bus and had even grown to love the guys and Antoni over the last few months. However, the person she'd developed the greatest affection for was Brady. We'd often find him with Mama perched on his shoulder as he read a book.

When we needed to take her off the bus, she had her own clear kitty backpack that she traveled in. Jax loved carrying her around in that thing, and we'd been photographed by the paparazzi carrying Mama around so much that she now had her own Instagram account where people could tag her in their Mama sightings. More often than not, people were more excited to see her than they were to see us, and we loved it that way.

We gazed off the deck into the sea of vibrant trees in shades of red, yellow, and bright orange. "It's so peaceful out here." I sighed as he tightened his arms around me.

"Hell of a view." Jax grinned as he took in the scenery, but I was looking at him.

"Sure is," I whispered. "Hell of a view."

THE SATURDAY BEFORE THANKSGIVING, WE WERE BACKSTAGE at the Ryman Auditorium for our last show of the year. I was nervous before every show, but this was on a whole new level.

The Ryman had been my dream for as long as I could remember, and on this night I could swear those stained glass windows were sparkling even more than usual.

I took a deep breath as I looked at my reflection and the sparkly champagne-colored gown I was wearing for the show. With it being our last show before the holidays, we'd all decided to dress up for the occasion. We had ten minutes till showtime, and I could feel each painful second tick by.

"You're going to kill it, Liv." Ella pulled me into her arms as Grace sandwiched me from the other side.

"And you look hot," Grace added.

"You mean H-A-W-T, right?" Ella laughed. "A total smokeshow."

"Back to the scene of the crime." Jax waggled his eyebrows at me.

"I can't believe that was only a little over a year ago." Katie shook her head in disbelief as she took a seat on the couch beside Dallas. "It feels like yesterday, but it also feels a little like you guys have been together forever."

"What's hard to believe is that I ever survived without your delicious pastries," Dallas said, taking a bite out of a chocolate croissant, one of the many treats Katie had supplied for us backstage. "This woman is a witch! A temptress! I love Nashville!" At least, I think that's what he said. He said that last part with half a croissant in his mouth.

"It's a shame *everyone* doesn't live here," Derek said pointedly at Luca. "The gang's all here, except for you."

"I do what I want." Luca shrugged, taking a drink of what looked like bourbon from the clear glass in his hand. "Besides, I'm with you guys all the time. Isn't it nice to be away from me on occasion?"

"You do have a point there." Dallas leaned forward and

attempted to retrieve another croissant from the box on the coffee table when Luca elbowed him. "Hey now! I've got precious treasures here." He made a big show of taking a bite out of his second croissant.

"How are you doing, Liv?" Antoni asked. "Are you ready?"

"Yes. No. I don't know," I admitted. "I don't want to forget to take in what it feels like to be on that stage."

"I don't think we have to worry about that." Jax grinned, pulling me into his arms.

Before I could worry anymore, Cash knocked on the door to the dressing room. "It's showtime, guys." He clasped his hands together, and I glanced up at Jax nervously.

"You're going to be perfect," he said, lacing his fingers with mine.

We all piled out of the dressing room where Brady was posted outside, holding Mama who was sound asleep in her backpack. "Break a leg." He waved as we walked by.

We wound through the backstage area that I remembered like the back of my hand, despite having only been there once. I was bursting with gratitude that I was getting the chance to play the stage where so many legends had played before me. It was even more special now because this was where my love story with Jax began.

A stagehand passed me the guitar Jax had given me and handed me my in-ear monitors. My nerves reached a fever pitch as the house lights darkened, and the crowd erupted in cheers.

"I'm so fucking proud of you, babe," Ella said in my ear, giving me one last squeeze.

Jax peered down at me, his boyish grin stretched across his face. "Are you ready?"

"Ready," I answered, and we took our spots on the stage as the crowd continued to roar. We began to play the notes to our opening song, and the stage lights went up. My stomach twisted, but like I'd done every night on every stage we played, I looked over at Jax, and the nerves subsided.

We made it through our first two songs before Jax took his break to allow me to sing my two solos. I tried to memorize each magical moment as I poured my soul out onto that stage. The crowd was lively and happy as they sang along with me. At one point, I turned the mic to them and watched in awe as the Ryman Auditorium sang me a love song.

At the end of my last number, the audience thundered their approval. I gazed out, trying to memorize every face that stared back at me.

"Thank y'all so much," I said. "We've got one more so…" I trailed off as dozens of audience members stood, hoisting white boards over their heads. I watched as the squares were raised in a wave that appeared to ripple across the crowd. I squinted, shielding my vision from the spotlight with my hand so that I could see what was happening. Suddenly, a message written amongst the boards became crystal clear:

Turn around.

I turned to find Jax standing beneath an archway that looked as though it was made entirely of tequila sunrise roses. Grace appeared at my side, taking my guitar from my hands with a knowing smile. I walked to where Jax waited for me, the butterflies in my stomach threatening to take flight and send me zip lining across the stage.

Jax reached for me, taking my hands in his as I approached.

"Liv," he said my name with tears glistening in his eyes. "I could live a thousand lifetimes, and that still wouldn't be long enough with you. You're everything to me. You're the love of my life, my best friend. You're my home. I don't know what forever holds for us, but I know I want to spend every second of it with you." He dropped to one knee, extracting a black velvet box from his pocket. Tears streaked down my face as the crowd cheered and applauded around us. "Olivia Faith Sinclair, will you marry me?"

I gazed down into his storm-cloud eyes and nodded profusely, unable to make my mouth form words.

"Yeah?" Jax asked as a glittering smile spread across his face. He slid the stunning pear-shaped diamond set in rose gold on my trembling finger, and I pulled him to his feet.

I took his face in my hands and crushed my lips to his, in awe that I'd get to kiss this man every day for the rest of my life. "Yeah."

Acknowledgments

Nicole, you've believed I could do this since we were kids, and you never let me forget it. You've helped me mold this series into something I'm proud of. This is only the beginning for us both. Because of you, I'm a better writer and a better person. SSMATBMDBFFAATE. Love you.

Jen, you've been my biggest cheerleader, and you never let me give up the many times I threatened to set my laptop on fire. You talked me through dozens of plot points, and you never held back. This story wouldn't be what it is without you. I love you a million shrimp emojis.

Katie, thank you for asking the difficult questions that helped shape Liv and Jax into who they are. This book, and my life, are infinitely better because of you.

Lauren, aka Wonder Woman, what would I do without you? I could fill this page, plus ten more, with all the ways you helped make this story what it is and the ways you've helped me grow as a writer. Any friendship born out of Richonne love was destined to be something pretty amazing, but this one is extra special. Thank you for everything.

Dee, my 11th-hour hero. By the time my manuscript made it to you, I was full of doubt. You reminded me why I wrote this story in the first place. You are such a blessing.

Samantha, you are the best and a thousand exclamation points combined. I adore you!!!!!!

Jena, thank you for reminding me to take care of myself. We've shared many tears, laughter, and love throughout this process. Ready to do this four more times, plus a few more? You're my soul sister. So much love and gratitude for you.

Kia, you've always reminded me I had something to say that people needed to hear. So many times when I've doubted myself, it's been your voice in my ear reminding me what I'm capable of. You are one of my greatest blessings. I love you, and I love us.

Erin my OG since birth. I wouldn't be me without you. You're my person forever. Love you.

Gaby, we've been each other's sidekick for years. Your friendship has been one of my life's greatest gifts. I'm so proud of you. Love you always.

Carina, for always knowing I would make it here. Love you to the moon and back.

Suzanne, The Loving Pie Co will forever be a place that magic happens. Love you.

Thank you to Sydney, Chelsea, Ali, Brooke, Amanda, Sam, Andrew, Tai, Neal, Erin C… You all touched this book in one way or another. I'm so lucky to have friends like you guys. Love y'all!

To Nat for everything. Always. Love you.

Mrs. Ross, you always believed I could, and I finally did. Much love and gratitude for your influence in my life. You're still my favorite teacher.

To Glendon, for being the most patient formatter ever. You are an angel!

Elle Maxwell, thank you for bringing Liv and Jax (and Mama) to life in such beautiful detail. You are a rockstar.

To my patient, loving husband. You taught me that not all love stories have to be grandiose. Sometimes the ones that sneak into your heart quietly are the best. You've supported my every dream. Love you and our sweet fur babies more than anything. You're the Jim to my Pam. Let's go to Target.

To Mama and Daddy, you fueled my reading obsession when I was a kid. You helped me become a voracious reader and that allowed me to become a better writer. This book wouldn't exist without all the hours you let me get lost in a book or in the countless family 'newspapers' I forced you to read. Love you both special.

To Matthew, the world's okay-est brother. Love you always, little brother.

To those who have been with me since my podcasting days... Y'ALL. We did it! When I spoke into a mic for the first time, I never could have imagined the support that would come from such beautiful, amazing women. You all have been the wind in my sails more times than you'll ever know.

To every woman over thirty, forty, fifty, and beyond who has ever felt like Liv... you are a million, billion, trillion, times enough. You are worthy of the dreams you have for yourself. Never give up.

Lastly, to Granny, you taught me to love freely and self-lessly. You are proof that the greatest love stories are often the ones that don't have anything to do with romance. They're in the quiet resiliency of our families and the sweetness of the friendships we form throughout our lives. I miss you more than I'll ever be able to put into words. I'd give anything if you were here to celebrate this with me. I hope I can make you proud. Love you special. Forever.

Melissa Grace is a freelance writer whose work has been featured in publications like *Medium, Thought Catalog,* and *The Mighty.* She resides just outside of Nashville, Tennessee with her husband and five (yes, five) fur children, including her hostile kitty, Mama. This is her first novel.

Learn more and stay in the loop about Melissa's future projects, including the next installment of the Midnight in Dallas series at: www.melissagracewrites.com.

Find her on social media:

facebook.com/heymelissagrace

twitter.com/heymelissagrace

instagram.com/heymelissagrace

goodreads.com/melissagrace

amazon.com/Melissa-Grace/e/B08LMS2237/ref=dp_byline_cont_pop_ebooks_1

bookbub.com/authors/melissa-grace

Printed in Great Britain
by Amazon

17899070R00205